MY
NAME
IS
Cain

DEAN SPARKS

My Name Is Cain
© 2021 by Dean Sparks

Published by Insight Publishing Group
contact@freshword.com
www.freshword.com
918-493-1718

ISBN: 978-1-943361-75-5
E-Book ISBN: 978-1-943361-76-2

Library of Congress Control Number: 2020924512

Printed in the United States of America.

DEDICATION

To my four daughters, Sela, Aleska, Hannah, and Mykaela.

Chapter One

Hannah had never lived in a place as strange as the Abbey of St. Margaret. The fortresslike convent, with three stories of solid exterior walls, a moat with a drawbridge, and modern defenses, housed more than a hundred nuns, some of whom worked with Vatican Intelligence researching potential threats to the Catholic Church.

Fog from the Thames River a few blocks away obscured Hannah's view of movements around the drawbridge the abbey's Mother Superior entrusted her to protect. She glanced at Mykaela, her friend of two months, and knew that today's goings-on equally baffled her. Mykaela had not taken her vows yet, so she was still a novice.

The Mother Superior and a few nuns knew more about her than they should. She also believed that an attack was imminent; but Hannah knew that in its long years of existence, no one had ever breached the security of the abbey.

Today, however, the lowering of the drawbridge heralded a new dawn. Sister Hannah felt, rather than heard, the great metal chains as they rotated off their posts and vibrated through the thick stone walls. To the outside world, all appeared normal and safe. However, the air was thick with tension. According to the ancient Mother Superior, the boys were coming.

As Hannah looked at her computer, she wondered why she had been selected to monitor the only entrance to the abbey. Maybe it was because she was at least thirty years younger than anyone, except Mykaela, who was twenty. Perhaps it was a test for her to keep her scholarship to Oxford. She switched views to a different camera hidden within a false stone above the entry. Other nuns monitored cameras that scanned the perimeter, roof, and courtyard. Motion detectors zeroed in on any object larger than a sparrow around the drawbridge.

Only women could enter the Abbey of St. Margaret. Hannah watched as Mrs. Brockhurst, who was always the first to arrive, crossed the bridge and entered the single ironclad gate to say her morning prayers in the Glass Chapel. She listened to Sister Mabel greet her in the small foyer and knew another nun had pressed the release button so she could be escorted through the thick iron doors and into the inner sanctum.

"Incoming worm," another sister, Gertrude, said from the computer station beside Hannah. Sister Gertrude was responsible for computer security. Her chair creaked when she shifted her weight. Though she was six inches shorter than Hannah's nearly six-foot height, she outweighed Hannah by at least two hundred pounds. Sister Gertrude typed a command and smiled. "Identity confirmed. Our attacker is Lawrence McKinney, sophomore, computer sciences, Oxford University, Kappa Lambda Omega."

A cheer rose from the twenty-six nuns who hovered in anticipation. *This is too weird,* Hannah thought, but she knew the history. Sixty years earlier, the young men from the KLO fraternity thought it might be fun for the freshmen pledges to try to get into the abbey as part of their initiation. A pledge received a demerit if caught by a nun or the police. If he succeeded in entering the abbey, he would avoid the humiliating induction process and be granted immediate membership into the prestigious fraternity.

After every pledge had failed, a much younger Mother Evelyn had sent the president of the fraternity a letter accusing the pledges of not being innovative enough. Since then, the abbey challenged them to set foot within its confines during pledge week.

Mother Evelyn had established a few simple rules. First, no permanent harm could come to either the nuns or the students, eliminating the use of firearms or explosives. Second, the public must never be aware of the contest. Third, if a pledge succeeded in his quest, the abbey would reward the fraternity with one hundred thousand pounds. Fourth, if either of the first two rules were broken, the contest would end permanently. The fraternity president accepted the challenge.

Some pledges tried to talk their way in. Many attempted briberies. A few were more clever. Pledges who tried parachuting were hit by a powerful wind that blew them off course and into the chilly moat. The ropes were cut for those who tried to scale the walls. In 1973, a group of engineering students dug a tunnel under the moat, but even they were stopped.

Mother Evelyn leaned on her black cane with a white angel's head carved in the handle and white angel wings flowing down the upper part of the shaft. With her shoulders hunched over as if time were curling her body back to the fetal position, she walked to the master control station to the left of Hannah. She wore heavy wool robes and a veil covered most of her face. Her rich brown eyes normally expressed her warm and caring nature, but this morning, they were sharp as razors.

"Places, ladies. The game is afoot. Let's see if the boys can give our defenses a real test this year," Mother Evelyn said with a touch of humor in her clear alto voice. The majority of the nuns filed out of the room to go to their assigned positions. Hannah watched as Mother Evelyn sat at her massive antique desk overlooking a dozen computer screens in a half circle. The Mother glanced at the large screen on the front wall, surrounded by a frame with small cherubs carved in the mahogany. Every computer screen was duplicated on it in twelve separate boxes. "Did you use your new reverse-worm attack, Sister Gertrude?"

"Yes, ma'am."

"Did it melt the poor boy's computer?"

"No, ma'am," Sister Gertrude replied, and Hannah noticed her grin with suppressed pride. "I'm not sure that's possible, but his computer will soon be wiped clean."

Gertrude began explaining the design of her attack, but Hannah ignored her as she noticed a motion detector alert on her own screen. "Second entrant approaching the bridge," Hannah said over the faint strings of Mozart playing in the background. She felt annoyed that her voice quivered with nervousness.

The Mother switched the view of the drawbridge to the main screen and remained silent for a few seconds longer than Hannah expected. Then she loudly cleared her throat. "Sister Hannah, did you forget about the fog?"

Hannah looked up at the main screen and saw only milky white. She felt her cheeks heat with embarrassment as she typed a command on her keyboard. "My apologies, Mother. Switching to infrared."

The large screen flickered and showed the moat below the bridge as cool blue. The drawbridge was dull green, retaining some of the heat from the abbey. A sole pedestrian, in stark shades of red, pink, and yellow, strolled across the fog-shrouded bridge. Two big blue circles glowed on the person's chest.

Hannah snickered as she spoke to Sister Mabel. "One male approaching disguised as a woman. He used water balloons to enhance his chest but wasn't wise enough to use warm water."

Hannah split her screen to include the view of the small entry foyer where Sister Mabel sat behind a simple desk reading from her Bible. Hannah cringed as Mabel's gruff voice came through the speaker. "Sister Hannah, this may seem like a game, but it is very serious, so please don't insert any of your silly Americanisms."

If any nun at the abbey looked like an old hag, it was Sister Mabel. More than forty years ago, she had come to St. Margaret asking for sanctuary. Her husband had beat her so badly that half of her teeth were missing as well as her left eye. Due to a damaged larynx, her voice sounded like a truck traveling down a gravel road.

Before the man crossing the bridge arrived, Sister Mabel removed her dentures, leaving spaces where teeth were missing. She removed her eye patch, revealing a yellowed, off-center eye with a blood-red iris, which was actually a miniature camera. She looked scary enough to make a soldier shudder.

A young lady in a bright blue dress with gold cross-stitch embroidery entered the foyer. Her hat, purse, gloves, and shoes matched the dress. She approached the desk and placed her purse on its edge. The fog from outside swirled around her feet.

Hannah turned up the volume.

"How may I serve you today?" Sister Mabel asked.

"I seek entrance into the Abbey of St. Margaret," said an obviously false soprano.

Sister Mabel closed her Bible and pulled a sheet of paper from her desk. "Your name?"

"Beth Winsomore."

Sister Mabel quirked a bushy eyebrow. "Your place of residence?"

"Lambeth."

Sister Mabel increased the sternness in her voice. "Miss Winsomore, the abbey is only open to women. Men may not enter. Are you male or female?"

"Female."

"I believe you are male. Therefore, entrance is denied."

"You are mistaken," the young man replied. He placed his hands on his hips and thrust out his exaggerated chest. "I am a female and wish to enter."

"Then disrobe and prove me wrong," Sister Mabel growled.

The man nearly lost his balance as he stomped a high-heeled shoe defiantly. "It's obvious I am female. You're a sick woman wanting to see my personals. Now let me in!"

"Mabel, show him the folly of his ways," Mother Evelyn commanded.

Sister Mabel rose from her chair and revealed her intimidating six-and-a-half-foot frame with broad shoulders. A touch of fear crawled across the visitor's face as she hobbled closer and loomed over him. She bent down slowly, as if it caused her pain, and peered into his eyes. Then, without warning, she punched his left breast with a classic karate chop.

The water balloon burst, drenching the front of the blue dress. The lad rolled his eyes in annoyance. Muttering under his breath with a distinctly masculine voice, he stalked out of the foyer and back across the bridge.

Mabel's laughter was not pleasant, but it was genuine. Through Mabel's camera in her false eye, Hannah watched as she opened the purse the boy had left sitting on her desk. Hannah noted a small video camera inside, but Mabel didn't touch it.

A warning note sounded from Hannah's computer and drew her attention to another person crossing the bridge, also dressed in a bright blue dress with gold cross-stich embroidery. She wore a matching hat, purse, gloves, and shoes. Although the dress looked the same, Hannah noticed an oddity and scanned the visitor with another sensor embedded in the drawbridge. "Mother Evelyn, the embroidery in the first dress was simply colored thread. The threading in the dress of our current visitor is made of real gold. There are also electronic components built into her shoes."

Mother Evelyn peered at Hannah, and the wrinkles around her eyes deepened. "Is our visitor male or female?"

Hannah double-checked her readings. "I believe female, ma'am."

"She may enter," Mother Evelyn stated and leaned back in her chair.

Seeing how the gold embroidery connected to the electronics in the shoes, Hannah felt it wise to object. "But she's up to something."

"Of course she is. It's your job to figure out what. It's not your job to deny entrance to any woman."

Hannah felt her heart flutter from the Mother's rebuke, so she transferred an electronic schematic of the dress and shoes to a file. She watched the girl's face as she entered the foyer and noticed she looked almost identical to the first visitor. As she approached the desk, Sister Mabel stood. "I believe your sister left her purse. I'm sure you'll want to return it to her."

The girl chuckled. "I'll be glad to return it. But that was not my sister; he is my twin brother."

"Of course," Sister Mabel replied and sat back down. "How may I serve you today?"

"I seek entrance into the Abbey of St. Margaret," the girl said in a genuine soprano with identical inflections as her brother.

"Your name?"

"Beth Winsomore."

"Your place of residence?"

"Lambeth."

Mabel increased the sternness in her voice. "Miss Winsomore, the abbey is only open to women. Men may not enter. Are you male or female?"

"Female and willing to prove it." She placed her purse against the identical one sitting on the desk.

"That won't be necessary. You may enter."

Hannah heard the lock on the heavy iron door click. The door opened slowly. Mabel said, "Another nun will escort you to the Glass Chapel or the library. Enjoy your visit, and may the Lord God bless your day."

As the young lady approached the opening door, Hannah saw Mabel look down at the two purses remaining on her desk. "Miss Winsomore, you forgot your purses."

"No, I didn't."

As Mabel watched, Hannah saw green gas billow out from where the two purses touched. She sucked in a breath of horror as Mabel closed her eye and the camera turned dark. She cringed as she heard Mabel's forehead slam against the table.

Hannah felt the blood drain from her face, and her hands began to shake. "I am so sorry. I should have caught the chemicals coating the purses. They weren't dangerous until they came in contact with each other."

Mother Evelyn typed, "I thought it was clever. Lower the portcullis. Lock the main door. Fill the foyer with a concealing fog at plus twenty psi pressure."

Hannah felt relieved that the Mother didn't make a big deal out of her mistake. She punched keys without looking. Her attention remained focused on her computer. "Two men crossing the drawbridge. They're wearing gas masks and carrying welding torches."

"Activity at the power juncture on Bell Street," Sister Gertrude interjected.

"They are well organized this year," the Mother replied.

Hearing Gertrude's calm, Hannah reduced the excitement in her own voice. "Miss Winsomore is blocking the door with her body, so I can't lock it."

Mother Evelyn's chair squeaked as she leaned forward and spoke into her microphone. "Team one, remove Miss Winsomore from the door and take her to the dining room. Team four, retrieve Mabel from the foyer. The boys will cut through the portcullis in a few minutes. Hannah, as soon as team four is clear, close the secondary doors and prepare to drop the foyer floor."

Everyone hurried to fulfill the Mother's instructions. Hannah barely noticed when the lights went out since her computer screen didn't flicker. Within ten seconds, the emergency lights came on, bathing the room in a reddish glow.

"They've cut the electrical lines," Gertrude reported. "There's no electricity in a ten-block radius."

Sister Mary Ruth, who sat between Hannah and Gertrude monitoring the exterior of the abbey, spoke. "I have s-simultaneous activity on the n-north, south, and w-west lawns." Her ancient body shook with tremors of Parkinson's disease. "There is s-seismic activity in the s-sewer lines beneath Boragan S-street."

Mother Evelyn split the large viewing screen into four quadrants. The view from the foyer moved to a smaller monitor beneath the main. In the top left quadrant, a lone teenager struggled with a jackhammer that bounced against the wall. He stood knee deep in murky water.

The other three quadrants looked blurry because of the fog, but it was thinning as the sun rose higher. The bottom left quadrant showed a large flatbed truck backing toward the east side of the moat. Six young men pulled a tarp off the rear of the truck, revealing a large catapult holding a white ball about six feet wide. Six more young men in black skin suits filled the top right quadrant. They stood across from the west moat holding coils of rope attached to grappling hooks. The bottom right quadrant showed the Bank of England parking lot behind the abbey. It bordered the moat on the south side across from the Glass Chapel. An old Toyota pickup with a wooden crate in the bed sat unoccupied at the edge of the parking lot where it had been left two days earlier. According to Gertrude, the truck belonged to a local company contracted to paint the interior of the bank.

Hannah turned to report the activity at the gate and noticed the Mother Superior staring so intently at the four views on the screen that she seemed to straighten the hump in her back. "Why are they avoiding technology? Everything they are trying failed fifty years ago. They're not even using video cameras to record anything. What are they up to?"

"I don't detect any cell phones in use," Gertrude said.

"Team three, prepare your pikes and bolt cutters to remove grappling hooks. Ignore the sewer. It's a decoy. Raise the magnetic repulser on the east roof and focus on the catapult. I'm sure there's a boy in that sphere. Try not to send him into the moat. Sister Hannah, is the door secure?"

"Yes, ma'am. But they have nearly cut through the front gate."

"As expected," Mother Evelyn stated. "Mary Ruth, this does not feel right. Someone is coaching them. I can almost sense his . . . Mykaela, give me an infrared view of the truck behind the Glass Chapel."

The main screen switched to a computer-generated three-dimensional view. Having sat in the bank parking lot all night, the truck looked similar to the ambient air. In the back of the truck, a large metal machine, inside a crate, took shape with various shades of orange and red as it started to warm up. Hundreds of small wires led from a rectangular machine into a large dark-red sphere.

"Two p-paragliders riding in from the w-west. Air compression t-tanks and fans ready to b-blow. Estimated t-time of arrival is three m-minutes."

The Mother stood so suddenly her chair crashed to the floor. "That's not paint equipment. Emergency! Gertrude, move to defense level five. Mary Ruth, tell all those protecting the roof to secure themselves against the wind. Wait fifteen seconds, and then move all fans and compressors to full power. Form vortex pattern gamma. Hit the catapult with the magnet at one hundred percent. Turn the truck over if you must. Hannah, drop the foyer floor ninety degrees and raise the drawbridge. Mary Ruth, get Sisters Hildegard, Maura, and Teresa to the infirmary immediately."

Mother Evelyn left her desk and headed toward the door. "I must get to the courtyard. Gertrude, after the wave hits and assuming we are safe, take Hannah and Mary Ruth with you to my office."

"What wave?" Gertrude and Mary Ruth said in unison.

The Mother did not answer. Everyone stabbed at their keyboards, sending emergency instructions all around the abbey. Hannah dropped the foyer floor and plunged the boys wielding the torches into the moat. The drawbridge began to rise at her command. On the main screen, she saw the truck with the catapult flip on its side. Nuns on the west roof used bolt cutters to clip the ropes of the young men trying to scale the wall.

Hannah was still typing when the wave hit her. She didn't scream, although she felt like it. For a few seconds, her skin felt as if a million ants were crawling under it. Sweat beaded on her brow, and she grew warmer. Her ears rang as if someone had clapped a symbol behind her head. The computers shut down.

Hannah could no longer see. For a few seconds, all she heard was Sister Mary Ruth's panicked breathing. "I n-need to be r-replaced. I am b-blind." Hannah pulled out the lighter she kept with her to light candles. She flicked it, and the flame shed a little light. "You're not blind. The lights went out."

In the darkness, Hannah heard the Mother descend the stairs, her cane striking every third step.

"W-what in the b-blazes happened?"

"I believe the boys used an electromagnetic pulse," Gertrude replied.

Chapter Two

The Mother Superior ran down the stairs, being careful as she rounded the corner to avoid slipping on the stones worn smooth by three hundred years of nuns' footsteps. She could hear senior nuns shouting commands to light candles and move to the roof. She felt proud of them for not panicking. She hoped the three nuns with pacemakers would survive.

Upon reaching the ground floor, she entered the courtyard. She saw sisters on the roof of the east and west wings, which held the individual cells for the seventy-eight nuns who called the Abbey of St. Margaret home. The voices above and behind her told her that more nuns protected the roof on the front of the abbey containing offices, the dining hall, infirmary, and classrooms. The rising sun reflected off the Glass Chapel, with its stained-glass roof, in front of her. She arrived at the Pool of Secrets in the center of the courtyard, where for the first time in many years no water splashed from the cherubic fountains.

No man had ever set foot within the abbey. Mother Evelyn's ancient heart fluttered as she reached the fountain and gazed at the open sky. "We are vulnerable."

The fog vortex swirling above the abbey dissipated as the fans stopped rotating. Two red paragliders approached from the west and descended toward the courtyard. The Mother glared at them as if sheer force of will might blow them off course.

The gliders came closer. Less than twenty yards from the west wall, both pilots dipped their left flaps and tacked due north. The nuns on the roof cheered as the gliders splashed in the moat. At the foot of the fountain, Mother Evelyn collapsed to her knees and bowed her head to pray.

⁓

"An electromagnetic pulse?" Hannah asked.

"The EMP corrupts electronics in a small area." Gertrude removed a large candle from a bookshelf and lit it. "Follow me. We have work to do."

"Where are we going?" Hannah asked as Gertrude led her down the hall.

"To the Templar Chamber. Security functions will receive emergency power first, and the backup computers should come online in about three minutes."

"What is a Templar Chamber?"

"The M-mother has many secrets," Sister Mary Ruth warbled. "She only sh-shares them with a s-select few. Gertrude will explain when we get there."

"You would have learned some of them when you were old enough, but I believe this emergency has moved your timetable up a bit." Holding the candle aloft, Gertrude approached Mother Evelyn's office, removed a large key from her bosom, and opened the door. Hannah gasped as Gertrude broke the rule and stepped inside without the Mother present. Mary Ruth followed and with reluctance, so did Hannah.

The office was spacious, with dark mahogany paneling, ivory inlays, thick Persian rugs, and a massive desk in the center. Hannah felt as if she'd walked into a room of ancient wealth. Two antique couches faced each other, and a small table with four chairs sat in the corner. A computer screen on the desk was the only visible electronic device. The large leather-bound books on the ornately carved shelf behind the desk, and the scrolls encased behind crystal glass, showed that the Mother was a collector of ancient texts.

The single candle cast an eerie glow, and the walls seemed to absorb the faint light. Gertrude walked to an alabaster table against the far wall, which prominently displayed a large Bible. She opened the book to Genesis 1 and placed her right palm on the center of the page.

"Genesis?" Mary Ruth said. "The c-code page changed t-to Exodus chapter 34 y-yesterday."

"I missed devotions yesterday," Gertrude confessed as she turned to Exodus 34. "Mother Evelyn says there is more wisdom behind the words in the Bible than in all the other books in the world put together."

Mary Ruth touched Hannah's hand. "When w-we are alone, you can dispense with p-proper titles."

"Thank you, but I don't think I can call the Mother Superior just by her name."

"Mother will do." Gertrude placed her hand on the center of the page, and a faint green glow emitted from the open Bible. The table receded into the floor, revealing a stone staircase leading into darkness.

Hannah felt a cold breeze from below, but the chill that ran up her spine wasn't from the temperature. *What's happening?* Hannah thought. *An EMP, backup computers, secret codes that worked on a green Bible with no electricity, and what in the world is a Templar Chamber?*

Gertrude picked up two more candles from the bookcase and lit them before starting their descent. The steep, narrow stairs led straight down without twisting or turning.

Hannah jumped when the door slid shut behind her. A faint musty smell emanated from the rough-hewn stone walls as they traveled down at least fifty uneven steps.

The stairs ended in a small chamber of gray stone with only one door to Hannah's right. Mary Ruth approached a recessed shelf in the stone wall across from the stairs where a small vase with three plastic daisies sat. She waved her hands in her jerking fashion over the fake flowers, and Hannah assumed the flowers contained a pheromone sensor like the ones she monitored on the drawbridge. She also assumed it would unlock the thick iron door, so she turned toward it and waited to hear it unlock. The room went dark. Hannah spun around and groped for either of the two sisters, but they were no longer there. Swallowing to keep panic out of her voice, she whispered, "Sister Mary Ruth, where are you?"

Mary Ruth's voice warbled through the wall to the left. "The iron door is a decoy. Please k-keep up, and why are you w-whispering?" Mary Ruth's shaking hand reached through the wall that appeared to be made of solid stone, grabbed Hannah's arm, and pulled her through.

Florescent lights flickered on, and Hannah found Gertrude already at a computer on the other side of the room. Six computer stations sat in a semicircle along the back wall contrasting with the large ancient cuneiform letters carved into the gray stone of a round room. Mary Ruth sat and directed Hannah to the chair beside her.

"Hannah, please check the g-gate. Then review what you can of the last ten m-minutes in your zone."

Hannah couldn't believe the calmness of the older nuns. Her hands shook, making it difficult for her to log in, but she succeeded. She scanned the foyer and saw a man in a rappelling harness wedged in the top of the inner iron door. He was cutting a hole in the door with a blowtorch. Hannah zoomed in and saw three sides of a large square already cut. She typed a command, but nothing happened. "Blowtorch guy is about to cut through the inner door. Can you give me any power?"

"Rerouting emergency power," Gertrude responded as she glanced at Hannah's screen.

Hannah retyped her command, and the blowtorch flew out of the man's hands and stuck to the door, the blue flame burning harmlessly to the side. He tried to pry the torch off the wall but failed. With a look of resignation, he cut the strap hanging from a spike he was hanging on and plunged into the moat. Hannah sighed in relief.

Mother Evelyn stormed into the room, her cane striking the stone floor with sharp clicks. "Gertrude, update me on our current security status."

"Security protocols are at level four. Emergency power has restored the magnetic repulsers and wind generators. Both must be directed manually, which team three is handling. I reviewed the potential points of entry for the last six minutes and found no evidence of trespass. Internal sensors are active, and I don't detect any unauthorized personnel. The boys are vacating the area. A tow truck removed the Toyota, but the boys are having difficulty with the flatbed I tipped on its side. I've yet to scan for local air traffic."

"Do so," the Mother quipped. "Sister Hannah, welcome to the Chamber. You must solemnly swear to keep secret what you learn today."

Hannah turned and looked at the Mother, sensing the seriousness of her request. "I do."

Mother Evelyn's gaze softened. "Very well. Gertrude, what is our electronic status?"

Gertrude looked grim. "The upstairs mainframe computer rebooted automatically, but all the memory has been wiped. Primary functions are being restored. We must replace or restore every device in the abbey that uses a battery and all stored data that has been wiped. It will take days to recover everything from the backup system. I severed all Internet links temporarily."

"Remain at defense level four. Return to level five as soon as possible. When the mainframe can resume full security functions, transfer control back upstairs. Return one at a time in case the boys make another attempt. I need to make a phone call." Mother Evelyn pulled her phone from a pocket and pressed a key. She slammed the phone down on the desk and looked at Hannah. "Hannah, please go upstairs and see if Mabel has recovered. If so, ask her to go into town and get me a new phone."

Chapter Three

Mother Evelyn climbed the stairs to her office. Before she reached her desk, someone knocked on her door. "Enter."

Mabel appeared, carrying a cell phone. "A young man just crossed the bridge to deliver this, courtesy of Kappa Lambda Omega."

Mother Evelyn took the phone. "I assume Miss Winsomore is still in the dining room. Please make her comfortable. I would like to have a chat with her after vespers."

Mabel nodded and left. A few seconds later, Beethoven's "Fifth Symphony" filled the room, courtesy of the phone Mother Evelyn held.

She answered and put it on speaker. "Do you concede?"

"Yes, ma'am, we concede." The pleasant tenor voice held the refined accent of the wealthy aristocracy of Britain.

"That was a dastardly trick you pulled today. It caused a power outage in a ten-block radius."

"But within our set of rules."

"Perhaps we should more properly define permanent damage," the Mother quipped.

"Yes, I have a severely damaged truck."

The Mother allowed the phone to remain silent for a minute. "I trust you will have an explanation for the media?"

"An article appeared several days ago in the *London Times* concerning a transformer that exploded in Wales. Apparently, the electrical currents arced to other transformers, causing several city blocks to have unusual electrical damage. Since the article was sanctioned by the Oxford Science Department's newsletter, of which I'm the editor, there should be no questions."

"And where did you find an EMP?"

"It was loaned to our university by Cal Tech. An anonymous alumnus suggested we use it to eliminate your defenses. Perhaps I may ask a question?"

"Certainly."

"How did you fool my paragliders? With no electricity, you could not have pushed them aside or projected a hologram."

Mother Evelyn chose her words carefully. "I do not need electricity for smoke and mirrors. We see what we want to see and believe what we want to believe. You made a good effort this year, Mr. Winston. Although you did not win, I will give you a bonus for your team's inventive efforts. I will transfer fifty thousand pounds into your fraternity's account as soon as my computers are back online, half of which you will discreetly distribute to my neighbors whose electronics you damaged."

"Thank you for your generosity. I apologize for the inconvenience we have caused you."

"Goodbye, Mr. Winston." She hung up the phone and laid it on her desk.

Mother Evelyn spent the rest of the day supervising repairs to the abbey. The foyer was reset, the inner door replaced, and computer systems partially restored. Vespers came as a relief from the day's stress. Only twenty nuns chose to attend since Mother Evelyn excused anyone wishing to rest.

Sister Mabel led the evening devotion. Miss Winsomore sighed loudly from the pew behind Mother Evelyn. Gertrude, sitting beside the young lady, cleared her throat in admonishment.

Mary Ruth sat in her customary place across the aisle, and Hannah, feeling sleepy, sat behind her right under the air-conditioning vent, a spot no one usually occupied.

As peace descended upon Mother Evelyn, she went through her personal evening litany: contemplation of the past, prayer for the present, and hope for the future. With her knees pressed against the floor, she said the concluding prayers by rote. Her gaze wandered to the beautiful stained-glass ceiling and the stars twinkling on the other side of it.

No man had ever seen the beauty of the chapel, with its finely polished woods and handcrafted alabaster carvings of angels and saints. No man had ever touched the floor where Mother Evelyn knelt. No male voice had ever spoken within the sanctity of the chapel.

"Hello, Mother," said a distinctly masculine voice.

Chapter Four

Hannah jerked awake from her near-slumber prayer at the sound of a deep voice dripping with malice. Gasps of surprise and anger filled the chapel as everyone stood to see the man who had entered their sacred abode.

Where Miss Winsomore should have been sitting in the pew behind the Mother, a man sat, looking smug. Mother Evelyn rose from where she had knelt and swung her cane at him. It struck him on the arm, but he didn't flinch.

The man's dark-brown, wrath-filled eyes focused squarely upon Mother Evelyn. "That was rude. Do you always greet your guests with violence?"

His casual black wool shirt, unbuttoned low, exposed a well-muscled physique. His wavy black hair framed a strong jawline and chiseled features, but a huge blood-red birthmark ran from his right jawbone, coloring the right cheek, continuing across his nose and brows, and branching into five directions like a handprint.

"How dare you enter this sanctuary," Mother Evelyn spat with a low voice.

He glanced around the chapel, looking at each nun. "You are older than I—remember, Mother. Shall we have this conversation in front of an audience?"

Mother Evelyn's eyes remained locked on the man as she commanded, "Clear the chapel."

The nuns, who had been standing in mute shock, quickly and quietly filed out of the room. Mother Evelyn motioned for Mary Ruth, Gertrude, and Mabel to remain. Hannah felt unnerved as the man stared at her. As Hannah turned to leave, the man's voice stopped her. "She stays."

Mother Evelyn pursed her lips but nodded her consent.

Hannah felt trapped as the sound of the closing door reverberated throughout the chapel. "Who are you?"

He smiled. "My name is Cain."

"How awful," Hannah quipped.

His smile grew wider. "You have spunk. I like that. But what's in a name? After all, Sister Hannah, your real name is Mary Louise Johnson. You were born and raised in Tulsa, Oklahoma. You graduated valedictorian from Broken Arrow High School and attended Hendrix College in Arkansas, where you heard the calling of the Church. Because of your eidetic memory and a gift for data analysis, the FBI offered you a job, but you turned them down. Instead, you applied to work for Vatican Intelligence, but unfortunately, you are the wrong gender. Not wanting to lose your talents, the Vatican placed you here with the Mother and her troop of old ladies, analyzing how world events will affect the Catholic empire."

Hannah gaped at the man sitting on the pew. She wondered how he got his information and what he wanted from her.

"Has that great mind of yours figured out how I got in here?"

Hannah stammered the first thing that came to her mind even though it didn't feel right. "The boy with the jackhammer in the sewer wasn't really a decoy."

"Very good. There is a new tunnel from the storm sewer to your underground maze created by a powerful organic acid produced in the Amazon forest, where I have a research lab. Do you know who I am?"

"You still get distracted too easily," the Mother interrupted. "Stop toying with her and tell me why you are here."

Mary Ruth spoke, but her voice shook so violently, her words were barely discernable. "She d-does not know, b-but I r-remember."

"S-sister M-Mary R-Ruth," Cain stammered mockingly. "Y-you have n-not aged w-well. You know, for the price of the stem cells from one fetus, you could get that little shaking problem fixed."

Mary Ruth grasped the back of the pew next to Hannah. Her knuckles turned white, but her voice turned calm. "I would n-not sacrifice even your l-life to provide myself c-comfort. Why would I s-sacrifice a life with more p-potential than yours?"

"You're so sanctimonious, it makes me nauseous."

"G-good for me."

Hannah felt relief at having his attention drawn away from her, but the question he asked still rang in her mind: *"Do you know who I am?"* Even though he had an American accent, from the mark on his face, Hannah deduced that he was a member of the Red Hand Defenders from Belfast, a terrorist group founded in 1998 by Protestant hardliners. They killed Catholics for sport.

Cain looked at Mary Ruth. "So, Lady Aleska, have you told them who their father is?"

"Th-that is n-none of your b-business."

"We have unfinished business, you and I." Cain's mocking tone turned vicious. "What did you two do with my *führer*?"

"I thought you killed him," Mother Evelyn said as she shifted to block Cain's view of Mary Ruth.

Hannah looked back and forth between Cain, Mary Ruth, and Mother Evelyn. She knew both elderly nuns had lived through World War II but didn't know they were working with Vatican Intelligence. By their reactions, they knew Cain personally from the war, which didn't make sense since he appeared to be in his early forties. She watched his blood-red birthmark turn brighter with anger, and she wondered if he would stand up and physically harm the Mother. Then she realized he had not moved anything but his neck since he arrived.

Cain seemed to hold his breath for a few seconds, and his birthmark returned to its normal color. He rolled his eyes. "I did not kill him. I assumed you and your Church buddies locked him up somewhere, which suited me since he already served his purpose."

"His purpose?" Mother Evelyn exclaimed. "What possible purpose was there in the slaughter of six million Jews? What purpose did eighty million deaths and the destruction of half of Europe serve?"

Cain sighed. "I explained this to you years ago. Conflict breeds progress. Wars fuel technology, like jet planes, nuclear energy, microwave ovens—"

"You are insane," Mother Evelyn interrupted.

Cain's birthmark brightened with anger again, but he still didn't move. "My unique talents kept the Cold War cold. I kept Kennedy from attacking the Soviet subs around Cuba. Now that the atomic age is upon us, I help keep the wars small. Having the planet turned into a nuclear wasteland would upset my plans."

"But the cost in lives has been enormous."

"I don't disagree that the coin is expensive, but it is necessary."

"Were you responsible for the destruction of the World Trade Center?"

"No, that one caught even me by surprise." The tension drained from his face, and he smiled. "Now, if you want to know why President Bush and his advisors believed there were weapons of mass destruction in Iraq—"

"Enough," Mother Evelyn shouted. "Why are you here?"

Cain stopped smiling. "All this talk about death is certainly appropriate since it is time for you to die. Goodbye, Mother."

Hannah wondered how he could kill Mother Evelyn without moving, and then she understood the real game he was playing. She opened her mouth to warn the Mother, but Mabel leapt from beside the pulpit and crossed to the first pew, trying to reach the man who had threatened to kill the Mother.

"I don't think so." Mother Evelyn lifted her cane and pressed the wings of the angel on each side of the handle. With her other hand, she secured her veil firmly across her nostrils.

A dark green gas spewed out of the angel's mouth, surrounding Cain in a thin cloud. His eyes widened with surprise as he puffed his cheeks out, holding his breath. But he was too late and slumped sideways onto the pew.

Hannah covered her face with her veil as the Mother had and held her breath until her lungs ached. She was thankful for her choice of seats as the air conditioner blew the poisonous gas away. The air currents didn't protect the other three nuns. Gertrude slumped onto the pew beside Cain, her chin tucked down to her chest. Mary Ruth landed with a thump in her pew while Mabel tried to stop her forward momentum but tumbled in a heap on the stone floor.

"That was simpler than I thought it would be," Mother Evelyn mumbled.

Hannah longed to tell the Mother what she knew but had to wait for the green gas to dissipate.

From the pew, Cain laughed. "Did you really think it would be that easy to incapacitate me? If I really wanted to kill you, you would already be dead."

Hannah could not see any green vapor and hoped she was safe, but even if not, she had to tell the Mother. "There's no tunnel in the sewers. The blue dress with real gold cross-stitch embroidery creates an electronic net for a holographic projection. You just gassed Miss Winsomore's body, and Mr. Cain is nothing more than a hologram."

Mother Evelyn stiffened. "That would have been nice to know about five seconds ago."

Cain laughed. "I love technology. Please set me up. I hate to slouch."

Mother Evelyn motioned to Hannah with her finger. Hannah moved across the aisle and grasped what appeared to be Cain's black wool shirt, but she felt silk under her fingers and heat emanating from the gold wires. Although it looked like Cain's muscular arm, Hannah could feel that the arm beneath the hologram was thinner and softer.

"I thought I detected your hand in the use of the EMP." Mother Evelyn jerked her veil loose and leaned closer to Cain. "If you wanted to chat, you could have called."

"Where's the fun in that?" His voice sounded odd as the holographic Cain began to fall sideways back to the pew. Hannah caught him, and being cautious not to bruise Miss Winsomore, pushed her more firmly against the back of the pew.

"Why are you really here?"

"I wanted to beat you at your own game."

"Which you failed to do since you're not really here."

"Do you really want to challenge me?" Cain snarled. "The boys play by your rules. I have no rules. If I want in, I will get in."

"That's not why you're here."

"Fine," Cain sighed. "I came to ask you a favor."

Mother Evelyn leaned forward and grasped the top of the pew. "You must be kidding."

A smile touched Cain's lips. "As a leader in the Christian community, I want you to issue a warning to your flock."

"I am not the leader of any organization other than this abbey. If you want to warn the Catholic Church, you should talk to the Pope, or are you afraid you might burst into flames?"

"See, I knew you had a sense of humor. It's just buried under all those wrinkles." Cain laughed. "I know you regularly communicate with the Pope as well as the leaders of several Protestant denominations."

"We have interesting conversations, nothing more."

"You keep everyone on the straight and narrow."

"Obviously, I am failing at that job," Mother Evelyn snapped back.

"I know you have ways of convincing people. Tell the Pope, the general superintendents, the bishops, and the televangelists that the world will soon change in ways they can't imagine. Their personal doubts and petty sins will be revealed for all to see."

For the first time in Hannah's tenure as a nun, she heard the Mother laugh. "You went through this elaborate ruse to give me this ridiculous message?"

"Yes, because it's true."

"Excuse me," Hannah interrupted as a horrible thought came to her. "What type of battery are you using to power your hologram?"

The Mother looked at Hannah as if she had just turned into a lemon. Cain could not turn his head to see Hannah, but he snapped, sounding irritated. "A unique one. Mother, don't you teach your young ones not to interrupt?"

Mother Evelyn raised one eyebrow toward Hannah. "I'm sure she has a good reason, but back to your request, what do you mean by 'it's true'?"

Cain's face brightened as his smile radiated from his lips to the rest of his face. "After all these years, I've finally found a cure."

Hannah looked at Mother Evelyn, who seemed to be stunned into silence. Not knowing what they were talking about, she asked, "A cure for what?"

"Everything," Cain exclaimed. "Come on, old woman, it won't hurt you to say congratulations."

Mother Evelyn cleared her throat. "Are you sure?"

"I still have a minor deterioration problem to solve, but it works!"

"For anyone else I would say congratulations, but since it's you, I must question what you will do with it."

"Even you can't dampen my spirits, Mother. I've also decided to get married."

"To your test subject, no doubt."

"Of course not," Cain scoffed. "I can't build a new master race with a test subject."

Mother Evelyn rolled her eyes heavenward. "And who did you find to suit your ego?"

"I captured one of the *Bene Elohim*."

The color drained from Mother Evelyn's face. Hannah wondered why an obscure Hebrew reference meaning "sons of God" would frighten the Mother, but a greater concern weighed on her. "Excuse me."

"What now?"

"I don't know of any type of battery that can survive an EMP."

"Then I guess you don't know everything, Miss Valedictorian."

Keeping to the side of Cain and away from where she assumed he hid a camera, Hannah reached through his holographic neck and touched Miss Winsomore, whose own neck felt cold and clammy.

"Now where was I?" Cain asked. "Oh yes, my Elohim bride is quite lovely. We shall make beautiful children together."

Mother Evelyn shook her head in disbelief. "You have made a grave mistake."

"Unto him a child is born, and his name shall be Susej," Cain practically sang. "Kind of poetic, don't you think?"

"You are an even greater fool than I thought."

Hannah searched for a pulse. She could barely feel the slow rhythm. Remembering the electronics contained within her shoes, she started to remove them. "He's using Miss Winsomore's body as a battery. It's draining the life out of her."

"I suppose my time is up." Cain flashed a sadistic smile. "However, if you interfere, Mother, I will kill you."

The image of Cain faded, revealing a chalky white Miss Winsomore. Hannah raised her hand in front of Miss Winsomore's nose and realized she was not breathing.

Chapter Five

Hannah picked up Miss Winsomore's feet, shifted her to the side, and laid her body flat on the pew. "She's not breathing."

Mother Evelyn hurried over. "You breathe for her. I'll do CPR."

"She still has a faint pulse." Hannah tilted Miss Winsomore's head back and opened her mouth. A shallow cough emerged. "That's a relief, but her body temperature is too low."

Mother Evelyn picked up Miss Winsomore's limp right arm and rubbed it to induce blood flow. "Mary Ruth keeps a throw for when she gets cold."

Hannah crossed the aisle and returned with a small blanket. As the Mother tucked it around Miss Winsomore, Hannah searched a few other pews and found several more covers. She also checked on the other sisters. Mary Ruth and Gertrude slept peacefully and looked comfortable. However, blood covered Mabel's nose and lip from where she had struck the floor.

"Is everyone okay?" Mother Evelyn's voice sounded strained.

"I believe so." Hannah's hands shook as she handed the other blanket to the Mother.

"Sister Hannah, please sit down. You're trembling."

Hannah sat beside Miss Winsomore's feet and began rubbing them. "Who was that?"

Mother Evelyn tucked Miss Winsomore's right arm under the blankets and switched to her other arm. "I believe the better question is, why did he ask you to stay?"

"I asked myself the same question." Having perfect recall had its advantages. "He only asked me two questions. The first, about how he got in, I answered incorrectly. He then asked if I knew who he was and you interrupted me, then Mary Ruth answered."

"That's because Mary Ruth and I have dealt with him before. His first questions were a test for the two of us. If you knew his real identity, the consequences would have been dire."

"What do you mean 'dire'?"

Mother Evelyn tucked Miss Winsomore's remaining hand under the covers and leaned against the back of the pew. "He tends to kill anyone who can identify him. I brought you to my abbey because you're intelligent and you have a gift for seeing a coherent structure behind supposedly unconnected events. Your applications of mathematical equations to sociological events are unique. I cannot tell you who he is, but I need to know what you saw."

Hannah felt Miss Winsomore's feet getting warmer, so she covered them with the blanket as she considered Mother Evelyn's question. "There's not enough information to draw any conclusions."

"I don't need conclusions; I need your thoughts. What was your first impression of the man who invaded our sanctuary?"

Hannah closed her eyes to examine her memories. "My first impression was he is insane, but I changed my mind. Each accusation and command held underlying messages. Whole stories were contained in brief statements, which raises many questions."

"I'll answer questions that I can, when I can. Go on."

"The layers of deception and planning necessary to get Miss Winsomore into position indicates an extremely high intelligence. His distractibility and tendency to flit from one subject to the next is a sign of attention deficit disorder.

Mother Evelyn gave her a perplexed look. "Yes, Cain has ADD, but on a grand scale."

"His claim that he influenced Adolph Hitler and Presidents Kennedy and Bush seemed at first to be delusional megalomania. However, you and Mary Ruth accepted his statements as truth, which lends credence to what he claims. He doesn't look old enough to have lived during World War II. He must have invested heavily in plastic surgery. But if that were true, why not remove the big red birthmark?"

Hannah stopped for a second and looked at the birthmark in her mind, wondering if it was real or a tattoo. "If his facial markings are on purpose, he is a member of the Red Hand Defenders, which is bad news for us. His accent is rather flat, but with a touch of emphasis on his r's, which would suggest he hails from somewhere in the northeastern United States and not Belfast. If his claims are true, he must have some good political connections there. Political connections take lots of money, which I doubt is a concern for Mr. Cain. A portable EMP is worth millions and he lent it to college boys to play a prank, unless he stole it. The holographic dress is also nearly priceless, so he's rich and well versed in technology."

"From his expressions, could you tell if he was speaking the truth?" Mother Evelyn asked.

"I believe he was sincere when he spoke of a cure, even though I don't understand what that means. If he really does have a plan for a master race, I think the world would be safer if he were insane. He could cause a lot of damage just trying. I could not tell if he was speaking truthfully since I was more concerned with Miss Winsomore. He was not as excited about his bride as he should have been. There was something missing in his tone. That he told you his plans means he is arrogantly confident. I think he may want something from you, but I'm not sure what."

"Blessed Mary, Mother of God," Gertrude groaned. She rose quickly, and immediately grabbed her forehead. "Where is he?"

Mother Evelyn stepped to Gertrude and helped her sit up. "He has gone."

Mabel rose to one knee and covered her nose with a handkerchief. "What did I miss?"

"It's all recorded. You can view the drama later."

"Thanks for the warning," Gertrude said. "I had just enough time to position myself."

Hannah gave Gertrude a puzzled look. "I didn't hear any warning."

"That's because you haven't been taught how to listen," Mother Evelyn replied. "Do you have any other thoughts, Sister Hannah?"

"Just one. He mentioned unfinished business with Sister Mary Ruth. It seemed personal."

"I would have p-preferred for my little s-secret to go with me to the gr-grave." Mary Ruth rose from her pew. "But I think t-they are old enough to h-handle it."

Mother Evelyn walked across the aisle and grasped Mary Ruth's hand.

"Cain is the father of my children," Mary Ruth said.

"You have children?" Hannah exclaimed.

"He is our father?" Gertrude and Mabel said in unison.

"*They* are your daughters?" Hannah's mouth hung open.

Mother Evelyn smiled. "That is the least of the surprises in store for you tonight."

Chapter Six

Hannah wondered what was more surprising—being hit by an EMP, discovering that the abbey sat on top of an ancient Templar site, being deceived by a hologram, working with a megalomaniac as old as the Mother Superior, or hearing that two of the sisters she worked with were actually biological sisters and daughters of a senior nun. "I'm not sure any surprise could top what has happened already."

The four older nuns laughed long enough for Hannah to feel uncomfortable. "I didn't think it was that funny."

"Sister Hannah," the Mother spoke, "we do more than assimilate unusual information for the Vatican Department of Intelligence. Because of circumstances, it is time to include you in the Inner Circle of the Abbey of St. Margaret."

Hannah felt honored that the Mother trusted her. "Why me?"

"B-because I am d-dying," Mary Ruth stated.

Mabel and Gertrude bowed their heads. Hannah was about to make a sympathetic denial but looked at Mary Ruth and saw the truth in her eyes. "How may I help?"

"You can bring supper for five to my office, where we can talk in a more secure location," Mother Evelyn replied. "Mabel, please take Miss Winsomore to the infirmary. Remove the holographic dress and give her something comfortable and warm. Gertrude, see if you can trace a signal from the dress. Cain could not transmit a signal from very far. Mary Ruth, please reassure the rest of our flock. Tell them Kappa Lambda Omega pulled a prank and there is no danger to the abbey. That will be all."

As everyone stood to carry out the tasks, Hannah felt her sense of humor reassert itself. "You might say that's a killer dress."

∽

Gertrude helped Hannah roll a food-laden cart into Mother Evelyn's office. The aroma wafting from the covered dishes paid tribute to the talent of Sister Betty, a master of the culinary arts. After living off dorm rations and fast food, Hannah was thrilled with the gastronomic delights she'd experienced here for the past year.

Today, Sister Betty's talent exceeded her normally scrumptious presentation. As Gertrude set out plates and silverware, Hannah placed on the table individual servings of steak tartar with minced cilantro and green onions beside the escargot in garlic and butter sauce. They placed the side dishes of delicately spiced vegetables and rice, which complemented the lamb in rosemary and mint sauce, in the center of the table.

Hannah felt grateful that Mother Evelyn believed a nun's lifestyle should be chaste and pure but not dull and miserable. She poured iced tea for everyone, respecting the Mother's abstinence from alcohol. The Mother didn't even use wine during communion, using grape juice instead.

Mabel escorted Mary Ruth into the office and closed the door behind her. Hannah felt a draft of cool air cross her ankles as the alabaster table with the large Bible receded into the floor.

Mother Evelyn stepped up from the secret stairway carrying several thick folders under her arm, then she sat at the head of the table. "Let's say grace and enjoy this wonderful meal."

After Mother Evelyn said a short prayer, everyone ate in silence for a few moments. Hannah was too anxious to appreciate the delicate flavors of her food. Feeling restless, she opened the conversation from where the Mother left off in the chapel. "Are you saying we are more than the *Catholic Inquirer*?"

Mabel and Gertrude chuckled. After swallowing a bite, Mother Evelyn looked at Hannah. "Vatican City isn't just the home of the Holy Roman Catholic Church. It's a nation unto itself. Although it's the smallest country in the world, it boasts a higher population than any other nation except China. All members of the Catholic Church are citizens of Vatican City. Priests are ambassadors to their local communities. Like any nation, the Vatican has enemies. Sometimes the Church needs to take direct action against an enemy. The Vatican must remain on the high ground so we do what they cannot openly do."

"I'm not sure what you mean."

"Perhaps I should have said *discreet actions*. Let me give you an example. A week ago, Mykaela discovered a potentially dangerous rap song in development for the American market."

"It really upset her," Hannah said. Just a year younger, Mykaela was Hannah's closest friend. Mary Ruth recruited her from a convent in South Africa to give her a greater opportunity to develop her musical talent. When she played the piano, Hannah's heart would ache with the intricate beauty she created. Mykaela also had what Hannah considered the best job of all the researchers: analyzing music.

"The song will definitely be a bad influence. Did you hear the words?" Gertrude asked as she added a heaping pile of lamb and rice to her plate.

"There were words?" Hannah knew her timing was perfect as a small smile touched Mabel's lips.

"Yes, there were words," Mother Evelyn replied. "The lead singer did not enunciate well, but the words encouraged listeners to kill priests."

"What would you expect from a group with the name 'Satan's Ambassadors'?" Mabel rasped and then coughed. Hannah wondered if she got an escargot stuck in her throat.

Mother Evelyn reached over to pat Mabel on the back, but Mabel waved her off. "Hannah, do you think the Vatican could do anything to stop this?"

"Vatican public relations could organize a protest through the media."

"A public protest would cause an increase in sales, which is what the recording company intends for the Vatican to do. I think it's time to give Sister Hannah a demonstration of what discreet actions mean. Is everything ready, Sister Gertrude?"

Gertrude looked at her plate, reluctant to interrupt her meal. She took one more bite, then with a sigh, she lifted her laptop computer from beside her chair and opened it. "Aarco Records is producing the album. Production companies separate every sound bite, tweak it to perfection, and blend it back together. This process can take months. I've adapted a computer worm to delete every file containing a reference to Satan's Ambassadors."

"Gertrude took responsibility for most of the containment process," Mother Evelyn explained. "However, to prevent a reoccurrence, the corporate director who approved the song needs to be relegated to a less influential position. I accepted the challenge of dealing with the leadership at Aarco Records as well as the lead singer of Satan's Ambassadors, who also wrote the song. Three days ago, the IRS paid Aarco Records a visit, demanding to see their financial records. Yesterday morning, Aarco's best-selling artist switched to Sony Records. And guess what happened to the lead singer?"

Gertrude turned her laptop around for everyone to see and moved her plate back in front of her. "Here is the news report from California."

Hannah watched police arrest a dirty-looking longhaired man with "Satan's Ambassadors" tattooed across his chest. The news reporter smiled as she encouraged other deadbeat dads to catch up on their child support payments before the same happened to them.

Gertrude turned her laptop back around. "All that's left to ensure that Aarco Records and Satan's Ambassadors will never be a threat again is to purge their files. I just need the password to access Aarco Records."

"Th-that is where I c-come in." Mary Ruth spoke a string of numbers and letters. A moment later, Gertrude pressed a button. "It is done."

Hannah looked at Mary Ruth. "How did you obtain Aarco's password?"

Mary Ruth glanced at Mother Evelyn, allowing her to explain. "If you assimilated information for British Intelligence instead of us, do you think you could spot James Bond?"

"You mean James Bond is real?"

"I don't know. I don't work for British Intelligence."

"Then are you saying that the James Bond of Vatican Intelligence gave us the password?"

Mary Ruth laughed, and the other nuns joined in. "I n-never thought of m-myself as J-Jamie Bond."

That doesn't beat the EMP in the surprise department, but it's close, Hannah thought. "So, Sister Mary Ruth is a spy."

"And I'm her escort and protector," Mabel added.

"But Sister Mary Ruth is . . ." Hannah stopped herself, but Mary Ruth finished the sentence for her.

"Old. And, I t-take no offense. Would y-you expect a decrepit old nun and her one-eyed escort to be s-spies?"

"No."

"It's not really dangerous," Mabel said. "We are usually only after passcodes and tidbits of information so Gertrude can do her work. Most of the time no one even knows we've been there."

Hannah changed her personal password every week and knew it would be nearly impossible for anyone to discover it. "How are you able to get passcodes without being in danger?"

Mary Ruth laughed. "I am a t-telepath."

Okay, Hannah thought. *That beats the EMP.*

Chapter Seven

Hannah sat in stunned silence, unsure how to respond to Mary Ruth's bold statement. She felt as if her mental elevator had fallen a hundred stories while she remained suspended in midair at the top. She stared at Mary Ruth, who looked back with a pleasant smile. "Are you playing a joke on me?"

"No."

The Mother stood. "Ladies, I'm afraid we will have to continue this conversation tomorrow on the plane. Mykaela is approaching to inform me that Miss Winsomore is awake."

Even though she knew it was coming, the knock on the door made Hannah jump.

"Enter," Mother Evelyn called.

Mykaela opened the door slightly and poked her head through the opening. "I'm sorry to disturb you, but Miss Winsomore is insistent upon leaving. Should I call her a cab?"

"No, I shall escort her home myself. Please have her ready in ten minutes."

After the door closed, Mother Evelyn picked up the plain manila folders from her desk and handed one to each sister. "I believe Sister Betty has made a chocolate mousse, and you won't want to miss it. Get some rest and follow your instructions in the morning. We'll depart at noon."

"Where are we going?" Hannah asked.

"We'll be heading to Mexico. Wear your cool robes." The Mother's hand froze as she placed the remaining folders back on her desk. She picked up a cell phone Hannah didn't recognize, turned, and looked at Mabel.

Mabel stood. "Is it on?"

"I hung up, but it's powered." Mother Evelyn handed the phone to Mabel. "It's the cell phone from Kappa Lambda Omega."

Mabel opened the back of the phone and removed the battery. "That was not a conversation to be recorded."

"No, it was not." Mother Evelyn left and closed the door behind her.

Hannah turned to Mary Ruth. "You can't leave me hanging."

Mary Ruth turned to Gertrude. "Ex-explain it to h-her."

Gertrude grasped her mother's hand and looked at Hannah. "Your brain has many functions, but the two I will explain are memory and surface thoughts. Reading your memory requires a deep probe, which only an accomplished coercer can do. Having your memory read is easy to detect, because if the reading is forced or done carelessly, it can be painful.

"A telepath can easily read your surface thoughts. When Mary Ruth first became a telepath, she had to train herself to create a shield so the thoughts of the hundreds of people around her did not drive her insane."

Hannah didn't always appreciate British humor, which often contained a cutting edge. Her own humor tended to be more whimsical and sometimes convoluted. Narrowing her eyes, she thought Gertrude and the rest were paying her back for some of the jokes she'd told in the last year. Instead of laughing, however, she said, "Prove it."

Gertrude looked at Hannah with a bemused expression. "Think of something Mary Ruth doesn't know. Don't say anything; just think it."

Hannah decided to return humor for humor. She began telling a joke in her mind. *As you know, Mahatma Gandhi walked barefoot most of the time, which produced an impressive set of calluses. He also ate very little, which made him rather frail, and with his odd diet of garlic and curry, he suffered from bad breath. This made him . . . what?*

Mary Ruth frowned at Hannah. "You are thinking a b-bad joke. The punch l-line is he was a supercallused fragile mystic hexed by halitosis."

Hannah's mouth flew open in astonishment. "I've never told that joke before. How did you know?"

Mary Ruth yawned. "I'm t-tired. Answers are for t-tomorrow."

Gertrude touched Hannah's arm. "Come, Sister. I hear a mousse calling from the kitchen."

⁓

Mother Evelyn climbed into the delivery truck to take Miss Winsomore to her sorority house near Oxford. They rode in silence for the first ten minutes with Miss Winsomore staring out the side window. Mother

Evelyn broke the silence with an innocent question. "Did you enjoy your day, Miss Winthrop?"

The young lady snapped her head around in surprise but didn't reply, so the Mother continued. "Yes, I know your real name is Heather Winthrop. I know quite a bit about you. You and your twin brother are freshmen at Oxford on full scholarship. Your father works in a small pharmacy on the south side of London. Your mother is an elementary schoolteacher. Although they've provided for you adequately, they could not afford a school as expensive as Oxford. Your scholarship is for academic achievement and you must maintain a 3.0 GPA to keep it. Because of your low math grades, your scholarship was in jeopardy until Professor Cain began tutoring you several months ago. You've made straight As since then. How am I doing so far?"

"Why would you bother to learn so much about me?" Heather asked.

"This is the information age, and information is power."

"Just because you know who my father is and you've read my report card, you don't have any power over me."

"Do you really think your academic dean would look favorably upon Professor Cain's method of tutoring or your method of payment?"

The color drained from Heather's face. "Professor Cain's methods work. But my method of payment . . . could be awkward."

"Do not fear me, child," Mother Evelyn replied. "Your secrets are safe with me. I merely tell you what I know to demonstrate the power of information. Why don't you tell me a little bit about Professor Cain's tutoring method?"

Heather squirmed in her seat and looked out the windshield as she spoke. "He uses hypnosis. I go into a blissful state, aware of only his voice. When I wake up, I understand the math. It's quite simple, and it works. My calculus grade has gone from a C to an A."

"Where did he tutor you?"

"In his apartment. I figured he knew you since he lives across the street from your abbey and refers to you by name."

"And what can you tell me of the events today?"

Heather shrugged. "My brother is pledging Kappa Lambda Omega. Professor Cain is an alumnus and knew about the contest. He gave the boys some pretty good ideas. He also provided them with that electromagnetic pulse thingy."

"What was your role in today's events?"

"Once I got inside, I was to find a way to get close to you. I was then supposed to click my heels together to activate the holographic dress. But as soon as I turned on the dress, I blacked out. The next thing I remember was sitting in your infirmary, smelling butter and garlic, and my beautiful dress was gone. I hope Professor Cain didn't want it back."

"I don't believe he will miss it. Nor will he be returning."

"He told me he had to go to Belfast tomorrow. I'll miss him. He had a delightful sense of humor and was incredible in . . ." Heather hesitated and blushed. "Please don't make me listen to a sermon about chastity or to be fruitful and multiply."

Mother Evelyn chuckled. "Many Bible verses are misunderstood or used to excuse bad decisions. Fruitful and multiply is one of them. I believe God meant for us to be fruitful *before* we multiply. In other words, learn to make a living to provide for a family and then multiply."

Heather stared at Mother Evelyn for a full minute and then laughed. "You're the strangest nun I've ever met."

Mother Evelyn swerved to miss something dead in the middle of the road. "I've heard that before. I have a whole apothecary of anecdotes, but I think you would choose not to listen."

Heather laughed again. "I'll have to tell my dad that one. What a day. Here I am riding in a beat-up old truck in the middle of the night with probably the oldest nun in Britain, and she's telling me jokes. This is rich."

The truck hit a large pothole, and Heather winced. "What I would really like to know is how I got this huge bruise on my arm."

Mother Evelyn chose not to answer the question since her cane had caused the bruise. "I think you should be aware that the holographic dress used your body as a power source. It almost killed you. If you see the professor again, I would suggest running away."

"Is that why I feel so drained?" Heather sucked in a breath as she realized she answered her own question.

Mother Evelyn dropped Miss Winthrop off at her sorority house with a promise to provide her with a new tutor, free of charge, from the abbey. She didn't head directly home. Instead, she drove down several blocks and backed her truck up to the garage of Kappa Lambda Omega that was having a loud party.

~○

Hannah read the disappointing minimal instructions from her folder while helping Gertrude push a cart laden with dirty dishes back to the kitchen. Once in the kitchen, she glanced at Gertrude's much thicker and yet still unopened folder. "Mother Evelyn wants me to assist you and Sister Mabel. What do you want me to do?"

"You can be patient while I enjoy my dessert."

Hannah knew better than to get between Gertrude and dessert. "Sorry."

Upon reaching the kitchen, Gertrude opened the refrigerator where five cups of Sister Betty's wonderful chocolate mousse waited. Gertrude brought the desserts on a tray to a table and sat. Hannah joined her. "Can you tell me more about Mary Ruth's talent?"

"That subject can only be discussed in a secure location," Gertrude replied under her breath.

"Then I guess I can't confirm what I believe about Mother Evelyn or Mr. Cain," Hannah whispered with a touch of frustration.

Gertrude raised her voice back to a normal volume. "Mother Evelyn will tell you what she wishes you to know. She doesn't tell me everything. For example, I know very little about Mr. Cain, with whom she obviously has history. It would have been nice to know he was my father."

"How about the Elohim? Do you know who they are?"

"Only one of the ten biggest secrets on the planet, which, of course, I can't tell you about in an unsecure location."

"But no one is here but you and me."

"Don't use two buts in the same sentence, dear. It's uncouth," Gertrude amended absently. "We're not totally unknown to the intelligence community, and our security is still not fully functioning. Only the basement is secure, and even it's vulnerable to a portable device like a cell phone."

Hannah ate in silence for a moment, hoping to find a subject that was not off limits. "Can you tell me about your relationship with Mabel and Mary Ruth?"

"Certainly," Gertrude said after swallowing a mouthful of mousse. "It isn't a secret. Since everyone here calls each other 'Sister,' I can see how you didn't pick up on the fact that Mabel and I really are sisters."

Hannah saw no familial resemblance. Gertrude was large from excessive calories while Mabel was bulkier from sheer muscle. Her brute strength was not apparent beneath her heavy flowing robes, but Hannah saw her three times a week for morning self-defense class wearing spandex. Mabel's leg muscles were like tree trunks, and her arms were scary strong.

"Do you know Sister Mabel's story?" Gertrude asked.

Hannah shook her head.

"Do you believe that God directs our feet?"

"When we choose to let him," Hannah replied.

"I know he directed our paths. As an orphan, Mabel transferred from foster home to foster home. Several of her foster parents beat her regularly. With low self-esteem and skinny as a pole, Mabel married at the age of sixteen to escape from her miserable life. After a few months of marriage, she realized she had jumped from the frying pan into the fire. Her husband turned out to be more brutal than any foster father she'd ever had. She lost a tooth for adding too much spice to the potatoes. She lost her left eye on her second anniversary."

Gertrude paused to scrape the last of the mousse out of her cup. "After hearing about the Sisters of St. Margaret, Mabel fled to the abbey. I empathized with her plight. I was also an orphan but had led a sheltered life as a ward of the abbey. I didn't know Mary Ruth was my mother. Mother Evelyn told me the reason for the secrecy was to protect me from my father, who might kidnap me if he knew where I was. Now that I've met my father, I'm beginning to understand."

She picked a second cup of mousse from the tray. "As Mabel and I became more acquainted, we compared the similarities in our lives. We shared the same last name. Bujold isn't common. We are both refugees from Berlin. I researched the records in the abbey as well as several store-houses in London. With the aid of a British magistrate, I obtained our birth records from Berlin. Not only did I learn that Mabel is my biological sister, I also discovered I have an exceptional talent for research. Mabel became an expert at boxing and judo so no man could ever harm her again."

Mabel entered the kitchen and frowned at Gertrude. "Just because the saint you were named for is the patroness of gardeners doesn't mean you should eat the whole garden."

"Yes, well, you were named appropriately after the old, ugly hermit of Wales," Gertrude snapped back.

Hannah looked from one sister to the other. Neither seemed offended at the pointed barbs. The only family resemblance she saw was in their sharp wit. She looked at Mabel. "Mother Evelyn told me to help you. What will we be doing?"

"Grunt work," Mabel replied.

"Great," Hannah grumbled.

Chapter Eight

Hannah woke at dawn, having slept little. After her morning prayers, she waited in the gym for Mabel to finish her extensive workout. Hannah was too anxious to enjoy watching her kick a punching bag, so she opened her laptop and studied Mexico.

Upon arriving at Mother Evelyn's office, Gertrude greeted Mabel and Hannah with a cheerful "Good morning." The secret passage stood open. "We need some items from the vault. Hannah, you'll accompany us. Mother Evelyn has put her trust in you. If you ever breach that trust, many lives will be in danger. Do you understand?"

"Yes, ma'am," Hannah replied, aware that her throat had gone dry. "May I ask a few questions?"

"Why am I not surprised? The Mother said the conversation dealing with Mary Ruth's talent would be continued on the plane. I'm free to answer some other questions. Would you like to know what's for lunch?"

Hearing the touch of sarcasm in Gertrude's voice, Hannah changed her intended question to one she felt Gertrude would answer and resolved to let no surprise leave her speechless today. "Last night, you called the basement the 'Templar Chamber.' Was it really constructed by the Knights Templar?"

"Yes, it was," Gertrude said as she led Hannah and Mabel through the secret door and down the stairs. "This chamber was constructed over nine hundred years ago as their secret vault. Did you know the Knights Templar were the first bankers?"

"No."

"During the Dark Ages, it was unsafe to travel the countryside carrying treasure. The Knights Templar devised a way for the wealthy to deposit their treasure with the church for safekeeping. Merchants and the aristocracy could then travel to their destinations and withdraw an equal value of gold at another church when they arrived, minus a small fee, of course."

Hannah followed Gertrude and Mabel through the holographic wall and into the round room. "This room was the front vault where thousands of coins were stored," Gertrude explained.

"So, there is more than one vault?"

Gertrude and Mabel moved to opposite walls and faced the large ancient-looking cuneiform letters carved into the stone. Ignoring Hannah's question, the two sisters pushed two stones on each wall at the same time.

Hannah heard a faint grinding of stone rubbing against stone. On the east side of the room, behind the computer stations, a portion of the wall sank into the floor. Huge iron chains were attached to the top of the descending wall. Hannah assumed they led to a counterbalance somewhere. She saw a round vault door, about six feet tall where the wall had descended. The door looked old. She noticed two small dials with letters, a thick pull bar, and a large spindle in the center. The logo on the door said "Peltz Genuine German Manufacture." Gertrude dialed a combination on the left dial. Mabel did the same on the right then moved to the center of the vault and turned the spindle.

"The Templar sanctuary burned over six hundred years ago, but the vault remained intact. This vault has a second secret chamber. Whatever they stored in here was much more sacred to them than gold."

"Please don't tell me you have the Holy Grail hidden in here," Hannah joked.

Gertrude laughed. "Goodness, no. But some of our treasures are too controversial to keep in a museum or even in the secret vaults at the Vatican."

Mabel pulled the vault door open, and Hannah caught a musty whiff of rusting metal. Gertrude hit a light switch and florescent bulbs flickered on. Hannah followed Gertrude and Mabel down a long, narrow tunnel with several curves, which opened to a much larger chamber. Hannah stopped at the threshold of the chamber. Her jaw dropped. Fifty or more pallets of rough-hewn gold bars glowed in the florescent light. She estimated each pallet contained a hundred bars. Thick chains and interlocking metal bands secured the pallets to the floor. Hannah made a quick calculation. "There must be half a billion dollars down here!"

"You've heard our abbey is privately funded? Well, here is the private fund," Gertrude replied. "The gold is worth less than the other treasures in this room."

"Where did it come from?"

"Before building the abbey, our founder, Mother Guinevere, was an archeologist. It was an unusual occupation for a woman in the eighteenth century. Some of the gold is marked in Aramaic, indicating it came from the secret treasures of King Asa, and some is from ancient Egypt. Some are marked with runes from the Aztec and Mayan cultures. There are also a few bars with the Nazi emblem on them."

Hannah tore her gaze away from the pallets of gold, which formed a circle ten feet out from the walls, creating a broad path to the other side of the round hundred-foot-wide chamber. Narrow pathways meandered through hundreds of crates with boxes piled on top, a couple of desks with computer terminals, several large safes, and an assortment of glass cases lit from within containing jewels, swords, scrolls, and other items Hannah assumed were priceless. It reminded her of a junk store, except everything was valuable.

"It takes your breath away," Gertrude whispered. "I've spent days here just looking at the walls. After our trip, I'll bring you back and you can absorb everything at your leisure. The dimensions of this sanctuary are exactly like the dimensions of our Chapel of Glass, which is located above it."

Gertrude grasped Hannah's elbow lightly and led her into the chamber. Six-sided rough-hewn tiles interlocked beneath their feet. Carved into the stone walls were different scenes from the Bible. The paint had faded with time, but Hannah could see most of the detail. Starting on the left appeared a scene depicting Adam and Eve in the Garden of Eden, complete with the serpent and the apple. The next scene showed Enoch riding a chariot up into heaven while people and demons watched from below. The third scene depicted Noah and the ark, with intricate details of elephants and giraffes. Moses parting the Red Sea filled the fourth. The next contained the Star of Bethlehem shining over a stable, with a manger and baby Jesus. The last scene showed Christ on the cross, with three women kneeling before Him.

Gertrude pointed to the ceiling. Hannah looked up and saw thick sheets of raw iron covering it about ten feet above her head. Six massive stone pillars extended beyond the metal, and large square iron posts held up the rusting iron, marring the beauty of the chamber. "The resurrection scene is the most magnificent, but you can no longer see it. Mother Evelyn added supports to enhance the structural integrity after cracks formed during the bombing of London in World War II."

Hannah noticed a heavy iron door on the opposite side of the room. "Where does that lead?"

"It once led somewhere beneath the fountain in the courtyard, but it collapsed long ago. Huge boulders block the passageway."

Gertrude led the way through the maze of treasures. "I have work to do." Mabel's gravelly voice echoed off the metal. "Sister, please take Hannah on a quick tour. I need to pack a few things you cannot see."

Hannah looked at Gertrude and raised a questioning eyebrow.

"A telepath can easily read your mind," Gertrude explained. "Not knowing what Mabel is doing is for everyone's protection."

Hannah turned toward Mabel as she walked away. "Are you a telepath, like Mary Ruth?"

"No." Mabel turned back to Hannah and rapped her forehead with her knuckles, making an odd thumping sound. "My strengths are defensive. I have a metal plate in my head, thanks to my ex-husband. A telepath can't read through metal."

"Are we going to meet other telepaths in Mexico?" Hannah asked.

Mabel gave Hannah a one-eyed glare.

Hannah followed Gertrude to the center of the room, where several dozen glass cases circled each of the six massive stone pillars. She hoped Gertrude would show a little pity and give her a few answers. "Are you a telepath?"

"Just a little," Gertrude sighed. "You might call me an empath. I can sense emotions. I can tell when someone is lying and am good at leading conversations around to subjects I want to approach. My talent isn't as useful as I wish it were. Strong emotions can overwhelm me as I feel the same sorrow or pain. Now, there are a few treasures I would like to show you."

Gertrude directed Hannah to the first set of glass cases. Indirect lighting made them seem to glow. "Each container is vacuum sealed. If you touch the glass, it will feel quite cold."

Hannah approached the first display, which held a massive sword. Looking at its rough finish, she noticed runes carved into the metal. Leather cured to a beautiful maroon color wound around the hilt. The pommel held a huge, clear emerald at the end, and smaller emeralds adorned the crossbar. "We believe this was the sword held by Guillaume de Beaujieu." Gertrude said with reverence, "Grand Master of the Knights Templar from 1279 until 1291."

Hannah moved to the next case. Inside was a golden half-crown ornately shaped in leaves. It looked very lightweight. "Whose was that, Caesar's?" Hannah joked.

"Not quite that old. Although over there is the cup the Roman senate tried to poison him with, along with the cup used to poison Rasputin. This crown belonged to Constantine."

"You're kidding."

"No, it's real." Gertrude led Hannah to another stone pillar surrounded by glass cases. "Let me show you a couple of my favorites."

The two nuns passed several interesting relics as they traversed the room. One held three plain, unadorned golden rods. Another held a simple iron spike. A good portion of the cases held scrolls and papyrus with pictograms. Several contained clay and stone tablets with cuneiform letters. One large case featured a chariot wheel with large metal spikes protruding out of the center. From open boxes, Hannah saw old comic books, sheets of stamps, and a few vintage toys.

As they entered the centermost section, Hannah passed a small case with an unusual computer keyboard. Strange markings figured prominently on the keys. She paused at the incongruity since everything she had seen so far looked old. "What is this?"

Gertrude turned and glanced at the keyboard. "I could never figure out what it is or where it's from. The internal components are melted. I think it must be a computer prototype or a toy. Mother Evelyn said I should throw it away, but you never know what might be valuable in a hundred years."

Hannah followed Gertrude to the largest case in the room. It was as tall as she was. Inside it sat a big, ugly, gray metal bomb, oblong, with four fins on the tail and a large white swastika on the side. "I'm sure you heard the rumor that Hitler was working on a nuclear bomb?"

Hannah nodded.

"This is it."

Hannah looked closely at the bomb behind thick glass. "How did it end up here?"

"Mother Evelyn worked with Vatican Intelligence before I was born," Gertrude replied. "She and Mary Ruth stole it out of a plane heading to London. When you get a chance, ask my mother to tell you the story."

"I will. Uh, is it radioactive?"

"No, dear. The uranium has been removed."

In the center of the room, Gertrude led Hannah to another large glass case with thin amber gas swirling inside and a long golden staff formed into a jagged lightning bolt. The gold swirled and twisted toward three curved prongs at the top as thin as a pencil. Leather wrapped around the center of the shaft, where a mighty warrior might hold it. Two curved wooden posts, about the size and shape of a gun trigger, stuck out of the leather grip. Two thick metal ropes, wrapped in leather, extended from the base of the shaft and joined a series of thirty or so gold triangular bricks about ten inches long.

"Who did this belong to?"

Gertrude hesitated. "It's our oldest artifact, and I'm not sure if you're ready for the answer."

"I can handle it."

"Zeus."

Hannah felt her knees go weak. "You're right. That's impossible to accept." She reached out to a chair sitting beside the glass case and sat down.

"Don't sit there!" Gertrude shrieked. "Jesus carved that chair!"

Chapter Nine

Hannah jumped to her feet, vacating the sacred chair. The guffaw from both sisters slowed her racing heart. Turning around, she realized she had sat on a simple wooden folding chair. She closed her eyes in relief then felt a little anger at the joke Gertrude had played on her.

When Gertrude caught her breath between laughs, she touched Hannah's arm. "After all these months of enduring your American jokes, I thought you could use a little dose of British humor."

"I thought you were German," Hannah muttered.

Gertrude burst into another round of laughter. "Born German but raised British."

"Were you joking about Zeus too?"

"No."

"But Zeus is a myth."

"Most myths are based in facts. Zeus was not a god; he was a man, a very intelligent man. There are few records still in existence, but from the information Mother Guinevere gathered, Zeus could have been less than ten generations removed from Adam and Eve. According to ancient Greek text, he was born of the purest blood. His life span could have been close to a thousand years."

Gertrude motioned Hannah to look closely at the staff. "According to the tests, it's at least four thousand years old. Gold is an excellent conductor of electricity. Zeus discovered this, probably by accident. The shaft of the staff is hollow, as is each gold triangular brick. The triangles acted as a primitive but effective electrical capacitor. Zeus would have his servants drag them through dry sand, each triangle building a powerful static electric charge. Using thick leather gloves, the servants attached gold wires in a series to the staff. By pulling the two wooden triggers, a massive arc of electricity sprang from the prongs at the tip."

Hannah imagined Zeus facing an army of a thousand men with their primitive bronze swords and helmets. He says something dramatic, pulls the triggers, and boom! The first wave of enemy soldiers lie dead from electrocution. The smell of burning flesh would be enough to rout the rest.

Though the ancient technology lay before her, the story was still difficult to believe. Hannah wanted to see more, but Mabel said it was time
to go. Before joining Mabel, Gertrude approached one of the posts that
held up the iron ceiling and gently removed a large piece of jewelry from
a hook attached to it. She marveled at the jewelry, an ornate wooden ankh
with small gems on both sides. The center held a large blue stone like a
sapphire. The perfectly smooth sphere stood out from the ankh to make a
hemisphere on each side. "What is it?"

"I don't know," Gertrude replied. "The museum manifest lists it as the
Ankh of Anak. Mother Evelyn instructed me to retrieve it."

~⟂

After carrying a thirty-pound box up fifty steps, Hannah felt like the
box weighed a ton. After three trips with more boxes, Hannah thought her
arms might fall off, and her legs felt like rubber. Gertrude had stopped at
the lower control room to do some computer work, so all the transport
duties fell to Mabel and Hannah. "What are we carrying?" Hannah gasped
during their fourth trip, carrying two heavy briefcases.

"Mostly electronic equipment and money," Mabel rasped.

Hannah had no breath to spare for talking. The last piece of equipment
was a large satellite dish. Although Mabel carried the brunt of the weight,
Hannah had to carry the other end and go up the stairs backward. "Can I
ask what this is?"

"It's the alternate relay for adjusting our satellite," Gertrude replied,
also out of breath, climbing the steps behind her.

Hannah had helped her father install a satellite on their roof back in
Tulsa. Lining the dish up correctly hadn't been difficult. "Can't you just
adjust it by hand?"

Gertrude and Mabel laughed. "No, dear," Gertrude replied. "This
doesn't adjust our satellite dish. It adjusts our satellite."

"Oh," was all Hannah could say.

~⟂

Hannah helped Mabel load the cargo van as Gertrude escorted Mary
Ruth to the garage across the street from the abbey. Mabel took the driver's

seat with Mary Ruth and Gertrude sitting up front, leaving Hannah to sit with the boxes in the back. They didn't head to Heathrow or Gatwick Airport, as Hannah had expected. Instead, they headed toward the coast. They traveled for a couple of hours along narrow country roads and arrived at a small private airport overlooking the English Channel. Hannah heard waves from the Atlantic crashing against the shore and smelled the salt air.

Mabel pulled the cargo van into a large hangar. As Hannah crawled out of the back, she saw Mother Evelyn directing a man using a forklift as a crew unloaded a large wooden box from one of the abbey's trucks. They put it into the cargo hold of a sleek-looking, pearly white jet.

"Isn't she b-beautiful?" Mary Ruth exclaimed. "We've only h-had her for a few m-months. She is a custom-made Bombardier Global 7500. She can t-travel halfway around the w-world without refueling and at n-nearly Mach 1."

Hannah breathed a sigh of relief when the Mother directed the men to unload Hannah's van. Mabel walked inside the plane and retrieved what looked like a large metal detector. She waved the round end over the outside of the plane. Before Hannah could ask, Gertrude said, "She's sweeping for bugs. We don't wish anyone to know what we do or where we go."

Seeing that Mary Ruth's tremors had intensified, Hannah assisted Gertrude as she led her mother up the stairs and into the plane. Down a short passageway of storage lockers, six oversized leather recliners filled the first compartment. Mary Ruth sat beside the window with her back to the front of the plane. Hannah assumed the Mother would sit beside Mary Ruth. She chose to sit across from the Mother's seat so she could continue the conversation from the previous night if the opportunity arose.

After sitting on top of a box in the back of a truck for two hours, Hannah felt grateful when she sank into the plush, warm chair, feeling it contour to her body. She discovered several control buttons and a small trackball on the right arm of the chair. The first button lowered a thin LCD display, about ten inches across, from the roof of the plane. It stopped at eye level about two feet in front of her face. Another button allowed her to choose between computer functions and television. The last button caused rollers in the lumbar support to massage her back, making her close her eyes as the tension left her.

Mary Ruth chuckled beside her. "You m-might want to take a quick t-tour before we d-depart."

Hannah reluctantly rose from her chair and headed aft. After the passenger section, she found a workroom with two swivel chairs on each side, facing desks secured against the outer wall of the plane. Four computer keyboards sat on the desks with flat screens attached to the walls. In one corner, Gertrude struggled to connect wires from a large metal box to the satellite dish attached to the top. Hannah had to duck under the dish to get to the next compartment.

She helped herself to a bottled water from the refrigerator in the third compartment, which contained a small kitchenette and pantry on one side and a bathroom, complete with shower, on the other. Two bunk beds filled the last compartment. Hannah felt she could easily sleep in her chair, leaving the beds to the older ladies.

She headed back to the front and peered into the cockpit, where the pilot and copilot were pressing buttons and checking them off a list as they turned green. The pilot noticed Hannah. He smiled.

"Welcome aboard," he said with a deep baritone. "I'm Captain Bob Mino. James, your copilot, and I will be escorting you to Mexico."

Noting the Texas drawl, Hannah looked into eyes as green as fresh limes. "How long will this flight be?"

"It's roughly six thousand miles. It should take about ten hours. We don't expect any bad weather, so make yourself comfortable and enjoy the flight."

Hannah sat facing Mother Evelyn. Mabel secured the door and took a seat across the aisle.

"I n-noticed you did not return t-to the abbey last n-night," Mary Ruth said to Mother Evelyn.

"I needed to pick up a few things." The Mother yawned. "Our visitor, Miss Winsomore, gave me the address of Professor Cain's apartment. I took the time to visit."

"Did you f-find anything interesting?"

"Old books and a few knickknacks, none of which fit his personality. I believe he used an interior decorator to make it feel personal. One room was full of hypnotism equipment. I also picked up the controls for the holographic dress. The kitchen looked unused, and the closet was full of new clothes. He probably rented the place to seduce Miss Winthrop and to spy on us."

"Where is it?" Mary Ruth asked.

"Right across the street from the abbey."

"Then he has b-been watching us for a while."

"I believe so. I found a parking stub from Heathrow Airport and a notepad with 'LAX' indented inside it. I believe he left for Los Angeles this morning. He also left me a little present. I needed to diffuse it before opening it."

"He left you a bomb?" Hannah exclaimed.

"Yes."

"Are you c-certain it was for y-you?" Mary Ruth asked, her voice shaking more than usual.

"It was a gift-wrapped box with a Mother's Day card attached."

Hannah gulped and wondered what she was getting herself into.

Chapter Ten

As the plane accelerated down the runway, Hannah appreciated the contour-forming chair. Instead of rocketing skyward, they flew what seemed like only a hundred feet from the surface of the ocean for twenty minutes. Flying low made for a bumpy ride, but Mother Evelyn explained that their flight was not registered, therefore they needed to fly under the radar until they were far enough from land.

By the time they leveled off, Hannah was itching to continue the conversation from the previous night. From the weariness around her eyes and occasional yawns, she could tell that Mother Evelyn was fatigued, but she did not want to postpone this conversation any further. "Mother," she said, "I feel like I'm drowning in a pool of questions."

Mother Evelyn sighed. "What would you like to know?"

"Who is Cain?"

Mother Evelyn closed her eyes for a few seconds. "In 1934, a talented botanist named Dr. Cain lived in Leiden, the tulip capitol of Holland. Dr. Cain amassed wealth not only from his tulip hybrids but also by developing new strains of herbs and fungi from which he created health-improving pharmaceuticals.

"He catered to royal houses, wealthy merchants, and high-ranking government officials all over Europe. He preferred to keep a low profile, refusing to have his picture taken because of his facial deformity. Many influential people trusted him, and everyone respected his apothecary talents."

"But no one realized he was a telepath," Hannah interjected, hoping to confirm what Gertrude could not tell her the previous night.

"I'm glad you picked up on that," Mother Evelyn replied. "As a telepath, he gathered private information from the elite. I don't know what he did with it, but I do know that he was searching for a pharmaceutical way to enhance telepathic ability. Although they didn't realize it, Cain was using royal bloodlines to test his theories on racial purity. He never succeeded in enhancing the telepathic gene, but some of his concoctions were effective against genetic flaws in infants. He began working with Hitler in 1938 because of Hitler's racially pure views expressed in *Mein Kampf*."

"Hitler believed in the superiority of the Aryan race," Hannah said. "Is Dr. Cain of German descent?"

"Not exactly," Mother Evelyn said, and Hannah noticed her lips quiver with a suppressed smile. "Cain's goal to breed telepaths was much grander than what Hitler planned. Although telepathy is a recessive trait, many people have a slight touch of it. Most don't recognize the experience when it happens. You may have experienced one or two episodes."

"I don't think so."

"Do the words 'women's intuition' or '*déjà vu*' sound familiar?"

Hannah thought about her grandmother and grandfather, who responded to each other's needs without speaking. She also remembered riding in the car with her best friend in high school and knowing what her friend was thinking. "I'm beginning to understand."

"Some nurses and doctors are low-level empaths. This is especially true of those who dedicate their lives to pediatric care. Young children can't communicate what hurts, but a good nurse or doctor knows anyway. They can feel the strong emotions coming from the child and can interpret them correctly."

Hannah felt an itch under the hood of her veil. Gertrude entered the cabin and took the seat beside her, and Hannah used the distraction to discreetly reach up and scratch her head. "So, Sister Gertrude is a low-level telepath?"

"Hardly." Gertrude puffed out her chest. "I'm aware of my gift and can seek out other people's emotions. I can also project emotions, so I am a midlevel telepath."

Hannah looked back at Mother Evelyn. "Is there a test to tell if a person has the gift?"

Mother Evelyn raised an eyebrow. "Why don't you ask the real question on your mind?"

Hannah felt a lump in her throat. "Okay. Am I a telepath?"

Mother Evelyn and Mary Ruth stared at Hannah intently. Hannah felt awkward as the stare lingered on for nearly a minute. She wondered what they were doing. Her head itched again, and she hoped whatever bug was under her bonnet wouldn't come crawling out while they were staring at her.

"There are no tests, but telepaths can sense each other," Mother Evelyn replied. "You have the potential. Your genetic background is diverse, which is good. You have a twin brother, which is also good. High intelligence is virtually a prerequisite for telepathy. Unfortunately, most talents do not manifest except under extremely traumatic conditions."

"Why would my diverse genetic background be a benefit? I thought Cain was working with people with pure racial bloodlines."

"Dr. Cain discovered that the closer knit a gene pool is, the less likely the genetic trait for telepathy would manifest."

"He did not t-tell the *führer* that," Mary Ruth added.

"How do you know?"

"I was there. I was part of his g-genetic experiments."

Mother Evelyn grasped Mary Ruth's hand. "Dr. Cain discovered Mary Ruth in 1938, when she was a teenager living in Paris. Her father was French and Italian. Her mother was Greek and English."

Mary Ruth shuddered. "One cold, rainy night as I was crossing the S-Seine River, a horse carriage passed too close and swept me off the b-bridge. I caught the rail but could not lift myself back to safety. D-dangling over the river, I screamed knowing the ice-cold water would be my d-death. No one was on the b-bridge to hear me, but Dr. Cain, who was visiting P-Paris, was close enough to hear my mental scream. Just as my numb fingers lost their grip, he reached over the side and s-saved me. My name was Aleska Bujold."

"A beautiful name, fit for a queen," Mother Evelyn added. "Several years later, as Aleska was about to take her final vows to become a nun, Cain kidnapped her and took her to Berlin, where he fathered three children with her."

Hannah looked at Gertrude and Mabel as a tear trickled down Mary Ruth's cheek. "What happened to the third child?"

"I don't know," Mother Evelyn replied. "In 1944, during a covert operation in Berlin, I helped Aleska escape. I needed her help to prevent a nuclear attack against London. Unfortunately, we could not find the secret location where her children and several other potential telepaths were hidden. Five years later, I found Gertrude in an orphanage in London, but I could never find Mabel, but she eventually found us. I found a paper trail for Mary Ruth's son Karl, and believe he traveled to America with his father. Once they arrived in America, their trail disappeared."

Hannah discreetly scratched her itching scalp again. "Do you think her son could be a full telepath like Cain and Mary Ruth?"

"It's possible, since that was his goal. But Cain is more than just a telepath. He is a coercer."

"Sounds ominous."

"A telepath can read your surface thoughts and can communicate over short distances. A coercer can make you do things against your will. He can do a deep scan and retrieve memories you're not willing to share. If the coercer is strong enough, he can alter or even erase your memories. A normal mind has no defense. A telepath has defenses dependent upon his or her mental strength. The art of coercion is subtlety. For example, if I wanted you to remove your veil—"

At that moment, the little bug in Hannah's hair bit her. She stood, shrieked, and tore off her veil. She flung it across the plane and viciously scratched her curly hair.

"I might try to make you feel like you have a bug in your bonnet," Mother Evelyn finished.

Hannah glared at Mother Evelyn. She no longer felt an itch. For a second, she was shocked, then angry, and finally embarrassed. "That was rude."

"It was m-my idea," Mary Ruth said, chuckling, and the others hid their mirth behind raised hands. "French humor."

"I would have removed my veil. All you had to do was ask."

"If I asked, you wouldn't have understood the lesson. Subtlety is the key. Until I said so, you had no idea I was manipulating your mind. That is what a skilled coercer can do."

"And Cain is a skilled coercer," Hannah said, then sat back down.

Mabel tapped her forehead and again, Hannah heard an odd clanging. "If you were wearing a metal helmet or even a metal band beneath your veil, you would be protected."

Mother Evelyn spoke, but her lips didn't move. *"However, if you wear metal, I cannot communicate with you privately."*

Hannah felt a slight tickling sensation behind her ear. "You just spoke in my mind."

"Yes," Mother Evelyn replied with her mouth.

Hannah's talent for making connections clicked in her head. "I once read that all Roman soldiers were required to wear metal helmets. Do you think telepathy was common in ancient times?"

Gertrude cleared her throat and turned in her chair to speak to Hannah. "The Bible tells of many prophets and a few with the ability to heal. Healing and precognition are two more of the higher-level gifts, like coercion. Most rulers of every ancient culture wore a crown of gold or a headband of metal. The oldest metal artifacts are not swords, shields, or even plowshares. They are helmets. I believe they wore metal to protect the mind."

"What happened to all the telepaths?"

"Poor nutrition and close-knit gene pools have diminished the trait over the years. If you were a king in ancient times and suspected a man of trying to read your mind, what would you do?"

"I would brand him a traitor and kill him."

"And you would kill their families. Eventually, the paranoia of the royalty nearly eliminated the genetic trait for telepathy from the gene pool," Gertrude said and looked to the floor sadly.

"Obviously, they didn't eliminate it completely," Hannah interjected, looking at Mary Ruth and Mother Evelyn.

"As the various cultures of Europe started crossbreeding, mental gifts began to manifest again. However, what man does not understand, he fears. In 1184, the Pope wrote a letter titled *Ad abolendam,* which translates to 'for the purpose of doing away with.' That letter instituted a process for the Church to deal with heresy, witchcraft, and other crimes against the faith."

"The Inquisition," Hannah stated, not wanting to review that ugly chapter in history.

Hannah felt a wave of sorrow flow from Gertrude. "The Church canonized a few people with the power to heal into sainthood. They burned anyone exhibiting any other telepathic trait. Years later, the same thing happened in colonial America, but they called the cleansing 'witch hunts.'"

"Then there are not many left?"

Mother Evelyn stifled a yawn. "There are probably several million low- or midlevel telepaths. A stockbroker who rarely makes a mistake, gifted doctors, and schoolteachers are the most visible examples. Some high-level telepaths reside in insane asylums because they did not learn to tune out the noise. There are probably no more than a few hundred high-level telepaths on the whole planet."

The Mother continued, "I apologize, but I've not slept in two days and I'm feeling my age, so I'm going to bed. Mary Ruth, I suggest you do the same. Gertrude, Cain left us a few interesting clues last night. I left a folder on your desk with a few details of his activities I've pieced together over the years. There's also a recording of our conversation in the chapel last night. His hologram was perfect right down to his fingerprints. Check with the FBI and Interpol to see if there are any records. Dig wherever you can to see what he has been doing."

Gertrude rose and headed toward the workroom. Mother Evelyn turned to Mabel. "There are six new satellite phones in the workroom. You need to link them to our satellite, put security protocols in place, and program the speed dials. After Hannah tells you where the Elohim are, talk to Captain Bob and see if he knows anyone in Mexico. I have a one-ton box that will need to come with us, so we need a large helicopter and a pilot."

Hannah looked at Mother Evelyn and knew her eyes were open as wide as they could be. "Me? I don't even know who the Elohim are, much less where they live."

Mother Evelyn leaned toward Hannah, her wrinkled brow creasing more deeply. "Hannah, some things are on a need-to-know basis. Not knowing who the Elohim are is for your own safety. You don't need a who to find a where."

"That will make it more difficult."

"Our satellite will be over Mexico in two hours. Have Gertrude teach you how to use the sensors. Most of the functions are locked. I wouldn't want you to crash our secret and very expensive satellite. You'll be looking for magnetic anomalies within the Sierra Nevada."

Hannah felt the weight of the overwhelming task placed in her lap. "Ma'am, I'm not sure how sensitive your satellite is, but the Sierra Nevada is a volcano belt that's nine hundred kilometers long. It's nothing but magnetic anomalies."

"Volcanoes are measurable, fairly predictable, and quantifiably logical. You need to look for something that does not fit the pattern."

"Yes, that's what an anomaly is." Hannah sucked in her breath, realizing what she'd just said. "I apologize if that sounded sarcastic."

"It did, but apology accepted."

Hannah concentrated on her words more carefully, making sure she didn't stumble with her dry mouth. "Should I look for a hidden village or something?"

"I doubt you would be able to spot it, so look for nothing instead."

Hannah was careful not to roll her eyes at the Mother's choice of words, but when the Mother smiled, Hannah felt her mouth turn even dryer. "Is your level of telepathy on a need-to-know basis also?"

"Absolutely."

Hannah watched Mother Evelyn as she helped Mary Ruth to the bunkroom and wondered how many years it would take her to learn not to think the thoughts that too often came out of her mouth.

Chapter Eleven

It took Hannah several hours to learn how to use the satellite. The multitude of scanning options amazed her, and she wasted a little time switching from infrared to ultraviolet, magnifying close enough to see individual animals and observing the statistical information of vegetation proportions and geological compositions. Several functions were not only blocked, they were unnamed, making her wonder what else the Catholic satellite could do. While Gertrude worked on a terminal across the aisle, Hannah wondered why the Vatican would need such a sophisticated satellite.

The satellite remained stationary over the Sierra Nevada, so Hannah took her time examining active volcanos. Every volcano was a little different, but when she compared the magnetic field with the metallic composition of a volcano, nothing seemed unusual. As the clock sped forward, she began to doubt whether she could find anything that could be defined as an anomaly. Mabel popped in every thirty minutes to ask if she'd found anything yet, adding to Hannah's stress. Starting on the East Coast, she looked at every dormant volcano hoping to find anything unusual. Papers with quickly scribbled notes lay scattered all over her desk along with several graphs and a few pictures. As the end of the eighth hour approached, Hannah compared her observations from the satellite to the data from the United States Geological Survey and finally found something more than odd. She hurried to tell Mabel so that Captain Bob would know where to land the plane.

The four sisters and Mother Evelyn met in the passenger compartment. Mabel served a simple supper of sandwiches and salad. Mother Evelyn glanced at Gertrude. "Why don't you start?"

Gertrude looked at her notes. "Cain's fingerprints were not in any database. I followed the money trail from his last known persona in 1947. He established three American holding companies in 1953 to manage his stock portfolios. His investment record is remarkable but not a surprise, since he is a telepath. He made major purchases of Disney, IBM, Walmart, Chase, and Microsoft stocks early on. All these companies were worth billions when he dissolved them a week before Black Monday in 1987. At that point, he took on a new persona, and I suspect he set up at least seven new holding companies."

"You suspect?" Mother Evelyn raised an eyebrow.

Gertrude clenched her fists. "I could only trace him to one company, Enoch Enterprises. He used one-seventh of his assets and reinvested primarily in the same stocks."

"Where is Enoch Enterprises located?"

"The main office was in the World Trade Center in New York. After the attack, he moved the office to Atlanta. There are branch offices in Los Angeles, Washington, DC, Tokyo, Sydney, Cairo, and Paris. Mr. Cain must be using a different identity for his other companies. In the last five years, Enoch Enterprises has purchased large tracts of open wilderness all over the world. A major construction project is under way in the Colombian jungle."

"Were you able to verify his claim of influencing the American presidents?"

"Yes, ma'am. I found a picture in the Kennedy files with Cain in the background. I didn't recognize him at first because he wore a beard and covered his birthmark with makeup. The photo caption identified him as Dr. Slayer, a professor of political science from Harvard. Harvard has no record of a Dr. Slayer. I found no evidence that he has been around any recent president, but he would only need to be in the White House as a tourist and close enough to the president or one of his advisors to plant a few telepathic suggestions."

"Excellent work, Sister Gertrude. Please find the architectural firm that designed the building in Colombia. I would like to know what he's constructing."

"Yes, ma'am." Gertrude sank back into her chair.

Mother Evelyn turned to Hannah. "Did you find a magnetic anomaly?"

"According to the USGS, the Colima volcano is the most active volcano in Mexico. However, its magnetic signature suggests that it's dormant."

"I knew you could find it," Mother Evelyn replied. "I assume you told Mabel?"

"Yes, ma'am, and there are a few villages about ten miles away."

As they descended beneath the clouds, Hannah glimpsed the afternoon sun reflecting off the Pacific Ocean. The plane banked over the water and approached the white beach that formed a half circle several miles long. Several sailboats played in the wake of a huge cruise ship leaving the bay. Mountains rose abruptly from the jungle a few miles from the shoreline. The plane flew past a luxury hotel with a well-manicured golf course and landed at a small airport.

Captain Bob parked the plane next to a large brown helicopter with "Albro Helicopter Tours" painted on it in bold white letters. The helicopter reminded Hannah of film footage she'd seen of the military copters used in Vietnam. However, large windows took the place of thick steel plating on the side.

Mabel exited first and walked toward the helicopter. A forklift approached the back of the plane and Mother Evelyn walked to meet it, her cane clicking sharply against the tarmac. Gertrude, carrying two metal suitcases, led Mary Ruth to the helicopter and Hannah followed.

The pilot, a short, middle-aged man who obviously ate well, stepped out of the copter as the nuns approached. He spoke English with only a slight Mexican accent. "Good afternoon, sisters. Welcome to Manzanillo. My name is Albro Sanchez, and I'll be escorting you to your destination."

Mabel handed Albro a large bundle of American dollars. "Here is the fee we discussed. There are to be no questions and no records."

Albro pointed to the large wooden crate on the forklift. "And there will be no drugs or weapons, as we also discussed."

"Agreed," Mabel replied, and Albro accepted the money.

A snowcapped mountain rising nearly three miles high filled Hannah's view. "It's beautiful!" She shifted her gaze slightly to the south. Another conical mountain rose close to the first and was almost as tall, but without snow capping the top. A faint cloud of smoke rose from it.

"Do you have the coordinates?" Albro asked.

Mother Evelyn handed Albro a topographical map with an X marked in the middle. "Just circle the volcano about three miles out. We will let you know where to land."

Hannah wondered exactly what the Mother was looking for. From the satellite, she knew there was nothing within three miles of the volcano.

Mother Evelyn sat in the copilot seat while the rest sat in the second row. Hannah felt overjoyed to sit by the big front window. It gave her an incredible view of the mountains. Being her first time in a helicopter, she was exhilarated as they rose several miles straight up to reach the level of the smoldering volcano. The vibration of the rotating blades tickled her ears.

From her sound-dampening earphones she heard Albro speak in a dramatic voice. "From atop their thrones of fire and ice high above the Valley of Colima, legends say the gods look down upon their ancient domain."

"A narrative will not be necessary, Mr. Sanchez," Mother Evelyn interrupted. She pointed to a picture of Albro with his wife and five children attached to the console and spoke with him in Spanish. Hannah understood a few words and was amazed at Mother Evelyn's linguistic skills.

Hannah tapped her mic. "Is this where the Elohim live?"

Mother Evelyn replied immediately. *"Careful, this is an open mic and our guide is fluent in English."*

Hannah thought that was a rude thing to say in Albro's presence until she realized the Mother hadn't stopped her conversation with him. Hannah's hands shook with more than just the vibration of the helicopter as it dawned on her that she hadn't heard the Mother's voice with her ears but with her mind. She took three calming breaths then spoke with her own mind: *"Mother, can you hear me?"*

Mother Evelyn continued her conversation with Albro in Spanish but answered Hannah in English. *"Yes, dear. But since it's not polite to pry, I only listen when a thought is directed specifically to me."*

"You are holding a conversation in Spanish with Albro at the same time. Isn't that difficult?"

"It's like playing the piano and singing a song at the same time. With time and practice, it becomes easy."

"How far can you listen?"

"That depends on the power of the sending and receiving minds. It's similar to short-wave radio. If the transmitter is strong, the signal can go for miles. If the receiver is also strong, the signal will be clearer. I can speak to you if you are within a short distance. I can speak to Mary Ruth from much farther away. Metal and the curvature of the planet will block any communication."

"So, if Mr. Cain were within a few miles, he could hear our conversation."

"Only if I were shouting, which I am not. If I thought he was close, I could touch you and our conversation would be private."

"Mr. Cain spent a lot of money on the EMP and holographic dress to only ask you to send a message to the Pope and other Christian leaders. He also spent a lot of time setting up the fraternity to get Miss Winsomore inside. He doesn't seem like the type of person to incur such large expenses unless he expects a good return on his investment. I don't think the message was important. I think he wants something from you."

"I will take that under advisement."

Hannah remembered her original question, which the Mother had not answered. *"I know that Bene Elohim means 'sons of God.' When Mr. Cain mentioned them, you seemed shocked. Are they the result of Hitler's genetic experiment?"*

Mother Evelyn's mental laughter sounded much younger than her normal voice. *"Not even close."*

"Then who are they?"

The Mother sighed into her microphone. *"A group of people I have spent my life avoiding."*

Hannah waited a full minute for the Mother to continue. *"Can't you tell me more than that?"*

"Not yet. We may not find them, and you will be safer not knowing."

It took about fifteen minutes to reach the volcano. Then Gertrude announced that she had found a magnetic spike, interrupting Hannah's thoughts. Hannah looked behind her at the wooden crate and wondered what was inside. It rested where two rows of seats normally sat. She could sense the helicopter descending toward the base of the volcano. A few minutes later, they landed in a flat spot between two jagged cliffs. She saw nothing but scrub bush and weeds in the barren canyon.

As the helicopter blades slowly wound down, Mother Evelyn and Gertrude opened their doors and stepped out onto dry gravel. The smell of sulfur permeated the air, but it was cooler than Hannah had expected. The setting sun caused dark shadows to fill the canyon.

The Mother flicked a scorpion away with the tip of her cane. Gertrude opened one of the suitcases she'd brought and pulled out an electronic device that looked like a large walkie-talkie, except two long metal prongs protruded from the top. When she turned the devices on, a faint beeping sound invaded the stillness of the canyon. She approached the side of the southern canyon wall, and the beeping intensified.

Mother Evelyn stepped up to the canyon wall. She rapped three times on the rock with her cane and spoke loudly. *"Anoun ismith plaka. Ankh do Anak boo eva dustath."*

Hannah glanced at Albro. He was busy checking his helicopter and seemed oblivious to the odd language the Mother was speaking.

Mother Evelyn removed the Ankh of Anak from her right pocket, held it in the air, and repeated, *"Anoun ismith plaka. Ankh do Anak boo eva dustath."* She then switched to English. "I have asked for entrance politely and bring a valuable gift. I am here to help you in your time of need. Do not force me to be rude."

She stared at the wall for two minutes. Nothing happened. "Very well. Just remember, I knocked first." She turned, looked at Mabel, and pointed to the back of the helicopter.

Mabel moved to its rear and opened the cargo hatch. With a pallet jack, she tugged the heavy crate down the ramp until it hit the ground, where its wheels sank into the hard dirt. A metal band surrounded the crate and two large hinges connected the lid to one of the side walls. Four zeros glowing in red appeared on a small electronic box attached to the metal strap.

Mother Evelyn approached Albro. "How long will it take you to start your bird, take off, and fly out one mile?"

Albro's brow wrinkled. "Four minutes to start and one minute to reach altitude."

"Start your engine. Everybody, get back on the copter."

As the nuns climbed back inside the helicopter, Mother Evelyn walked to the wooden crate and set the numbers to six minutes. She then climbed aboard.

The helicopter lifted with dizzying speed. Hannah saw a brief flash of light from two ridges over, but she ignored this distraction and focused on the crate.

Everyone watched the crate as the time on the clock began to tick down. One minute after reaching a mile up, the metal band snapped loose, and all four sides collapsed. The hinged side carried the lid with it. Inside the crate was the electromagnetic pulse from Kappa Lambda Omega.

Chapter Twelve

A bright flash of light emanated from the EMP. Hannah didn't close her eyes as she prayed that they were far enough away for the magnetic wave to shut down the electronics in the helicopter. She breathed a sigh of relief, knowing they were safe when Mother Evelyn asked Albro to land. Upon reaching the ground, Hannah looked out the window and saw the seams of two doors in the canyon wall where Mother Evelyn had previously knocked. One door was the size of a typical house door. The second was large enough to allow a small plane to pass through. Hannah surmised that some sort of hologram had previously covered them.

Before leaving the helicopter, Mother Evelyn touched Albro's arm and told him, "Fly to a safe location and wait for my call." She then handed him her satellite phone.

Looking a little pale, Albro nodded and took off. Hannah followed the Mother and wondered what kind of people would live inside an active volcano. Mother Evelyn approached the small door and motioned Mabel forward. "The locks are magnetic, so the door should open with a strong push."

Mabel pushed on the door with her shoulder, and it opened into darkness. Gertrude removed a large flashlight from her suitcase and handed it to Mabel. The flashlight penetrated the darkness, revealing a large hangar. Gertrude handed Hannah a second flashlight and kept one for herself.

Hannah felt a rush of adrenaline as she directed her flashlight to the right. It illuminated a flying craft of some sort, but its dull gray paint diffused the light. It looked similar to a shuttle pod from *Star Trek*, sitting on top of a circular platform. The sleek craft was slightly smaller than the helicopter. A large windshield sloped up the front and three window ports lined the side. Mabel ignored it and led the way with Mother Evelyn behind her. The Mother lifted her cane and twisted the angel clockwise. A bright blue flame emanated from the bottom of the cane. A second craft sat behind the first, which was as long as Mother Evelyn's plane but shaped like a wedge. Two rows of viewports indicated two levels. Hannah couldn't see any engines or exhaust ports.

The hangar brightened as a few overhead lights flickered on, revealing empty spaces for several more ships. Mother Evelyn shut off the flame and tapped her cane on the smooth rock floor as they crossed the hangar. Everyone walked toward the double doors on the left side of the back wall. A set of wide stone stairs in the center led to a balcony and another door.

As they approached, the lower door opened, and a blue man walked through. He was tall, well-muscled, and ruggedly handsome in a pair of sandals and a thin white tunic. Not a hair was visible on his smooth azure skin. The blue skin shaded darker in the curves of his muscles and lighter around his eyes and hands. His pale blue lips held an angry frown. Hannah's eyes widened in shock. Two more men and one woman followed the blue man. They were also dressed in simple tunics. The woman looked pretty, but her bronze skin sparkled, and Hannah detected small scales, which made her look like a human reptile. The two men appeared normal, except their hair and eyes were bright green. The two green-haired men carried weapons. If Hannah had not already seen spaceships, she would have thought them to be art deco toys.

She felt lightheaded. "Am I seeing what I think I'm seeing?"

"If you see four aliens, then yes or a fantastic illusion," Gertrude replied.

Mabel snorted. "They are real."

Telepathic Catholic spies, an EMP, spaceships, and aliens living inside an active volcano is about all I can take, Hannah thought as her head began to spin.

The blue man crossed his arms and spoke with a deep bass voice. "You are not welcome here."

Mother Evelyn lifted her chin at the blue man. "I knocked first."

"And then forced your way in," the blue man replied with anger.

"I apologize for the intrusion. I asked you not to force me to be rude. The choice was yours."

"No matter. Your memory will be wiped of everything you have seen."

"I don't think so," Mother Evelyn replied with total calm.

The blue man flashed an arrogant smile and stared at Mother Evelyn. After a moment, she gave an exaggerated yawn. The blue man stopped smiling and began to sweat.

Mother Evelyn raised an eyebrow. "Must we continue, or have I made my point?"

Hannah was not sure what was happening and could only surmise that some sort of telepathic battle of wills was transpiring between Mother Evelyn and the blue man.

Blue blood trickled from his nose. "Enough!" He stepped behind his three companions and wiped his nose with his arm. "Stun them."

Hannah closed her eyes as the three aliens raised and clicked their weapons, but nothing happened. She opened her eyes and heard three more clicks as they tried to fire.

"No battery can withstand an electromagnetic pulse," Mother Evelyn spoke to the three aliens. "Sister Mabel, please teach them that stunning an old woman is not only rude, it can be dangerous."

Mabel took six steps forward. The aliens crouched into defensive postures. She punched the first man's jaw, knocking him out cold. The second man received a sidekick that sent him gasping for air. The bronze woman retreated behind the blue man, who raised his fists like a prize boxer.

"Yield, Lotan," a musical female voice commanded from the balcony above.

The blue man lowered his fists reluctantly and took one step back.

Hannah looked to the balcony and saw a beautiful woman wearing a sleeveless, gossamer gown that shimmered with all the hues of the rainbow and enhanced her ample bosom and narrow waist. Her lustrous pale silver hair reached to the middle of her back. Slightly angular facial features made her appear even more exotic as did her large, bright purple eyes. Her flawless skin was so white it glowed. Hannah blinked to be sure and concluded that light actually radiated from her skin.

The woman with the musical voice spoke. "With all the trouble these half-breeds have gone to, the least we can do is listen."

"It is against the rules," Lotan replied.

"But not against the laws."

She descended the stairs gracefully, approached Mother Evelyn, and extended her perfectly smooth hand. "You have us at a disadvantage. We are just observers, not warriors. My name is Sela, Princess of the Eloshin."

Mother Evelyn didn't accept the handshake but answered politely, "It is a pleasure to meet you. You may call me Evelyn."

"How did you find us?" Princess Sela lowered her hand.

"More than a hundred thousand people saw one of your saucers during the solar eclipse in Mexico City in 1991, many with video recorders. There are many pictures of your triangular ships. A Mexican Air Force plane tracked eleven craft for more than fifteen minutes in 2004. There have been more recently. I triangulated your general location and then looked for magnetic anomalies. I have long believed that your technology would allow you to tap into the Earth's magnetic field to generate free, clean, and virtually unlimited power."

Sela's reply held wry humor. "The incident in 2004 was regrettable. All those ships were an honor guard for me. We did not even know of our error until the video appeared on the national news. Fortunately, your newscasters are cynical and incapable of giving an unbiased report. The reporters on CNN were especially helpful to debunk the story as a hoax."

"Did something happen to your stealth technology?" Hannah asked.

The princess turned toward Hannah. "One of the volcanoes must have laced the air with ferric oxide, which negated the Doppler shift shield we use to mirror what is around. From the ground, we are invisible."

Hannah excelled in chemistry but was reluctant to correct the beautiful alien. "Isn't ferric oxide a manufactured chemical used as a harmless coloring agent?"

Princess Sela smiled, and Hannah noticed that her straight, white teeth also glowed. "We live in a volcanic region. You would be surprised what the core of a planet can cook up."

"Why did you call us half-breeds?"

"It is not my place to teach you geology or your own history. Read your Bible."

"Enough, Hannah," Mother Evelyn admonished.

The princess turned back to Mother Evelyn. "When you approached, you spoke the ancient language. How did you come to such enlightenment?"

"I collect ancient scrolls."

The alien Mabel had knocked unconscious stirred, and she helped him regain his feet. He stood slowly, shaking his head. Princess Sela moved closer to the man with green hair and touched his jaw. Her hand glowed, and his green swelling bruise immediately disappeared. "You mentioned something about the Ankh of Anak. Do you have it?"

Mother Evelyn removed the relic with the blue stone from her pocket and handed it to Sela, who took it and held it reverently as she gazed into the large gem in the center. "Do you know what this contains?"

"It's a gift of great value I offer as a token of trust. The ankh is ancient technology dating back six thousand years."

"Yes, it is. It holds the life recording of Anak, overlord of the race of giants called the Keldian. After murdering thousands of his own people, he and his followers traveled to dozens of worlds, blazing a path of death and destruction wherever they went. He was also a powerful transmuter. His army was eventually defeated, but Anak and a few of his children escaped to Earth in a small spacecraft. He is the Nephilim written of in your Bible."

Nephilim must mean sons not of God, Hannah thought.

Sela gazed at the relic, and her purple eyes glowed brighter. "No one knows why Anak traveled from world to world or why he murdered so many people. Perhaps this recording will provide answers to long-debated questions. I thank you for the gift. But please tell me why you are here."

Mother Evelyn placed her hands on top of her cane. "There is a man of great power and as evil as Anak. He met with me yesterday to warn me not to interfere with his plans, but I am not inclined to follow his orders. He told me he had kidnapped one of your females. I know you do not wish to interfere with events on our world, but we are not so constrained. We are here to help recover your missing person."

Sela's laughter sounded like a faint lullaby. "There is no one missing from our people."

Mother Evelyn looked perplexed. "Are you sure? The man went to great lengths to inform me that one of your women has been abducted."

"There are only seventeen of us at this observation station and one hundred and twenty-three scientists and observers from the Elohim worlds on your planet. If someone were missing, I would know. Who is this man?"

"A man who is obviously capable of lying to me," the Mother quipped. "He goes by the name of Cain."

"Cain!" Lotan shouted.

Mother Evelyn looked toward Lotan. "You know of him?"

"We've met," Lotan replied with bitterness. "It has been many years since we crossed paths. Is he not dead yet?"

"He is still alive and is apparently toying with me. I take it your meeting was unpleasant?"

"He lured me into a trap." Lotan clenched his fists. "He sent a mental distress call in the ancient language. No one on your planet knows the ancient language. When three of our scientists and I flew to investigate, he shot our shuttle out of the sky. We landed in a remote desert in Nevada."

"Roswell, I'm guessing," Mother Evelyn replied.

Lotan nodded. "My friends were killed on impact. I had some serious bruises but no broken bones. When I exited the craft, a man was waiting for me holding a metal gun. I could not affect his mind, for he had a strong mental shield. He introduced himself as Cain."

"I mourn for your loss," Mother Evelyn said with sympathy. "I'm surprised you survived."

"He forced me back into the shuttle at gunpoint and became angry when he discovered my companions were dead. He screamed at me for being such a poor pilot, raised his gun, and shot me. Had I not been wearing my inertia armor, I would surely be dead. He did not notice that I was not wounded, so I took the opportunity to jump out of the craft and ran as far and as fast as I could."

Lotan continued, "I nearly didn't survive after that. I come from a very cold planet. The heat of the desert was a death sentence for me. I would have died within the hour had the military not set up a roadblock on the local highway. A truck carrying frozen meat was my salvation."

Hannah listened to the blue alien and tried to keep her jaw from dropping open. She glanced at Gertrude, who was very pale, and felt better for not being the only one in shock. Lotan's story made her wonder exactly who Cain was.

"A few hours later, I heard Cain being interviewed on the radio pretending to be a dirt farmer, whatever that is. I spent five miserable days in a meat freezer waiting for a rescue."

Mother Evelyn turned back to Princess Sela. "I apologize for our intrusion. Since you are now aware of the threat, I would suggest that you be extra careful for the next few weeks."

"You breached our security," Princess Sela replied. "We are already shutting down this facility. We appreciate your warning and will inform the rest of our people."

A distant look clouded Sela's eyes, and Lotan cocked his head slightly to the side as if he were listening to someone else. After a few seconds, Sela smiled. "I'm afraid you will have to exit through our southern door. It opens in another secluded canyon to the south."

"Is there a problem?" Mother Evelyn asked.

"Nothing serious. Occasionally, wilderness groups and hunters make camp for the night in the canyons close to the volcano. A large troop of Boy Scouts from Los Angeles just landed two helicopters in the north canyon."

"From *Los Angeles*?"

"So it says on their arm patches," Sela replied. "Troop number 666. The boys are thirteen or fourteen years old and have paint-ball equipment. They look cute with their faces painted red. The holographic wall is back in place, so there is nothing to fear."

Sister Mary Ruth shook violently. Mother Evelyn's eyes were wide with surprise. "Show me!"

Sela's face hardened. "Forgive me if my smile makes you believe I trust you or that we are friends. I don't, and we are not friends. I will not allow half-breeds any deeper into my facility. The whole place will explode if you pass through that door. I can read two of your companions like paper, but three of you are well shielded, especially you, Evelyn."

"Then bring a monitor here," Mother Evelyn demanded.

The princess stared at the Mother for several seconds before she motioned to one of the green-haired men. A moment later, a dainty young woman with a large spiral horn protruding from her forehead entered with what looked like a three-foot-long thin pipe. She set it on the floor and touched one end. A window formed in the air, with the pipe as the base.

Hannah looked through the window and saw a three-dimensional view of the canyon. Forty or so young teens, dressed in Boy Scout uniforms, were unloading equipment from two large helicopters. The boys placed eight huge stereo speakers facing the hidden doorways. Each boy sported a helmet and a red hand painted on his face.

"Those are not Boy Scouts," Mother Evelyn stated.

Chapter Thirteen

Hannah watched the three-dimensional scene within the alien electronic window. The Boy Scouts moved in a quick orderly fashion. Lotan spoke a quiet command in a language Hannah didn't understand. The view in the window zoomed in on a gun strapped to a boy's back. The gun looked real, except for the orange paint on the end of the barrel.

Mother Evelyn slammed the tip of her cane against the rock floor. "You must flee. Now!"

The princess narrowed her eyes. "Your fear is unwarranted. Our technology is much greater than yours. The magnetic pulse will not work again. You want us to run away so you can advance several thousand years with the knowledge you gain here. Do not bother to deny your scheme, unless you would like to open your mind to me."

Princess Sela stared at Mother Evelyn, who said nothing. "I thought not."

Hannah moved closer to Lotan. "Excuse me, Mr. Lotan."

Lotan shifted his attention to Hannah. "Just Lotan."

"Can you change the view to see the holographic rock wall?"

Sela sighed. "They cannot detect where the door is. Besides, they are just children."

Lotan spoke a few alien words, and the view pivoted. Hannah watched two boys climb the rock wall. Lotan zoomed in on one of the boys as he slapped a large wad of a puttylike substance against the rock and placed a small metal rod into the putty. He climbed higher and repeated the process.

"Can your door withstand multiple blasts of C-4?" Hannah asked.

"No, it cannot," Lotan answered. "This complex is designed with low fracture and melting points so we can erase any evidence of our presence."

"All your technology is defensive, and your door is about to be blown away," Mother Evelyn stated, emphasizing the point with a tap of her cane. "You are facing the most devious mind on the planet. You must flee."

"No."

"Don't be a fool." Mother Evelyn pointed to the monitor. "Cain does not need your technology to advance our race. He needs you!"

The view pivoted again, and Hannah saw a man exit the helicopter. Cain smiled like a predator that had cornered its prey. Sela touched Lotan on the shoulder. "Can you coerce them away from the door?"

Lotan closed his eyes. Upon reopening them, they widened with distress. "No, they are wearing metal helmets."

Princess Sela turned to one of the green-haired aliens. "Marshalon, have our stunners been recharged?"

"No, ma'am. Reconfiguring our defenses against an electromagnetic attack took priority."

Sela stood straight, projecting confidence. "Flood the northern canyon with sleeping gas. Once they are asleep, we will alter their memories and depart before they awaken."

"Too late." Mother Evelyn turned toward the outer doors.

Hannah looked back to the window. Cain and the boys pulled gas masks over their faces. Every boy stepped back, and many nodded or tapped their fingers against their guns to the beat of the music.

"If any human steps into the hall past the hangar threshold, this compound will explode," Princess Sela said.

Mother Evelyn sighed. "You will soon seek my forgiveness for your arrogance."

Hannah felt her knees grow weak. The throb of deep-base kettledrums came from outside and vibrated the stone floor.

Lotan stood beside Hannah. "He is good."

"What do you mean?"

"The intense rhythmic music enhances psychic defenses."

Hannah's voice squeaked as her fear intensified. "If that door is going to be blown off, shouldn't we get behind something?"

"The princess has everything under control," Lotan replied. "It will all be over soon."

The explosion blasted the doors inward, and the wind and heat slammed into Hannah with the force of a hurricane, knocking her to the floor. Her ears throbbed, and her nose twitched as the dust settled.

She lay on the floor, momentarily stunned, then rolled over, expecting to see an army of Boy Scouts wearing helmets and gas masks carrying large guns, racing toward her. Instead, they marched slowly, dancing in unison to a music beat, which was more intimidating.

The blast had curled the huge door around the nose of the front shuttle. Techno music blasted her eardrums. Cain led from the center, wearing a scoutmaster's uniform. He removed his mask and handed it to one of the boys. He smiled victoriously.

It took nearly two minutes for the troops to reach the back of the hangar. Even though their guns had orange paint on the end of the barrel, Hannah could tell they were real. Several of the boys took strategic defensive positions around the perimeter. Hannah climbed to her feet, and Gertrude assisted Mary Ruth. Mabel grabbed the pipe from the 3D viewer and moved in front of the doorway. Princess Sela stepped behind the two men with green hair.

Hannah felt uneasy seeing a red hand painted on each face as the boys, in unison, removed their gas masks. The troops stopped twenty feet from Lotan. Cain pointed a stereo remote control behind him, and the throbbing music disappeared.

"Ah, Mr. Blue," Cain mocked. "It is so nice to see you again. You ran away into the desert so quickly the last time we met. I'm surprised you survived."

"You will not survive this day," Lotan replied coldly.

"What a sense of humor!" Cain laughed. "And Mother, I want to thank you. I could not have made it this far without you. Please remain standing beside Hannah and keep your precious cane where I can see it."

"You will make it no farther," Mother Evelyn declared. "I have warned these people. This place will explode if you enter that hall."

"You are mistaken." Cain walked to the front of the troops. "The Elohim will not kill, especially not children. That is why I brought them."

Hannah looked at the boys and saw kids of many races. She saw no fear in their eyes, just loyalty Cain could buy with money or coercion. There would be no sympathy or help from any of them.

Cain looked at the six aliens. He glanced past the men but focused intently on the three women, looking them up and down. The bronze-skinned, reptilian-looking one drew a deep frown from him. He raised an eyebrow at the second woman with the horn protruding from her forehead.

Hannah prayed silently, hoping that Sela would remain hidden from his view. God didn't answer her prayer—Princess Sela stepped from behind the green-haired men and gathered the attention of everyone in the room. Her bright purple eyes seemed to dance with pleasure as her beauty transfixed everyone, including Cain.

Mother Evelyn rolled her eyes and muttered something under her breath to Mary Ruth, who shrugged.

Cain took three steps forward and bowed formally before Sela. "I was hoping to find a beauty but did not expect to find a goddess."

Sela slapped Cain across the face. "Do not blaspheme!"

"And spirit too." Cain laughed while rubbing his cheek. Without taking his eyes off Sela, he called out, "Mother, I think I will take this one."

"My name is Sela, Princess of the Eloshin. And you will be taking nothing and no one."

"Eloshin," Cain replied. "The word means 'daughters of God.'"

Lotan placed himself between Sela and Cain. "So, you know the ancient language. Do you understand the words *non takoth*?"

Cain took a half step backward, withdrew a sleek long-barreled pistol from his jacket, and pointed it at Lotan. "Mister Blue, you were in such a hurry last time, we were not formally introduced. My name is Cain."

"I know who you are, Mr. Cain. You shot down my spacecraft."

Hannah felt her pulse increase as Cain's eyes flashed with anger. "I am not Mr. Cain or Professor Cain or even King Cain. I was born over six thousand years ago speaking the ancient tongue. I am *the Cain!*"

Chapter Fourteen

From the gasps around her, Hannah knew the aliens felt as shocked as she did. Lotan's hairless body turned pale blue. Princess Sela stopped glowing. The Boy Scouts continued to nod and sway to the rhythm of the music playing inside their helmets, making them oblivious to Cain's proclamation. Hannah glanced at Mother Evelyn, who wore a sour expression, as did Mary Ruth. *They already knew Cain's real identity,* Hannah thought.

Sela took a step back. "That is not possible. None of God's creatures live longer than a thousand years."

Cain laughed. "Surely in all the worlds you and your cohorts have visited you've met at least one person cursed by God?"

Sela looked down her nose at Cain. "On the Nephilim worlds, the founding parents who ate from the tree of knowledge traded eternal life in heaven for eternal youth where they lived. But they were not immortal. Eventually, their descendants discovered the truth and the founders were killed. You are not a founding parent."

Cain shook his head like a teacher to a student with an incorrect answer. "Before coming to my world, did you not read our history book? Try Genesis chapter 4, verse 12: 'A fugitive and a wanderer shalt thou be.'"

"I am familiar with the passage. I see God's curse written upon your face. But He did not say you were cursed to wander forever."

"When Moses wrote Genesis, he had a limited supply of papyrus scrolls. He crammed the first several billion years in the first chapter. He left out most of my history, but you can read between the lines. He told the age of every male at the time of his death except me. That is because I never died."

"If you are who you say you are, then you are the reason this planet is full of half-breeds. Your race is the lowest of the Nephilim."

Cain placed his free hand atop his heart. His other hand still pointed the gun at Lotan. "I am so insulted."

Sela crossed her arms and sneered with disgust. "God sent his Son to die here so that even the lowest of the Nephilim could find a path to salvation and heaven. The human race is barely above the animals. God should not have wasted his time trying to redeem you!"

"So, you're now entitled to judge God?" Cain sneered back. "Too bad 'Thou shalt not be arrogant' was not one of his commandments."

Sela lowered her eyes. She spoke in a low, quiet voice. "You are responsible for the contamination of your bloodline. You are the cause of the diminishment of the genes and the lessening of life spans. You are the reason your people become sick and lack the gifts. All the pain and suffering of your people is entirely your fault."

"Actually, I think my mother has some fault in there somewhere." Cain's mark darkened to a deeper red as he glared at Princess Sela. "If you want to place blame, then accept your own. The Elohim chased Anak here and left him."

Hannah wanted to know who Anak was and why he was so important, but she heard Mother Evelyn's voice speak to her mind. *"Hannah, listen. When his attention is elsewhere, discreetly reach into my left pocket. Inside you'll find a small metal case. Open it. Inside is a miniature keyboard. Type 'C,' then the pound sign, then press Enter. Do you understand?"*

"Yes, Mother."

Hannah looked back at Cain and saw him roll his eyes. He lowered his gun and took a few steps toward Sister Mabel. As soon as his back was turned, Hannah slipped her hand into Mother Evelyn's pocket and removed the small metal case.

Cain held his gun casually in his right hand and glanced at Mabel. "Is this place really rigged to explode, daughter?"

Mabel spat at Cain's feet. "Don't ever call me daughter." She raised a 3D window pipe and took a step forward. One of the teenagers on the front line raised his orange-tipped paint gun. Hannah dropped to the floor, as did several of the aliens as the roar of the gunshot reverberated around the cavernous hangar. Gertrude screamed.

Mabel grabbed her stomach and toppled forward. Blood covered her hands.

Cain spun around and pointed his weapon directly at the face of the boy whose gun was smoking, then he aimed lower. The second gunshot sounded more like a cough. The boy grabbed his thigh and fell, withering in pain. Cain pulled the stereo remote control from his pocket, raised it to his lips, and screamed, "I told you, no one fires unless I give the order!"

The boys cringed.

"Do you understand?"

All the boys nodded. Cain looked to the boy crying on the ground. "If she dies, you die. Your share is now forfeited to the others."

A few of the boys smiled. Mother Evelyn, Mary Ruth, and Gertrude rushed to Mabel. Hannah moved to help but stopped when Mother Evelyn cleared her throat and realized Cain had turned his back. Lotan also noticed and moved closer to him.

Cain pointed his gun at Lotan even before he turned back around. "Don't even think about it. I have had six thousand years of target practice and have killed more people than you can imagine. I never miss."

Hannah turned further from Cain and carefully opened the small metal box. She saw eight bug carcasses lying in padded foam and a small pen beside a tiny keyboard. She took the pen and typed "C," then the pound sign, then Enter. Six tiny mosquitoes and two dragonflies flew out of the box.

Sela walked over to Mabel and crouched down. With her back to Cain, she said softly, "Move your hands. I may be able to help."

Sela placed her hands on Mabel's stomach and closed her eyes. Her lips moved as if she were praying, and her hands glowed. She opened her eyes. "She will be fine."

"You have the gift," Mother Evelyn whispered. "Thank you."

"I have the faith. The gift is God's. Only He can heal if He chooses to intervene."

Cain stepped closer to Princess Sela and Mother Evelyn. Hannah opened her mouth to distract him, but his withering glance stopped the words before they could start.

"Princess Sela, it is time to go," Cain said, keeping his weapon aimed at Lotan.

Sela stood and wiped her bloody hands on her white gossamer gown. "What do you mean?"

"Surely the dear Mother told you. I have no need of your technology. I only need you."

Panic showed in the princess's eyes. "Why?"

"I intend to take you for my wife and create another race of half-breeds."

Sela's skin turned pale gray. The glow in her eyes disappeared. "I already have three husbands."

Cain chuckled. "I am happy to hear that God has not outlawed polygamy. It always confused me why adultery was a sin while multiple marriages was not. Besides, I love a woman with experience. I threw a big party on Mount Vesuvius about a thousand years ago to celebrate my millionth woman. It was a cataclysmic event, although not many survived. I don't think you will be disappointed in me as a husband. You might even learn a thing or two."

"I am an Eloshin," Princess Sela said as she gagged and grabbed her stomach. "No other race may touch an Eloshin. God forbids it."

Cain's face lost all expression as he stared at the princess. Although he frightened Hannah when he was angry, she realized he was more terrifying when he was calm. "Do you really think I care what God forbids?"

"And if I refuse?" Sela asked in a small voice.

"The first to die will be Mr. Blue, then the weird-looking woman with the horn, then the rest of your team, then the five nuns. Afterward, I will press a button and every helmet on those little boys' heads will explode. Then I will shoot you in the leg, throw you over my shoulder, and take you with me anyway. Or you could come peacefully."

Sela raised her hand to her mouth. She turned to Mother Evelyn with tears in her eyes. "You were right, Evelyn. I apologize."

Cain looked at Mother Evelyn with a gloating smirk quivering on his lips. "Thank you for being so predictable and running to the rescue. If not for you, I never would have found this lovely creature." His smile turned cold. "However, the next time I see you or any of your cronies, I will shoot you."

"You cannot go with him, princess," Lotan pleaded.

"I will not be the cause of so much death."

"Come, my queen to be." Cain took Sela by the arm and walked toward his boys.

"You will die a slow, painful death for this!" Lotan shouted. "I will find you and kill you."

Cain stopped and looked over his shoulder at Lotan. "'And the Lord said unto him, therefore, whosoever slayeth Cain, vengeance shall be taken on him sevenfold. And the Lord set a mark upon Cain, lest any finding him should kill him.' I am sure Princess Sela is flattered that you're willing to become a Nephilim for her sake. Are you seriously willing to sacrifice your sons, their sons, and their sons for seven generations just to kill me?"

Lotan clenched his fists in frustration.

"Seven generations, Mr. Blue," Cain said viciously as he marched through the middle of his boys, who turned and followed. The last two boys grabbed their bleeding friend and dragged him with them.

Lotan followed a few feet behind. Not sure what to do, Hannah looked at Mother Evelyn, who motioned for her to follow Lotan. Hannah caught up with him at the hangar door and saw tears flowing down his cheeks. He looked at Hannah. "There are times I wish I could disobey our primary commandment."

"And what is that?" Hannah asked.

"Thou shalt not kill," he said, gritting his teeth.

Hannah touched his arm and noticed that his skin felt at least thirty degrees cooler than her skin. "Lotan, that's our commandment too."

"Maybe you obey, but not the rest of your world," Lotan replied absently. "I can do nothing. Your world is under interdiction. We cannot interfere, only observe."

Hannah clasped Lotan's cold hand. "You aren't alone. We'll think of something."

They watched the troops climb into the two helicopters, taking the EMP with them. The helicopters rose into the sky and headed south. Hannah walked outside with Lotan. A few seconds after the helicopters cleared the top of the canyon, a missile shot out from one and streaked into the next valley. A massive explosion lit the night sky.

"Albro!" Hannah screamed.

Chapter Fifteen

Hannah ran out to the center of the canyon and watched a cloud of black smoke mushroom into the sky. Lotan approached from behind and placed a hand on her shoulder. Her head began to throb. A cold drop of water struck her arm. She noticed that it was blue. She took a deep breath, swallowed her pain, and laid her hand atop the blue one. "This isn't over. We will find a way to bring the princess back."

As she turned to face Lotan, he looked into her eyes. "Your faith is strong."

Lotan turned her to face where he pointed in the sky to the west. The stars lit the dark sky. "Do you see that bright star there, the one with the reddish hue?"

Hannah looked and nodded, knowing if she thought hard enough, she could remember its name.

"Beyond that star is another star, which is completely blue. My world circles the blue star. When the Council of Elders elected me to be an observer on your world, my entire planet rejoiced. Millions of scientists from thousands of races apply for this opportunity. I am the first of my race selected for the privilege. I left my wife and my eighty-seven children to come here. If I do not rescue Princess Sela, my race will be disgraced. My children will be shamed."

"But Cain kidnapped her. It's not your fault," Hannah said gently.

"It happened on my watch. I am a climatologist but also second in command. Sela is an Eloshin, one of the most respected races in the galaxy. If Cain carries out his plan, the repercussions will shake many worlds, including yours and mine."

"How many races are there?"

"According to ancient texts, there are 144,000 races. The Council of Elders represents twenty thousand races. The rest we have not found yet."

Hannah felt surprised that Lotan had answered her. She looked at him and noticed his glazed eyes. Taking advantage of his distraction, she asked another question. "Are all races telepathic?"

"All but yours."

"Why do you call us 'half-breeds'?"

Lotan's eyes focused, and he moved his hand off Hannah's shoulder. "You should do as Cain suggested. Read your Bible, and read between the lines."

He returned to the hangar. Hannah followed, her head still throbbing.

Upon reaching the back of the hangar, Hannah saw Sister Mary Ruth lying on the floor. She looked pale, and she rocked back and forth. Mabel held her mother's hand. She also looked pale. A considerable amount of blood stained her robe. Mother Evelyn knelt at Mary Ruth's head, holding a small cup of water, and gave her two pills.

"Do you have another healer?" Mother Evelyn asked Lotan.

He tilted his head and looked at Mary Ruth. "Princess Sela is . . . was the only healer at this facility. Even if she were here, I do not think she would be able to help. Mary Ruth is simply . . ."

"Too old," Mary Ruth finished when Lotan politely faded off. "Y-yes, I am. B-but I will see this th-through."

Mother Evelyn stood and looked at Lotan. "I need her strong to be able to rescue the princess. Is there anything you can do to help her?"

"I am sorry," Lotan replied with sympathy. "There is no cure for old age, but compared to me, she is still a young woman. I am at least four times her age. If I could help, I would, but truthfully, your own medical technology is more advanced than ours."

"You've got to be kidding," Gertrude exclaimed.

"It is true," Lotan replied. "In our society, healers mend broken bones and close wounds, but we have no sickness or disease. Unless we are exposed to radiation, we have no cancer. We have no need for medicine."

"I will be f-fine," Mary Ruth stammered.

Mother Evelyn straightened her back. "In that case, I believe we should leave. If we are to rescue the princess, we must follow Cain as soon as possible. I tried to call Albro, but he's not receiving my signal."

Hannah felt a lump in her throat. "Cain killed him."

Mother Evelyn closed her eyes. "Are you sure?"

Hannah forced back her tears. "I saw a missile shoot from one of Cain's helicopters, and a huge fireball exploded in the next valley."

Mother Evelyn looked at Lotan. "Can you fly us to Manzanillo? Night has fallen, and no one will see us."

Lotan raised one hairless eyebrow. "Princess Sela did not trust you, and neither do I. You led Cain straight to us and negated our defenses. I can read Hannah's thoughts but not yours. We have recharged our stunners. If you approach our shuttles, you will wake up in the middle of the jungle."

Mother Evelyn snapped her cane against the floor. "Time is of the essence. How would you suggest we catch up to Cain without transportation?"

"There is an American-made Hummer at the southern exit."

Mother Evelyn pursed her lips. "I thank you for your generosity."

"I have no further use of it, and it would not survive being encased in lava when we destroy this base in a few hours."

"Are you able to track the princess's location?"

Lotan closed his eyes for a few seconds. Hannah surmised he was communicating telepathically with someone. "The princess is wearing a Life Ankh. It records everything within her visual range, or within range of the ring she wears. She is heading toward the city of Colima."

Mother Evelyn reached in her pocket and retrieved her phone. "Would you be willing to call me periodically to update me on her location?"

"I will be glad to. Of course, we will remove the GPS unit from your phone first. I see no need for you to track me. Do not try to find us again. We will find you."

"After we rescue your princess, would you rather we deliver her to one of your other minor stations like the one in Nepal, or should we take her to Antarctica?" Mother Evelyn snapped.

Lotan turned a darker shade of blue as he raised the phone in his hand. "Call me, and I will meet you at a discreet location."

Hannah tried to catch a glimpse of the alien habitat as Lotan led the five nuns through the door at the back of the hangar. Other than a few grim-faced aliens, she was disappointed that all the doors remained closed. She spent the next thirty minutes traveling through a maze of underground passageways bored through volcanic rock. Her headache gradually abated, but she grew weary of watching Mabel's back as she walked in front of her. They arrived at a small hangar with no aircraft, just a few filthy trucks and motorcycles.

"Why do you have these old wrecks here?" Hannah asked.

"We often observe your people directly," Lotan explained. "Who would look twice at someone in a beat-up old truck?"

Hannah touched Lotan's arm as she prepared to enter the Hummer. "We won't allow Cain to father a new race with Princess Sela."

Lotan turned a sickly shade of light blue. "You are Sela's only hope. You must prevent this travesty."

"We will not fail," Hannah replied with more conviction than she felt.

Lotan handed Hannah the keys as Mother Evelyn and Mabel helped Mary Ruth climb into the Hummer. Hannah grew concerned when she saw full harnesses instead of seatbelts and wondered how rough the roads would be. As she pulled forward, Lotan opened a garage-size door and Hannah drove into another barren canyon. There was no road, only rocky ground with large eroded trenches flowing down the canyon. The automatic headlights brightened, revealing a man sitting on a rock thirty feet in front of the Hummer. Hannah pulled closer and offered a prayer of thanks when she realized that the man was Albro.

Hannah stopped the truck and got out. As she approached, Albro didn't look at her or the Hummer. Hannah touched him lightly on the shoulder, but he didn't respond. Looking down, she saw a scorpion on top of his boot. She kicked it off but didn't see any wound or blood. "Albro, did a scorpion sting you?"

He still didn't respond. Hannah shook his shoulders and shouted his name. She heard a door to the Hummer open and saw Mabel approach.

After a few seconds, Albro shook his head and looked at Hannah. "She's gone."

"Yes, but we will rescue her."

"But she's been destroyed," he sobbed.

"No, only kidnapped."

"They shot her." Albro wiped tears from his eyes.

Hannah felt her throat constrict with fear. "Albro, where is she?"

He pointed down the canyon.

Hannah looked to where he pointed and saw the smoldering ruins of his helicopter. She sighed with relief realizing he was not talking about the princess. "I'm sorry they shot your helicopter."

"Is there a problem?" Mabel asked.

"I think Albro is in shock. Cain destroyed his helicopter."

Albro looked at Mabel, and his eyes widened. Mabel looked down at the bloody hole in her robe. "Believe me, I've had a worse day than you."

Hannah and Mabel assisted Albro to the Hummer and helped him climb in the back. Hannah drove slowly down the canyon, the rough terrain bouncing the passengers against one another. She gripped the steering wheel, grateful that the Mother asked her to drive since it gave her something to hold herself in place.

Mary Ruth's medicine made her giddy. Every time they bumped over a rock or bounced down into a gully, she let out a loud "Whoop!" and giggled with abandon. She told the same joke a dozen times. "Has anyone seen my left kidney? It seems to have popped out on that last bump." Mary Ruth was having a blast, but her antics made Hannah's job of navigating across gullies and around boulders through the dark canyon harder.

It took nearly an hour to crawl down the canyon, even though it was less than ten miles. They reached a partially paved road and turned toward Manzanillo. Every few minutes, Albro sniffed loudly and cried quietly into his hands, "My baby is gone."

The nuns sat in silence listening to Mary Ruth giggle and Albro cry. When Albro started hiccupping, Mother Evelyn exclaimed, "Oh, for pity's sake!" A moment later, Albro began to snore, which was not much better.

Hannah needed to think, but the roar of the tires and the stress of driving on the curvy mountain roads in the dark prevented her from doing so. The snoring from the back seat and the occasional "Whee!" from Mary Ruth as she navigated around a sharp curve distracted her further. Every time she tried to put her thoughts in order, the Hummer would hit another bump or pothole. She wanted to talk to Mother Evelyn. After several close brushes with abandoned vehicles parked on the side of the road, she believed even a mental conversation would be too distracting.

By the time she parked next to their plane, her hands ached from gripping the steering wheel. Mother Evelyn motioned everyone to be quiet and allow Albro to remain asleep. Hannah followed the Mother while Gertrude and Mabel assisted Mary Ruth up the stairs and into the plane. Hannah wanted to ask so many questions, but the stress of the drive and the tension in her back and arms made her first question come out with anger. "Why didn't you tell me Cain's real identity?"

Mother Evelyn stopped and turned around. Her deep frown made Hannah regret her emotional outburst. "I allow you to seek knowledge and ask questions of me because you have an extremely gifted mind. You now know some of the greatest secrets on the planet. However, I am your Mother Superior. If you can't treat me with respect, I will remove all the knowledge you have gained from me. You will find yourself in a hospital in Mozambique wondering why you can't remember anything from the past few days."

Hannah's anger turned to fear.

"Do I make myself clear?"

Hannah bowed her head. "Yes, ma'am. Please forgive my impertinence."

"I forgive you. As soon as we are in the air, you may ask a few questions. Right now, you'll retrieve the briefcase with the blue tab from the storage locker. Wake Albro, and give him the briefcase as compensation. Tell him the title for the Hummer is in the glove box. It now belongs to him." Mother Evelyn pulled out her satellite phone and pressed a button, implying dismissal.

Hannah walked to the locker and retrieved the briefcase with the blue tab. She noticed several other briefcases marked with different colors. Upon reaching the Hummer, she climbed into the back seat and woke Albro from his deep slumber.

He opened his eyes and frowned. "You're not Saint Peter."

Recognizing he was still in shock, Hannah spoke gently. "No, I'm not, and you're not dead. Albro, it's Hannah. Do you remember me?"

"Yes," he replied. "I had a terrible nightmare. I dreamed someone blew up my helicopter."

Hannah touched him gently on the shoulder. "That was not a dream." She saw his eyes begin to water and handed Albro the briefcase before he could start to cry. "The title for this Hummer is in the glove compartment; it is now yours. Also, the content of this briefcase is compensation for your loss."

Albro opened the briefcase and sucked in a deep breath. It was full of American currency. He smiled.

Hannah heard the engine start and quickly boarded the plane. She saw Mabel and Gertrude helping Mary Ruth get into bed, then she took a seat facing Mother Evelyn.

Mother Evelyn looked at her. "You have questions?"

"Yes, ma'am," Hannah replied politely. "You and Mary Ruth knew he was the real Cain, didn't you?"

"Yes. He revealed himself to Mary Ruth in Germany the first time she tried to escape. I knew him before that."

"And I gather this isn't the first time you have made contact with people from other planets."

The Mother hesitated a moment. "I met them in my youth."

Hannah felt disappointed with the Mother's brief answers. "Will you tell me why you didn't tell me before?"

"Cain tends to kill people who know his true identity. As to our foreign guests, I was not sure we would find them. Both are secrets best untold unless there is a need."

"Why didn't Cain kill us when he had the chance?"

"He owed me a favor. The details are private."

Hannah noticed the plane was already in the air. Realizing the Mother was giving answers but little detail, she shifted her thought to the task that lay before them. "What was in the little metal box?"

"Bugs."

Hannah was careful not to roll her eyes. "But they were not alive until I typed in your code."

"The six mosquitoes are GPS units I can track anywhere in the world. The two dragonflies have miniature cameras and are programmed to follow the mosquitoes. The mosquitoes were set to follow Cain, who is now heading to Los Angeles. By the way, I can hear you roll your eyes. You must control your thoughts."

"Yes, ma'am." Hannah wondered how the Mother knew in advance to program the bugs to follow him and hoped her thoughts were private.

"That's all for now. I need to talk with Mary Ruth." The Mother rose from her chair.

"Mother," Hannah said. "There is a major piece to this puzzle missing. I can feel it. You're not telling me something."

"You're wrong, my dear." Mother Evelyn smiled. "There's a lot I'm not telling you."

~⌒~

Mother Evelyn stepped into the dark sleeping cabin to check on Mary Ruth. Mabel and Gertrude's peaceful snores flowed through the air. Not wishing to wake them, Mother Evelyn turned around to leave.

"I'm sorry."

Mother Evelyn sat on the edge of Mary Ruth's bed. *"You have nothing to be sorry for."*

"I'm sorry for growing old on you."

Mother Evelyn smiled. *"The resident aliens gave us permission to blame Cain."*

"I could sue him." Mary Ruth's mental tone lightened with humor.

"Are you feeling better now?"

"I hate that medicine. It makes me feel drunk," Mary Ruth growled. *"How bad was I?"*

"You would have been quite entertaining had the circumstances been different."

"You should tell Hannah the truth." Mary Ruth's tone turned serious. *"She will soon figure things out for herself."*

"Were you eavesdropping?" Mother Evelyn joked.

Mary Ruth's tone remained serious. *"You will need to replace me soon, and Hannah is a good choice."*

Mother Evelyn bit her lip. *"No one will ever take your place."*

"When I'm gone, you'll need someone who can continue our work."

Mother Evelyn twisted the bedspread in her hand. *"Hannah and Mykaela shine brightly with potential. I had hoped the shocks Hannah has received in the past two days would break through her mental walls."*

"That will require terror, and you know it. You must put her life in jeopardy."

"With her personal commitment to self-sacrifice, I'm not sure terror will work."

"Then you should tell her the truth,"

"She's not ready," Mother Evelyn snapped.

"No. It is you who are not ready. You don't trust her."

Mother Evelyn rubbed the crumpled covers back down. *"As I must earn her trust, so she must earn mine."*

"The choice will soon be taken from you, and you will regret the opportunity you wasted to build trust both ways." Mary Ruth crossed her arms under the covers.

"I will take your comments under advisement."

Mary Ruth sat up. "Sometimes, you are so pompous."

Mother Evelyn laughed aloud and stood. "You're right. Now, get some rest. I have a feeling your talents will be needed in the next phase of our quest."

Chapter Sixteen

Hannah woke in the workroom with her chin resting on her curled fist. Captain Bob's voice traveled through the speaker. "Please fasten your seatbelts. We are making our final approach into Los Angeles."

Mother Evelyn, sitting across the aisle, closed her computer terminal and the screen slid back into the table. Hannah was about to do the same when Mother Evelyn's phone rang. She answered, stood abruptly, and yelled, "What did you say?"

The Mother lunged across the room while hitting the speaker button on her phone. Then she tossed it to Hannah. Hannah scooted out of her way as the Mother took over her keyboard. Lotan's voice shouted from the phone, "They are heading right toward you!"

Typing quickly, Mother Evelyn accessed a video viewing program. "Are you sure?"

"Yes!" he screamed. "In another thirty seconds, you can reach out and grab Princess Sela!"

Hannah looked out the window and saw another plane approaching their trajectory from a much lower altitude. It looked like the same type of plane as Mother Evelyn's, but it was coal black.

Lotan's tension carried through the phone. "Two thousand meters, one thousand meters."

Mother Evelyn lifted her fingers from the keyboard. "Lotan, what is their altitude?"

For a few seconds, the phone was silent. Then Lotan said a word that Hannah didn't understand. However, she gathered from his tone that it was an alien curse word. "You are still on the plane, aren't you?"

"Yes, Lotan. But I didn't know that they left Los Angeles. Do you know their trajectory?"

"I feel very foolish," Lotan replied. "The velocity should have been an obvious clue. I was so excited that she was close; I didn't stop to think. They're heading southeast."

Hannah looked at the computer screen and saw the interior of a plane from the perspective of an overhead luggage rack. She realized she was viewing a video feed from one of Mother Evelyn's dragonflies. Cain sat in a comfortable chair, reading a newspaper. Princess Sela slumped in the chair across from him, apparently asleep or drugged.

Mother Evelyn tapped a command, and the dragonfly turned to show the rest of the cabin. Two large men in black suits sat behind the princess. Across the aisle from Cain, a tall woman with long platinum-blond hair painted her nails with bright pink polish. Her perfectly symmetrical face highlighted pale blue eyes. She wore a micro-mini skirt, revealing well-muscled thighs, and her low-cut blouse displayed the work of a plastic surgeon. In less than a minute, the image became fuzzy and then disappeared.

Mother Evelyn hit the intercom button. "Captain Bob, our quarry has left Los Angeles. You must change course right now. Turn the plane southeast."

"I'm afraid I can't do that, ma'am."

"Why not?"

"I'm on final approach into LAX. If I deviate from my flight path, the American Air Force will assume we're terrorists. We'll all be dead in seven minutes."

Mother Evelyn rubbed her forehead. "How long will we be delayed?"

"We need to refuel, and I'll have to submit a flight plan. I won't know how long until they put us in the queue, but I'd estimate a two-hour wait."

Mother Evelyn sighed. "Hannah, please ask Gertrude and Mabel to join us. Try not to disturb Mary Ruth."

"Yes, ma'am." Hannah woke Gertrude and Mabel. All three returned to the workroom and buckled in.

Mother Evelyn shut down Hannah's computer. "Cain has left LA. He could be headed toward Colombia. Gertrude, see if you can hack his architectural firm's computer to see what the construction project is. Mabel, after we land, we will have two hours to kill in LA. Would you like to take Hannah hunting?"

Mabel rubbed her hands together. Hannah anticipated the opportunity to find a fifteen-year-old boy with red paint on his face for the Mother to interview.

Mother Evelyn's voice held a trace of mirth. "Two of our mosquitoes and one dragonfly lost their way and are somewhere in the airport. One mosquito has already died. Would you please retrieve my million-dollar bugs for me?"

"Yes, ma'am," Mabel replied, sounding disappointed. She retrieved the small metal box that once held the eight bugs.

As Hannah rose from her chair, Mary Ruth entered the workroom and looked at Mother Evelyn. "Doesn't that itch?"

"Horrendously so," Mother Evelyn replied.

Mary Ruth laughed.

Hannah didn't get the joke. Maybe it was something only a telepath could understand.

Hannah rested until the plane bounced from turbulence. She entered the workroom and saw Gertrude bent over one of the desks, examining a large set of blueprints. "Where are we?"

"A little north of Bogotá, Colombia," Gertrude replied.

Hannah proceeded to her seat in the passenger compartment across from Mother Evelyn. Everyone looked more refreshed except the Mother, whose face appeared pasty, pale, and dry. Mabel handed Hannah a turkey sandwich, which she gratefully accepted.

Mother Evelyn looked up from her computer as Gertrude took her seat next to Hannah. "Sister Gertrude, what have you found?"

"I found a second company owned by Cain. I looked at any company with the names of C-a-i-n, C-a-n-e, C-a-i-n-e, and K-a-y-n-e. By transposing the letters, I found Niac Inc. Its net worth has increased twentyfold since 1987. Cain retains controlling interest in thousands of Internet porn sites and a healthy percentage of several large casinos. The corporate office is in Las Vegas."

"Which fits his personality profile," Mother Evelyn interjected.

"I may be able to find other companies by cross-checking the charitable contributions. Both Enoch Enterprises and Niac Inc. made donations to many of the same charities, most of which are organizations dealing with the environment or education. They made some small donations to several textbook publishing companies, which I'm researching now."

"Excellent work, Sister Gertrude. Keep looking. I'm sure with your talent the truth can't stay hidden long. I spoke with Lotan about an hour ago. According to my tracking bugs, Cain's plane has left Bogotá. However, Lotan insists Sela is in a valley thirty miles south of there. One of us is wrong. But the coordinates Lotan sent are the same location as the construction project for Enoch Enterprises."

"What's he building?" Mary Ruth asked.

"An enormous warehouse," Gertrude replied. "When it's complete, it will be one mile wide and a half mile long. Construction will take three more years. According to Lotan, Cain is holding Princess Sela in what will be the executive offices in the center of a large atrium. The offices and atrium will be completed first, so there could be a secured area already."

Mother Evelyn returned her attention to her computer. "The kind brothers of the Catholic church in Villavicencio have consented to rent us their van. The warehouse isn't far from there. I'll be surprised if the princess is there, but we will be prepared just in case. Gertrude, please pack your toys."

~⌒

Hannah lurched in her seat as Captain Bob reversed the engines to brake the plane on the short runway. Out the window, she saw neat rows of dark green coffee bushes extending to the rugged hills that blocked the setting sun. The cool evening air felt invigorating as she stepped out of the plane.

Using her cane, Mother Evelyn tapped her way to the priest standing beside a brown passenger van and handed him a manila envelope. They spoke briefly, then he gave her a set of keys. The nuns got into the van. Mabel drove with caution down the rough dirt road of the coffee plantation and pulled onto a wider gravel road, crossing shallow gullies where rain had washed part of the road away. A short while later, they reached a newly paved road that cut through the dense jungle, twisting with the contours of the broad valley and erratic hills.

About a mile before reaching the location of the gate, according to the blueprints, Gertrude told Mabel to turn off the headlights. Mabel stopped before the last turn.

Mary Ruth whispered to Mother Evelyn, "I sense two g-guards watching television."

"Confirmed," Mother Evelyn replied. "Gertrude, I need the signal jammer to avoid the security cameras. Once I've disabled the guards, you can reroute the video feeds."

Gertrude handed her a small black box. Mother Evelyn quietly opened her door and moved to the edge of the road. Her black robes blended with the darkness. The only thing Hannah could see was the white angel head of her cane. A moment later, Mother Evelyn walked around a bend in the road and disappeared.

That none of the other nuns accompanied the Mother Superior surprised Hannah. Traveling down a dark jungle road could be dangerous. Wild predators probably lurked in the dense jungle. An elderly lady could fall and break a hip. Hannah was about to ask if they should check on the Mother when Mary Ruth's voice spoke in her head. *"She is older than I am, but she is in much better condition. She knows what she's doing. Trust her, child."*

Mary Ruth tapped Mabel on the shoulder. Mabel started the van and drove it forward to the gate. Mother Evelyn stood beside the small guardhouse. A twenty-foot-tall chain-link fence stood behind her. The road continued to a closed wide iron gate. Hannah followed Gertrude as she got out of the van, carrying one of her metal suitcases.

Beyond the gate, the structure under construction looked at least three stories tall. Massive, evenly spaced steel girders extended in both directions as far as Hannah could see. Small incandescent lightbulbs burned inside the open structure, turning the dark jungle into a galaxy of stars. Hannah felt awe at the massive size of the project. "There are whole cities smaller than this."

Gertrude walked to the guardhouse and opened her suitcase. She pulled out what looked like a handheld TV with several knobs and a miniature keypad. Carefully reaching around the sleeping guard, she attached two wires to the control panel for the security monitors. "The cameras are being monitored from a remote location. I've set them to run on a loop for the next three hours. There are no sound detectors."

Everyone walked to the large lock holding the gate shut. Gertrude removed a flat pouch from her suitcase and pulled out three small wire picks. When she touched the first pick to the lock, a bright streak of electricity arced out to the pick, sending Gertrude to the ground. She landed on her large padded bottom and covered her mouth to stifle a scream. Mother Evelyn and Hannah rushed to assist her. Gertrude whispered, "That was stupid."

"Lesson 21 of the thieves' guild: Always check for traps," Mother Evelyn said with sympathy.

Gertrude removed a voltage meter with two long prongs from her suitcase. With an annoyed look, she touched the prongs to the lock and then the fence. "The fence is electrified. I guess they haven't put up the warning signs yet."

Mother Evelyn moved to the chain-link fence. She grasped both ends of her cane and twisted the angel head clockwise. A blue flame sprang from the bottom of the cane extending four inches. She raised the flame to the fence and cut the metal wires. A minute later, she had cut a hole large enough to drive the van through.

Hannah looked at Gertrude's hand with sympathy, seeing her thumb and index finger swollen and burned. She bandaged her burnt hand as Mabel drove them through the opening, right to the edge of the building. The concrete foundation stood three feet above the ground. Hannah could not see a ramp for vehicular access. Concrete blocks formed a stairway onto the foundation.

Mother Evelyn sighed. "I guess we walk from here. The atrium is about a quarter mile inside."

The faint swishing of the black robes and the light tap-tap-tap of Mother Evelyn's cane broke the stillness of the night. Hannah looked in all directions, fascinated by the steel structure. She saw movement to her right and heard a loud bark.

Everyone spun around. Mabel stepped protectively in front of Mary Ruth and Mother Evelyn. Hannah feared she would see a massive

Rottweiler run at her, ready to rip out her throat. Instead, a small, ugly dog stood beside one of the iron pillars, barking loudly.

"What in the world?" Gertrude said.

Hannah giggled. "It's a peekapoo!"

"A *what*?" Mabel rasped.

Hannah clapped her hands with joy. "It's a cross between a Pekingese and a poodle. My aunt has one. They're really sweet, but they'll bark at anything. My aunt used to say her Sweetie would bark at a cockroach."

Mabel scratched her head. "They're using a peekapoo as a guard dog?"

"Come here, Snookums." Hannah squatted and spoke in a baby voice. Several more sets of eyes glowed red in the dim light behind the peekapoo. She froze as a deep growling reached her ears. Now, *those* were massive Rottweilers.

Chapter Seventeen

Hannah didn't move. She didn't even breathe. Four of the scariest dogs she had ever seen were staring right at her. With teeth bared, jowls quivering, and drool streaming from their lips, they crept toward her. Six more Rottweilers appeared from the gloom behind the first four.

She extended her hand in a gesture of friendship and little Snookums bit her. She yanked her hand back, and blood welled from her middle finger. She stuck it in her mouth in hopes that the Rottweilers wouldn't smell her blood. The lead Rottweiler tensed to lunge.

Mother Evelyn said one word: "Sit!"

Hannah plopped to the ground. So did the Rottweilers. When Mother Evelyn commanded, "Lie down," the dogs obeyed, but Hannah remained sitting.

"Come here, boy," Mother Evelyn cajoled. All ten Rottweilers wagged their stubby tails and hindquarters as they bounded toward her.

Hannah turned to see four nuns petting ten huge Rottweilers. Mary Ruth laughed as two dogs competed for her attention. Hannah turned back around and noticed little Snookums sitting in front of her. She reached out her uninjured hand but drew it back quickly when the peekapoo growled and bared her teeth. "Evil little dog."

Hannah looked at Mother Evelyn in amazement. "What did you do?"

The Mother smiled and pushed down a dog that was trying to lick her face. "God gave us dominion over the animals. I simply told them we were their friends."

"You could have done that sooner," Hannah said. "I thought I was going to die."

"You lose again," Mary Ruth muttered to Mother Evelyn.

Hannah didn't understand Mary Ruth's comment, but she saw the glare the Mother returned to Mary Ruth.

"Does anyone have anything to feed these pups?" the Mother asked.

Everyone looked to Gertrude. Her face turned red as she reached in her pocket and pulled out four packs of peanut butter crackers. "They're for emergencies," she said sheepishly.

"Were you expecting an earthquake?" Mabel asked.

Gertrude handed the Mother the crackers. Once all the dogs were sitting again, Mother Evelyn gave each dog a cracker. "Here you go, big boy. I know it's small, but to you, it will taste like chicken."

The little peekapoo started yapping again. Mother Evelyn glared at the ugly little dog. "Be quiet. You bark loud enough to wake the dead."

The dog quieted, but Hannah felt her heart flutter as she scanned the darkness looking for any movement that might be the walking dead. She flinched when Mother Evelyn touched her shoulder.

"It was a poor choice of words. Once you are dead, you are dead. There are no such things as zombies."

"In the last few days I've discovered that I'm surrounded by telepaths, that there are blue aliens on the planet, and that Cain is still alive. Finding that zombies are real wouldn't shock me."

"Let's move on," the Mother said. The dogs obediently moved away when she told them to go to bed. Gertrude pulled a GPS tracker from her briefcase and pointed the way. The five nuns proceeded deeper into the massive open-air warehouse.

After walking for half an hour on hard concrete, Hannah's feet began to ache. Mary Ruth had to lean on Mabel's arm, and Gertrude breathed heavily. The Mother tapped her way without any indication of weariness.

Hannah noticed a patch of darkness ahead, where no lightbulbs burned.

"Finally," Gertrude moaned. "According to the blueprints, this should be the location of the future atrium."

The thick concrete floor ended abruptly, and concrete block stairs led down three feet to exposed dirt. The atrium was about the size of two football fields, the stars and moon providing the only light. Compared to the jungle along the road, the ground foliage looked thin, but an assortment of large trees remained, creating a natural garden. Mother Evelyn led the way down the stairs, which ended on a winding path made of concrete and pebbles. Gertrude handed Mabel and Hannah flashlights from her metal case, and Mabel led the way. They waded through an ankle-deep, stone-bordered stream where a footbridge was under construction.

From the back of the line, Hannah marveled at the brightness of the stars peeking through the trees and drank in the fragrant aroma of the tropical flowers.

Gertrude stepped backward, and Hannah almost ran into her. She jumped off the path onto the springy loam to save her toes and became alarmed when everyone else backed up too.

"What's the problem?" Hannah whispered.

"Snakes," the Mother replied with a shudder. She lifted her cane, and four inches of blue flame sprang from the bottom. "I loathe snakes."

The beginning of a thought tickled at the edges of Hannah's mind, wanting to resolve itself into a full-blown realization. She began to chase the thought, knowing it was important as she looked around Mother Evelyn and saw an anaconda as thick as a small tree trunk sprawled across the path. The dark spots covering its ten-foot length blended with the pebbles of the footpath. Although not moving, it looked directly at the Mother. Hannah laughed.

Mother Evelyn glared at her. "You find this funny?"

"It's just an anaconda. It won't hurt you."

"Just an anaconda?" The Mother took another step back, keeping the blue flame of her cane between herself and the snake.

"My brother has one for a pet."

"How revolting."

Hannah noticed leaves move in the tree beside her and saw a smaller boa constrictor curled around a branch. "This is a snake garden. Why don't you make it obey you like you did the dogs?"

"I cannot touch the mind of a reptile," the Mother stated flatly.

Hannah's expression remained neutral as the thought she was chasing resolved itself. She quickly buried her realization for later examination. "May I borrow your cane?" she asked.

"Please." Mother Evelyn handed it to Hannah. "Kill it quickly!"

"I most certainly won't," Hannah exclaimed. "Snakes don't attack anything they can't eat, unless threatened. You're far too large for this baby to swallow. Besides, do you see that large lump a few feet behind the head? Someone fed it recently. It's big enough to eat a large rabbit . . . or maybe a peekapoo."

Hannah grasped both ends of the cane and twisted the head counter-clockwise as she had seen the Mother do. The blue flame disappeared. She tapped loudly on the stone path and approached the anaconda. It looked at Hannah, stuck its black tongue out a few times, but didn't move. Cautious not to get too close, Hannah tapped the snake lightly on the side a few times and it slithered in the opposite direction. With a few more encourag-ing taps, it cleared the path. Hannah handed the cane back to the Mother.

Mother Evelyn tucked her trembling hands inside the pockets of her robe. "Keep it for a while. You may need it again."

Hannah used the cane two more times to clear snakes from the path and had to go around one that refused to move off the warm sidewalk.

The path led to the center of the garden, and another set of concrete block steps allowed them to reach what Gertrude said would eventually be the senior executive offices. Wooden studs divided the area into several dozen separate rooms. Electrical wires hung loosely from the stud walls, and the aluminum air-conditioning ducts reflected Mabel's flashlight beam when she directed it toward the ceiling. The corner office contained a dozen large pots with healthy-looking tropical plants with long, pointed leaves. A slight breeze carried a fragrant aroma from the large black flowers growing on the branches.

"Black orchids," the Mother stated. "Cain's favorite and difficult to grow. I'm surprised to see them outside of a greenhouse. Gertrude, are these the coordinates Lotan gave us?"

Staring at the numbers on the blue-lit GPS screen, Gertrude walked a little closer to the trees. "According to Lotan, this should be Sela's location."

Hannah saw a small reflection in one of the pots as her flashlight drifted by. She walked over to it and peered inside. A shiny object glitter-ing in the black dirt caught her eye. She picked it up. She recognized the large diamond. *Princess Sela's ring!* She showed it to Mother Evelyn. "Do you think Cain made her take it off?"

"No. If he suspected she had any special technology, he would keep it for further study. She must have removed it herself."

"But why?" Hannah asked. "She knows the ring is the only way we can track her."

Mary Ruth spoke up, her voice wavering. "Perhaps S-Sela has decided t-to join C-Cain."

Mother Evelyn shook her head. "From the dedication to God I sensed, I don't believe she would. It is more likely she left the ring here for a reason. She would have known her people would find it. Maybe she left a message recorded on it."

Gertrude walked across the room, stared at a steel pillar in the corner, and touched an air duct that ran along its side. "This isn't on the blueprints. And why would they need an air duct that goes into the floor? Unless . . ."

"A secret room is beneath this one," the Mother suggested.

Hannah turned back to the pot where she found the ring. Seeing a few slight scuffmarks on the cement, she called everyone over. "This pot has been moved recently. All the other concrete shows evidence of a rainfall within the past few hours. The rain should have removed these scuffs."

Mabel moved the large pot to the side to reveal a square piece of metal about six inches wide with a one-inch hole in the center. Gertrude opened her suitcase and pulled out the voltage meter she'd used on the fence. After a quick scan, she put her finger in the hole and lifted the metal plate, finding beneath it a ten-digit keypad with a green-glowing electronic display with six zeroes. Gertrude pulled out a small aerosol can. She sprayed the keypad, and five of the digits turned white. She looked up. "The oil from his fingertips is still there. The combination is a six-digit code, using only five numbers. I'll have this open in a jiffy."

With another gadget, Gertrude attached two wires to the lock, and within a minute she found the correct code. Hannah heard a grinding behind her and turned to see a section of concrete sliding out of the way, revealing stairs descending into darkness.

Hannah peered into the stairwell, fearful of lurking predators. An awkward scream made her jump back. She realized the sound hadn't issued from the dark stairwell but from the snake garden. Everyone turned as a male voice yelled again.

At the edge of the garden stood a man in a dark blue parka and thick pants with his back turned to the nuns. A large snake entwined his left leg and he struggled with the head of the snake, trying to prevent it from wrapping around his torso as well.

"I thought you said they were harmless," Gertrude exclaimed.

"Relatively harmless," Hannah replied as she moved to the steps that led back to the garden.

Hannah ran toward the man to help him remove the snake. He turned at her approach, and Hannah saw his distressed blue face.

"So nice of you to join us, Lotan," Mother Evelyn quipped.

Chapter Eighteen

Hannah grabbed the snake's head with both hands. She twisted it in the direction opposite which it was trying to encase Lotan. But the snake didn't want to cooperate. Reluctantly, Mabel unwound the tail from Lotan's leg. Five frustrating minutes later, the snake let go and slithered into the garden.

Hannah looked at Lotan as she caught her breath. "I take it you don't have snakes on your planet."

Lotan leaned on a tree and massaged his leg. "One of the advantages of living on a cold planet is no reptiles."

"In the future, I advise that you not use your boot to move one out of the way."

"I will certainly remember that."

Hannah noticed that Lotan's dark-blue suit fit him snugly and a large crystal gem hung on a chain around his neck. Where the snake had wound around his leg looked flat and green instead of blue. "Why are you wearing a parka?"

"This is a cool-suit. Your planet is too hot for me. It also protects me from your mosquitoes, which find me quite tasty."

Mother Evelyn descended the steps from the office area, having waited for the snake to disappear. "I'm surprised to see you here since you're not allowed to interfere. Are you not taking a risk exposing yourself?"

Lotan stood straight, wincing as he put weight on his leg. "There are only two other humans within ten kilometers, and they are sound asleep. My superiors made an exception in order to rescue Princess Sela. They do not trust you to do as you said."

"Are there no military types more suited to assist in a rescue operation?" the Mother shot back.

Lotan turned a shade darker. "They are busy shutting down several observation sites that have been recently compromised. The safety of the scientists and observers took priority."

"As you can see, Sela is not here, but she left her ring," the Mother said.

Lotan examined it. "If she removed her ring, it was to leave us a message that is more important than her own life."

"We discovered a secret passageway. You're welcome to join us if you like," Mother Evelyn offered politely.

"I would prefer for you to leave and let me take it from here," Lotan replied, placing his hands on his hips.

"Is there a problem?" the Mother asked, her voice chilling.

"You altered the Ankh of Anak."

Mother Evelyn crossed her arms. "You know as well as I do that the recording crystal in the ankh cannot be altered. It recorded more than seven hundred years of Anak's life. Are you telling me you've already viewed it all?"

"Others are examining it now. I reviewed a few highlights. Imagine my surprise to see a familiar face. You must have altered the recording when you were younger."

"I gave you a priceless treasure. General Anak was one of the most notorious villains in galactic history. And now you accuse me of altering it?" Mother Evelyn shouted.

"How else would you explain your presence on a six-thousand-year-old recording?"

The Mother stood silent. She glanced at Mary Ruth then Hannah. She replied with a cold voice, "I was Anak's prisoner for twenty-three years."

Lotan rolled his eyes. "Sure you were."

"Sh-show him," Mary Ruth said.

Hannah held her breath. The Mother peeled the rubbery-looking wrinkles off her face. She then removed a thin layer of latex off the back of her hands. Straightening her back, she appeared to be in her mid-thirties. Hannah thought she looked even more beautiful than Princess Sela.

Lotan shook his head and narrowed his eyes. "That's the face I saw on the video clip. Who do you think you're trying to fool?"

"Sh-show him," Mary Ruth repeated.

Mother Evelyn removed the veil covering her head. Hannah saw her hair for the first time. It was not gray; it was a rich, thick chocolate brown. She loosened it from her clasps, and it flowed freely to the middle of her back. The Mother reached behind her and a prosthetic hump fell to the ground. She unzipped the back of her robe, and it fell to her feet, revealing the figure of an athlete in her prime.

She crossed one arm discreetly over her brassiere and the other in front of her panties. Hannah looked at the slim, well-muscled torso and noticed she had no belly button. Standing in the middle of a beautiful forest garden with a large boa constrictor hanging from the branch of the tree behind her, the scene could not be more perfect. "My name is Eve."

Chapter Nineteen

The Mother looked at Hannah and seemed disappointed that she had not surprised her again. Hannah didn't understand why the Mother wanted to do so. Weren't telepaths, aliens, and Cain enough?

Lotan took a step back. His blue skin turned almost white. "This is not possible! That would make you—"

"Over six thousand years old," Mother Evelyn purred. "When I ate from the tree of knowledge, I exchanged eternal life in heaven for eternal youth on Earth." Mother Evelyn retrieved her robe and zipped it back up.

Lotan turned to Hannah. "I scanned your mind a few hours ago, and you did not know she was Eve."

"It has been an enlightening week," Hannah replied. "Mother Evelyn is devoutly devoted to God. She is a powerful coercer. She possessed the Ankh of Anak. When Cain calls her 'Mother,' it's not a title of respect; it's a name. I put the pieces together when the Mother reacted with extreme loathing to snakes. She really is the Mother Superior."

Lotan turned back to face Eve. He clenched his fists and spoke in a low voice. "You are the reason humans are born with sin."

Eve bowed her head. "I've been paying penance for more than six thousand years. The tortures I endured in Anak's prison were nothing compared to what my son has caused me to suffer."

"You deserve it."

"Perhaps, but you are not my judge, and we have work to do. You may join us, or you may leave."

Hannah saw Lotan bite his lip. Eve strode past him and headed for the secret stairway. Gertrude followed, lighting the way with her flashlight. Mabel assisted Mary Ruth. By their lack of surprise, obviously Mary Ruth, Gertrude, and Mabel already knew Eve's real identity. Hannah believed that God could forgive anyone, even Eve.

Their footsteps on the metal stairs echoed as they descended to the bottom. Hannah estimated they were thirty feet underground. The final landing opened to a twelve-foot-square concrete room.

Gertrude took out her voltage tester and brought it close to a light switch at the base of the stairwell. Apparently satisfied with her readings, she flipped it on, and florescent lights brightened the room. A large, round vault door took up half the opposite wall. A computer screen and keyboard took the place of a combination wheel in the middle of the vault. Mother Evelyn motioned for Gertrude to proceed.

Gertrude stood in front of the keyboard. Glancing at the screen, she smiled and spoke quietly. "I think we've found another company owned by Cain."

A logo bounced across the screen, spelling "Eden Pharmaceuticals."

Lotan sneered, "Cain is dealing in drugs."

Gertrude whirled around. "Please keep your voice down," she whispered. "The walls may have sensors that will trip an alarm from sound or vibrations."

"This is a construction zone," Lotan whispered back. "These walls get major vibrations all day long."

Mother Evelyn glared at Lotan. "She knows more about security than the rest of us put together. If she says be quiet, then be quiet."

Lotan stepped back, crossed his arms, and leaned against the wall.

Gertrude set her suitcase on the floor and opened it. She pulled out a laptop computer and turned it on. She removed a stainless-steel dentist's tool with a small mirror. Kneeling in front of the vault, she ran the mirror along the bottom of the door. She stopped a few feet up the left curve, placed a jeweler's monocle to her right eye, and peered at the mirror.

She sat back and typed a long series of numbers into her laptop. A few seconds later, a message flashed on her screen and she frowned. She pulled out the small spray can she'd used earlier, stood, and lightly sprayed the vault keyboard. She frowned again.

"Problem?" Mary Ruth asked.

"This isn't going to be easy, especially with our limited time. This is a high-quality Mosler vault door. The security firm that installed it changed the manufacturer's code. I can't use the combination based on the serial number listed in my program. They also modified the safe when they interfaced the combination with a keyboard. The keys are made of a special polymer that evaporates fingerprints, so I can't dust them as I did with the keypad upstairs. This is high-tech so I must be careful, or it will lock out the combination and set off an alarm. This model requires an eight-digit combination, and I only get three tries. A simple combination would have ninety-nine numbers or fifty-two letters using the upper- and lower-case alphabet. The keyboard adds punctuation. The ALT key and control key multiply the possible digits to three hundred seventy-two. There must be a billion possible combinations."

"You are the b-best," Mary Ruth warbled. "I know y-you can do it."

"If half your population weren't thieves, you wouldn't need such elaborate security," Lotan sneered.

Gertrude gave Lotan a sour look. "Mr. Blue, I'm an empath. If you can't dampen your feelings of superiority, contempt, and anger, you must leave."

"Princess Sela left her ring here for a reason, which is most likely inside the vault. I will not be leaving."

"Can I knock him out?" Mabel asked the Mother.

Eve looked at Lotan. "I hope that won't be necessary."

Lotan spoke with an artificially sweet voice. "I apologize and will attempt to think of you more kindly. How are you going to bypass the security code?"

"I can't," Gertrude replied. "Safe designers are like architects, bureau-crats, and middle managers. To keep their high-paying jobs, they must find new ways to make a perfectly good piece of equipment work differently. The improvements sound great and look fancy, but the original design was more secure. I'm going to analyze the circuits beneath the keypad to see which keys are most commonly pressed. Only eight keys should show any sign of use."

Gertrude attached a USB cable to her laptop. A microthin wire, about four inches long, with what looked like a miniscule suction cup at the end, extended from the cable. She brought out a small metal syringe from her briefcase and moved the needle to the upper edge of the keyboard, dripping a drop of clear fluid onto four spots across the top. Wisps of smoke rose from the drops. When the smoke cleared, the fluid left four tiny holes in the keyboard.

Gertrude maneuvered the wire into the first hole, bit her lip, and removed the wire. She gently entered the second hole. "Five or percent sign. Six or up arrow. H and N." She removed the wire and entered the third hole. "Eight or asterisk, J, and O. The last digit is a colon or semicolon."

She removed the wire. "I'll enter the digits into my computer and see what comes up."

"Don't bother," Hannah said. "It's a Bible verse—John 6:58 or John 8:56."

"What about John 5:68 or John 5:86?" Lotan questioned.

Smiling with just a touch of superiority, Hannah answered, "There are only forty-seven verses in the fifth chapter of John."

Eve's lips tightened as she spoke to Gertrude. "Try the first verse." She stood beside Mabel and swatted a mosquito on Mabel's shoulder. A few mosquitoes flitted about, but most hovered around Lotan, who occasionally shooed them away from his face.

Hannah wondered if any of the mosquitoes might be mechanical.

"What does John 6:58 say?" Lotan asked.

Hannah opened her mouth to quote the verse from memory, but Eve interrupted her. "It's not our place to teach you our history."

In private, Hannah examined the verse. *This is that bread which came down from Heaven: not as your fathers did eat manna, and are dead: he that eateth of this bread shall live forever.*

"Why would Cain choose a Bible verse for his password?" Lotan asked.

Eve smiled wryly at Lotan. "If you were to choose one word to describe Cain, what would it be?"

"Murderer," Lotan responded.

"Mary Ruth, you know him better than most. What word would you use?" Eve asked.

"Evil," she replied.

Eve clasped her hands behind her back and walked slowly. "I knew him as a child. If I had to choose one word, it would be 'cunning.' Since he set events in motion several days ago, we have been dancing to his tune. We scanned for tracking devices and flew under the radar. He flew to Los Angeles before we left England, yet less than thirty minutes after we arrived in Mexico, so did he. Hannah, how did Cain know we would go to Mexico?"

Hannah looked at Eve with confusion. "I don't know, Mother."

Eve gently touched Mary Ruth's hand as she passed and headed for Mabel. "The boys of Kappa Lambda Omega delivered a cell phone to my office right after our phones were rendered useless. We know the ruse at the front gate was to get Miss Winsomore inside so she could get close to me."

Gertrude was patching the tiny holes she had made in the computer keyboard. Eve squeezed her shoulder in encouragement as she circled past. "I believe he used the electromagnetic pulse to get the cell phone into my office. He heard every word we said and listened to every plan we made."

Eve continued, "He used children as his soldiers, knowing the Elohim would never harm them. He hid this vault in a place no one would suspect and left no obvious security to draw attention to its location. He planted snakes around the secret door to keep me out, which might have succeeded had Hannah not been with us."

"I'm glad I have a knowledge of snakes," Hannah replied, feeling pleased.

Eve turned and paced back toward Hannah. "Just in case we made it to the vault and were able to decipher the code, he sent me a personal message, which is John 6:58."

"What was the message?" Lotan asked.

Eve quirked an eyebrow. "It's personal."

Lotan raised his hands in exasperation. "Then why—"

Eve cut him off. "Sister Gertrude, are you ready?"

"Yes, ma'am." Holding her breath, she pressed the space bar and the screen saver disappeared. A log-in box appeared in the middle of the screen with the phrase "Please Enter Your Password."

Hannah felt Eve touch her hand. *"Do not react."*

"If Cain is as cunning as you say," Lotan said, "how do you expect to beat him?"

Eve smiled. "He may be cunning, but I am smarter."

Still touching Hannah's hand, Eve spoke to her mind. *"I am touching you so Lotan cannot eavesdrop on what I have to tell you. When we get into the* vault, I think I know what we will find. It is imperative that you ask no questions in front of Lotan. I will explain later."

Eve broke contact with Hannah's hand. *Cain isn't the only one who is cunning,* Hannah thought. *Eve orchestrated the whole conversation so she could move around the room and discreetly touch each person.*

"Of course, I could be wrong about the message," Eve said. "When guessing a combination, the first try usually fails."

Gertrude typed in "John 6:58," with no space between the "n" and the "6." The large vault door clicked three times and swung open.

Chapter Twenty

A s the door swung open, Hannah smelled the sweet fragrance of honey. She and Lotan followed Eve into the vault. Gertrude, carrying her suitcase, escorted Mary Ruth. Mabel took up a guard position beside the door. Hannah estimated the vault to be about thirty feet wide and thirty feet deep. A row of about twenty metal file cabinets stood against the left wall. Shelves, with white plastic medicine bottles about ten inches tall, lined the opposite wall. A long metal table with medical equipment occupied the center. Hannah noticed three centrifuges, an electron microscope, and several machines she could not identify. A computer displayed the Eden Pharmaceuticals logo bouncing across the screen.

"It's a drug lab," Lotan said with disgust.

"Cain has many hobbies," Eve said. "Drugs are a surprise."

"Nothing about this planet or you people surprises me anymore."

Hannah sucked her lips between her teeth to keep from saying anything. She examined the lab equipment while Eve, Gertrude, and Lotan moved to the file cabinets. Mary Ruth sat in the computer chair.

"I'll have these open in a jiffy." Gertrude reached into her briefcase and brought out her lock-picking tools. Hannah moved closer to watch.

"Try this key," Mary Ruth called. "It was taped to the b-bottom of the d-desk."

Gertrude retrieved the key, turned the lock, and gently tugged on the first drawer. It didn't open. Rolling her eyes, she turned the key back to the original position, opening the drawer. "It was already unlocked."

Eve smiled. "If a thief can get this far, why worry over locking anything else?"

Gertrude moved to the computer, and Hannah looked inside the first file cabinet marked "A." Many alphabetized tabs stuck out of the drawer dividers. A thick file with a tab that read "Adam" caught Hannah's attention. There were files for many people she didn't recognize like *Ibn al-Baitar*, but she did recognize *Idi Amin*, *Archimedes*, and *Atilla the Hun*. She opened a few, but they were written in a language she didn't know. On a hunch, she found the cabinet marked "H" and the file labeled "Adolph Hitler." She opened the file and could tell it was written in German. "Wow!"

"What is it?" Eve asked.

"Cain's personal notes," Hannah replied. "His observations and comments throughout history."

"That may be important to you," Lotan said, "but it does not help us find Princess Sela."

Hannah looked at Eve, who nodded that she should continue. "Do you have any suggestions?"

"Try 'alien.' I will look for 'genetics' and 'Elohim.' Someone try to find his home."

"Cain has no home," Eve explained. "He cannot stay in one place for very long. It's part of his curse. He must wander."

Hannah pulled out a picture from the Adolph Hitler file and saw people who looked familiar. She took it to Mary Ruth. "I believe you might want this."

Mary Ruth looked at it. "This was t-taken during W-World War II. It is of my th-three children and me."

"You were very beautiful. I recognized Mabel and Gertrude. The third child must be your son. He must have grown up to be a handsome man."

Gertrude set her laptop on the desk and plugged a wire from it into a desktop computer port. Hannah watched as she pressed a few keys simultaneously and the screen saver disappeared. Then a log-in box appeared in the middle of the screen with the phrase, "Please Enter Your Password."

"This is too easy," Gertrude stated. "I don't think Cain expected anyone to find this place."

Eve moved to examine the medical equipment on the tables. While Lotan's back was turned, she took four bottles off a shelf and discreetly dropped them into Gertrude's suitcase. Beneath the Eden Pharmaceuticals logo, printed in big bold letters, was the word "MANNA."

Lotan called out, "Has anyone found anything?"

Mary Ruth replied, her voice wavering very little, "He has s-some interesting ideas on Social Security, but n-nothing that will help us."

Lotan sighed. "He has a huge file on genetics, but it is all mathematics and human research. I cannot find anything describing his plans with an Elohim."

Gertrude stared at her laptop screen. "Everything in the cabinets is also in here, plus much more. I'm downloading the data to my laptop. We can peruse his files at our leisure."

"Good work, Gertrude." Eve touched Gertrude's shoulder.

Lotan walked to the computer. "Can you make me a copy?"

Gertrude looked at him. "I didn't bring any flash drives, but I can email the important information to you later. What is your email address?"

"I don't believe our computers are connected to your Internet," Lotan replied.

"Too bad. I would have enjoyed testing your firewalls. I can access a satellite from here." Gertrude typed for a moment. "You're now the proud owner of your own email address. It's lotanblue@yahoo.com. Your password is Arrogant1."

"Thanks," Lotan replied between gritted teeth.

Eve strolled to Hannah and opened the next cabinet. She casually touched Hannah on the arm. *"I am clouding Lotan's mind, but he will notice it soon. I don't want him asking questions. Find a way to distract him and get him out of here."*

Lotan turned toward the shelves, but Hannah interrupted him. "Did you say earlier that you read my mind?"

Lotan turned a darker shade of blue. "Yes."

"Is that why I got a splitting headache in Mexico?"

"I'm sorry for that. I was careful not to make your nose bleed."

Hannah knew she had picked the right thing to distract Lotan when she felt anger building inside her. She slapped him hard across the face. "How dare you! Do all the Elohim practice rape?"

"I have never been with any woman other than my wife."

Hannah put her hands on her hips and glared. "You entered me. You took what you wanted without my consent. I call that rape!"

Lotan looked at Eve and raised his hands defensively.

"We are done here," Eve said. "Hannah deserves better from you."

Hannah burst into tears and ran out the vault door toward the stairs. As she did, she heard Eve tell Lotan to go make things right. Hannah faked a stumble on the bottom step and, looking back, saw Lotan heading toward her. Behind him, Eve smiled at her. Hannah turned and headed up the stairs.

Angrily, Hannah wiped tears from her face as Lotan reached the top step. "I am sorry," he said. "Of all the souls I have encountered on this planet, yours is the most like the Elohim. You remind me of my beloved wife. You are honest, sincere, gentle, and intelligent. I would never intentionally harm another person. I am deeply sorry for offending you."

As he stepped closer, Hannah moved farther away. She felt confident that her true anger at his invasion of her mind would cover her desire to distract him from Eve. "One day I'll be able to forgive you, but not today. Don't ever touch me again."

"I wish I could make that a promise, but frankly, there is too much at stake. Princess Sela is far more important than you know. She is the last-born daughter of the Queen of Eloshin. When her mother dies, she will be queen of an entire race. Her mother insisted that she come here to learn leadership and Nephilim sociology. We must get her back. If it comes to a choice between Sela's safety and harming you, I will choose the princess."

Hannah heard footsteps on the stairs behind her and believed she could let go of her anger a little bit. "I understand your commitment to Sela, but promise me you'll ask first before searching my memories. You may read my surface thoughts without invading the privacy of my mind. It's not the sharing of knowledge I resent but the method of force you used."

"Then I promise to treat you with respect."

Mabel's face was flush as she carried Mary Ruth up the stairs, with Eve and Gertrude following. Gertrude reset the keypad in the floor and the concrete slab slid silently back into place.

Eve looked into the atrium and shuddered. "I wish we could avoid the garden."

"On that at least, I agree," Lotan replied.

Eve flicked her eyes at Hannah, who understood Eve's fear. "Why don't Lotan and I clear the path ahead of you?"

"Thank you," Eve, Gertrude, and Mary Ruth said simultaneously.

Lotan pressed a button on the arm of his cool-suit and a beam of light shone from his sleeve. Hannah accepted Eve's cane but felt no need to use the flame. "Don't your people have laws against invading another person's mind?"

Lotan laughed. "Our culture is different from yours. Our level of innocence would be difficult for you to grasp."

"If it's not a breach of your ethics, I would enjoy being enlightened."

"We have no laws governing the right to privacy because we have nothing to hide from one another."

"I don't understand."

Lotan shined his light on a snake beside the path, and it moved away on its own. "You seem comfortable around Eve and Mary Ruth, even though you know they can read your thoughts. Why?"

"I trust them. Besides, I have no thoughts I would not be willing to share with them."

Lotan pointed a finger at Hannah and smiled. "Exactly. That is the nature of Elohim society. I trust my brothers and sisters, even those of other races. I have no thought I would not share with any other person. I have nothing to hide."

Hannah coaxed a python off the garden path. "What if your neighbor stole your copy of *Galaxy Today* or some other trivial object? Would they not wish to hide that fact from you?"

"There is not a person on my planet who would steal anything from me. It would go against our nature."

"I suppose having telepathic neighbors is a deterrent."

"We do not need a deterrent since no one ever steals."

"Never?" Hannah asked.

"Well, almost never," Lotan conceded. "Occasionally, someone chooses to go against God's laws. There was actually a murder on my world over eighteen hundred years ago. When someone breaks God's law, our Council of Elders holds a trial. My imaginary thieving neighbor would be given the opportunity to apologize, make restitution, and return to the path of enlightenment or be exiled to a Nephilim world."

"Are Nephilim worlds that bad?"

"You live on a Nephilim world. Truthfully, your world is one of the worst. The people on most Nephilim worlds believe in God and follow His laws even though they are born with sin."

"It's difficult to imagine a world without lying, cheating, stealing, murder, graft, and corruption." Hannah laughed as a thought occurred to her. "What do your politicians do?"

"Represent their people," Lotan replied. "Our worlds are not perfect by any means. We have trade disputes, disagreements, distasteful personalities, and profiteering. Our politicians and courts have plenty to do."

Hannah was amazed at Lotan's willingness to open up to her. She silently prayed that no peekapoo would disturb their conversation as they climbed out of the garden back to the concrete floor. "You said I remind you of your wife. Is she attractive?"

"No, she is beautiful." Lotan's smile was wistful with longing.

"What is she like?"

Lotan closed his eyes. "She is as lovely as a morning sunrise over the Corammi Glaciers on my world. Her eyes are the color of the purest icicle reflecting the radiant light of our bright blue sun. Her skin is softer than new-fallen snow. Her long tresses are so dark, they are hardly blue at all. She is my glory of the morning and my dream at night. Her mind is like a bright shining star breaking through the clouds on the darkest of nights. Her soul sparkles with humor like the waves of our frothy oceans."

Hannah smiled. "Why, Lotan, I believe there is a poet inside you."

Lotan returned her smile. "I never thought of myself as a poet. But fifty years of writing love letters has caused me to appreciate the creativity of the written word."

"You haven't seen her in fifty years?!"

"I get a vacation every three years. We also correspond holographically so I can share with her the wonders of your world and she can share with me the adventures of our eighty-seven children. God blessed her with the gift of transmutation, and she works in one of our recycling centers."

Hannah imagined eighty-seven blue children resembling Lotan. She kept from laughing by focusing on the need to keep his mind off Eve.

"What if a man didn't know she was married?"

"Anyone who spends more than two minutes with her could read her surface thoughts and emotions. They would understand that she loves me and is as devoted to me as I am to her."

"What if he only wanted to have sex with her?"

Lotan laughed. "We do not have casual sexual encounters. You and your people can only experience the physical side of sex, which is so shallow. The pleasures of the body are only about ten percent of the ecstasy God intended. When two telepaths love each other and become intimate, they conjoin in a way you cannot comprehend. The two truly become one. The passion of the body is nothing compared to the passions of the mind and the soul. The depth of understanding and love that flows between us is profound. No other man could break our bond. I am sorry you will never partake of the experience."

"I have no regrets. I choose to be a nun."

"I was referring to your lack of telepathic ability," Lotan corrected. "We obey God's laws naturally because we are born without sin. Your philosophers of old describe the seven deadly sins as vanity, greed, envy, wrath, lust, gluttony, and sloth. We have none of those."

"But you have emotions. I've seen you show anger, arrogance, and pride. I assume you're one of the best of your society. I doubt all Elohim control their emotions and model the behavior you do."

"Emotions are not sins." Lotan's voice trailed off as he looked out into the warehouse. Hannah followed his gaze. She saw several pairs of eyes reflecting the dim light and heard a "woof" as the Rottweilers turned and trotted off to the side.

Lotan continued as if nothing had interrupted him. "Even God expresses anger, as do the angels. Emotions are like food. Used in moderation, they are beneficial. Their absence can cause debilitation, and if used to excess, can turn into sin. There are lazy or sloppy Elohim, but none to the point of slothfulness. We admire beauty and wish to make ourselves more pleasant to the senses, but that is not vanity."

"The Elohim worlds sound like heaven," Hannah said wistfully.

"Oh no. Heaven is much grander. We have accidents, and we eventually grow old and die. There are times when our winters are too cold, and our summers are too hot. If we do not plant our crops wisely, there is famine. If we overpopulate our world, there is suffering. My world is not perfect, but at least we don't have mosquitoes!" Lotan swatted a bug off his face.

As they approached the stairs leading out of the warehouse, Eve said, "It was nice of you to join us, but it's time for us to part ways. My tracking devices indicate that Cain is heading to Chicago. We are already four hours behind him. Too bad it's against your rules to give us a lift. I'm sure your craft could get us to Chicago before Cain."

Lotan surprised Hannah with his response. "It would be my pleasure to offer you a ride. I will ask permission to offer you some limited assistance." He turned, walked away, and suddenly disappeared.

"Where did he go?" Hannah asked.

"Obviously into his ship," Eve replied, sounding displeased.

"Is his ship invisible?"

"Nothing in the material world is invisible. Lotan's technology only makes it seem that way."

"He's up to something," Gertrude whispered.

"Perhaps he only wishes to assist us to help return the princess," Hannah responded, feeling Gertrude was too harsh.

Gertrude pursed her lips. "There's an advantage to being an empath. Telepaths can shield their thoughts, but they rarely shield their emotions. Since our first contact with him, his emotions have been radiating out of him like a poorly tuned radio. Two minutes ago, he shut them off completely. I don't trust him."

Lotan reappeared. "I have been granted permission to give you a lift."

Eve cocked her head. "Why would your superiors allow us to enter your ship and see your technology?"

"This is a simple shuttle. There is not much technology to see."

Eve stood silent for a moment. "I don't know what to say."

"How about 'thank you'?"

Hannah could read Eve's expressions better now that she'd removed her artificial wrinkles. The tension around her eyes conveyed her suspicions. "Of course. Thank you for the unexpected escort. We will need to retrieve our laptops from the van."

"I will wait here for you."

As the nuns walked back to the van, Eve whispered, "Mary Ruth, Gertrude, and Mabel, you'll return to England. Dig through Cain's records. Look for places he could hold a telepath securely. We also need to test Cain's manna. The three of you and Mykaela must be the guinea pigs. Follow the directions on the bottles, and stay secluded in the basement for five days. Hannah will come with me."

Mabel grabbed Hannah's arm. "You are Eve's protector now. She is not invincible and can die as easily as you and I. Do not allow that to happen."

Hannah sucked in her breath as the enormity of that responsibility hit her.

Before she could leave the van, Mary Ruth spoke to her mind. *"Trust Eve and do whatever she asks, except for one thing. If you value your sanity, you must not let her drive. Ever!"*

Chapter Twenty-One

H annah watched the van pull away, then she turned around to face Eve. "What's so important about the manna?"

"When Moses led the children of Israel through the wilderness for forty years, God provided them with manna to eat. A small amount fed them for a day."

"I know the reference. Do you think Cain has found a way to end world hunger?"

"Not in a pill form, but manna did more than provide nourishment," Eve whispered. "And it's prophesied that manna will be given to the Church during the tribulation. There are references in Exodus, Numbers, and Deuteronomy. The children of Israel had no sickness until they stopped eating the manna. They were also rewarded in their later years. In other words, while eating the manna, they aged slowly. If Cain's manna does that . . ."

Lotan appeared in the darkness. "Are you coming?"

"That's what Cain meant when he said he had found the cure for everything," Hannah whispered.

Eve nodded affirmative to Hannah while replying to Lotan, "Yes, it's unfortunate that Cain will know we've been here."

"So?" Lotan said.

"If Cain knows we're tracking him, he'll look for my bugs."

"Hopefully, we'll catch him in Chicago," Hannah said.

Eve touched Hannah lightly on the arm. *"He can't read you well while he's concentrating on his shields. When he relaxes, be careful not to think about the manna. Sing a song in your head or do some calculations."*

Lotan took a step back and was no longer visible.

When Hannah reached the spot where Lotan disappeared, an odd tickling sensation accosted her. One second, she was seeing the warehouse structure right in front of her. The next, a small alien spacecraft sat less than ten feet away. It looked like a sleek minibus sitting on top of a disk. Hannah took a step backward, and the craft became invisible. She stepped forward, and the craft reappeared. She followed Eve to an open hatchway from which light streamed, then she stepped across the threshold and gulped.

The interior looked like a small airplane, with two seats in front for a pilot and navigator and six passenger seats behind them. An aisle led to a doorway and several closed lockers. Hannah felt a touch of static electricity as her veiled head brushed against the low ceiling. Three small green lights glowed over each of the passenger seats.

Eve sat behind Lotan. Across the aisle from Eve, by the door, Hannah sat in a fluffy, comfortable chair with small holes along both sides and the armrests. She wondered if the holes were for personal atmosphere and temperature comfort, though she saw no controls.

As Lotan checked his instruments, Hannah glanced at the cockpit and thought there should be more gauges, dials, buttons, and screens for a spacecraft. Lotan pressed a button, and the hatch closed. Hannah looked out the starboard window and saw the craft rise from the ground, though she felt no motion.

"This is not a long-range craft," Lotan said. "Only the seats contain inertia-dampers. The restroom is in the rear, but you may find it difficult to walk while we are accelerating."

Hannah gazed out the window and noticed that the lights below passed much quicker than in a normal plane. "So, this craft is only for travel in the solar system?"

"Yes."

Hannah noted the smooth texture of the walls and cabinets of the cabin. "Is the entire ship made of plastic?"

"And ceramic compounds. Metal is the bane of any type of mental activity."

"I didn't see an obvious method of propulsion," Hannah said. "How does this ship fly?"

"I am not allowed to explain any specifics of our technology."

Hannah watched Lotan fly for a minute, observing how the craft responded to his commands. He used a joystick to guide the craft and foot pedals to go faster. "Since the passenger section sits on top of a disk, you must be using a magnetic drive."

Lotan frowned over his shoulder at Hannah. "You are very observant. The details are secret, so don't ask."

"Magnetic propulsion isn't a secret," Hannah corrected. "We already have maglev trains. My physics class in college did an experiment with a wafer of superconductive material. When we placed the wafer within an electromagnetic field, it floated in the air and rotated. We also observed a decrease in gravitational pull over the magnetic field."

Lotan sighed. "But you have not discovered how to purify superconductors or tap into one of the five largest magnets in the solar system."

"You mean our own planet," Hannah stated.

"When you do, all of your power needs will be solved. Electricity will become virtually free. You can also use the planetary poles to reach escape velocity and go into space as cheaply as traveling from one city to another."

Eve sat with her arms crossed and her eyes closed. Hannah hoped she was satisfied with her continuing distraction of Lotan. "How fast can this thing go?"

"That would depend on the strength of the magnetic field," Lotan replied. "This is a simple shuttle, not an exploration vessel or teleportation ship. If we were in close orbit around your sun, we could reach a velocity of about five percent of the speed of light. I doubt we could maintain even two percent for more than an hour using the Earth's magnetic field."

Hannah was surprised that Lotan answered her question and hoped she would get a straight answer to her next one. "Is this the craft you use to abduct people on Earth?"

Lotan sputtered, "Not me. I am a weatherman."

Hannah felt a little anger build as she thought about what the Elohim were doing to her race. "But your people abduct humans to study, do they not? How do you justify kidnapping?"

"Is it wrong to pick up a stray dog to see what types of fleas are on its body? We do not understand humans. Some act so much like animals, we are not sure they have souls."

"How do you test for a soul?"

"I am the wrong person to answer your questions," Lotan replied. "I know our psychologists sometimes choose highly intelligent individuals to measure your telepathic growth."

"Then why do you choose alcoholics out in the middle of nowhere?"

"We pick up some of the lesser intelligent examples of your race so our sociologists can understand genetic abnormalities in the brain. We cannot understand sheer stupidity. Of the two billion people on my planet, everyone tries to make the most of their lives. We do not understand why many of your teenagers lose their desire to learn while in school. We do not understand why so many humans choose to destroy what little brainpower they have with drugs and alcohol. We do not understand why so many of your people choose to sit in front of your entertainment television learning nothing."

Hannah quirked an embarrassed smile. "Don't feel too bad. Our sociologists don't understand it either."

"Besides, we erase the memories of the abductees before they are returned."

"Not always, apparently," Hannah snapped back.

"Tampering with a person's memory is tricky. Even the best coercer can miss something, especially with a highly intelligent or extremely dumb person. We return the subject quickly, replacing their memory with the feeling of having taken a nap. Most of the time there is not a problem."

"As Elohim," Eve interjected, "you follow the teachings of Jesus. Since Jesus said to treat others as you wish to be treated, should I assume you would prefer for me to erase Princess Sela's memory before she is returned?"

"Absolutely not," Lotan shouted. "That would be—"

"Exactly what you do to my children."

Hannah looked at Eve then past her out the window. The moonlight created shadows on the tops of the clouds. Goosebumps traveled across her flesh as she realized that while she was distracting Lotan, he was distracting her. Hannah touched Eve's hand. *"Mother, if we are traveling north, shouldn't the moon be on my side of the craft?"*

Eve looked out Hannah's window and then looked out her own window. She opened her satellite phone and checked her GPS. The moonlight was not as cold as Eve's voice. "Lotan, is there something you would like to tell us?"

Chapter Twenty-Two

Lotan's hands froze above the control panel. After a few seconds, he touched several buttons and rose from his chair. His forehead creased with stress, and his skin turned so dark, Hannah thought it looked purple. "Eve of the planet Earth, I hereby place you under arrest for the crimes you have committed against your children."

An icy wave stirred in Hannah's heart then traveled to the top of her head and down to the tips of her toes.

Eve glared intently at Lotan. "Do you have a warrant?"

Lotan's defensive stance told Hannah that he had prepared for denial, anger, or even a potential violent reaction, but not for a calm question about legality. He opened and closed his mouth twice before answering with a simple, "No."

"Are you taking it upon yourself then to make a citizen's arrest?"

Lotan remained rigid, not even allowing his fingers to move. "My authority derives from the Galactic Council of Elders. They do not believe you have the princess's best interest in mind."

"So, are you a police officer?"

"We do not need police officers," Lotan sneered.

"This is kidnapping," Eve snapped. "You do not have jurisdiction here. You will turn this craft around and take us to Chicago, as you told us you would do."

"Actually, I told you I would provide transportation. I never said I would take you to Chicago. Either way, the decision is out of my hands. You will face the consequences of your actions. You are the originator of your race and are responsible for billions of souls being lost. No originator who transgressed against God has ever lived long enough to explain to a court the reason for their crimes. You provide us with an unprecedented opportunity to examine your memories."

Eve's face turned dark. "I have been facing the consequences of my sin for more than six thousand years. I have watched as billions of my children die in sin."

"That is not enough!" Lotan screamed.

Hannah held her breath, not sure what to do or think. From her time spent with Mother Evelyn, she knew in her heart that Eve was a good person and served God with all her might. She also understood that Lotan and the people he represented were born without sin. She now understood why Eve was reluctant to contact the Elohim. With their advanced technology and the weight of a galactic civilization behind them, Eve had every right to conceal her identity.

Eve took a deep breath. "How much have you seen from Ankh of Anak?"

"I was shown a short clip of you having a conversation with General Anak."

"And the Council of Elders wishes to examine my memories of these events?"

"And much more."

"Then I will share a memory with you, and they can examine your memories!"

The spacecraft turned dark. Hannah smelled the heavy scent of blood. She looked around and saw that she was in a small room carved out of stone. Torches burned fitfully along the four walls and a rough-hewn door remained closed on the far side of the room. Hannah's eyes widened in surprise, for although she felt the seat of the spacecraft beneath her, she seemed to be no longer in the craft. A window in one wall allowed air to pass, and a faint whiff of urine and feces wafted by. The sound of a dog whining in pain echoed through the room.

Hannah looked down and shuddered. Eve lay naked on a slab of rock, with blood covering her stomach and legs. The sound of the whining dog came from her lips.

The door opened, and the largest man Hannah had ever seen ducked into the room, his head almost touching the eight-foot ceiling. He wore no shirt, and sweat greased his heavily muscled, hairy chest. He removed the Ankh of Anak from a woven leather chain around his neck and placed it inside one of the thick leather bags attached to his belt. His massive leg muscles bulged beneath black leather pants. A large chicken squirmed in his left palm, and his right held a rope that wound around the neck of a small, grimy man, dressed in rags, who followed him into the prison cell.

The giant held out his huge hairy hand and smiled at the chicken through his thick beard. The chicken squawked once and seemed to melt before Hannah's eyes. Then it transformed into a snake, which Anak dropped to the floor and crushed beneath his sandaled foot. The giant spoke with a deep guttural voice in a language Hannah didn't know. Yet somehow, she knew what he was saying. "Healer, if she dies, the consequences to you and your family will be much worse than death."

"Yes, Master Anak," the grimy little man replied with a shudder. "I will do as you wish."

Hannah covered her mouth to prevent herself from uttering a sound. She realized she was witnessing a deep, painful memory from Eve's ancient past. She bit her lip as tears welled in her eyes. She looked closer and realized that blood didn't cover Eve's skin. There was no skin. Her torso and thigh muscles glistened in the guttering light, where someone had flayed her living body. Each finger and several toes looked twisted and broken. Hannah wondered how anyone could endure such pain.

Anak opened one of the pouches tied to his belt. He poured white sand into his massive palm and leaned over Eve. The room began to spin, and suddenly Hannah was lying prone on the slab of stone. Her hands and feet felt numb, but even so, she knew that many bones in her body were broken. Her stomach and legs felt like fire. She opened her mouth to scream, but her throat was too raw and swollen to do so.

"Tell me what I want to know. Tell me where the second tree is," Anak demanded as he poured the white sand on Hannah's stomach. Every nerve shattered as Hannah realized the sand was salt. *Then* she screamed. In the distance, she heard Lotan screaming too.

The pain stopped as suddenly as it began. Again, Hannah found herself sitting in her seat inside Lotan's spacecraft. She threw up on the floor. Lotan's hand covered his mouth. He looked more white than blue.

Lotan stared at Eve as he reached for a compartment on the side of his chair. He brought out a thick rope of gold and tied it around his head. "You will not manipulate me again, Eve. You are a coercer and illusionist. I should have realized as a racial founder you would have three talents. What is your third talent?"

"None of your business," Eve replied in a low voice. "I apologize for your two minutes of discomfort. I endured Anak's torture for twenty-three years. Do you really think there is any punishment your Council of Elders can do to me that would equal what I've already suffered?"

"The decision is not up to me. You will be given a fair trial, and I am sure the council will listen to whatever you have to say."

"A fair trial?" Eve retorted. "And who will be my attorney?"

"I do not know," Lotan replied. "We have no laws or lawyers to suit your crime."

Eve quirked a small smile. "What Anak did to me is nothing compared to what my own son has done."

"You sinned directly against God," Lotan returned. "All the suffering you and your race have endured is your fault, not Anak's and not Cain's. You have never stood before a judge and explained why you sinned."

"I stood before God Almighty and He judged and punished me. You and your council have no right to second-guess God!"

Lotan's brow caused the gold rope around his head to shift up and down as he thought about Eve's words.

"Lotan, we've spent a lot of time and energy trying to track down Cain," Hannah said. "He has stayed hidden for six thousand years and has vast resources. You'll never find Princess Sela without Eve's help. Please, turn this ship around."

Lotan sighed. "I wish I could, but it is not my decision. I trust you will not try something rash like a physical attack. I would hate to have to restrain you."

"I thought you did not trust me," Eve snapped back.

Lotan tilted his head. "I don't." He pressed a button on the arm of his chair, and a gooey ropelike substance shot out of the small holes surrounding Eve's chair. A thick mesh formed around her, securing her to the chair from the neck down. She squirmed but could not get up. Only her face was free.

"I told you I will show you respect," Lotan said, looking at Hannah. "I hope I do not have to ensure your cooperation also."

Hannah bowed her head in submission. Out of the corner of her eye, she noticed Eve's cane resting against the chair, not entwined in the rope mesh.

Lotan swiveled his chair back around to check his instruments. He didn't notice Hannah slowly reaching out and grasping the cane. Then she stood, and he swiveled his chair back around, looked at the cane, and laughed. "What are you going to do—rap me on the head?"

Hannah grasped both ends of the cane and twisted the head clockwise. A bright blue flame shot out four inches from the base. Lotan stopped laughing. He reached up to remove the gold rope from around his head but shifted his eyes toward Eve and changed his mind. "Hannah, you are no more capable of killing than I am. Put down your weapon."

"You're right, I don't believe in killing; but I do believe in defending myself and the people I love." The calmness in Hannah's voice surprised even her. "How well can you drive this thing with only one hand?"

Lotan extended his right hand. "Even if you can cut off my hand, I will not turn this craft around."

Growing up with a twin brother, Hannah had learned how to fight dirty. She swiftly reversed the direction of the cane and aimed the blue flame at the one place any man would protect.

Lotan reacted exactly as she expected. His hands instantly crossed in front of his groin, and he sucked in air to his chest to minimize his diaphragm. With the flame almost touching Lotan's groin, Hannah brought the top of the cane in front of his nose and she squeezed the angel's wings as she had seen Mother Evelyn do. Suddenly, a green gas streamed directly up Lotan's nose. Within a heartbeat, he slumped, and the back of his head struck the buttons in the center of the control panel.

An alarm blared, and the craft suddenly accelerated skyward. Hannah tumbled back into her seat upside down with such force her head swam.

As her sight dimmed, Hannah watched the blue flame of the cane rake across the navigator station, causing sparks to cut through the navigator's seat. Lotan shot past her down the aisle and landed against the back wall with a sickening thud. The blue flame of the cane followed him, barely missing Hannah's face as it hurtled past. As she lost consciousness, she had just enough time to pray that it wouldn't skewer Lotan.

Chapter Twenty-Three

Hannah snuggled deeper into the soft, warm, and oddly green cloud. A soft breeze drifted across her forehead, and the faint sounds of raindrops enhanced the serenity of her slumber. Birds sang in perfect harmony in the key of G. Vaguely understandable words formed.

"Wake up, Hannah."

The song repeated the same verse over and over and kept getting louder. With a sigh, Hannah parted the cloud with her hands. Looking down into the trees below, she spotted a large bird staring back at her while it trilled even louder. She floated her cloud closer to the bird, then said, "Please stop annoying me. I'm trying to sleep."

"You breathed in some sleep gas and you need to wake up," the bird sang back.

"But it's warm and safe here."

"You are running out of time."

Hannah looked closer at the bird, which was actually a duck-billed platypus. Its tone sounded familiar, like the Mother Superior. Hannah could not understand why the Mother would be in her dream looking like a duck-billed platypus. She rolled over and pulled a cloud over her head. The platypus sang a discordant tune. Hannah tried to shut out the song, but every time a verse repeated, thunder rocked her cloud. She closed her eyes tighter. Just when she thought the song could not get worse, a big drop of rain landed on her eyelid. With a sigh, Hannah asked the platypus, "Why are you raining on me?"

"Because we are in serious trouble. Wake up!"

Hannah's eyes flew open and saw that the platypus sat precariously on the tree branch looking disgusted. The raindrops turned into a downpour, dissolving her cloud. Her stomach turned over, and her ears popped as she began to fall. She tried to grasp the tree branch the platypus sat on as she passed by, but it slipped through her fingers. Hannah landed on her head and seemed to bounce once and remained upside down. She felt awkward with her feet sticking up in the air.

"Hannah, you must wake up!"

Hannah sensed the urgency in Eve's voice and opened her eyes. She was upside down in her chair, her feet pointing toward the ceiling of the spacecraft, but she didn't feel upside down. Then a wave of panic shook her as she remembered slamming into her chair. Her neck and face bent forward on the seat cushion. She wondered if she had hit the cushion with enough force to break her neck.

Her face felt warm and soft. Her wrist ached where it had hit the arm of the chair, but the rest of her body felt numb. Her eyes focused on the ceiling, and her ears picked up faint beeps from the pilot's area. An odor that reminded her of burnt plastic and another kind of chemical smell wafted across her nose. Hannah commanded her foot to move, and relief coursed through her when her foot wiggled. When her shoe came off, she closed her eyes in case it fell toward her face. After a second, she opened them and noticed that her shoe hadn't fallen toward her. It was floating lazily toward Eve.

Why would my shoe float? Hannah wondered. The truth woke her to full alertness. There was no gravity.

She tried to flip over and land on her feet. Instead, she slammed into the ceiling. As she bounced off and floated back to the floor, Eve gagged beneath her.

"Help!" Eve gasped. "I can't breathe!"

Hannah tried to spin in midair, but the lack of gravity made movement clumsy and difficult, so she pushed gently on the ceiling. As she turned slowly to face Eve, she saw rubbery-looking ropes loosely securing her body to the chair. Embarrassment heated Hannah's face when she saw her shoe had floated right under Eve's nose. Using the ceiling and chair, Hannah swam to Eve and removed her shoe. Eve gagged and gasped again. Hannah tried to fan some fresh air toward Eve's face but only managed to spin herself around backward.

Eve said, "Remind me to buy you some new shoes when we get to Chicago."

Hannah avoided looking directly at Eve, knowing her face was flushed. "Sorry about that."

"Right now, we have higher priorities. The sleep gas should be wearing off Lotan soon. Where is he?"

Hannah looked to the back of the spacecraft and spotted an arm and a leg protruding from a large mass of what looked like lime Jell-O. "He's stuck to the back wall encased in some sort of green goop."

"Is he breathing?" Eve asked.

Using the next row of seats for leverage, Hannah moved closer to Lotan. "I can't tell."

"The green goop is an automatic safety precaution, like an airbag for Zero G. Go check on him. If he's alive, remove the gold rope from around his head."

As Hannah made her way back to Lotan, she asked, "Where are we?"

"I'm not sure," Eve replied. "According to Lotan, this craft could reach up to five percent of the speed of light. We accelerated for about an hour and have been coasting for several more."

"We could be twenty million miles from Earth by now," Hannah reported after a brief calculation.

"This craft is powered by planetary magnetic fields. The emergency escape program probably sends the craft toward the nearest powerful magnetic field."

"That would be the moon," Hannah replied.

"Think bigger. Imagine yourself as an Elohim space captain fleeing a Nephilim warship or a galactic catastrophe. You want to get away as fast and as far as you can and boost yourself again with the next magnetic field."

Hannah reached Lotan and saw that green goop encased his entire body. She heard shallow breathing as air passed through two small holes in the goop. She touched the day-old-bubblegumlike-feeling substance near the holes, but the goop hardened against her fingertips. "I can detect shallow breathing, but the goop has thickened. I can't tell how seriously he may be injured, nor can I retrieve the golden rope."

"We must keep alert. He may be hurt, or he may just still be unconscious from the sleep gas. He is capable of physically overpowering us."

"Could you control him if he were not wearing metal?" Hannah asked.

"I'm stronger than he, but his mental shield is formidable. It would take me time to penetrate it. A battle between two coercers can take a while. Do you see my cane?"

Hannah's eyebrows rose in surprise as she looked at the back of the craft and spotted it. "It's buried up to the hilt in what I believe is the bathroom door. It's only about a foot from Lotan's head." Hannah looked closer. The shaft had burned through the door. She shuddered to think what would have happened had the cane burned through the rear of the craft.

"Would you please make your way forward and find the release button for this chair?"

Hannah could tell that Eve was speaking through gritted teeth, obviously frustrated. Hannah turned a little too quickly and spun in a circle again. Grabbing the back of a chair, she maneuvered back up the aisle to the pilot's seat. "If the ship's emergency protocol boosted us to the nearest magnetic field, but the moon is too weak, then we are heading to Venus, right?"

"Venus is on the other side of the sun right now, and Mars has virtually no magnetic field," Eve replied as Hannah passed her.

Hannah recalled a map of the solar system and knew that Jupiter was five times farther from Earth than the sun. "Would the ship exclude stars when searching for a magnetic field?"

"No. The ship would use a star to recharge the engines so it could sling-shot around it and boost the acceleration enough to flee a solar system. Look out the front window."

Having reached Lotan's chair, Hannah looked. The window was almost completely black. A pinprick of light shone through the upper left corner. Hannah looked closer and picked out another faint light in the upper right. "Is the window polarized?"

"Yes."

Hannah gulped. "How close are we to the sun?"

"I can tell you if you can find a way to release me from this chair."

Hannah looked at the arm of the chair, remembering that Lotan had pressed a button to cause Eve's chair to become a prison. She saw two rows of eight buttons on the front of the left arm. All were blue, except the top left one, which was red. Hannah pushed it, and it turned blue. The ropes surrounding Eve withdrew back into the holes on the sides of her seat.

"Thank you," said Eve, who then moved to sit in the pilot's seat. She didn't exhibit any of the clumsiness Hannah felt in free fall. Eve pressed buttons and read the alien words that appeared on the screen.

"You know how to fly this thing?" Hannah asked as she took the copilot's seat.

Eve's hands froze in place. "Maybe . . ."

Hannah raised one eyebrow as the stories she'd heard in the past few days rumbled through her mind. One story in particular stood out, fitting what she observed as Eve read the alien text. "So, you must have learned to fly Anak's ship."

Eve slapped a hand on the console in front of her. "And you think you deduced this how?"

Hannah cringed. "How else would you understand how to fly alien spacecraft and read their language?"

A muscle in Eve's cheek twitched. "That's stretching your talent a little far, don't you think? The basics of flying any craft are simple. Yaw, pitch, thrust, and roll are the four principles of air flight. As far as the language, I have known galactic standard for eons, and it has changed very little."

"But you did fly Anak's ship, didn't you? You apparently know what each button does, and you understand all the graphs and numbers on the screens."

"Hannah," Eve exclaimed, "everything we do and say is being recorded. I don't need Princess Sela and her people to know everything about me."

Hannah looked around the cockpit, hoping to spot a camera lens. "I'm sorry, Mother. I will be careful what I ask in the future. Since you gave Princess Sela the Ankh of Anak, won't her people be able to gather that information?"

Eve cocked her head to one side. "I suppose so."

"Can you tell me how Enoch stole Anak's ship?"

Eve sighed. "How did you draw that conclusion?"

"The book of Genesis traces the lineage of Noah but only singles out a few individuals. Biblical scholars assume Enoch ascended into heaven, but there are no details of his life. Ancient artwork depicting the ascension shows him riding a chariot. Making the leap from a flying chariot to a spaceship isn't difficult."

Eve pressed buttons and read the data on a holographic screen. "By the time Anak arrived on Earth, the genetic trait for telepathy and the higher gifts had almost disappeared. The family line that produced Enoch and eventually Noah was one of only a few that maintained the gifts and longer life span. For their own survival, they hid their talents and Anak underestimated the primitive humans. Enoch learned to fly Anak's spacecraft from one of Anak's wives. Thankfully, galactic technology has not changed much in five thousand years."

"Then you know where we are?"

Eve grasped the control sticks and manipulated the pedals on the floor. The spacecraft flipped over so the back of the craft faced the sun. "Do you see that bright star in front of us?"

"Yes."

"That is planet Earth," Eve said calmly.

A shiver flowed down Hannah's spine as she realized how far away from Earth they were. "Can't you just press the gas pedal and take us back home?"

Eve pointed at the huge gash in the console in front of Hannah where her cane had cut through several electronic components. "We no longer have a navigation computer, and we are traveling at about five million miles an hour away from Earth between magnetic fields. I don't think we can generate enough thrust without another magnetic field to halt our momentum, much less reverse direction."

Hannah looked at the polarized window as Eve turned the craft back around. "Are we heading directly toward the sun?"

"The ship is following the emergency protocol. It will slingshot around the sun so we won't burn to death."

Hannah let out a breath. "How long will it take to get back to Earth?"

Eve pressed a few buttons, and a map of the solar system appeared on the window. A small blinking triangle and a line projected their course around the sun. "Our current trajectory won't take us back to Earth. Our velocity will increase substantially as we slingshot around the sun and are propelled out to the Oort Cloud."

"That's farther from the sun than Pluto." Hannah shuddered. She studied the map to look for a solution. Jupiter was too far away to slingshot around and maneuver back to Earth. Hannah noticed lines indicating planetary orbits and fainter lines representing the paths of asteroids and comets. She also saw a green triangle close to the Oort Cloud, which dissected their projected trajectory. "What is that green triangle near the Oort Cloud?"

Eve typed a few commands and grimaced. "That would be the Elohim mother ship."

"Out of the frying pan . . . ," Hannah mumbled. "Any other problems I should know about?"

"We'll reach the sun in about thirteen hours where a good solar flare could burn us to ash as we slingshot around it. I don't think things could get much worse."

Hannah looked to the back of the spacecraft. "We have one more problem."

"Is he awake?" Eve asked and spun her chair around.

"Not as far as I can tell," Hannah replied. "But he's stuck to the bathroom door."

Chapter Twenty-Four

Hannah rose from her seat and floated toward the back of the ship. "Wait," Eve commanded. "Before moving Lotan from in front of the bathroom door, we must first ensure he can't control you."

"Won't the gold band around his head block him?"

Eve looked in the compartments around the pilot's station. "It will, but should he remove it without either of us noticing, you would be vulnerable." She glanced around the spacecraft and spotted their laptop computers on the floor beside the chairs. "Remove the power-charging cord from your computer and wrap it around your head."

Hannah did as requested. The heavy converter box dangled beside her ear.

Eve stared at Hannah and said, "I can still hear your thoughts. Do you feel anything?"

Hannah felt a tingle behind her ears. "Yes."

"One cord is not enough metal. Use the power cord from my computer too."

Hannah puffed out her cheeks as she removed the power cord from Eve's computer and wound it around her head, dangling the converter box beside her other ear. "I feel ridiculous."

"You look ridiculous, but it's better to be safe than sorry. Lotan is an unknown danger."

"Can I cut off the converters?"

"No. We'll need them to recharge our computers."

"You're enjoying this," Hannah accused.

"Only a little," Eve smiled. "You almost asphyxiated me with a stinky shoe."

"I apologize for that, but it wouldn't have killed you since you're immortal."

Eve's face darkened. "I am not immortal. Adam ate from the same tree as I did, yet he looked no older than I do when he was killed. I don't grow old, but a knife to my heart will kill me as easily as it would you. I have just managed to avoid all the knives."

Mentioning the forbidden fruit caused several awkward questions to roll through Hannah's mind. She was glad the metal around her head made it impossible for Eve to hear them.

Eve's eyes narrowed. "I don't need to read your mind to know what you're thinking. I will answer the question you're afraid to ask. The forbidden fruit contained more than the knowledge of good and evil. The knowledge was not what tempted me. Satan approached me the day my pet lion died of old age. He showed me how I would look and feel when I grew old. Disobeying God was not a lighthearted decision. During your short life, you've disobeyed His simple commandments for frivolous reasons. Tell me, granddaughter, if you were given the opportunity to remain young forever, would you take it?"

Hannah looked at the floor, unable to meet Eve's eyes. "I don't know if I would have the strength of character to say no."

"The fruit of the tree of good and evil provided eternal youth but not immortality. The fruit from the tree of life granted immortality, but I never touched it."

"But why—"

"Right now, we have more important issues to address. Go see if you can move Lotan."

Hannah tried to pry Lotan off the bathroom door. Every time she got one arm unstuck, the other arm would touch the wall or floor, and the sticky green goop would adhere to the surface. She wedged herself between the door and Lotan so he would only stick to her. Once he was unstuck, the lack of gravity made moving his bulky body easier. She placed Lotan in the seat she'd previously occupied, and he slowly molded to the contours of the chair. Eve pressed a button on her chair and wrapped Lotan in the rope webbing that had recently encased her.

After an awkward moment learning how to use the alien restroom, Hannah returned to the front where Eve was deciphering their speed and course.

"I think I've found a solution, but it's dangerous. Without the navigation system, we must use our laptops to calculate our course and fly the ship manually."

Hannah looked at Eve and spoke with more confidence than she felt. "If you give me our velocity, location, and vector, I can plot a new course. I've no desire to go to the Oort Cloud."

"Your calculations must be exact."

"When we slingshot around the sun, our exit velocity will exceed thirty-five million miles per hour, and we would pass Earth in three hours. Our velocity will be too high to stop. We could reach Pluto in four days, but it will take at least a day to brake, find another gravity well, and slingshot back to Earth. Are you thinking a second slingshot run around Jupiter? Even if it is in a good position, it will take a long time."

Eve reduced the polarization of the front window and light flooded in. "We're not using the sun's gravity well. We are going to slingshot around Mercury."

Hannah watched the plasma of the sun swirl and flow in random patterns. A solar flare erupted, and, for a moment, Hannah's eyes were mesmerized as the flare seemed to move in slow motion. She noticed a small black spot on the left side of the sun and realized it was Mercury. She stood abruptly and regretted it. After bouncing off the ceiling again, she retrieved her laptop. "Mercury orbits the sun in eighty-eight days. It will be out of range in about ten hours."

"I made a course adjustment but had to estimate where Mercury will be in three hours."

"Can you get exact measurements from the ship's sensors?" Hannah's voice raised an octave. "I need a gravitational gradient for the sun and Mercury."

Eve called out information while Hannah built mathematical formulas to balance the multitude of factors that would affect their course. In less than an hour, Hannah had a rough estimate for a course correction that would bring them close to Mercury's orbit.

Eve typed in the course correction, and the ship thrummed with power as it altered their trajectory. Hannah spent the next two hours refining her calculations. By the time she balanced the gravitational pull of the sun with the miniscule pull of Mercury, they were almost there. "If everything is correct, our velocity will increase by twenty percent as we pass around Mercury, but the sun's gravity will decrease it by thirty percent over a six-hour period as we pull away. We will return to Earth at four million miles per hour, braking at full power for the last four hours and be back home in thirteen hours."

"If?"

"I'm good at math, but I'm not a rocket scientist."

Eve sighed. "You've been itching to say that for a while, haven't you?"

"Yes," Hannah confessed.

Eve pressed a few buttons. "I'm shutting down all nonessential systems to conserve power."

Hannah gulped. "Why?"

"We used a lot of our reserves to change our vector. I shut down the Doppler shield, but we are so far away from Earth, no one will see us."

"I was more concerned about melting," Hannah quipped.

"I'm leaving the heat shields on as well as the magnetic absorption system. The closer we get to the sun, the faster our magnetic drive will recharge. Mercury's magnetic field will also give us a boost. We should be safe enough."

Hannah rechecked all her equations. She felt constantly distracted by the mesmerizing yellow-orange glow of the sun bleeding through the polarized front window. A dark sunspot rotated slowly into view, and it undulated like a jellyfish in the sea. Mercury was still a tiny black spot in the middle of the sun.

Thirty minutes before their approach to Mercury, Eve turned all the systems back on. The slingshot around Mercury was almost anticlimactic. Eve turned the windshield into a magnified view of Mercury. The surface of the planet reminded Hannah of butterscotch pudding. The craters and small hills were liquid smooth from millennia of molten rock settling on the barren surface. With a diameter of a little over three thousand miles, Mercury was behind them in a few seconds.

As they retreated from the sun, Eve checked their course. A bright star appeared near the center of the windshield. Eve told Hannah not to get up from her chair, for it would be several hours before their velocity steadied enough to leave the inertia-dampening field.

With nothing to do but look out the window, Hannah's mind buzzed with questions. Careful not to raise any issues the aliens would want to record, she made her first inquiry a simple one. "What was the Garden of Eden like?"

"We were landscapers with a lot of pets."

"Seriously? Is that all I get?"

"I apologize. I'm a little stressed. It was a beautiful forest similar to what you saw in Colombia, filled with lots of fruits and vegetables. Flowers bloomed everywhere, so it smelled wonderful. Animals roamed freely, and we did not fear each other. But there were no structures, paved pathways, or giant clamshells to stand in. We didn't know what a weed looked like. The best part was that the bugs did not bite or sting. Is that better?"

"Yes. Thank you. Why did you look like a duck-billed platypus in my dream?"

Eve laughed. "When a coercer enters a person's dream, he or she must obey the rules in the dreamer's world. I entered your dream to coerce you to wake, and although I can influence your dream, I can't control it. The best defense against a coercer is to fall asleep. The subconscious mind can protect the conscious mind even against the most powerful coercer. If I touch you too lightly, your mind will reject me. If I touch too harshly, your mind will put you into a deeper sleep. Subtlety is a coercer's greatest tool."

"But why a duck-billed platypus?"

"If you really want to know, I can share a memory with you."

Hannah's pulse quickened. The last time Eve had shown her a memory, it had been rather painful. "Will it hurt?"

Eve glanced at the cords wrapped around Hannah's head. "No. You'll have to remove the metal cords you're wearing, and I'll keep an eye on Lotan."

Hannah closed her eyes. "I'm ready."

"Then open your eyes," Eve said. "You can't experience an illusion with your senses blocked."

Hannah heard a man laughing. She opened her eyes and saw that she was no longer in a spaceship. A small fire crackled in front of her, the heat banishing the cold from the cave that surrounded her. An aroma of baking bread filled the cave. Hannah figured she had just eaten, for she felt fuller than she had ever felt in her life. She touched her stomach and looked down. She sucked in her breath and almost screamed. She was pregnant!

She sensed her arm resting on her cushioned chair and realized she was living one of Eve's memories. She ignored the chair and felt something poking her thigh. It was straw, scattered on the ground beneath her.

"I think there are two within me," Eve said as she gently rubbed her belly.

The male voice laughed again, and Hannah sensed him moving closer. She raised her eyes and beheld the most handsome man she'd ever seen. His black eyes, shining like onyx, looked lovingly back at her from a face so perfect that tears welled in Hannah's eyes. His voice sounded like rich chocolate flowing over fresh strawberries. "May I see?"

"Of course, my beloved."

Adam gently placed his muscular hands on her belly. Hannah felt her heart flutter with the warmth of his smile. He closed his eyes and held his breath. "You are amazing. Two girls live within you."

"I thought I sensed two minds waking this morning."

"Now our sons will have mates and experience the joy I have with you," Adam said, finishing with a hiccup.

Eve stroked his cheek. "We should not inhale the smoke from those odd weeds."

Hannah looked closer at Adam's eyes, which were a little red.

"I think you are right. My head does not feel as it should, and my healing talent is not clearing it up."

"Perhaps the smoke poisons the mind."

Adam sighed and massaged his forehead. "We have too many ducks."

"Excuse me?" Eve said, reflecting Hannah's confusion.

"We have too many ducks. The lake is crowded with them. There are duck droppings everywhere, and I don't like the way duck tastes."

"I can still travel," Eve replied. "I will go to the lake tomorrow and coerce them away."

"There is no need," Adam said almost sheepishly. "I turned them into trout and otters. I like the taste of trout, and the boys like watching the otters play."

Eve laughed. "I'm sorry I missed the fun."

Hannah heard a noise from the front of the cave. Two boys walked in wearing animal skins. One carried something like potatoes, and the other held two ducks. Hannah recognized Cain even without the mark of God on his face, though he appeared no older than twelve. The younger boy spoke, and Hannah knew him to be Abel. "Dad, I caught two more ducks. Can you change them into something different to eat?"

Cain shuddered as he turned his back.

Adam's voice turned harsh as he spoke to Cain. "How do you expect to grow strong if you won't eat meat?"

"Husband," Eve pleaded. "Let him choose his own path."

"Abel eats meat," Adam said with another hiccup.

Eve grasped Adam's hand, and Hannah felt his warmth in her fingers. "Abel tends his sheep and lures other animals with illusion, but he does not empathize with them. Cain is a coercer. He feels their pain when they die."

Adam tensed with anger. "I am his father, and I am not pleased. I do not believe God will be pleased with his offering either."

"And you know the will of God so well," Cain mocked quietly.

Adam stood abruptly. "Do not talk back to me, boy."

"I like meat!" Abel interrupted with jubilation.

Adam seemed to calm down, "Of course you do. Bring the ducks here, and I will change them."

Abel placed the ducks in front of his father. "For you, I will change them both at the same time."

Eve shifted awkwardly. "Are you sure? If your healing talent is not working properly, perhaps you should wait until tomorrow to change anything."

"I think I can handle it." Adam smiled, and Hannah watched as he began transforming the ducks into otters. As he did so, he hiccupped again. The transformation turned out wrong. The two creatures were no longer ducks, but they were not quite otters either. Adam looked at Eve, and Hannah could see he felt embarrassed. "I am sure they will taste just fine."

"No!" Cain screamed. Before anyone could do or say anything, Cain commanded the creatures to come to him. He gathered them up in his arms and fled the cave.

Adam called out, demanding Cain to return. "Bring them back here. You will not defy me. You are going to kill them yourself!"

Eve stood and moved to Adam's side. "Please, husband. Don't make him kill something he loves. He will learn to accept death in his own time."

"If I don't kill him first," Adam mumbled.

Hannah heard Abel sigh as he walked out of the cave. "I will go catch a few fish."

Adam and Eve sat in silence. After a while, Adam spoke. Hannah could tell that he felt more sober. "I believe I shall make my first law. No one should use anything that alters the mind."

"Adam's first law. That sounds good," Eve spoke with warmth. "But I have a feeling the law will be ignored."

"Is that a vision?" Adam asked.

"I'm not sure," Eve replied. "But I know the best way to ensure the law is not ignored. We must set the example."

"I agree," Adam said as he reached over and clasped Eve's hand. "I promise you I will be more careful."

"And I promise you the same."

Hannah realized she was holding her breath as the cave faded and the spaceship returned. "So, you must have been thinking of Cain when you entered my dream."

"I've been thinking of him a lot," Eve admitted. "The subconscious plays its own games."

"Now I understand why you abstain from alcohol."

"Even for the ungifted, alcohol and drugs lower inhibitions and cloud judgment. A telepath loses their ability to control their gift."

Hannah gazed out the window as Eve changed the view to confirm that their trajectory would take them to where the Earth would be in thirteen hours. Hannah examined their lines of intersection and was again amazed as the alien computer displayed the orbits of every planet and major asteroid in the solar system. She looked far out to the Oort Cloud to see the green triangle representing Lotan's mother ship. She blinked then sat up straighter. "Why is the green triangle blinking?"

Eve began checking her instruments but froze as a strained male voice answered from behind them, "Because if you can't get Muhammad to come to the mountain, then the mountain will come to Muhammad."

Chapter Twenty-Five

Hannah whirled around, causing one of the power cords wrapped around her head to slap her ear. She winced, but more so in sympathy at Lotan's painful expression. "Are you hurt?"

Lotan looked up and started to laugh. He immediately stopped with a major groan and a sharp intake of breath. "Please turn back around, Miss Hannah. It hurts too much to laugh."

Hannah heard Eve suppress her amusement with a cough and felt her face turn hot, but she refused to turn around. "I'm sorry for your pain."

"I trusted you," Lotan said, sounding as wounded as he looked.

"I'm only human," Hannah replied without apology.

"And that is why I forgive you."

"I did not—"

Lotan shouted a phrase in a language Hannah didn't understand.

"I've disabled voice commands," Eve interrupted. "Are you injured?"

Lotan was quiet for a moment. "My left arm is definitely broken as well as half of my ribs. I may have a concussion."

Hannah raised a curious eyebrow as she observed the green goop drip off Lotan and fall to the floor, where it was immediately absorbed. "I regret that I caused you harm."

"What are you doing with my ship?" Lotan asked Eve, ignoring Hannah.

"Returning to Earth," Eve quipped.

"Returning to Earth from where?"

"You accidentally hit the emergency escape button when you fell," Hannah explained.

"Which would send us to slingshot around the sun. But, how could you . . . ," Lotan stammered and then fell silent as something on the other side of the window caught his attention.

Hannah noticed the amount of light increase in the cabin and turned around. "Are we supposed to be glowing?"

Out of the corner of her eye, Hannah saw Eve turn to look out the window. Hannah was too fascinated to watch Eve check her instruments since liquid light danced and swirled in front of her.

"How close are we to the sun?" Lotan asked with concern from behind Hannah.

Eve was busy, so Hannah answered. "We're flying away from the sun and are about forty million miles out."

"How did you reverse our vector?" Lotan asked with a touch of urgency.

"We used Mercury to slingshot back around."

"Please tell me you shut down the magnetic absorption system as you left."

Hannah looked at Eve, who shook her head in the negative. "I'm afraid not. Is it important?"

Lotan growled with frustration. "Untie me, or we are all lost."

"That's not an option," Eve said through gritted teeth.

Hannah looked toward Eve, but the multiple flashing buttons and messages scrolling in front of Eve drew her attention. An alien voice emanated from an unknown speaker. Hannah could not understand the words but recognized the tone. She figured it translated roughly to *"Warning! You are about to blow up!"*

Hannah felt the temperature rise as the polarized windshield turned completely dark. "What's happening?"

"You created a magnetic wake when you swung around Mercury," Lotan shouted as the spacecraft began to shudder and buck. "Just like a high-speed boat on the lake, you have drawn plasma from the sun, and it has caught up to us."

"We caused a solar flare?" Hannah squeaked.

"You should never play with a star," Lotan yelled over the rumble emanating from the walls. "Shut down the magnetic absorption system."

"I already have," Eve shouted back.

"Reverse the polarity, and turn it back on."

Eve typed commands and said with relief, "Thus creating an eddy of tranquility in the river of chaos."

"You should be thankful I am a galactic weatherman and know how to manipulate solar flux," Lotan stated with a touch of arrogance.

"Will it work?" Hannah asked.

"It should," Lotan replied. "I don't think anyone has ever been foolish enough to cause a solar flare and test it."

Hannah was sweating and not just from the heat. The shuddering of the spaceship subsided and the view out the window dimmed. She breathed a sigh of relief as she gazed at the bright point of light before her that she knew must be Earth. "Will the radiation reach Earth?"

Eve checked a few readings before answering. "We are on a direct trajectory to Earth, but it will take us another twelve hours to get there. The radiation is traveling much faster. It won't hit Earth directly, but the planet will pass through the residual radiation cloud. The atmosphere and magnetic field will protect the planet, but we'll have some interesting aurora borealis."

"How do you know how to fly this ship?" Lotan asked in a suspicion-tinged tone.

"I read the instruction manual," Eve snapped.

"There is no instruction manual. Anak taught you how to fly his ship," Lotan shouted his accusation.

Hannah cringed as Eve snapped her head around. Hannah tugged on one of the cords wrapped around her head and shrugged. "The conclusion is obvious."

"Anak did not teach me anything willingly," Eve hedged as she glanced at Lotan.

"Then you stole his ship," Lotan continued. "You and some of your children hid in Peru. My people have always wondered why the Nazca Indians carved glyphs that can only be seen from the air."

"I believe your concussion has addled your brain," Eve said dryly.

"The Nazca Lines are only two thousand years old," Hannah added.

Lotan stared directly at Eve. "They were carved by the Amerindians that migrated from Asia, across the Bering Straits, and south all the way to Peru. But you and your children were already there, weren't you? They worshiped you as gods."

Eve slammed her fist on the arm of the chair, stood, and whirled to face Lotan. "Lotan, you do not understand the enemy. Cain spent two thousand years murdering every one of my children and their children. He nearly succeeded in killing all my descendants not of his blood. That's why the line of Noah is special. His family was one of the few that hid among Cain's people. Have you read our Bible?"

"Of course," Lotan replied.

"Every person in Noah's line lived nearly a thousand years and produced hundreds of children. Noah did not marry until he was nearly five hundred years old. Do you know why?"

"No."

"Because he could not find a female not of Cain's blood," Eve shouted. "Cain is the father of humankind, not Adam. Noah married a common woman because he was the last of Adam and my line untainted by Cain."

"But you and your children fled before Noah was even born," Lotan accused.

"Let's just suppose your speculations are correct and a few of my children survived and hid in Peru. Do you know what Cain would do if he sifted your theories out of your mind?"

"I can keep Cain out of my mind," Lotan growled.

"Your mind leaks like a sieve," Eve mocked. "If he thought a single child of mine survived, he would hunt down every descendant and kill them."

"I can keep Cain out of my mind," Lotan insisted.

"But she can't," Eve spoke quietly and pointed at Hannah.

Lotan looked at Hannah and tried to shrug, but the chair bindings prevented him from doing so. "I apologize, but the damage is done. You will have to keep her away from Cain."

Eve placed her hands on her hips in exasperation. "She has a gift I need. She sees answers where others see only questions. I need her to find the princess. I believe there is a high probability that she will eventually come in contact with Cain."

Lotan began asking Eve questions about her plans to locate the princess, and Hannah wondered why. Then she remembered the last time

Lotan had been in a conversational mood and Hannah turned around. "Mother, Lotan didn't intend to upset you."

Eve whirled around and directed her anger toward Hannah. "Why are you defending him?"

"Because his intentions are to distract," Hannah said calmly. "The mother ship is gone."

Eve froze in her chair and looked at the planets displayed on the front window. The blinking green triangle was gone. Hannah noticed that Lotan was silent. Eve typed commands, and after a few minutes shifted the view on the window. "I found them."

Hannah looked and saw the green triangle blinking in a different location between the orbit of Jupiter and Mars, but high above the solar ecliptic. "How did it get there so fast?"

"They teleported," Eve stated, and Hannah could sense the tension in her voice.

"Wow." Hannah breathed quietly. "A telekinetic can teleport that far?"

"Distance isn't relative when teleporting," Eve explained while typing. "However, a telekinetic can only teleport a limited amount of mass. No telekinetic could move something the size of a spaceship."

"Then how . . . ," Hannah began but changed her question. "If they are after us, why didn't they teleport here?"

"Because it's afraid," Eve stated.

"It?" Hannah asked, puzzled.

Eve glanced at Hannah as if debating whether she should answer the question. Hannah was not sure whether she had won or lost, but Eve answered. "It is a leviathan."

Hannah almost laughed. "You mean like a whale?"

"A whale feeds on plankton, one of the smallest creatures in the sea," Eve explained. "A leviathan feeds on interstellar hydrogen, so it is much larger. People can ride inside."

Hannah's jaw fell open again. "You mean like Jonah?"

"Something like that," Eve mumbled distractedly.

"You know more than you should, Eve," Lotan spoke softly.

Without turning around, Eve sarcastically replied, "According to your theory, we had a spaceship with a galactic database and thousands of years to learn how to use it. You figure it out."

Lotan sputtered, and Hannah knew without looking that he was turning dark blue. "Then you—"

"I'm kind of busy right now," Eve interrupted. "Hull integrity is down to thirty percent."

Lotan's tone changed to one of concern. "What else is damaged?"

"I don't know yet," Eve replied shortly. "Answer Hannah's questions, and leave me alone."

Hannah turned toward Lotan and smiled sweetly. "Why is the leviathan afraid?"

Lotan sighed but answered, "A telekinetic can't teleport though metal. A leviathan moves solely by telekinesis. Since they are so large, even the metallic molecules floating freely within a solar system can cause them pain."

"So it won't pass through the asteroid belt?" Hannah asked.

"No."

"And you travel inside their body?"

"A full-grown leviathan is about twenty miles long, and we can build a whole town inside them as long as we don't use metal."

Hannah was beginning to understand. "Leviathans can teleport between the stars."

"God set up the laws of physics so they cannot be broken. There are only two ways to travel between worlds. A powerful telekinetic can move something about the size of this shuttle and maybe twenty people. A leviathan can move anything inside itself."

"Are they sentient?"

Hannah noticed a slight smile touch Lotan's lips. "They are sort of like a puppy."

"A puppy twice the size of Manhattan?" Hannah exclaimed.

"They are loving and kind. They like to play, and even though they can be coerced to teleport vast distances, if they sense metal, they are frightened and refuse to obey."

Hannah chuckled. "I had to give my aunt's dog a bath once. He hated water. It was not a pleasant experience. The little mutt—"

Lotan turned serious. "My people were able to coax the leviathan much closer to Earth. They will catch us long before we reach orbit."

"Math is not your strongest talent, is it, Lotan?"

Lotan frowned. "I get by."

"We are thirty million miles from Earth. Your people are over three hundred million miles from Earth. Our maximum speed right now is one percent of the speed of light. Our pursuers need to reach six percent to catch us before we reach Earth. Somehow, I think they can't do that what with the laws of physics and all."

Lotan's frown deepened. "We have telekinetics."

"And if they could reach us, they would already be here. If I were a telekinetic, I wouldn't want to try to teleport in the middle of a solar flare. The space around us is probably loaded with heavy metal particles."

Lotan stared at Hannah for a moment and then spoke in a low, angry tone. "Eve, you know every detail about this ship, but you somehow forgot to shut down the magnetic absorption system when accelerating away from the sun. You caused the solar flare on purpose."

A jolt of shock traveled through Hannah. She had not figured that out. Eve looked at her. "I think it's time for you to be quiet, my dear."

Hannah's astonishment rendered her mute. She sat forward, placed her hands on her lap, and stared out the window.

"You did not answer my question," Lotan stated flatly.

"I liked you better when you were unconscious," Eve replied.

"I can't believe you would risk destroying your planet just to avoid a trial," Lotan said harshly.

Eve dismissed his accusation. "My planet is not in any danger. There will be some interference with delicate electronics, but that's about it."

"But why risk it?" Hannah asked but immediately closed her mouth when Eve narrowed her eyes.

"You have not lived long enough to see clearly when God opens a door for you. God gave me an unexpected opportunity, and I took it."

"I don't understand," Hannah mumbled.

"You will," Eve whispered.

"How much damage did the ship endure?" Lotan demanded.

"There's nothing wrong with our propulsion system," Eve shot back. "You lost a few scientific sensors. I've ordered your repair nanites to ignore navigation and concentrate on the hull. Integrity should improve to forty percent by the time we reach Earth, but we'll have to enter the atmosphere the old-fashioned way."

"This ship was not designed for an atmospheric burn," Lotan protested.

"Not that old-fashioned," Eve replied. "Hannah, keep watch and keep quiet. I need to take a nap."

Hannah sighed in disappointment. Then she stared out the window, watching Earth grow larger. The moon became a second pinprick of light. It was the most beautiful sight Hannah had ever seen.

Chapter Twenty-Six

Hannah felt frustrated because the two most fascinating people on the planet, well technically *near* the planet, were sleeping less than ten feet away and she could not ask a single question. With their perfect genetics, they didn't even snore. At least she had a beautiful view as Earth grew larger in front of her. As she strained her eyes to see the cloud patterns swirl around the planet, a faint beeping from the console woke Eve.

"Is something wrong?" Hannah asked.

Eve checked several readings, and Hannah felt frustrated again because she could not read the language. "No," Eve replied. "The solar flare is having the effect I hoped it would."

"What affect is that?"

"Effect, not affect, and I'd rather not say." Eve nodded toward Lotan.

"Sí, *señorita,* I can see the sea when you sing in the key of C at CiCi's Pizza if you wish to discuss semantics," Hannah quipped.

"What?" Eve said and turned to look at Hannah.

Hannah whispered, "I'm confident I can create a conundrum of complicated constructs considered confusing for conspiring kidnappers to comprehend without coercion."

She could almost hear Eve roll her eyes. "I don't think so," Eve said.

Hannah continued to whisper, "He's still asleep."

"I doubt that."

"I've been watching him for hours. He has not even twitched."

Eve placed a finger in front of her lips to indicate silence and spoke quietly. "Do you think I should turn this ship over to the Americans? With their technology we could solve a lot of problems."

"You claim to follow God's laws, yet you would steal my ship," Lotan sneered.

Eve said, "I knew you were not sleeping."

"It would be unwise to steal this ship."

"Lotan, we don't need your technology. We will soon reach your level and surpass you."

Hannah expected Lotan to laugh. The dread in his tone surprised her. "That is what we are afraid of."

"You're afraid of us?" Hannah nearly laughed.

"We use the tools God gave us to conquer space and cultivate new worlds. We use the natural magnetic field of the planet to supply us with clean, unlimited power. You destroy the land, contaminate the water, and pollute the air. Your scientists force molecules apart to produce energy, destroying tiny pieces of the universe God gave us. Your intellectually elite are now playing with black holes. We are frightened because you might actually succeed."

"But your science is much more advanced than ours," Hannah began.

"We understand black holes," Lotan interrupted. "We do not play with them."

"Why would the twenty thousand races of your confederation be afraid of one?"

"Because we do not kill."

Hannah felt her face turn red.

"And you kill without a conscious," Lotan continued. "You strap bombs to your children and tell them to die for a false god."

"You can't judge us based on a minor sect," Hannah objected.

"Oh, but we can. They are part of your race."

"We're not all like that!" Hannah exclaimed.

"Hannah," Lotan asked quietly, "you are an American, correct?"

"Yes."

"If the radical Muslims had their way, they would invade America, kill your leaders, and destroy your culture. Do you honestly believe that your people would not use children to help destroy your enemies?"

Hannah clenched her fist. "We value our children above all else. We wouldn't sink to their level no matter how desperate we got."

Lotan looked sad. "Not all Americans do. One of every four daughters is sexually assaulted before they turn eighteen. The same men who would rape a child would not hesitate to strap a bomb to their backs."

Hannah opened her mouth to object but could not find it within herself to defend a child molester. Eve spoke with sympathy beside her. "Hannah, you can't win this argument."

Hannah looked at Eve and felt ashamed. "You're siding with him?"

"The truth doesn't take sides," Eve replied. "It just is."

"Is there any hope?" Hannah asked.

"It is why God sent his Son here," Lotan replied.

The faint beeping sound caught his attention. Eve pressed a button, and the beeping stopped.

"Is there a problem with the Doppler shield?" Lotan asked.

"Nothing to concern yourself with." Eve cleared the planetary schematic overlay from the window. "We will be entering Earth's atmosphere soon."

Hannah watched the big blue marble hanging in space. She could make out points of light from the eastern seaboard. Eve steered the ship farther north.

"Every internal component on this ship will melt if someone tries to tamper with it."

"I know," Eve replied.

"What do you intend to do with me?"

"Lotan, I don't wish to harm you. At any time, I could have removed your gold band and scanned every thought in your pretty blue head, but I chose not to. I could have downloaded your entire computer database, but I chose not to. I am not your enemy. I would release you, but I don't trust you. Therefore, you shall remain under temporary restraint. I will free you when we are back on the surface of my world. That is the best I can do. As for Hannah and me, we still have a princess to rescue."

"I do not believe you will make it back to the surface of the planet," Lotan said with sincerity. "However, if you do, please heed this warning. We have become very good at making discreet abductions. I will try to buy you some time for Princess Sela's sake, but eventually we will find you and you will be imprisoned."

"I appreciate the warning, but I would expect nothing less. Now, please heed my warning. I've been using sophisticated technology for thousands of years. If any of my pureblood children survived, they undoubtedly focused on developing ways to hide from Cain. They have developed stealth technology far beyond yours. I know about your main bases in Antarctica and Nepal. I know where your research stations are, and when your leaders panic and move, I will know where they go."

"Is that a threat?"

"No, I wish you and yours no harm, but I can expose you," Eve replied solemnly. "You referred to your Council of Elders. Why do you revere your elders?"

Eve's question perplexed Hannah, and she sensed that it puzzled Lotan too. "Because the elders are wiser, and the older they grow, the stronger their mental gifts are," Lotan replied.

When his eyes lit, Eve looked kindly at Lotan while he made the connection. "I was a powerful coercer at the beginning, and now I am over six thousand years old. None of your people has ever crossed a coercer as powerful as me. You have no idea what I am truly capable of."

"You are bluffing."

Eve simply smiled. "Your wife's name is Jadzillia. Your firstborn's name is Lori. Your second born is Jillian. Your youngest is Libbie. Shall I continue?"

Lotan paled slightly and glanced at the gold rope around his forehead. "That is impossible. No one can read through gold."

Eve simply laughed.

"Then why did you allow me to capture you?" Lotan asked with skepticism.

"I am not infallible. You actually caught me by surprise."

Lotan frowned. "If you are the most powerful coercer in the galaxy, why did you not stop Cain from kidnapping Princess Sela?"

"Because Cain is the second most powerful coercer in the galaxy. He also had forty boys with explosives in their helmets, and just to get Sela he would have sacrificed all of them right after he killed each and every one of your people."

"But he could not use his powers. He was wearing a metal helmet!" Lotan nearly exploded.

163

"No, he wasn't," Eve replied calmly.

"Yes, he was. I saw him."

"The helmet was plastic. He was powerful enough to make you believe it was metal. The art of coercion is subtlety, and Cain knows his art well."

"Then why have you not just . . . ," Lotan stuttered to a stop.

"Killed him?" Eve finished the sentence. "Because I obey God's commandment, *Thou shalt not kill.*"

Eve checked the readings on her screen, made a few adjustments, and took hold of the control sticks that grew out of the armrests. She slowed the ship and approached the North Pole.

The brilliant white ice reflected sunlight in a dazzling display. Eve descended slowly to prevent any damage to the atmosphere. Hannah wondered when Lotan's alien allies would show up.

Eve descended almost to the surface before heading south. Hannah chuckled to herself since every direction from the North Pole was south. It didn't take long to enter Canadian airspace. A few minutes later, Eve and Hannah's phones beeped. Eve was too busy to answer, so Hannah looked at her phone. A message in a computerized voice said, "You have twenty-three new messages in your mailbox."

Hannah smiled at the familiar electronic voice. "I guess we're back under the satellites."

Eve replied quietly, "That will have to wait. Right now, we have company."

A strong male voice spoke in English through an overhead speaker. "Unidentified craft, you will land immediately!"

Eve banked the ship and increased their speed. She touched a blue button and spoke politely. "I'm sorry. Who did you say you are?"

"You know who we are. What have you done with Commander Lotan?"

Eve pushed the blue button again and continued to speak in a polite voice but with a touch of humor. "Commander is such an appropriate name for a coercer, don't you think? Commander Lotan seems to have broken his arm, and I am not quite ready to land."

"We cannot hear his mind. You have killed him. You will land now, or I will blow you out of the sky."

"I thought they wouldn't kill us," Hannah said with concern.

"After Cain attacked my craft fifty years ago, we added a few safety features. If this craft crashes, we will be surrounded in green protection gel that will probably keep us from dying."

"Not with our hull integrity at thirty-five percent. Talk to them."

"This is Lotan. You cannot hear my mind because I have a band of gold around my head. Please don't shoot. A solar flare damaged our hull. We would not survive a crash."

Eve banked again and descended farther. She made a small screen appear in the middle of the window, showing the view from the rear of the ship. The tops of the trees bent over as the craft screamed past. Snow sprang up, and a cloud of white ice particles followed in its wake. The inertia-dampers surrounding their seats were turned off to conserve power, so the contours of the rugged Canadian Rocky Mountains made each dip and turn sickening. Eve spun their tiny craft three hundred sixty degrees around the crest of a tall mountain, creating a whirlwind of snow larger than any natural tornado Hannah had ever heard of.

Hannah closed her eyes and prayed silently. The two pursuing crafts increased their altitude and flew above. Eve braked suddenly, bringing the craft to a near stop as two lines of bright blue energy streaked in front of it. She pivoted and shot straight into the early evening sky.

"Do we have any weapons?" Hannah exclaimed.

Eve spoke through gritted teeth. "This isn't a military craft, but don't worry. They're not used to flying within an atmosphere. I can fly circles around them."

Hannah held the arms of her chair as the craft reached what seemed like the top of the atmosphere, and Eve pivoted again and headed straight back toward the ground in a spiral pattern, circling the two attacking ships as they were still ascending. A streak of blue light flashed across the window, blinding them for a second.

"That was close," Eve muttered.

"Perhaps you should land," Lotan said.

"A third craft entered the fray," Eve said. "I am aware of it now."

"We have more," Lotan warned.

Eve wove in and out among the three alien ships. She danced, nearly touching each craft, so that if they shot their weapons again they would risk hitting one of their own ships. She dipped low in a snow-covered canyon, causing an avalanche, which slowed two ships considerably. Outracing the third, Eve curved southeast. The lights of Calgary shone brightly in the darkness.

Hannah watched as the alien craft dipped and twisted behind them and wondered why she could see the alien spacecraft. "Mother, are we immune to their Doppler shielding? I mean, should I be able to see them?"

"No, and it is about time I pointed that out to them." Eve pressed the blue button again. "I will be ready to land soon. From this point on, I will be flying over major cities, so I would not recommend using your bright blue lights anymore. By the way, have you noticed the solar flare has shorted out your Doppler shield?"

An alien word Hannah didn't understand came through the speaker. A smile touched her lips. "That's another reason why you caused a solar flare."

"It was an added bonus," Eve admitted.

"You are scary," Lotan mumbled.

Eve pressed the blue button again. "If you would like, I'll land in a discreet location north of Chicago and Lotan can take this craft back to Antarctica. However, if you continue trying to follow me, I will land on the front lawn of the White House. I prefer the first option, but the choice is yours."

The pursuing ships peeled off one by one. Eve slowed down to below the speed of sound and danced between cities, staying within clouds when she could to avoid highly populated areas. Through a break in the clouds, Hannah saw millions of lights surrounding the perimeter of the blackness of Lake Michigan.

Eve remained within the clouds as long as she could, then she landed in a small park a short distance south of Milwaukee, Wisconsin.

Pressing another button, Eve released Lotan from his netting. He had difficulty standing, so Hannah helped him get into the pilot seat. As the two nuns headed toward the opening hatch, Lotan called out to them.

They stopped. Lotan removed the gold rope from his head. "May God be with you and protect you as you search for the princess."

Eve and Hannah bowed their heads in acceptance of the blessing and stepped onto the melting slush on the grass of the small park. After a few steps, Hannah stopped and turned around. As the spaceship lifted silently above the trees, a sense of awe fell over her and she laughed.

Eve stopped and turned around. "What's so funny?"

"It all makes sense now."

"What?"

Hannah pointed to the bottom of Lotan's spaceship. "Do you see the four concentric rings of light surrounded by a ring turning clockwise and another ring turning counterclockwise?"

"Yes," Eve replied. "That's the electromagnetic propulsion system."

"You don't see it?" Hannah asked.

"See what?"

Hannah started singing an old hymn:

"*Ezekiel saw the wheel, Way up in the middle of the air.*

Ezekiel saw the wheel, Way up in the middle of the air.

And the big wheel is turned by faith, And the little wheel is turned by the grace of God.

It's a wheel in a wheel . . ."

"Do be quiet," Eve scolded. "We are trying to be inconspicuous."

Chapter Twenty-Seven

Hannah didn't understand the need to be inconspicuous. "Who are we hiding from?"

"Lotan's people," Eve whispered.

Hannah felt confused. "I thought you could protect us from them."

"Good. Let's hope Lotan believes the same thing. We need to find lots of people."

The two nuns headed to a shopping mall two blocks away then walked briskly across the parking lot and into the front mall entrance. A fair number of shoppers were looking for bargains during the Saint Patrick's Day sale.

"What do you mean 'hope'?"

Eve ducked inside a high-priced coffee shop and took a seat with a clear view of the entrance. "I might have exaggerated a little."

Hannah's voice rose an octave as she whispered, "You were bluffing?"

A teenage boy approached their table to take their order. Eve ordered the house special café latte for both of them. Before the boy turned away, he looked at Hannah and raised an eyebrow.

Eve hid her smile behind her hand. "I think you can remove your earrings now."

Hannah felt her cheeks turn red and removed the two power cords from around her head and dropped them inside her bag. When the teenager brought their drinks, he tried to keep a straight face but was unable to look directly at Hannah.

After he left, Hannah asked, "You get more powerful with time, correct?"

"Yes."

"Then are you the most powerful coercer in the universe?"

Eve took a long sip of coffee. "Probably. It's not like there is a test I can take."

"Then why are you afraid?"

"Because I'm susceptible to a stun gun."

Hannah sat back in her chair and held her cup in both hands. "Your illusions seem powerful to me, but I don't have anything to compare them to."

"Illusions are like second nature to me. You've seen my illusions many times, but you were unaware of them. I don't normally wear latex makeup or a prosthetic hump. I usually make myself look old with illusion. God gave us coercion to have dominion over the animals. He gave us illusion to teach our children."

"Is that why there's no evidence of a written language for the first two thousand years?"

"Yes, for a while there was no need for a written language."

"In the beginning, we used illusions to teach and entertain. It takes a great imagination and a lot of practice to weave an effective illusion. However, an illusionist affects the senses of the viewer directly. Any telepath, with a little effort, can see through it. Metal-filtered glass can allow the viewer to see through an illusion."

Hannah sipped her coffee as Eve watched the crowds of shoppers. She wondered if Eve was scanning for any aliens using illusion to hide among the people. Eve seemed satisfied with what she saw. "You flew circles around Lotan's comrades. It was as if you knew where they were going and when they would shoot beforehand. God gave you and Adam three powers. Is your third power divination?"

Eve frowned. "I prefer to call it precognition. I would prefer for Lotan to believe my third power is one of the more useful and powerful gifts."

"Your gifts seem useful and powerful to me."

"A healer is difficult to hurt, a telekinetic is hard to catch, and a transmuter is just plain dangerous. Precognition is a confusing and fickle gift and is rarely useful. Most precogs have an affinity toward something. One can find water, while another can search for a lost item, and a third can follow the historical path of an object. A few precogs have visions of the future, sometimes the distant future. The birth of Jesus Christ was prophesied more than a hundred times in the Bible. Some of the prophecies were made thousands of years in advance."

"Then I assume you can see into the future. How did Lotan surprise you?"

"I can only see a few minutes into the future clearly. My style of precognition takes a tremendous amount of concentration and is sometimes confusing. The Heisenberg uncertainty principle is in full force. The very act of glimpsing the future can change it, so there are sometimes too many paths to see anything clearly. After a few minutes, the multiple choices of other people's free will make the future too convoluted to comprehend. In all my years, I've never had a mysterious vision of the future, as some precogs do."

Hannah sighed. "Well, at least you're not hampered by metal."

Eve laughed. "Oh, but I am. I can no more read through gold than you can sprout wings and fly."

"But you read Lotan's mind while he wore gold."

Eve glanced around to see if anyone had noticed Hannah's outburst. "Please keep your voice down. I didn't read Lotan's mind through metal. The name of his wife and some of his children were on the surface of his mind while he was telling you about them back in the Eden Pharmaceuticals warehouse. No telepath can read through metal."

"You were bluffing."

Eve smiled. "Let's just hope Lotan and his superiors will believe the bluff."

Eve's phone buzzed, and she answered. Hannah could only hear one side of the conversation.

"Yes, Gertrude, we've been out of range. I'll have to explain later. I'm sorry you were worried, but we would have called if that had been possible. The mosquitoes are still in Chicago? Good. That's disappointing. What? I told all three of you to stay secluded in the basement for five days. Why did they go to Paris? I see. What time is it there? Use an express courier as soon as possible and send me another cane. I don't know where we will be staying, so send it to the vicar-general for the Archdiocese of Chicago. Yes, a few hours. A taxi? Don't be insulting. I'm glad she's feeling better. Goodbye."

Eve spoke to Hannah. "Gertrude believes Cain is still in Chicago. His airplane is in a private hangar at the airport. We have one mosquito and one dragonfly still functioning, but they've been stationary for two days.

They were programmed to follow Cain, so he must have left the building he entered by a different exit."

"Where are they?" Hannah asked.

"Somewhere close to the Willis Tower. Unfortunately, our sisters have been unable to locate an office or residence for Cain in Chicago. Mary Ruth and Mabel are in Paris trying a different approach to finding his location. We need to get to Chicago tonight, but first we should do a little shopping. I promised you a new pair of shoes, and you'll need civilian clothes. Looking like everyone else is the best disguise."

⁓

Eve purchased several sensible and conservative outfits for herself and Hannah, and they changed in a restroom. After eating supper in the food court, they took a taxi that would drive them ninety miles south to Chicago.

About a mile from the interstate, Eve yelled, "Stop the car!"

The taxi driver braked to a stop, and she asked him to turn around and pull into a used car lot a block back. As he entered the lot, Hannah read the sign: "Westshore Custom and Classic Cars." Some beautiful vehicles sat on the lot, including an older-model Jaguar and a dozen or so Corvettes. A Rolls Royce, several Mercedes Benzes, and a whole section devoted to muscle cars from the sixties occupied the lot too. Eve got out and headed straight to two Chrysler Prowlers built to look like roadsters from the forties but with all the luxury of modern cars.

A dignified salesman wearing a black suit approached with a warm smile.

Hannah felt self-conscious about wearing clothes other than a nun's habit. The cool wind ruffled her hair, and she noticed the salesclerk glancing at her ring finger, seeing her simple gold band. She returned his smile.

"Good evening, ladies. Can I get you some coffee or hot cocoa?"

Eve stroked the side of the first Prowler. The dark purple highlighted the highly polished chrome perfectly. "I've always wanted one of these."

"These two fine automobiles are both 2002 models. The Chrysler Prowler is one of my favorites. It's a little chilly to put the top down, but would you like to take one for a spin?"

"I don't think that will be necessary."

"With any luxury car you would expect the standard amenities, such as air-conditioning, power windows and locks, cruise control, and an illuminated entry system. There are also some extra features, like the delayed/fade courtesy lights and the peripheral antitheft protection. It also provides the joys of a convertible while still being a safe car. It has driver and passenger airbags, secure but comfortable three-point reel-in front seatbelts, and state-of-the-art run-flat Goodyear tires. It also comes with a three hundred twenty-watt sound system with a six-disc CD changer and seven speakers. Would you like to hear the sound system?"

Eve didn't even bother to look at the salesman. "I'm sure it also has a makeup mirror on the sun visor, but I'm more interested in hearing the 3.5-liter, twenty-four valve V6, which offers two hundred fifty-three horsepower."

The salesman was too experienced to act surprised. "Then you're of course familiar with the wishbone front and rear independent suspension with a stabilizer bar and coil springs. It can go from zero to sixty in 5.8 seconds and tops out at one hundred forty-eight miles per hour."

"How much?" Eve asked, still stroking the car.

"They don't make these beauties anymore, so their value has increased. It's a steal at forty thousand."

Hannah looked at Eve and saw lust in her eyes. "Wait a minute! You're not really considering buying this toy, are you?"

Eve glanced coyly at Hannah. "We might be in Chicago for a few days, and we need a set of wheels."

"We can rent a set of wheels for $59.99 per day."

"But not a Prowler."

"But you can buy a small house in Tulsa for forty thousand dollars!"

"I don't need a small house in Tulsa, but I need a car in Chicago."

"But, but, but . . . it probably gets real poor gas mileage."

"Actually, it does quite well for a sports car at twenty-three miles per gallon on the highway," the salesman interjected.

Eve glanced at the second Prowler. "How much for that one?"

"That one is even more special. It has been specially modified for even more speed, with a twin-cam V8 and a six-speed transmission for high-velocity driving. The interior has been updated with today's technology. It's reasonably priced at fifty thousand."

"But it's pink!" Hannah exclaimed. It was not just a calm pink, but a bright Day-Glo pink.

"It's a one-of-a-kind color. Not only is it the only Prowler with this particular shade, it's the only automobile with this particular shade."

"That isn't a shade even in full darkness! It probably even glows in the dark!"

When the salesman didn't deny it, Hannah saw that he was blushing. "It does! It really glows in the dark."

"I'll give you forty-five for the pink one," Eve said.

"What!" Hannah exclaimed. "You've got to be kidding. But, but, but . . . I hate pink!"

"Do you have cash?"

"Do you take a debit card?"

Thirty minutes later, Hannah sat fuming in the passenger side of the Day-Glo pink Prowler. Eve revved the engine. Using the manual shifter, Eve slammed the car into first gear and left a wide track of rubber on the cement. The acceleration threw Hannah's head back into the headrest.

As she buckled her safety belt, she recalled what Mary Ruth had said to her. *"If you value your sanity, you must not let her drive. Ever!"*

Chapter Twenty-Eight

Hannah cringed as Eve screamed the Prowler onto the entrance ramp at ninety-two miles per hour, and they were not even on the highway yet. Gripping the sides of her seat, Hannah asked, "Are we in a hurry?"

"No," Eve replied. "I just want to see what my new baby can do."

"'Baby,'" Hannah muttered. "If this car were a baby, they wouldn't have called it a Prowler."

Hannah could not hear the engine over the howl of the rear tires as they tore down the interstate. The sound was not unpleasant. It was almost as if the tires were singing. She tried to relax, thinking this might be just a little bit fun when Eve whizzed past the first semi as if it were sitting still.

Eve wove through four lanes of light traffic heading into Chicago. Hannah carefully opened the glovebox to ensure her emergency airbag was activated. Several dozen multicolored glow-in-the-dark condoms fell out on the floor. Hannah blushed, but Eve was too preoccupied to notice.

After a few minutes, Hannah's left leg began to twitch. She realized she was pressing down on an imaginary brake pedal. Eve slammed on the real brakes. For a few seconds, Hannah could not breathe as the seatbelt compressed her lungs. She looked out the front windshield and read a vanity license plate on the back of a Mercedes a few inches from the front bumper: "B4DKCME." Hannah figured the car belonged to a dentist. Eve blew her horn and scooted around the car.

Traffic became thicker as they approached the more populated outskirts of Chicago. Eve wove a dance among the many cars, SUVs, and semis. Slamming her open palm against the steering wheel, she used the shoulder to avoid several cars traveling in a pack. Hannah whimpered as the tires growled down the edge-of-the-road warning rivets, but Eve continued to use all four lanes and both shoulders of the interstate.

Hannah noticed pure pleasure blazing on Eve's face. She was so intent on the intricate dance that her eyes were barely open. With that realization, Hannah began a litany of Hail Marys. It didn't help, so she began a litany of "Please slow downs." Eve ignored her. When fear prevented her from speaking aloud, a new litany flowed through her mind. *"If you value your sanity, you must not let her drive. Ever!"*

As Hannah looked at the speedometer, it read "135" miles per hour. She closed her eyes. Swaying back and forth as Eve wove through more traffic, Hannah heard Eve speaking softly to herself. "Move to the left . . . Tap your brake . . . Hang up your phone, you're too stupid to drive and talk . . . Move to the right . . . Speed up a little . . . Brake now . . . Move to the right."

Hannah believed Eve was using precognition to see where the traffic currently was and would soon be. She was also using coercion to cause the other drivers to clear a path for her. Eve was dancing on several different levels.

Time flew as fast as the Prowler, and Hannah felt thankful to be alive still. Her heart pounded almost as fast as the rivet song on the edge of the road. With eyes closed, she tried to calm her breathing and slow her heart rate. Just as she thought she might succeed, Eve screamed. So did Hannah.

"Why are you screaming?" Eve shouted.

"Because you screamed."

"I'm screaming because there is too much metal."

"Thank God," Hannah whimpered.

Traffic was heavier than the last time she dared to look. Bright orange construction barrels prevented it from using the far right lane, leaving Eve with only three lanes. The Prowler approached two semis traveling side by side on the left and in the center. Hannah braced herself, expecting Eve to slam on the brakes. Instead, she sped up to one hundred and fifty miles per hour and shifted into the right lane traveling within inches of the orange construction barrels.

Hannah's eyes grew wider as a delivery truck switched lanes and blocked the right lane. Eve flew right behind the truck, and Hannah heard a commanding voice in her head scream, *"Lean to the right!"*

She immediately leaned to the right, pressing her body directly against the door. A temporary concrete safety barrier approached fast, taking the place of the orange barrels. The first concrete slab began a few inches from the road and rose sharply at an angle to a height of about three feet, meeting the same level as the rest of the wall.

At the last second, Eve swerved farther to the right and used the sloped barrier as a ramp to rocket the right side of the car into the air. The Prowler screamed past the delivery truck on its two left wheels. Hannah screamed. Eve screamed with her, but it sounded joyful. Hannah stopped screaming when the right tires bounced back onto the pavement. Her teeth hurt from grinding them.

Eve laughed. Hannah stopped screaming and said a few choice words in her mind that she hadn't used in a long time. Eve said, "Watch your language, dear," and laughed again.

A minute later, Eve started mumbling and frowned. Steeling her nerves, Hannah looked up and saw another wall of semis. Hannah said a prayer of thanks because there was nowhere to go. Eve slammed on the brakes and sent the Prowler into a spin. Hannah was not sure how many times they spun, but when they stopped they were right behind the center truck traveling at a sedate sixty miles per hour.

Hannah cried again. Eve sighed. "Good grief, you're as bad as Gertrude."

Eve drove at a slower pace for several miles, and they reached the Jackson Avenue exit. Hannah had never been so glad to reach an exit in her life.

She watched the monstrous buildings and bright lights of Chicago as Eve drove past. She knew Cain must be somewhere among the millions of people in the city.

Eve pulled in front of the Hotel Allegro, a historic lodging spot in the heart of downtown Chicago. It maintained its classy art deco design from the 1920s but looked like it had been remodeled recently. Eve got out of the car but stopped when she noticed Hannah had not moved. She walked back to Hannah's door and opened it. Hannah was shaking still. "Please tell me you did not pee on my nice leather seats."

Hannah looked up at her. "No, but if you ever drive that fast again, I promise you, I will."

Chapter Twenty-Nine

Hannah's hands were still shaking, so Eve opened the door to their hotel room. Two four-poster beds, a plush couch, two wingback chairs, and a desk made the room feel luxurious. A large TV hung on the wall between two paintings depicting life in the roaring twenties.

Eve pulled out her satellite phone. She sat in a chair, placed the phone on the desk, and made a call. "I'm sorry to wake you, Gertrude, but we have some privacy now," she said on speaker phone mode.

"There's no need to apologize. I had to get up anyway. The phone was ringing."

Eve chuckled. "Well, since you're up, please give me the coordinates of my dragonfly."

Hannah heard Gertrude moving around as she spoke into her phone. "If we get disconnected, just call me back. We might have connectivity issues for the next several days due to a solar flare."

"Sorry about that."

"It's not your fault."

Eve cleared her throat but didn't correct Gertrude. Hannah heard typing, and then Gertrude gave the latitude and longitude. Hannah stood behind Eve as she typed in the coordinates and watched her computer screen. The screen was completely red. Eve tilted her head. The picture cleared but held a greenish hue. Hannah saw the roof of a car traveling down a wide boulevard. There were buildings on each side of the street and tall skyscrapers in the distance. On the closest building, Hannah saw a name—"Willis Tower."

Eve pulled up information about the tower on her computer. "This isn't good."

"What's wrong?" Hannah and Gertrude asked at the same time.

"The Willis Tower has one hundred ten floors and thousands of people working there. Within a mile, there are many thousands of places Cain could be. He might not even have an office in Chicago and was just visiting someone. We need an address."

"We might know more tomorrow when Mary Ruth and Mabel return," Gertrude replied.

"They may not have even be here. We lost a lot of time," Eve said with some exasperation.

"Where did you go?" Gertrude inquired. "Lotan must have scrambled your phone signals or taken you deep underground for the satellite to not be able to find you."

"You were right," Eve explained. "I should not have trusted Lotan. He and his people decided to arrest me for crimes against humanity and God."

"But they're not human, nor are they God," Gertrude joked. "At least it was a quick trial. How did you win?"

"We didn't exactly make it to the trial. There was a slight detour along the way. Hannah wanted to see the sights around the world. I'll explain later. We need to focus. What in the world is wrong?"

"Is there a problem?" Gertrude asked with concern.

"Yes," Eve replied. "I ran a diagnostic on the dragonfly, which showed nothing out of order. The image was red for a few seconds when I first connected. Then the picture cleared but had a green hue. A minute ago, it turned a sickly yellow and is now red again."

"As much as we paid for the dragonflies, it should work perfectly. Let me check the manual. There could be an issue with the camera or the transmission."

"Don't bother," Hannah interjected and tried not to laugh. "It's really quite simple. The dragonfly is sitting on top of a traffic signal."

Eve sighed. "Well, that should have been obvious. It recharges itself with light and is safe from the wind."

"That's a relief," Gertrude said. "I don't think we would be able to get a refund."

"What have you found from all the data you extracted from Colombia?" Eve asked.

"It's fascinating reading, but not useful in helping us figure out what Cain is up to. It's a historical overview of Cain's adventures. Did you know he was the power behind Genghis Khan?" Gertrude asked.

"Yes, and he advised Caesar Augustus, Osman I, and Napoleon. He also spent time in China and India, but I'm much more interested in his current projects and location."

"Ah yes," Gertrude stammered. "I found out why he is donating money to independent textbook companies through Enoch Enterprises. Each company produces textbooks for either Christian- or Muslim-based homeschooling."

"Supporting Christians is out of character for Cain," Eve stated. "He must have an ulterior motive."

"I believe he is supporting them to keep the creation conflict going between religious and secular groups."

"That sounds more like him," Eve replied. "There have been more arguments over the first ten chapters of Genesis than everything else combined."

"I've been drawn into that argument a few times," Hannah admitted.

"Why bother?" Eve asked.

"Because the Bible says God created everything in six days."

"Hannah, God never lies. If carbon dating proves dinosaur bones are eighty million years old, then they are eighty million years old. He did not place them there to test our faith. If a star is a million light-years away, then light has been traveling for a million years to reach us. You seem confused because God said he created the universe in one day. When Mary Ruth has celebrated over ninety birthdays, did you not assume that she celebrated them on ninety consecutive days?"

"No, because birthdays are only celebrated once a year."

"God told Adam about the six days of creation. Which verse states that the second day followed immediately after the first?"

Hannah fell silent.

"Anything else you can tell us about Cain?" Eve asked Gertrude.

"From his files, I know he enjoys influencing political leaders. By following the money, I found four more holding companies. Among them he has enough shares to attend stockholder meetings in many different companies."

"Which allows him to use his talents to manipulate the political and financial environment in the direction he wants," Eve added.

"Could he control a whole room of stockholders?" Hannah asked.

"He could influence a whole room of stockholders briefly, but he would really only need a few key leaders. Have you found anything connecting him to Chicago?"

"We may have a new source of information when Mary Ruth and Mabel return from Paris."

Eve frowned. "I distinctly remember asking the three of you to stay within the confines of St. Margaret's basement out of view from everyone unless there was an emergency. What was the emergency?"

"We tried to contact you for two days. Mary Ruth believed it wise to proceed with the mission as if we were working alone."

"Why did she go to Paris?"

"We have our entire flock of sisters analyzing the data from Colombia. Mykaela read a research paper from 1979 concerning the uniqueness of palm prints and how they are more accurate than fingerprints. Cain purchased controlling interest in DuBoise Security, which uses the technology. Mabel recognized their logo from a warranty sticker on the inside of the safe door in Colombia. We're hoping Cain uses DuBoise Security for all his systems. I can't get past their firewall without a password. My probe was detected and nearly traced. Mary Ruth took Mabel and flew to Paris to retrieve a password in her usual way."

"Is Mary Ruth feeling better?" Hannah asked.

"Remarkably well. She told us she hasn't felt better in thirty years. By the way, your debit card charges just showed up. I noticed you've activated your Genevieve McAdam persona. Wait a minute . . ."

The phone went silent for half a minute. When Gertrude spoke, her tone was suspicious. "Mother Evelyn, did you buy a house?"

"Not exactly. We needed transportation while in Chicago."

"But you spent nearly fifty thousand dollars on a car?" Gertrude exclaimed.

"Well, the taxes were more than I expected, but it's a really nice car."

"And I suppose it goes really fast too."

"You might say that."

"And did you drive it on the highway?"

"Just for a little while."

The phone "clicked" as it disconnected. A few seconds later, Hannah's phone rang. She answered, and Gertrude sounded sympathetic. "Are you alright, dear?"

"No, it was awful." Hannah sobbed.

Eve looked disgusted. "Good grief. If you two are going to have a pity party, I'm going to bed."

Chapter Thirty

The next morning, Hannah awoke and turned on the television to watch the news. It showed a volcano blowing smoke with the words "Colima Volcano" in bold letters at the top of the screen. "Mother Evelyn, you might want to see what's on TV."

Eve entered the room with a thick white towel wrapped around her head. Hannah turned up the volume as a blonde newscaster spoke. "Although the mighty Colima Volcano is still spitting smoke, the citizens of Colima, Mexico, are returning to their homes today. Volcanologists had feared there might be a major eruption after a minor vent erupted three days ago.

"Four other volcanoes, also thought to be extinct, have erupted in different parts of the world this morning. Several members from the United States Geological Survey are gathering more information concerning the volcanoes in Fiji, Greece, Japan, and Canada. With us now is Simon Feldspar, director of the USGS. Director Feldspar, can you hear me?"

A deep male voice broken by static said, "Loud and clear," although he was neither loud nor clear.

"Can you tell us what's happening with these volcanic eruptions?"

The director spoke over an odd buzz. "Beginning at 2:43 a.m., Eastern Standard Time, a minor tremor of 3.2 on the Richter scale was detected, with the epicenter near the Nazko volcano in British Colombia, Canada. Within the next six hours, we detected minor disturbances near volcanoes in Tokachi, Japan; Milos, Greece; and the Fiji Islands. The seismographic data suggests there were minor volcanic events at all four locations. We have compiled photographs from NASA for each of these sites and detected small amounts of volcanic smoke in each of these regions. We already have agents in British Colombia, and their preliminary report suggests only minimal lava flow and almost no damage to the surrounding environment. Other agents are traveling to the other three sites."

"Director Feldspar, what could cause these five volcanoes to return to life at the same time?"

"We are uncertain. Two days ago, a solar flare erupted as the planet Mercury passed between Earth and the sun. NASA and the European Space Agency recorded an unusual magnetic wave inbound from Mercury. This could affect our own magnetic field."

"Did you notice the way he looked to the left?" Eve said. "His reply is a subtle misdirection."

"Director Feldspar, why did the USGS not give any warning of any of these eruptions?"

"Because Mother Earth doesn't always warn us in advance. Seismic prediction is complex and difficult. Most of our budget is spent analyzing data on our own continent."

"Director, in the last few years we have had several major earthquakes. There is one question on the top of everyone's mind this morning: Are we safe?"

The director chuckled. "Well, you are in New York, so of course you're safe from volcanoes and earthquakes. The rest of the world is difficult to predict."

"Thank you, director," the newscaster concluded, then picked up, "Another event occurred last night in the Rocky Mountains of Canada. Meteorologist Hal Lincoln will explain what may have been a tornado where no tornadoes have ever been reported."

The camera shifted to a portly man standing in front of a map of the North American continent. "Thank you, Lydia. A surprising north wind blew through parts of the Canadian Rocky Mountains last night, toppling trees and setting off avalanches along the upper mountain ridges. The great Chinook of the North traveled a narrow path before dissipating west of Saskatchewan. Several ham radio operators reported seeing flashes of strange lightning and a loud thunderous boom. Because of the nature of the damage, local mountain men believe it may have been a freak tornado. Meteorological reports cannot confirm this but suggest that the damage came from straight-line winds in excess of one hundred twenty miles per hour; but we don't believe there was an actual tornado. No one should be afraid of the wind today on the West Coast. Our forecast calls for sunny skies over California and—"

Hannah turned the volume back down and looked at Eve. "That was interesting."

"Yes," Eve replied. "I didn't expect the Elohim to shut down their observation posts so quickly."

"Will you be able to find them again?" Hannah asked.

"Eventually," Eve stated flatly. "They'll improve their shielding, which will make it much more difficult. It would be nice if they would just leave the planet."

Hannah pulled a chair behind Eve to watch as she maneuvered her dragonfly camera to different windows of the Willis Tower, looking for Cain. The temperamental winds prevented her from peering into the windows on the west side of the tower, which still left thousands of windows to examine.

Soon, she grew bored looking through office windows on a computer screen from behind Eve's shoulder. "I think I understand coercion. Perhaps, while we are searching for Cain, you could tell me a little more about how illusion works."

Eve remained silent for a minute before replying, "I suppose a little education could not hurt. Coercion and illusion are more powerful than telepathy. Illusion is like viewing a hologram. You know it's there, but you may also know it's not real." She opened the desk drawer and reached for something inside. "Let me give you a little demonstration. As an illusionist, I can create an object that seems totally real even though you know it isn't."

She tossed the object she had removed from the desk in Hannah's direction. "Here, catch."

Hannah reached out and caught the apple Eve tossed to her. She examined it carefully. It looked like an apple. It smelled like an apple. It felt firm like an apple and even had a small soft bruise.

"Taste it," Eve requested.

Hannah reluctantly took a bite, and it even tasted like an apple. It was tart and chilled, as if it had just come out of the refrigerator. "That's amazing!"

The illusion disappeared, and Hannah realized she was holding a paperweight with the hotel logo on it.

"The eyes are the easiest to fool. A skilled illusionist will create an illusion that has texture, smell, taste, temperature, and sound, if necessary. These are very complex illusions and can only be done for small numbers of people. The larger the crowd, the simpler the illusion must be. Normally, when I appear as an old woman, it's only an illusion. When I stand before the sisters of our order, there are nearly a hundred present. I only have to create wrinkles on my hands and face and a hump on my back. I wear my makeup and prosthetics only when necessary, like on the day of the annual invasion by Kappa Lambda Omega. If I'm distracted or surprised, I might lose concentration and the illusion would fade. I need my mind free to use all my skills against the boys. The two flying paragliders thought they were landing in the courtyard, for that's what they saw. In reality, they flew right past."

"That's why you ran outside to the courtyard," Hannah exclaimed.

"Yes," Eve replied. "Illusion has some of the same mental characteristics as coercion but is definitely different.

"That makes you extremely powerful."

"Against an individual, and only because this world is populated with nontelepaths," Eve agreed. "The worlds of the Elohim are wonderful because their cultures choose to be open and honest. They do not practice or even understand deception. Against another telepath, especially another coercer, I wouldn't be nearly as effective. Coercion is God's gift to help us have dominion over the animals, not each other. Illusion is for teaching our children and entertainment."

"The worlds of the Nephilim must be terrifying," Hannah added.

"They are probably much like our own. For the past six centuries, the physically strong have held power over the physically weak. In more modern times, the financially strong hold power over the financially weak. On the Nephilim worlds, the telepathically strong hold power over the telepathically weak."

Hannah shuddered. "Cain is a coercer too."

"Oh yes," Eve replied with candor. "He's almost as strong as I am. Because of his nature, he has used his formidable powers much more than I have."

"That's why he is so rich and is able to manipulate everyone around him," Hannah said.

"Yes, but a coercer's influence lasts only as long as they are present, unless their suggestions are in line with the personality they are dealing with. He might be able to force a preacher to steal a piece of candy, but he could not change who they are. The preacher would feel guilty as soon as Cain's influence relented. The preacher would probably make restitution. For coercion to be effective, it must be subtle."

"So, if I ever see a dragon flying in the air, I should just believe it's only an illusion," Hannah joked.

"There's just one problem with that," Eve warned. "Against a powerful illusionist, whatever he or she creates will seem real to you. An illusionary knife through your heart can still kill you. Your mind might die from shock."

"I think I want to invest in some metal hats."

"I don't think that will be necessary," Eve comforted. "Low-level telepaths are developing slowly all over the world, but as far as I know, there are a limited number of high-level telepaths on the planet."

"I know I have nothing to fear from you, but we are in a battle against Cain."

"Good point."

"I have another question for you. Why don't you just switch identities like Cain does every twenty years or so?"

"Because Cain does not care about the people he may hurt. When he closes one of his companies, thousands of people lose their jobs. The last time I changed identities was in 1938. I had to stage my own death and leave. I had to relocate the majority of the sisters over a period of three years to other convents, and new sisters transferred in. When the new Mother Superior arrived, no one knew what the previous Mother looked like when she was young. I have done that every so often since I built the abbey in 1758. It's not a pleasant experience to pretend to die and lose all of the friends that are important to you, so I try to live as the same person for as long as I can."

Hannah felt her heart grow cold, for she now considered Eve to be more than her Mother Superior and a relic from the past; she was her friend.

At nine o'clock, Eve halted her search to prepare for her meeting with the vicar-general. She expected the courier service to deliver her cane by ten o'clock. Eve carefully maneuvered the dragonfly back to the ground and skimmed it past the front entrance. As the dragonfly flew over the pedestrians, Hannah saw a woman who looked familiar. "Stop!"

Eve stopped the dragonfly in midflight. "Did you see something?"

"The blonde in the yellow outfit looked like the woman on the plane with Cain."

Eve turned the dragonfly back toward the entrance to Willis Tower and zoomed the camera to see the blonde's face.

Hannah looked at her face and recalled the memory of the woman. "That is definitely her."

The dragonfly showed the woman's face briefly but clearly. She wore a hat that matched her yellow outfit, and her long platinum-blond hair blew in the wind. The yellow latex outfit advertised her overly large breasts, and the miniskirt accentuated her shapely long legs. Her lips were painted a bright red, and she maintained a small smile, as if enjoying the constant stares of the men around her.

She passed through the door, and the dragonfly dove after her. Suddenly, the camera angle changed and the dragonfly flew in the opposite direction.

"What happened?"

"Automatic defensive maneuver," Eve replied. "The dragonfly must have sensed a bird under the awning of the door." Eve looked at the clock and sighed. "We'll have to follow her later. Right now, we have an appointment with the vicar-general."

"I can stay here and use the dragonfly, if you want," Hannah suggested.

"No. I'll look too old to travel alone, and I might need your assistance with distractions if there are too many people."

"What do you mean?" Hannah asked.

"I seem to have left my prosthetic hump back in Colombia," Eve replied as she headed into her bedroom.

Hannah donned her nun's habit. When Eve came through the door, Hannah's jaw dropped.

"How do I look?" Eve asked, her voice trembling with age.

"Like you always do."

Eve looked like an old woman, stooped over. Huge liver spots and thick blue veins covered her face and hands. Large crevices crossed her face with lines and wrinkles radiating from around her eyes like the spokes of a broken bicycle wheel. Her eyebrows were gone, and her lips looked parched.

"Good." The illusion faded, and she looked youthful again.

"I thought you wore a disguise to look old."

"Heavens no," Eve exclaimed. "That getup is incredibly uncomfortable, and the fake skin itches terribly. I only wear the latex applications when I go out in public. I can maintain the illusion of being old for a large group of people in a close area, more if I wrap up in my robes and wear my veil across my face. Sometimes, I wear gloves to reduce the area of illusion."

"Can anyone on the streets see through your illusion?"

"A camera has no mind to affect. It records reality, not illusion. Sister Mabel would see through it because of the metal plate in her head. She has become immune to illusions. She sees me exactly as I am."

"Should I line the inside of my habit with tinfoil in case we run into Cain?" Hannah asked as they headed out the door.

Eve stopped in front of the elevator as she wrapped her veil around her face. "I think that would just annoy him."

"So?"

"Cain kills people who annoy him."

"Oh."

"I will try to teach you a few ways to protect your mind to prevent Cain from hearing your surface thoughts. Without a mental shield or metal helmet, your best option is to submit."

When the elevator arrived, a chill raced through Hannah's heart. "If you're going to look like an old crone, would it not be better for me to drive?"

"I think it would look awkward for nuns to drive the Prowler, but two young nuns could walk. It's less than a mile and after being cooped up in Lotan's ship, I need some exercise."

"Thank God," Hannah said, the words escaping before she realized her mouth was open.

Chapter Thirty-One

Hannah tried not to gawk as she walked past the monstrous steel-and-glass skyscrapers. Pedestrians crowded the sidewalks, rushing to wherever they needed to go. Eve didn't create an illusion to change her youthful appearance. Hannah felt thankful for the protection her nun's habit provided since the street vendors and game players ignored them as they walked by.

As they crossed the Chicago River, Hannah noticed the stone-lined channel held a greenish tint around the edges from the Saint Patrick's Day celebration. Street-sweeping machines were cleaning up green confetti from the festivities. Hannah wished she could have seen the parade, but she was a day late. The bright green shamrocks on the lampposts were cute, but after passing numerous leprechaun-covered storefronts, Hannah grew weary of green.

The office of the vicar-general was in the beautiful gothic-architecture-filled historic district. The arches, columns, and handcrafted masonry made each building a work of art. New spring flowers poked to the surface in planters along the streets. The two nuns walked up the steps of the magnificent old building housing the Archdiocese of Chicago. Eve grasped Hannah's arm and leaned into her as they passed through the first set of doors. A second set of doors created a barrier between the cold temperatures outside and the warmth within. Eve changed her appearance in the small vestibule between the doors, stooping over with age as she leaned heavily on Hannah's arm.

A large staff of priests and clerks looked busy with their computers and paperwork. After confirming the appointment, a clerk escorted the Mother and Hannah into the vicar's office.

"Is it really you?" the vicar asked in a warm baritone as he rose from behind his desk. He looked like a healthy senior citizen, completely bald with a friendly, crooked smile.

"It is I," Eve replied.

"I thought I would never see you again." The vicar embraced the Mother gently. "I was puzzled when I saw your name added to my appointment book. Then I received a package from the convent I associated with you many, many years ago. It's so good to see you again."

"It's good to see you too, Robert. Please allow me to introduce my assistant, Sister Hannah."

The vicar shook Hannah's hand and pulled out chairs for each of them. He offered refreshments, but Mother Evelyn politely declined. "I'm so surprised to see you again," he said. "Honestly, I'm surprised you're still alive. God has blessed you abundantly."

"More than you know," Mother Evelyn replied.

"If you don't mind my asking, how old are you?"

Mother Evelyn laughed. "You're still the same blunt Robert that I once knew. A woman never tells her age, but I can assure you, I'm older than you think."

"You're shorter than I remember."

"And you're taller," Mother quipped. "You have done very well for yourself being vicar-general and all."

"The Lord has been good to me too." He looked at Hannah. "Has your Mother Superior ever told you of her adventures during World War II?"

"I've heard a few stories. But I'm sure there's much more that I don't know."

The vicar leaned against his desk. "Your Mother Superior saved my life. She saved the life of my entire family."

"Now that's a story I would enjoy hearing." Hannah clasped her hands with anticipation.

A faraway look settled in the vicar's eyes. "It's a short but fascinating story. In 1942, my family resided in Berlin. My father lost his hand in a battle in Poland at the beginning of the war. He was a good Catholic. When Hitler rounded up the Jews and sent them to concentration camps, my father decided to oppose the Nazi party.

"The Americans contacted my father through the underground network. He became a janitor at one of Hitler's secret research facilities. We struggled just to survive. My mother worked in a bakery, making bread for the German soldiers. I was only thirteen, and my younger sister was eight. My father sent the Americans information about a superbomb Hitler was building. A man came to the research facility one day and talked briefly with anyone who had access to the building. Dad did not ever see his face. He kept it wrapped in a scarf.

"That afternoon, my father was arrested. So were my mother, my sister, and I. The commandant scheduled our execution for the following dawn. Late that night, the door to our cell was unlocked and a soldier walked in. He was short, and his voice sounded light. He had a limp and used a beautiful black cane with a white angel on top. He informed us he was to escort us to a priest who would administer our last rites before we continued to our execution.

"We were all chained together as we shuffled through the prison, but no one paid any attention. The guards at the front gate didn't even wake up as we passed by. We got in a car, and the soldier spoke quickly and quietly. He removed his hat and revealed himself to be a woman who worked with the British government. She made a deal with my father—the life of our family in exchange for information concerning the progress and whereabouts of the bomb Hitler was building.

"The next few hours were a blur." The vicar laughed and looked at Hannah. "You better be thankful she's too old to drive now. The drive through Berlin was terrifying. The countryside was even worse. I still have nightmares about being in a car balanced on the train rails at night with no headlights and feeling vibrations of a locomotive behind us as we both traveled at high speeds.

"When we arrived at a haven in France, I was surprised when the young lady donned a nun's habit. She arranged for my family to hide close to her abbey in England. A few months later, we migrated to Chicago. My family and I are eternally in Mother Evelyn's debt."

Hannah cleared her throat. "Thank you, sir. I learn more about the Mother every day, and it's nice to hear some of the exploits of her youth."

The vicar turned back to Mother Evelyn. "What brings you to Chicago?"

"We're trying to find someone here, and I broke my cane along the way. You're the only acquaintance I have in the city. My staff sent me another cane, and it should have been delivered to you this morning."

The vicar retrieved a long, narrow package from behind his desk. The Mother motioned toward Hannah. "She better open it. My hands are not as adept as they once were."

Hannah opened the package and removed the cane. As she handed it to the Mother, the vicar asked, "Is that the same cane?"

"Yes. I have several."

"Does it still have the green gas and the blue flame at the bottom?"

"Now, Robert," she admonished, "that was supposed to be our little secret."

"I apologize. There have been times I thought that cane was part of a dream. The memory is blurred. You cut our hand and ankle cuffs with a blue flame, did you not?"

"Yes," the Mother replied.

"My parents would never talk about it, and my sister didn't remember anything. It's nice to know my memory was real."

The vicar paused and then said, "Since you are still using your cane, then you are still playing the spy game. Who are you looking for? I know many people in Chicago. Perhaps I can help."

Mother Evelyn pulled a small piece of paper from her pocket and handed it to Hannah. It was a close-up picture of Cain with the red hand of God emblazoned boldly across his face. Hannah handed the picture to the vicar.

He looked at it for a moment and handed it to Mother Evelyn. "Yes, I know him. I had a lunch meeting with him yesterday."

"*What?*" The Mother stood abruptly and dropped the picture to the floor. Her hand and face wrinkles faded briefly. Hannah stooped to pick up the photo and noticed it was now a folded ten-dollar bill. The picture had been an illusion. She quickly stuffed the money into her pocket.

"I've never seen a red birthmark on his face, but that is definitely Michael Gentile. Now I understand why he always wears makeup."

Mother Evelyn sat back down. "I know him by another name. What can you tell me about Michael Gentile?"

"He is wealthy and reclusive. He immigrated here about . . . twenty years ago from Ireland and opened an advertising agency."

"What's the name of the agency?"

"Pair-O-Dice Advertising."

"Did you say 'Paradise'?" Hannah asked.

"No," the vicar replied. "Pair-O-Dice," he said and spelled it out. "They have contracts for almost every state lottery and many of the casinos that are popping up all over the country."

"If you don't mind my asking," the Mother inquired, "what were you meeting with him about?"

"Michael Gentile is a large contributor to the Saint Patrick's Day Parade. Although he has not admitted it, I believe most of his contributions come from the gambling consortiums. His company provides free leprechaun and lucky clover pictures to parade merchants. Personally, I find the man rather distasteful, but my office helps coordinate much of the Saint Patrick festivities and we sometimes cross paths."

Mother Evelyn's face pinched in disgust. "And when did Saint Patrick become the patron saint of luck?"

"Saint Patrick is the patron saint of Ireland, having brought Christianity to the island. He drove the pagans led by the Druids from Ireland along with all the snakes. That would include the belief in luck and any leprechauns. Secularists use the leprechaun the same way as the Easter Bunny and Santa Claus. In a hundred years, Saint Patrick will be called the God of Luck."

"That's sad. Did anything of interest happen in your meeting with Michael Gentile?" the Mother asked.

"He called a special meeting of the parade committee after the parade ended. He informed us that the clients his company represents were willing to guarantee a high gambling payout ratio for ten years if the city of Chicago would allow gambling during the week of Saint Patrick's Day."

"How did the committee respond?" the Mother asked.

"I objected, but I was the only one. If enough people sign a petition, it will be voted on by the general population during the next election."

"I see," Mother Evelyn said. Hannah heard disapproval in her tone.

The vicar's eyes narrowed. "Is Michael Gentile involved with the Irish terrorist group known as the Red Hand Defenders? They mark their faces the same way as the man does in that picture."

"There may be a connection," Mother Evelyn hedged. "I would suggest you distance yourself from him."

"That won't be a problem. Mr. Gentile is rarely in town, and we only have contact through the parade committee. I have a little piece of advice for you too, Mother Evelyn."

"I'm listening, Robert."

"If you're looking for Mr. Gentile, try to avoid his assistant. She is the spawn of the Devil."

Mother Evelyn raised an eyebrow. "I hope you don't mean that literally."

"It wouldn't surprise me," he replied. "Her name is Carla Babb, and she has probably slept with half the men in Chicago. She takes great pleasure in trying to seduce my priests. She will proudly tell you she worships Satan and resides where Anton Szandor LaVey was born."

"Who is that?" Hannah asked.

"He is the author of the Satanic Bible and several other satanic books," Mother Evelyn supplied.

The vicar's intercom beeped. "I'm sorry to disturb you, sir, but your appointment with the archbishop is in ten minutes and we must depart immediately."

Mother Evelyn stood and gave her old friend a hug. "May God continue to protect and bless you." She departed the office faster than a decrepit old woman should be able to and returned her appearance to her younger self. Upon reaching the street, she immediately hailed a taxi.

As they climbed into the back seat of the taxi, Hannah said, "You're in much more of a hurry than you were an hour ago."

"Yes," Eve replied. "We now know where to look and need to use our dragonfly and see what's going on at Pair-O-Dice Advertising."

The taxi pulled up to their hotel, and the two nuns rushed inside. In their suite, Eve called Gertrude and asked her to do a background check on Michael Gentile and Carla Babb.

Eve accessed the dragonfly on her computer, and Hannah watched over Eve's shoulder. To avoid the birds around the entrance of Willis Tower, Eve landed the dragonfly on top of a woman's hat as she entered the building. She kept the dragonfly on the hat until the woman entered the elevator and then flew it to land high on the elevator wall. Pair-O-Dice Advertising was on the eighty-second floor, and the dragonfly rode the elevator up and down at least a dozen times without stopping a single time on the eighty-second floor.

Eve directed the dragonfly to investigate the air-conditioning vent, but the grid covering it was too small to squeeze through. When the elevator was unoccupied, she tried to ram the dragonfly into the button marked "82," but the automatic safety programming prevented it from hitting hard enough to succeed.

Upon reaching the first floor again, a new group of people entered the elevator and Hannah noticed one lady staring at the dragonfly. "I think the tall black woman spotted it."

The woman rolled a magazine into a tight cone, then Eve flew the dragonfly to the corner of the elevator. Just as the woman raised her magazine to swat it, Eve dove it directly toward her face. Since the dragonfly didn't convey audio, Hannah wondered how loud the woman screamed. Eve kept the dragonfly in the far corner until the lady exited on the forty-seventh floor.

"I could get in the elevator and press button 82," Hannah volunteered.

"And what would you do if Cain got on the elevator?" Eve asked.

"What are the odds of that?"

"Slim," Eve admitted. "But are you willing to gamble your life on those odds?"

"You mean he would kill me?" Hannah asked, astonished.

"I'm sure he would make it look like a suicide, especially after you would write your own note."

"It's almost lunchtime," Hannah said. "Perhaps you can follow someone when they return from lunch."

Eve shook her head. "The Willis Tower has one hundred and four elevators and only six go to the eighty-second floor. Pair-O-Dice Advertising has a limited client base and probably only a few employees. We only know what Carla Babb looks like if that was her on Cain's plane. She might not go out to lunch."

Hannah's stomach rumbled as she anticipated lunch.

"I think I'll order something from room service. What would you like?" Eve asked.

Hannah paused for a second to think. "Why don't we order pizza and send it to the Pair-O-Dice Advertising."

Eve picked up her phone, but it rang before she could dial. She pressed the speaker button, and Gertrude said, "I have good news! Mary Ruth was successful. I have access to DuBoise Security until Mr. DuBoise changes his password. You need to look for an office on the eighty-second floor of the Willis Tower. The name of the company is—"

"Pair-O-Dice Advertising," Eve finished her sentence.

"Then you probably also know Michael Gentile is actually Cain."

"Yes. What about Carla Babb?"

"Her file says she's been in America for four years. She's originally from Lithuania. Her office is in the Willis Tower, and her condominium is in the John Hancock building."

"What floor of the John Hancock?" Eve asked.

"The sixty-sixth floor. She purchased her custom-designed luxury condo for $1.8 million. Her apartment rates a higher security level than her office."

"What do you mean by 'a higher security level'?"

"Cain has minor security systems at hundreds of locations, including the Pair-O-Dice office, medium security at fifty-four locations, and high security at seventeen. Carla Babb's apartment is a high-security site. Her condo entrance is under constant observation from Paris, and there is antisurveillance equipment installed. Your dragonfly will die if you send it in there."

"Do you know if Cain is at either location?" Hannah asked.

"Cain left the advertising agency yesterday afternoon and hasn't returned. He hasn't visited Miss Babb's apartment in the past year."

"Any clues as to the whereabouts of Princess Sela?" Eve asked.

"Not yet. There are lots of data and video logs to sort through. Mary Ruth and Mabel just arrived from Paris. I'll have an easier time since I have Cain's password too."

"You do?"

"Until he changes it," Gertrude quantified.

"Can you track where he is?"

"There is no trace of him since yesterday afternoon. If he logs in to one of the places under observation, I'll know where he is. His plane is still in Chicago."

"We'll try to follow Carla Babb. Perhaps she knows where Cain or the princess is." Eve hung up the phone. "Go ahead and order some pizza while I maneuver my dragonfly to intercept the delivery."

Hannah turned on her laptop and located the nearest pizza delivery. "I'm going to send this courtesy of the Iowa Lottery Commission."

"Good idea. Be sure and order a veggie pizza. Cain is a vegetarian."

"You're kidding."

"He always has been."

Thirty minutes later, the dragonfly perched on top of a pizza delivery man's hat. It flew to the ceiling as soon as he entered Pair-O-Dice Advertising. While Eve flew the dragonfly down the hall, Hannah kept her computer open to a Web page from a real estate company trying to lease a floor a few levels down. The eighty-second floor contained nearly thirty thousand square feet of space, with four large wings extending from the elevators in the center. She kept track of where the bug flew by keeping an eye on Eve's progress.

The main workroom was open from the north windows to the south. Only the elevators and a few support poles blocked the view. Eight employees worked at their computers while four others drew an advertising campaign for the state of Georgia. Two large television cameras focused on an empty desk in front of a blue screen. A glass sound room stood open and unused on the other side of the elevators. Pictures of highway billboards and magazine ads lined the east and west walls, framing double doors in the center of each wall.

"This looks like a legitimate business with artists and agents," Hannah commented.

"This may be a dead end, but we have to check it out." Eve flew her bug past a conference room and a breakroom on the west side. The open door to the office at the end of the hall commanded a view of the west side of Chicago. Carla Babb sat behind a monstrous desk, talking on the phone. The dragonfly remained close to the ceiling and perched behind the desk on top of a framed collage of articles about presidential candidates.

Eve zoomed the camera in and watched Miss Babb type an order for the California Lottery Commission, then she panned the camera around the room. Two large leather sectional couches and a bar turned one side of the office into a comfortable sitting area. Life-size wood carvings of animals, including a pouncing puma along with bearskin rugs, competed with the head, making the room feel warm, rich, and professional. Eve directed the dragonfly back out the door.

It traveled back down the hall, and Hannah noticed several employees eating pizza. At the end of the hall, the bug came to a closed door with a nameplate that read "Michael Gentile, CEO." A gap at the bottom of the door allowed the dragonfly to slip underneath it.

The office was larger than Carla Babb's and featured an all-glass desk. Not even an ink pen or computer keyboard disrupted the view of Lake Michigan reflecting in the midday sun. Except for the desk and two low-back leather chairs, the office was completely empty. Eve stopped in front of the only picture hanging on the wall. The large oil painting depicted two teenage boys, arms around each other's shoulders, carrying homemade walking sticks and wearing small animal-skin loincloths. They looked happy, and after a moment, Hannah recognized them from the memory Eve had shared with her earlier. The eyes of every animal in the background focused on the two boys. Hannah picked out three deer, two duck-billed platypuses, and several apelike creatures in the trees.

"It has been a long time since I've seen Abel in anything but a memory."

"Did Cain paint that?" Hannah asked.

"I doubt it. He has difficulty focusing on one task for a prolonged period. But the picture is perfect, so it definitely came from his memory."

Eve flew the dragonfly though the only other door in the room and found a small apartment that, except for the magnificent view of the John Hancock building and Lake Michigan, reminded Hannah of a hotel room.

The dragonfly returned to the reception area, entered the elevator, rode back down with a departing employee, and then exited Willis Tower. "Hannah, find some information on the Web about the John Hancock building. I want to examine Miss Babb's condo while she's at work."

Hannah checked a few Web sites. "Her condo is on the east side. The building will block most of the wind, so you can probably fly the dragonfly up to the sixty-sixth floor."

The dragonfly hitched a ride on a city bus traveling to Michigan Avenue. Upon arriving at the Hancock, Eve guided the dragonfly up the east side. When it reached the sixty-sixth floor, the sun was descending on the west side of the building. Eve parked it on a window brace so they could see inside. Hannah saw a plush bedroom decorated with erotic art, a leather harness attached to the ceiling, and handcuffs around the bedposts. Several whips hung on the walls, and sex toys sat on a bookcase. Hannah blushed.

Eve's phone rang, and she hit the speaker button. "I discovered why Miss Babb's apartment is one of the seventeen Cain keeps under constant surveillance," Gertrude said. "Hundreds of clips show everyone who enters and exits her apartment. Seven clips are protected with Cain's password. They show her taking young teenage boys into her place and never coming out. I did a cross reference with the Chicago Police. The first boy has been missing for three years. The others are spaced out about every six months."

Hannah felt sick to her stomach.

"I still need to interrogate her. Give me until dawn, Chicago time, and then contact the Chicago Police anonymously. Send them copies of all seven videos."

"Yes, ma'am," Gertrude replied.

"Please scan the video logs of the other sixteen high-security sites, and see if you can find a clip of the princess."

"I'm already in the process of doing so. I'll call you if I find anything."

Eve hung up the phone and moved the dragonfly to the next window, allowing Hannah to view a large open room with a kitchen, dining room, and a lavishly appointed living room with thick Persian rugs. Paintings and photographs of naked men lined the walls, and several life-size statues of young couples in the act of copulation stood around the room.

"This isn't a place where they would take Princess Sela," Hannah said.

At the last window, flickering candlelight illuminated the room, where a black stone altar stood in the middle. An inverted cross hung above it, and a large black book lay open on the altar. On the black marble floor, the tile was inlaid with pearl-colored stones that formed a pentagram. In the center of the pentagram sat a large golden bowl containing what looked like blood.

Chapter Thirty-Two

Hannah shuddered. "Can Carla Babb summon demons?"

"I don't think so," Eve replied. "But I've learned to never say a thing is impossible."

A jolt of fear coursed through Hannah. "Do you think Cain is trying to bring demons into this world?"

"It would be out of character for him since he believes in free will. He would not wish to become subservient to a demon who is beneath God's power. Cain likes to manipulate events without sitting on the throne himself. I'm beginning to wonder if he's using Carla Babb as a front to protect himself."

"Who is the greater enemy, the person in power or the person behind the power?" Hannah asked.

"Right now, Carla Babb is our target. Once she leads us to the princess, we will turn her over to the police and her threat will be contained."

Eve maneuvered the dragonfly back to the ground. The screen flashed red, and the dragonfly headed toward the nearest tree.

"What happened?"

"The emergency programming took over," Eve said. "There must have been a bird in the way that I couldn't see."

With no leaves to hide the dragonfly, it attached itself to the underside of a thick branch. A large bird's head peered upside-down looking at the dragonfly. Hannah said a little prayer, hoping the bird would move on. She recognized it as a raven, which she knew to be very smart.

Eve spoke to her computer screen. "Please don't eat my bug."

The raven tilted its head to the left, then to the right, then flew out of view. A moment later, it swooped up from underneath the tree and snagged the dragonfly. The screen turned black.

Eve slammed her fist on the desk. "That stupid bird just ate a million-dollar bug! Now we have to do things the hard way."

"You mean this has been easy? What will we do now?"

Eve picked up her phone and spoke to Gertrude. "Check the security log. See when Carla Babb usually leaves work and when she arrives home."

Eve received her answer and hung up. "Miss Babb entered the Wacker Street entrance, so we can assume she'll leave the same way. She leaves work at six o'clock and arrives at home by 6:20. She departs most nights around seven and returns at various times of the night, usually accompanied by one or more men. Whoever comes with her never spends the night. My illusions can fool the mind but not the cameras. Her security team will warn her or send someone to stop us.

"We will go to the lobby of the Willis Tower," Eve continued. "I'll disguise myself as a blind woman with a cane. I'll run into her, tangle my cane in her feet, and say, 'Pardon my cane.' Hopefully, the word association will cause her surface thoughts to reveal where Cain is."

"Is there a second option?"

"It's Friday night, and she does not seem like the type to stay home and watch TV. We can try something simple and direct. When she leaves her condo, we can follow her, and you could distract her until I rip her mind open."

A feral smile crept across Hannah's face. "I like that one."

"You won't if she's carrying a gun. We'll try the blind woman routine first and see what happens."

Hannah changed into a conservative business suit and accompanied Eve to the elevator. Eve wore a simple pantsuit, and her cane was a thin white rod with the bottom colored bright red. Her irises were milky white and her pupils nonexistent.

As they headed toward the parking garage, Hannah stammered, "Do we have to drive?"

"You'll be driving. I appear to be blind."

Hannah felt relieved. She drove through the heavy evening traffic and parked the pink Prowler in the Willis Tower garage. The two women entered the lobby and sat in the lounge. The lobby was bigger than she'd seen through the camera of the dragonfly. A large mobile filled the high ceiling of the foyer containing various shapes, colors, and movements. The modernistic lobby used transparent walls and escalators to pierce the vertical space.

While Eve tapped her cane in close proximity to the elevators, Hannah pretended to study the mobile. Pedestrian traffic was heavy for an hour but thinned out as the hands on the clock approached opposite positions.

At 6:04, Carla Babb strode out of the elevator. She didn't look to the left or the right, so she didn't see Hannah behind the modern art sculpture in the foyer nor did she notice the short blind woman tapping toward her.

Eve approached Miss Babb but didn't drop her cane, stumble, or even touch the woman as she strode past. Carla Babb exited through the lobby doors and got in the line for a taxi.

Something must have gone seriously wrong, Hannah thought as she approached Eve. When she got within speaking distance, she whispered, "What happened?"

Eve allowed her milky eyes to return to their normal rich brown, but they looked troubled. "Cain must have told her about telepaths and warned her she might be scanned. There is a metal band in her hat."

Chapter Thirty-Three

"Why would she wear metal in her hat? Do you think Cain knows we're here?" Hannah asked.

"It doesn't matter. We must proceed to the second plan," Eve said. "Miss Babb is heading home right now. When she exits her building, you must find a way to distract her and remove her hat."

"How will I do that?"

"I don't know, but you have about thirty minutes to think of something."

Eve drove to the Hancock while Hannah wracked her brain to come up with a plausible excuse to make Carla Babb remove her hat. She didn't need the extra pressure as Eve ran a red light. After failing to think of a good plan, she asked, "Do you have any suggestions?"

"None immediately come to mind. Mabel would bump into Miss Babb rather forcefully, and Mary Ruth would drop something in front of her and ask for assistance."

"I'm not strong enough to bowl her over or old enough to need assistance."

Eve parked the Prowler in a no-parking zone a half block away from the residential entrance of the Hancock. She and Hannah stepped into an alcove of a store for rent. City lights cast shadows on the street. Hannah wondered if Miss Babb would turn left to walk to one of the restaurants or clubs nearby or right and take a taxi somewhere else. Either way, they could follow her and wait for an opportunity to distract her.

The cool night breeze chilled Hannah, so she hugged her elbow to wrap her jacket tighter. As her teeth began to chatter, she spotted a tall blonde in a pink hat walking through the lobby doors—Carla Babb.

Hannah assumed Carla Babb's hat also contained metal or Eve would have let her know a distraction was not necessary. Tall black boots with bright pink heels also covered Miss Babb's feet. Her pink shirt matched her hat, and she obviously wore no bra. Her miniskirt made Hannah wonder how she could endure the cold.

Miss Babb turned left and headed straight toward Hannah. As she came closer, the Prowler caught her attention. She slowed down, moved closer to the edge of the sidewalk, stopped to admire the vehicle, and bent over to peer into a side window.

"Give me the car keys. I have an idea," Hannah whispered to Eve.

Eve handed her the keys, and Hannah strode toward the Prowler "She's for sale!"

Carla Babb looked up as Hannah approached. "Really? I didn't see a for sale sign." Her voice sounded rich and deep.

"A friend of mine works at Westshore Classic Cars," Hannah said. "You might have seen their advertisements. He let me borrow it for the weekend. He'd be very happy if I brought him a customer."

"I'm familiar with the place since I sold them this car a month ago," Carla said.

Hannah stood close and said, "Really? Well, you match."

"I beg your pardon?"

"Your hat and the Prowler are the exact same color."

Miss Babb stepped closer to the Prowler and held her arm against the side. "Why, so we do."

"I'm glad I ran into you. I think you left something in the glove compartment." Hannah pressed the auto-unlock on the key fob and the interior lights came on. Hannah pointed to the bright multicolored condoms still on the floorboard.

Carla Babb placed one hand on the doorframe and the other on the roof. As she bent down to look inside the Prowler, Hannah tipped off her hat.

The next instant, Hannah felt like her brain was on fire. It seemed like two hot branding irons had been thrust into her eye socket. She fell to her knees and grabbed her temples. She could not move or even breathe. Carla Babb opened her hand, revealing an ornate gold knife.

Chapter Thirty-Four

Hannah screamed and shouted with her mind, *"She's a TELEPATH!"* She watched the knife jab toward her heart. It pierced her blouse, but as it began to cut into her chest, Carla dropped the knife and put her hands to her ears. She looked anguished. Then Eve approached from the shadows, and Carla bolted across the street. Hannah was still too stunned to move, but she watched Carla half-run and stumble.

Eve knelt and touched Hannah's forehead. "I'm sorry. I never expected her to be a telepath, much less a coercer. I acted as quickly as I could." Eve closed her eyes, and the fire in Hannah's head receded to a dull ache.

Hannah struggled to her feet and asked, "What do we do now?"

"The pain you felt was a coercive attack. The game changes when two coercers collide. I will have to use brute force."

Hannah clenched her fist around the pink hat she still clutched. She stuffed it on her head. "I'm ready."

The two women took off up the street at a steady jog. Miss Babb was already two blocks ahead but traveling at a slower pace. "Were you able to get anything from her mind?" Hannah asked.

"I didn't have enough time to crack her mental shield."

"Thank you for saving my life."

"My pleasure. I also prevented the taxi drivers and the doorman from noticing anything."

Eve touched Hannah's arm as they moved up the next street. "You need to let go of your anger. Emotions are gifts from God, but you must recognize them as gifts in order to use them. Fear enhances your thinking processes. Anger diminishes them. Right now, we both need to think clearly so we can respond and not react."

Hannah felt chagrined and took several deep breaths.

Miss Babb headed toward a line of thirty or so people in front of a brightly lit dance club. She swept past them and walked right toward the bouncer wearing a Viking helmet at the door. He gave her a slight nod, and she entered the club.

Hannah slowed to a walk as they approached the end of the line. Eve noticed and glanced over her shoulder. "Is there a problem?" Eve asked. Hannah shook her head "no," then asked, "Do you know what kind of place this is?"

Eve looked at the large neon sign glowing bright blue above the door. It read "Rave of Chicago."

The people in line were all young, the oldest no more than thirty. The guys wore baggy jeans or long basketball shorts and T-shirts. The girls wore shorts or short skirts and spaghetti-strap tops or thin blouses. Everyone wore some type of athletic shoes. Loud colors were popular. A lot of people had piercings and tattoos. Many wore glow-in-the-dark necklaces. Almost all were holding glow sticks.

"It's a dance club," Eve said.

"No, it's a rave," Hannah replied.

"What's a rave?"

"A massive party that lasts all night. They've been banned in most cities."

"Why?"

"The theory behind a rave is to create mystical and spiritual awakening by celebrating peace, love, unity, and respect through sensory stimulation and dance. Egos and personal prejudices are supposed to be left behind to create what they call 'the Vibe.'"

"What's wrong with that?" Eve asked.

"They dance nonstop for hours to loud techno music and various lighting effects to create a sensory overload, which leads to some sort of spiritual nirvana. Many use drugs like Ecstasy or LSD to stimulate the senses. As inhibitions are lowered, the party often turns into a sexual free-for-all."

Eve smiled. "I walked Earth for twenty-five hundred years before God gave us the Ten Commandments. Hedonism was the rule of the day. This won't be my first time I've walked into a den of iniquity. We must hurry, or we will lose our target."

She took three steps past Hannah but stopped when she realized Hannah was not following. "I failed to realize that you've never been in a den of iniquity. It will be okay. Just stay close to me and try not to overreact if someone grabs your butt."

Eve took Hannah by the arm and led her past the crowd. Several of the young people smiled in welcome. As they reached the front of the line, a young girl called out, "Nice hat."

Hannah turned red and stammered, "Thank you."

As they walked toward the bouncer, Eve stopped and whispered, "There's metal in that Viking helmet."

"Then how do we get past him?"

Eve looked around the crowd and focused on a tall teenager nearby.

"Plur!" he shouted at Eve.

"Plur?" Eve asked.

He smiled and said, "Peace, love, unity, and respect. It's the raver's creed, lovely lady."

"Plur to you too."

"You're a raver baby, aren't you?"

"What's a raver baby?"

"They're both babies," the girl beside him said, and several people laughed. She approached and hugged Eve. "A raver baby is someone who's visiting for the first time. I think you'll find the experience enlightening. People are celebrated for who they are."

"Did you bring a glow stick?" the tall teenager asked.

"No. I didn't realize I needed one."

He pulled two glow sticks out of his pocket and handed one to Hannah and Eve. "You can buy more inside, but they cost three times as much. Be sure to drink lots of water."

"Thanks for the advice," Hannah replied.

"You're in for an adventure tonight. You'll have a visually astounding experience before the night is over."

"Great," Hannah drawled. "The last visual experience I had almost got me killed."

"Cool," several in the group said in unison.

"Do you come here often?" Eve asked the tall man.

"Every weekend."

"We're just visiting and were supposed to meet someone inside. Do you think you could help us get in?"

He smiled and called to the bouncer. "Hey, Thor, we got two raver babies tonight. Why don't you let them go in ahead of us?"

The big Viking crossed his arms. "We are at capacity, Chris. You know the rules."

"Ah, man, those are white man's rules."

"Aren't you a white man?"

"I wasn't in my previous life!" Chris responded with a laugh.

Several people said, "Cool."

Chris started a chant, and the whole crowd joined in: "Open the door, Thor! Let them in, Sven! Open the door, Thor! Let them in, Sven!"

After several rounds of chanting, the bouncer shook his head and rolled his eyes. "Perhaps I miscounted the customers." He motioned for Eve and Hannah to approach then used a handheld metal detector to scan them. He made Hannah remove her hat and examined it. "We don't allow violence in the club. The fire doors are alarmed, so be sure to exit through the front." Eve paid the entrance fee, and Thor opened the door.

Chris led the crowd in a cheer.

Eve and Hannah made their way down a ramp and entered the main building. The dance floor reminded Hannah of an oversized skating rink. A low balcony encircled the oval floor, with lots of tables and chairs around the perimeter. Young people drank from water bottles and partook of drinks served by skimpily clad waiters and waitresses. Hannah could smell an abundance of alcohol. One side of the building was a separate glassed-in room with big blue neon lights. Over the entrance hung a sign that read "Cool Room." The moisture condensing on the windows made it look cold. The opposite side of the building held the restrooms, displayed in bright red and green neon.

The club was a visual assault on the optic nerves. Multicolored neon tubing ran up and down the walls and on the ceiling. Bright colored lights lit each acrylic tabletop from underneath. More lights pulsed with the beat of the music under the dance floor while laser beams crisscrossed from above. Bright green lasers focused on four disco mirror balls, creating an effect of falling laser rain. A twenty-by-forty-foot projection screen filled one wall with computer graphics pulsing in time with the music. Every surface not blazing with bright colored light was flat black.

Eve and Hannah stopped at the edge of the balcony and looked over a sea of hundreds of undulating people. Many were jumping up and down with no apparent partner. Most of the dancers weaved patterns in the air with a glow stick, and several dancers' eyes looked glazed.

Hannah scanned the crowd for a tall blonde wearing a neon pink jacket. She saw several, but none was Carla Babb.

Three disc jockeys sat on a raised platform in the center of the dance floor. They kept a bass rhythm with a loud and fast drum machine. The computer-driven techno music varied as the disc jockeys modulated the music and lights.

Hannah, standing beside Eve, who was searching the crowd, sensed a presence behind her. She turned her head and saw a man, older than most of the crowd, standing very close. In a deep, scratchy voice, he said, "Good evening, ladies. Where have you been all my life?"

"For the first half of your life, I wasn't even born!" Hannah replied. She felt his hand squeeze her butt.

Hannah spotted a look on Eve's face that told her she had received the same treatment. The man screamed and looked at his left hand. He turned and fled toward the front entrance.

"I thought you said not to overreact if someone grabbed my butt," Hannah said to Eve.

"I didn't overreact. He only thinks I withered his hand. A little therapy will do him some good."

Hannah returned her attention to the crowd. "We will never find her in here. There are too many people, and they won't stay still."

"Then we will have to make them stay still."

"Can you do that?"

"There are too many to control but not too many to influence. Just watch and be ready."

Eve closed her eyes in concentration. A moment later, she opened them and shouted, "Gun!"

The music, lights, and computer effects screeched to a halt. Every person in the building dropped to the floor. Several people whose faces and scalps were covered with metal piercings stayed standing. Across the room, a tall blonde wearing neon pink stood defiantly.

Hannah cringed as Eve's eyes locked on Carla Babb, who stood looking like the ancient mountains that had weathered the onslaught of many storms without cracking or crumbling.

Carla Babb lowered the cell phone from her ear, and without losing eye contact with Eve, placed it inside her jacket. Her face conveyed thunder rolling deeply through the clouds.

Eve stepped down to the dance floor and walked around the bodies lying prone on the floor. Hannah followed Eve, anticipating the thrill of watching her ground Carla's lightning.

Halfway across the floor, Hannah sensed a lessening of the tension. People chuckled as if they had participated in a big joke. The dancers regained their feet.

A chill traveled down Hannah's spine as dancers closest to Miss Babb stood in unison. Their expressions turned from fear to anger and then hatred. Fingers curled into fists, and several turned their bodies sideways in classic martial arts attack posture. Many brandished their glow sticks as if they were daggers. They might not be trained warriors, but to dance all night, they had to be in excellent physical condition.

Eve stopped beside the disc jockey's station. Without saying anything, she raised her right hand and snapped her fingers. A second later, she snapped them again three more times. Several of the young people surrounding her stood and snapped their fingers in the same rhythm.

She glanced at the DJ, who chose a song that followed the same beat as the young people's snapping fingers. A second DJ modulated the tune with his equipment. The drum machine kicked in, and the tempo increased. The third DJ added visual effects.

Everyone on Eve's side started to dance. They began making wild, highly energetic gyrations, jumping up and down and flowing back and forth.

Eve continued to snap her fingers to the beat as she strolled forward. Several people bumped and jostled Hannah as she followed Eve through the community of energetic dancers. The dancing hoard drifted away from the angry mob until a ten-foot-wide empty circle formed around Carla Babb. Eve faced the angry mob of people, several of whom growled. Drops of laser rain made their angry faces look like the visages of zombies from a bad sci-fi movie. The glowing light sticks made the surreal scene even more bizarre. No one stepped into the empty zone, but Hannah believed any one of them would kill Eve before allowing her to encroach into Carla's territory. Carla gloated with victory behind the crowd that formed a human barrier.

Eve stepped into the isolation zone. With her eyes half-closed, she raised her arms in the air and swayed them back and forth. Her fingers continued to snap as she flowed with the music, as if her arms were made of liquid sensuality. When the music modulated to a more intense key, she moved her torso to the same pulse. Then she said, "Plur."

The crowd behind her repeated, "Plur."

Eve and the crowd said the word again, and the green rain of light began to change. From Eve's fingertips, the light flowed in waves around the crowd of angry young people and the tension faded from their faces. One of the young ladies close to Miss Babb said, "Plur." A minute later, all but four large men around Miss Babb started to dance and say the same.

The four protectors surrounded Miss Babb, and she pulled out her cell phone. While speaking into it, she backed up through the tables and chairs to reach the back wall. Eve closed the distance, and the people sitting at the tables nearby stood abruptly and left. Carla placed her back against the wall and stared at Eve.

Eve stopped ten feet in front of the four large men and said, "These are not the droids you are looking for."

The four men replied, "These are not the droids we are looking for."

"You can go on about your business."

"We can go on about our business."

"Move along."

The four men walked away.

Eve looked at Carla with cold eyes. "I've always wanted to say that. You should realize by now that you are far outclassed. Did you want to try something else, or are you ready to talk?"

Miss Babb growled like a crazed lion. "You can't harm me. I'm stronger than you think."

"Really?" Eve said as she stepped forward. "You seem like a frightened little girl who just realized she's not the biggest bully on the playground anymore."

"Who are you?"

"My name is Mother Evelyn, and this is Sister Hannah."

"Keep praying nun, for you will soon die." Carla glanced toward the main club entrance then turned her attention back to Eve. "You will get nothing out of me."

"Oh, I beg to differ," Eve replied. "Where has Cain taken Princess Sela?"

Carla laughed. "Wouldn't you rather know where they buried Jimmy Hoffa? I can tell you that without having to die."

"I have no intention of killing you, but if you don't cooperate, I will cause you considerable pain."

"It's not you I'm afraid of," Carla replied. "If I tell you where the Sacred Mother is, my father will kill me."

"Your *father*?" Hannah interjected.

Carla smiled. "Cain will not be pleased when he finds out you've assaulted me."

"Cain has many sons and daughters, and I doubt he really cares about any of them. You will end up a vegetable in the mental ward if I have to force my way in. Tell me what I need to know."

"Your threats don't scare me!" Carla screamed. "I know how to defend my mind. My future has been prophesied."

Eve raised an eyebrow. "You certainly inherited Cain's ego."

Carla stole another glance at the main entrance.

"She's stalling. She's expecting a rescue," Hannah whispered.

Carla looked at Hannah. "Your death is getting closer."

"I am far more powerful than you can imagine—even more powerful than Cain. I can peel your mind like a grape, and when I am done, the pulp will be ground into a very bitter wine. Now, tell me what I need to know."

Carla's face twisted in pain as Eve's coercion gripped her mind. Carla slammed the flats of her palms against the wall. She kicked out high, her bright pink stiletto heel heading directly toward Eve's face.

Eve moved a half second too slow, and the stiletto grazed her temple, leaving a bloody cut.

Hannah balled her right hand into a fist, just as Mabel had taught her, and punched Carla in the face. Hannah felt her nose snap as her head rocked backward into the wall.

Unable to breathe, Carla slumped to the floor.

Hannah heard several people scream from across the room. The music and dancing again screeched to a halt. She turned and saw six large men wearing black pants, black sweaters, and ski masks walking toward her, carrying automatic Uzis. Two of the men raised their guns, shot into the ceiling, and pandemonium broke loose.

Chapter Thirty-Five

Hannah crouched down to avoid stray bullets. She looked for the nearest fire door and saw the panicked throng swamping each exit. Eve had her hands full with the collapsing Carla Babb. Hannah's feet wanted to escape with the mob, but her soul refused to leave her Mother Superior.

Eve grasped Hannah's ankle. "Stay down, and be perfectly still. Pretend you're a chair."

Hannah squatted and watched Eve grasp the stunned Carla Babb. Her fingers encircled the left side of Carla's slender neck as Carla's eyes glazed over.

Hannah watched the pandemonium as the clubgoers and workers fled through the fire escape doors. The men in black scanned the fleeing crowd. Hannah saw a replica of herself and Eve fleeing through the farthest door. A few seconds later, Carla seemed to appear in the crowd and motion the men in black to follow her through a different door. The six men followed the illusionary Carla Babb outside. As soon as the dance hall emptied, Eve relaxed her grip on Carla's neck and gently slapped her face. "Wake up, Miss Babb. I need you conscious to scan you properly."

Carla's eyes rolled several times. She struggled to take a deep breath, coughed once, and regained consciousness.

Eve turned to Hannah. "That was a nice punch. I think you broke her nose."

Hannah had never hit anyone in anger before except her brother. "Thank you, I think."

Eve placed her left hand against the wall and her right hand upon Miss Babb's forehead. "Now, let's see what's inside this sick mind." She let out a moan of disgust. "You're a despicable character. Your mind is repulsive."

"It's in the genes," Carla replied groggily.

"No, something is missing in your jeans. Your mother will be disappointed. You're also much older than you appear. You've been taking Cain's manna."

"That's a secret." Carla giggled. "And you're much older than I, old woman."

"Much older and much wiser. You have several locked doors in your mind. Would you like to show me which door is hiding Princess Sela, or shall I open them at random?"

Eve closed her eyes for a moment. Opening them in sudden horror, she spit on the floor. Breathing heavily, Eve looked at Hannah. "She has tortured and murdered thirteen children."

"They were virginal sacrifices," Carla proclaimed.

"Your mind is more polluted than Hitler's."

"Hitler didn't have enough vision to carry out the master plan. I do!"

Eve closed her eyes again. "Stop resisting me!"

Carla grimaced and flailed her arms. "Hold her arms," Eve commanded.

Hannah moved closer and grabbed Carla's hands and then held them against the wall.

Carla slit her eyes. "Wouldn't you rather know about Al Capone? He had no secret vault. My father stole all his money to establish a new economic base when he and I came to America. Father visited Al Capone while he was losing his mind from syphilis in 1947. Father helped him remember. Too bad about the little stroke he suffered after his memory returned. After that—"

"Stop evading me," Eve interrupted. "Your little mind games won't prevent me from finding what I want to know."

"Did Cain really steel Al Capone's money?" Hannah asked.

"Yes, but it's not important. She's trying to misdirect me."

Carla clamped her jaw closed and struggled to free her hands. Hannah felt thankful for all the workouts she had with Mabel to build her strength.

Eve's voice turned cold. "If I have to rip open every door, your mind will be gone. I won't kill you, but the rest of your life will be empty. Now, show me the door!"

Carla cried out in pain, and tears fell from her eyes.

Eve looked at Hannah. "Her defenses are strong, and I don't have time to open every door. When I mention sex, a thousand doors move forward, but when I mention Princess Sela, I see nothing but a long, empty hallway."

Hannah thought for a moment. "She didn't call the princess by her name. She called her the Sacred Mother."

Eve leaned closer, using her hand against the wall to leverage more strength against Carla. She closed her eyes. "Ah, there you are. I have the door open."

"I know where the princess is," Eve told Hannah. "Now I'm going to try to find out where Cain is. Carla, where is Cain?"

Eve's sudden scream sent a shock through Hannah. Eve released Carla's forehead and reached for her left hand pressed against the wall. The hilt of a long dagger protruded from the back of Eve's hand, pinning it to the wall. Blood gushed from the wound and flowed down Eve's arm. Hannah released Carla, turned around, and froze. The rich brown eyes returned her stare with mirth.

"Hello, Mother. I understand you're looking for me."

Chapter Thirty-Six

Hannah gazed into Cain's eyes. Eve's scream halted abruptly, and she froze in place. Carla growled like a bear waking from a deep slumber and regained her feet, then she cocked her fist, preparing to slam Eve in the jaw. Cain prevented the attack with a few simple words. "Let's show a little respect. This is my mother and therefore your grandmother."

Cain nodded at Hannah. "You can hit *her* if you like."

Carla pivoted on one foot. Her fist caught Hannah on the corner of her jaw.

Pain stunned Hannah as she stumbled into the table behind her. She shook her head and tasted blood, then she ran her tongue along her teeth to insure they were all still there. None felt loose or missing.

Carla turned her attention to Cain. "What took you so long?"

Cain handed Carla a napkin off a table for her bloody nose but ignored her question and spoke to Eve. "This is twice in one week I've caught you by surprise."

"Congratulations," Eve said through gritted teeth.

"I must give you points for your mosquitoes! I didn't know anyone had perfected them yet. Where did you find them?"

"Japan. But they're not perfected yet."

"Miniaturization does have its drawbacks." Cain chuckled. "Expensive?"

"Extremely, and birds like them."

Cain laughed. "I will try to remember that if I ever buy any."

The casualness of the conversation struck Hannah as odd. Carla also looked puzzled, standing with her hands on her hips, tapping her foot.

"Would you mind removing your dagger now?" Eve asked.

"Not just yet." Cain reached inside his coat and pulled out the large handgun Hannah had glimpsed in Mexico. Using the long barrel, he flicked the hilt of the dagger, causing it to quiver in the wall and through Eve's bloody hand. Eve sucked in her breath but didn't scream.

Cain turned his attention to Carla. "What did she learn from you?"

Carla paled slightly. "Why don't you just kill them? We can discuss this later."

Cain's voice turned cold. "What did she learn from you?" he asked again.

Carla stammered. Cain raised his gun and pointed it at her face. "I have had millions of children and billions of grandchildren. You mean nothing to me. I tolerate the risks you cause only because of your gift."

Carla straightened and tilted her head. "She knows about Al Capone."

"Old news."

"She knows my real identity," Carla confessed.

Cain barked a laugh and glanced at Eve. "I would love to see Mary Ruth's expression when you tell her. What else?"

"She knows about the sacrifices," Carla admitted.

"How unfortunate." Cain sighed. "Your current identity has been compromised. You will pack up your essentials and get on your plane by dawn."

"But I love Chicago," Carla cried. "If you kill them now, no one else will know."

Cain lowered his gun. "You do not understand how Mother and her annoying nuns operate. She didn't run into you by chance. When she lost my trail, she followed yours. They knew about your indiscretions long before they approached you."

Cain then asked Eve, "How much time does she have?"

"At dawn, the Chicago Police will receive an anonymous tip accompanied by video footage of Miss Babb escorting seven young teens into her apartment over a period of three years. All seven are currently missing and presumed dead."

"You will be on your plane by midnight," Cain commanded. "I warned you, your little hobby would end up badly. What are you up to now, ten?"

When Carla didn't immediately reply, Hannah filled in the gap. "Thirteen! She has killed thirteen innocent children! Why would she do such an awful thing?"

Cain looked at Hannah. "She thinks she's communing with Satan. She wants to be the Antichrist's harlot."

"But—," Hannah began.

"Stop talking," Cain ordered. He got on his cell phone. "James, this is taking longer than I thought. You need to distract the police. Blow something up."

Cain paused as the other person replied, "I'll ask."

He looked at Carla. "I thought you sold your pink car."

Carla removed the handkerchief from her nose and smiled. Hannah noticed blood covering her teeth. "Your mother bought it."

"Oh, this just gets better and better," Cain said with exuberance and returned his attention to the phone. "Yes, James. That will do nicely. Blow it up."

As Cain hung up, he chuckled then snapped his fingers. He raised the gun and pointed it at Hannah's left eye. "Don't be so hard on her. Sometimes I kill just for the fun of it. You've interrupted my evening, and that makes me want to kill someone." Cain's dark brown eyes lined up with the sights on the barrel.

"Please don't," Eve pleaded.

"What's that, Mother?" Cain mocked. "Someone is going to die tonight, and the only other choice is you. Why don't you give me a good reason why this one shouldn't die?"

"Because she's gifted," Eve replied.

"Really?" Cain looked at Hannah and frowned. "Remove your hat."

Hannah crossed her arms in refusal. She didn't want Cain digging into her mind.

The gun coughed.

Hannah went deaf in her left ear as the bullet whizzed by. She touched her ear and, though swollen, hot, and wet, felt grateful it was still there.

"Remove your hat!"

Hannah did as instructed and tossed it on the floor.

Cain stared at her. She felt him touch her mind and flinched.

"Why, so she is. Remarkably gifted but surrounded by thick walls of mundaneness. Have you tried shocking her awake?"

"Several times," Eve replied as if she were a doctor discussing a patient. "But there was not even a glimmer of awareness."

"What about fear?" Cain asked with clinical curiosity. "I've found that absolute terror can sometimes be effective. Fear awakened Lady Aleska, or the one you call Sister Mary Ruth." Cain pointed at Carla. "I threw that one off an airplane. My skydiver almost didn't catch him in time."

"I tried. Fear is not her key."

Hannah stood in stunned disbelief. Her mind spun as recent events changed perspective, starting with why she had been included in Eve's inner circle and brought on this quest, and concluding with the terror she had gone through on Eve's little joyride.

"Now that she knows the potential is there, it will be more difficult to awaken," Cain said.

"I know."

"Very well, she may live. After all, if the princess proves to be genetically incompatible, I'll be looking for a new bride."

"You can't be serious," Carla mumbled.

"It would be rather entertaining for a corrupted nun to spawn your Antichrist," Cain mused.

"I would rather die," Hannah managed to stammer.

"I think I will take Miss Hannah with me. I've been experimenting with a new drug that might allow her talent to awaken." Cain continued to stare at Hannah. Her head throbbed with pain. "I can hear you singing a song in your head. What are you trying to hide?"

Cain's eyes widened in surprise. Every muscle in his face hardened with fury. He released his control over Hannah and turned to Eve.

"They live!" he hissed. Cain pressed his body against Eve's back and shoved her into the wall. She cried out as the dagger in her hand held her in place. Breathing on the back of her neck, Cain asked with a quiet yet terrifying voice, "Your children still live. Where are they?"

Eve managed a weak laugh. "You should kill me now, for you know you can never break me. With my death, you will never find them."

"Let me guess. You and Enoch stole Anak's ship. You gathered the rest of your children and hid somewhere. Where are they? Antarctica? Under the sea? Or did you build your own spaceships and go to another planet?

"You know I will never reveal their location. Anak tortured me for twenty-three years and achieved nothing. You can do no better."

"I am the father of the human race. Not Adam, not Seth, nor any other of my brothers. I shall hunt them down and kill them all." Cain snapped his right hand out, hitting the hilt of the dagger still embedded in the wall and Eve's hand.

Eve let out a shuddering scream as her pain intensified with the vibration.

"Grant me the peace of death and allow me to join my husband in heaven," she replied with mock kindness. Cain reached out his right hand and with the butt of his gun hammered the dagger deeper into the wall.

As Eve inhaled a breath of shock, he released her and took a step back. He raised his gun and placed the barrel to the back of her head. Hannah wondered if he had completely lost control, and at that moment, he lowered the gun and trembled. He raised the gun back up to Eve's skull and still hesitated. With a primal scream, he lowered the gun again.

"Just kill her," Carla interjected. "If you can't, then give me the gun and I will."

Cain closed his eyes. Without opening them, he asked Eve a question with a deadly quiet voice. "Why are you here?"

"What do you mean?" Eve asked.

"Why are you not with your children?"

Eve took a moment to respond. "Three reasons. First, they are my grandchildren. I want to be here to help them learn, grow, and survive. I had hoped that one day their genetics would improve enough to develop the higher mind powers.

"Second, I clean up your messes, son. I influenced the leaders of the world to end World War I, which you started. Had I not ended Hitler's atomic program, he would have destroyed everything you've worked for. I stopped the black plague when you could not."

Cain released Eve and backed away. "And the third reason?"

"I know that someday, someone will kill you." Eve turned away from the wall. With her pinned arm bent behind her, she faced Cain directly. "I am here to witness your death. When you are burned and your ashes tossed to the four winds, my children will return to this world."

Cain raised his gun again and placed it directly against her forehead. Eve didn't change her cold stare into Cain's eyes. "And when I kill you, what happens then?"

"Tomorrow, a hundred years, or a thousand years will pass. Someone will be watching. You won't know who they are or where they're watching from." Eve gave a tight smile. "They won't kill you, for God's curse still stands. But they will rejoice when your own children accomplish the task."

An outside explosion interrupted Cain. He smiled. "That's my distraction. I just blew up your car. You shouldn't have parked in a no-parking zone."

"I really liked that car," Eve replied.

A second explosion followed, which sounded much louder. The floor shook hard enough for Hannah to look at the dust falling from the ceiling. Sirens whaled in the distance.

"My cane was in that car. If you're going to kill me, you should hurry." Eve maintained her stare. "The SWAT team will be on their way, and they tend to shoot people with guns. You are still vulnerable to bullets, I assume."

Cain quirked an awkward smile and tucked the gun back into his jacket. "Next time, Mother, I will not hesitate." He licked the tip of his finger, pointed it like a gun, and touched her brow.

"Don't forget your dagger," Eve said.

"Thank you for reminding me." Cain retrieved a napkin from a table, dipped it into a glass of alcohol, and wiped the handle of the blade. Then he pulled out his gun and, using the hilt, hammered the knife deeper into the wall. "That should slow you down."

The front door of the club crashed in. "This is the Chicago Police! Raise your hands and make no sudden moves."

Hannah wanted to scream for help as the four police officers in full body armor burst in with guns raised. Cain trapped the words in her throat as he coerced her mind.

Carla, Hannah, and Cain raised their hands slowly. Eve raised the hand not pinned to the wall.

Cain turned around. "Begging your pardon, officer. My name is Dr. Millard Fillmore, from Cook County Hospital."

The officer relaxed and took several steps closer to Cain, although he kept his gun pointed at the group. "Do you have identification?"

"Not with me, but you probably recognize me. My name and face have been in the newspapers. I received the Chicago Humanitarian Award just last week. I've been attending the young lady with a broken nose. The other one's hand is attached to the wall with a dagger. She needs an ambulance, and you'll need a pair of plyers to remove the dagger."

Another officer lowered his gun, pulled out a radio, and called an ambulance.

"Yes, I recognize you," the first officer replied. "Do you know what happened here?"

"I had just arrived when four men burst through the door and screamed, 'Free Ireland!' They carried automatic weapons and shot a few rounds into the ceiling. Everyone panicked and evacuated the club. I stopped when I saw this helpless young lady attached to the wall. From her accent, she's obviously from England, so she must be involved in this attack. The one with the broken nose was unconscious."

Cain pointed to Hannah. "I'm not sure what happened here, but judging from the blood on this girl's hand, she must be responsible for the broken nose. Apparently, she's on drugs. She kept screaming about her pink hat, which obviously belongs to the woman dressed in pink. Now, she appears to be mute."

Hannah tried to open her mouth to deny being on drugs, but no sound came out. She glared at Cain.

"Excuse me," Eve interjected with a heavy English accent. "Would someone please remove this dagger from my hand?"

Hannah hadn't expected Eve to play along with Cain's game. She understood when Cain spoke to her mind. *"Would you rather I kill these fine officers?"*

"Wouldn't that bring the SWAT team in with guns blazing?" Hannah shouted back.

"My, my. I haven't met a nun willing to sacrifice the innocent since the Inquisition. You would make a great mother for the Antichrist."

Hannah stopped trying to scream. *"I submit to your kindness."* She felt her vocal cords relax.

Two more officers came forward to help Eve, and Cain spoke to the first officer. "If you don't mind, I would like to escort the young lady with the broken nose to the hospital. I don't think she needs an ambulance. You can interview her there."

The officer nodded his consent.

Eve screamed as one of the officers used a pair of pliers to remove the dagger from the wall and Eve's hand.

Hannah thought she heard Cain chuckle.

Chapter Thirty-Seven

Hannah sat in the hospital waiting room watching the news coverage of the explosion in downtown Chicago. She was thankful no deaths had resulted from the blast. The reporter stated that the streets were relatively empty due to a terrorist intrusion into a local dance club moments before the explosion. Security camera video footage captured the explosion, which sent the Prowler into the air. A second larger explosion occurred before the vehicle reached the ground. According to the reporter, an unconfirmed source claimed the Irish Republican Army was responsible for the incident.

The waiting room was full of sick and injured people, and it reminded Hannah of the waiting room she had sat in with her brother for his many mishaps. Just like the Tulsa hospital, the emergency room looked overcrowded and woefully understaffed.

She glanced at Eve, who sat beside her in meditative concentration. The ambulance paramedic had bandaged her hand in a large gauze cocoon on the way in.

Hannah looked back to the television. Fire trucks sprayed water on the damaged buildings. In the waiting room, several young people from the dance club sat in mute shock nearby, most with minor cuts and abrasions. Those with more serious injuries were already in treatment rooms. Hannah hoped Eve would be next to see the doctor.

Someone turned up the volume on the television when a reporter came on with breaking news of additional video. Hannah watched a black-and-white video feed captured from a John Hancock building security camera. According to the reporter, the new footage had been taken less than an hour before the explosion. The grainy image made it difficult to see the faces of the three women involved, but Hannah knew that other people in the waiting room might make a connection since she was wearing the same outfit as one of the women.

She watched herself in the video walk up to Carla Babb as she stopped to look at the car. They talked briefly, and eventually the camera showed Hannah tipping the hat off Carla's head. Hannah saw herself raise her hands to her temples and fall to her knees. Then Carla withdrew a knife and jabbed it at Hannah. Then Carla dropped the knife and grabbed her own ears as Eve approached from the darkness, and Carla ran away. A moment later, Eve and Hannah followed.

In the waiting room, Hannah touched Eve's arm and said, "I think we're in trouble."

"I know. I'm trying to find a path that will cause the least damage," Eve whispered.

Hannah placed her hand over her mouth to ensure no one else could hear her. "I thought you could only see clearly two minutes into the future."

"Clearly, yes. Then there are many paths I can follow for a little bit. In less than a minute, a police officer will make a decision. From that point, there are a half-dozen paths based on our interaction with him. During the next twenty minutes, we will flow through ten major decision points, the most drastic one based on whether a drunk driver three blocks from here turns left or right. Each decision point creates more paths. I have looked down several hundred paths and can't find an easy one."

Hannah looked to the emergency room exit, where a police officer talked on his cell phone. The television drew her attention when the reporter stated that two individuals involved in the bombing were about to be taken into custody. Hannah smiled, anticipating seeing a picture of Cain and Carla. Her blood turned to ice as her own picture appeared, followed by Eve's.

"Sit still," Eve said, "or this will take an ugly turn. I could bleed to death if I don't see a doctor."

Except for the television noise, the waiting room turned deathly silent. No one coughed, and one who'd been crying, stopped. Every eye looked at Hannah and Eve. Hannah glanced at the exit and saw four officers coming through the door.

Eve touched Hannah's arm. Eve spoke into her mind. *"My name is Genevieve McAdam, and I am a sister of the Abbey of Saint Margaret. We both work for Mother Evelyn in the Department of Intelligence for Vatican City. If they separate us, you know nothing and will say nothing. I don't know what's going to happen. I can't follow any future path."*

Eve removed her hand as the officers approached. One officer stepped in front of Eve. He asked in a polite but firm tone, "Are you Genevieve McAdam?"

"Yes."

"Do you own a pink Chrysler Prowler?"

Eve looked past the officer to the television, where the video of the Prowler exploding in midair was playing again. "Apparently, not anymore. Someone blew it up."

The officer placed his hand on his holstered gun. "Genevieve McAdam, you and your companion are under arrest under the provisions of the Homeland Security Act. Please come with me to the station."

Eve looked offended but spoke politely. "I assure you, sir, we had nothing to do with the explosion. We will come peacefully after I am attended by a physician."

The officer reached for the handcuffs attached to his belt.

"Officer," Eve said as she looked directly at him, "you have a decision to make, and I suggest you consider your actions carefully. My lawyers will treat you more kindly if you do not violate my civil rights. Placing handcuffs on me could cause more damage to my already injured hand. Removing me prematurely from the hospital will put my life in jeopardy. Please allow me to receive the physical care I need."

"Very well." The officer ordered another officer to find a doctor. "But any attempt to flee will be dealt with full force."

"Thank you for your kindness," Eve replied.

The officer asked Hannah her full name, told her to stand up, and handcuffed her wrists. Hannah felt disappointed when Eve didn't protest.

All four officers stayed in the surgical room with Eve and Hannah as a young doctor sewed up both sides of Eve's hand. "You have lost a lot of blood. Do you know your blood type?"

"O-positive," Eve said between gritted teeth.

As soon as the doctor finished, the four officers escorted Eve and Hannah to the police station.

The temperature in the interrogation room felt bitterly cold. Hannah spotted cameras in each corner of the room, and she assumed that they were also behind the large mirror in front of where they sat. Eve didn't speak while they waited alone. "How is your hand?" Hannah asked.

"I have a hole through it, so it hurts."

"Sorry."

Hannah thought she would freeze to death as they waited for someone to arrive. The metal chair she sat on and the metal table in front of her made it seem colder. She shook constantly and found concentration difficult.

Finally, two detectives walked into the room and sat. The tall, bald senior detective looked to be in his mid-sixties. The other detective didn't look much younger. His frown appeared to be permanent as did the two-day stubble on his triple chin. The overweight detective reeked of cigarette smoke.

The smelly one spoke in a dry, harsh voice. "My name is Detective Joseph Kriskoff, and this is Lieutenant Robert Thornman. We'd like to ask you a few questions. I trust you'll be cooperative."

"It's a little chilly," Eve remarked. A faint cloud of mist wafted out of her mouth.

"The air conditioner is broken, and we can't shut it off," Detective Kriskoff said with a little smile.

"If you expect the truth from me, you should make a greater effort not to lie yourself. The air conditioner is not broken, and I can speak more freely if my teeth are not chattering. Turn the heat on."

Hannah assumed that Eve was coercing him because the lieutenant motioned with his finger to the mirror behind him. A few seconds later, she sensed warmth flowing from the overhead vent. Hannah let out a grateful sigh, but Eve simply smiled.

"Now, perhaps you'll answer a few questions?" he asked Eve. "Miss Genevieve McAdam, of Great Britain."

The detective looked at Hannah. "Mary Louise Johnson, originally from Tulsa, Oklahoma. It seems you like to pull pranks."

"You found pranks on my record?" Hannah exclaimed.

"You put thousands of crickets in your high school auditorium right before graduation, didn't you?"

Hannah's face felt hot. "My twin brother did that."

"But you put the limburger cheese in the radiators of your college cafeteria, didn't you?"

"It smelled better than the turkey tetrazzini. Hasn't the statute of limitations expired on the cheese? No pun intended."

Hannah felt a muscle cramp and remembered she was supposed to keep her mouth shut. Eve cleared her throat. "So you've caught the cheese bandit. Fine her, and let us go."

"We're not interested in cheese," the senior detective sneered. "We have a record of an altercation between you two and Carla Babb at 7:15 this evening near a pink Prowler registered to you, Miss McAdam. You purchased it yesterday from a dealer near Milwaukee, and Carla Babb is the previous owner."

"Since you've done your homework, let's save ourselves some time, shall we?" Eve replied. "I'm not interested in wasting time. I need to fly out of Chicago before dawn"

"You won't be going anywhere," Kriskoff said. "We have lots of questions."

"I don't think so," Eve replied. "I'm entitled to one phone call. I would like to make that call now."

"I would like to remind you who is in charge here."

Eve looked Lieutenant Thornman right in the eye. "Hand me your phone."

The lieutenant reached inside his jacket pocket and pulled out his phone. As he handed it across the table, Kriskoff leaned forward and then froze in place.

Eve punched in a series of numbers and spoke into the phone. "Gertrude, send the files on Carla Babb to Joseph.Kriskoff@cityofchicago. org immediately. The team needs to leave for Taiwan within two hours."

Three police officers burst through the door. Eve glanced their way, and the first tripped over his own feet. The next two fell over the first one's back, and they tumbled into a heap on the floor.

"Oh yes, and bring me another cane." Eve hung up.

A large police officer stepped through the doorway with his gun pointing at Eve. "I'm not sure what you're trying to pull here, lady, but I'm about to throw you into a cell."

"Good evening, chief. I was simply asserting my right to make a phone call," Eve replied.

The chief stepped farther into the room. "Terrorists don't get lawyers. Give me the phone."

Eve tossed the phone to the chief and spoke kindly. "I'm trying to prevent a crime without causing an international incident. I would declare diplomatic immunity, but I would rather clear my name."

"Diplomatic immunity?" the chief asked with disbelief.

"I am with Vatican City Secret Service," Eve replied, rising from her chair. "We've been tracking a serial killer, and she's in Chicago. Several of the teens she's killed were from Catholic families, and we assert our right to help them find out the truth. Tell Detective Kriskoff to check his email. He'll find evidence of seven missing children in the Chicago area. We had a confrontation with the psychopath earlier tonight. Her name is Carla Babb."

The chief made a finger motion to Detective Kriskoff, who rose and left.

Hannah felt her head throb like it had with Lotan. The chief froze. Eve stood up and looked at the door. A short man dressed in a dark tailored suit walked into the room.

"My name is Blake Forester. I'm assistant director of the Secret Service. This investigation is now ours."

"The Chicago Police knows how to investigate," the chief replied.

"What Genevieve McAdam told you is true. She is no longer your concern."

"What does this have to do with the Secret Service? Don't you protect the president?"

Blake Forester looked at the chief. "Thank Vatican Intelligence for their help. Please escort us to a private room."

The chief didn't look happy, but he looked at Eve and said, "Thank you." He motioned his hand toward the door and said, "Please follow me."

Hannah clasped Eve's hand. *"Were you expecting him?"*

"No. He is a coercer and there is a precog nearby preventing me from seeing the future."

With eyes opened wide, Hannah gulped. *"Now what do we do?"*

Chapter Thirty-Eight

Eve, Hannah, and Assistant Director Blake Forester entered a conference room. "Please take a seat," Forester said. He then placed a black box about the size of a Rubik's Cube on the table and sat down.

Hannah's head throbbed again. A few seconds later, Forester grimaced in pain. He looked at Eve and said, "This black box creates electronic interference. What you say in here is private. Miss Johnson has shields, but they're weak. You, however, Miss McAdam, have walls. By the headache you just gave me, you must be a coercer."

Hannah's eyebrows arched.

"As are you, Mr. Forester," Eve replied.

"Why are you here?"

"As I told the police, we were following a lead on the serial killer known as Carla Babb."

"I hear you say the words, but Miss Johnson's mind says something else. What princess are you trying to rescue?" Forester asked. He grimaced again and touched his temples. "Please don't do that again."

"Then stop invading her privacy. You may call me Eve, and this is Hannah."

"Very well, Eve, why are you here?"

"We really are on a rescue mission, but that has nothing to do with the Secret Service."

Forester stared at Eve for a moment. "You may call me Blake."

"Very well, Blake. Why are you here?"

"The Secret Service has orders to lend you aid. My partner knew several hours ago that you would be in Chicago and would need our help."

It was Eve's turn to stare at Blake. "Who gave you those orders?"

"President Johnson. His advisor, Dr. Slayer, gave the president a demonstration and said that he should have psychic protection to keep anyone from forcing him into nuclear war. He left the Secret Service with three telepaths who found a few others. We've been protecting presidents since then. We were also told that you would be our instructor and to lend you aid if needed."

Hannah sat back in her chair and thought to herself, *Why would Cain want to protect Eve in the sixties?*

"That surprises me, but I will thank him sometime."

The door opened, and a young woman wearing a hijab entered carrying several boxes that smelled like Chinese food. Hannah was grateful and relaxed a little as the woman served her the food.

"This is Zara, my partner."

"Are you a precog?" Eve asked Zara.

"I am a seer," Zara replied as she sat beside Blake. "I foresaw the bomb in Chicago and your face on the news. We left Washington immediately."

"A helicopter landed on the roof of the John Hancock building a few minutes before the bomb exploded," Blake said. "The helicopter belongs to Enoch Enterprises out of Tokyo. Was this company involved in the bombing?"

"The bomb was personal not political. If you value your life, you should not investigate Enoch Enterprises."

"I think you'll find that I have a formidable talent."

"Compared to whom?"

"Compared to any other telepath I have met until now."

"The founder of Enoch Enterprises is almost as strong as I am, and Carla Babb has a formidable talent. This doesn't involve the safety of the president."

Blake quirked an eyebrow. "Okay then, how can we help you?"

"It would be nice to arrive in Taiwan before Carla Babb. Do you think you could help with that?"

Blake touched Zara's arm. They conferred in private for a moment, then Blake smiled. "We tracked Carla Babb's plane until it flew into Canadian airspace and used a jamming device to block radar. Her plane is pink, by the way. We can't find or communicate with her. But I think I know another way, but you might not like it. Will you agree to teach our people more about our talents?"

"I will," Eve replied.

"How would you feel about going to space?"

Hannah gulped.

Chapter Thirty-Nine

Hannah watched the lights of Chicago fade as the Learjet banked southwest. They had retrieved their belongings that the police had confiscated earlier from their hotel. She felt grateful to change from her bloodstained clothes and back into her habit. Eve, Blake, and Zara sat several rows behind her. No one spoke. Only occasionally someone laughed.

As Hannah opened her laptop, she sighed. Her computer was a mess after being scanned by the police specialist. She began a diagnostic and wondered how advanced Eve's computer must be since she'd had access to advanced technology for the past five thousand years. Now, Hannah flipped through her computer files ensuring that none of her notes contained references to any of the secrets she'd learned from Eve. She felt relieved when she found nothing obvious.

She gently touched her bruised jaw where Carla had struck her. Her memory kept circling around what Cain and Blake had said: "She has shields." Did that mean she might become a telepath? Was that why Eve kept shocking and scaring her? What did Cain mean when he said it would be more difficult to awaken? Would the manna Cain created awaken her talent? She wished she could talk to Eve, but she was busy. She distracted herself by studying Taiwan and hoped they would find the princess there.

"Hannah, will you please join us?" Eve said from behind her.

Hannah joined the others and buckled her seatbelt.

"We need to go over the plan," Blake said. "We will land soon at a secret military facility. There's a test flight of a spaceplane in a few hours. It will fly at an altitude of over fifty miles, taking it out of the atmosphere. I must warn you it won't be pleasant. It's scheduled to land at Midway. I'll stay in the control center and convince the controllers to change your destination to Naha, Japan. You're booked on a private jet from there to Taiwan. It will be up to you, Eve, to make sure the astronauts don't question their orders. They'll be able to see the weather around Midway with their instruments."

He continued, "Getting into the facility won't be difficult. Once inside, you'll take the place of the crash test dummies. Eve, you must be absolutely certain that everyone believes you're the real dummies."

"I can make that happen," Eve said.

Blake and Zara gasped as Eve suddenly appeared as a crash test dummy. "You have three talents?" Zara asked.

"Yes. Neither of you are an illusionist, so there was nothing to teach you."

"Are there any other surprises I should know about?" Blake asked.

"Not today," Eve replied.

"That's a relief. I'll have to explain to the president why I commandeered a spaceplane."

"I hope you won't be in too much trouble," Hannah said with sympathy.

"There are two portraits hanging in the boardroom of the Secret Service Telepaths," Zara explained. "One of them is a close rendition of Eve. The directive to assist her is a secret order from President Johnson. The president will not be happy, but he will accept it."

"You said two portraits," Hannah said. "Does the other face have a red birthmark that looks like a hand?"

Zara looked surprised. "How did you know?"

"We've met."

Zara stood and ran to the restroom. When she returned, she handed Hannah a travel can of hairspray. "Hannah, you will be responsible for spraying this on the cameras focused on the dummies. Eve can fool the people but not the cameras. Keep your faces covered. You've been on the news lately, and you will be recognized if not careful."

The plane tilted forward and descended beneath the clouds. Hannah saw nothing but darkness. The landing gear opened and as they approached, two rows of blue lights came on and allowed her to see the runway. The plane bumped three times as it gripped the pavement. There were no buildings, only hills on one side. The plane taxied to one of the hills, and as they approached, two camouflaged doors opened to allow the plane to enter a hangar.

Everyone walked down the stairs. Four other private jets sat inside. They approached the guards, and Blake spoke to them. The guards motioned to a door, and Hannah heard a click as the lock disengaged when they approached.

They walked down a long hallway with several doors. The door at the end was guarded, but the lock clicked and they went into a large hangar where three planes were joined together at the wings. The two on the outside had very large jet engines on their wings. The one in the middle was shorter and was mostly a rocket with a few windows at the front. They were all painted slate gray.

Blake opened a door at the back of the hangar. They entered a small room with one woman at a desk in front of a computer and two crash dummies sitting on a golf cart with wires attached to them. More dummies sat in chairs along the back wall. The woman started to turn around then stopped and refocused on her computer.

They moved to the back of the room, and Blake touched Eve and Hannah's arm. *"After the technicians remove the wires from the dummies, you must take their place. Don't make any noise."*

"How do you know all of this?" Hannah asked.

"I'm often close to the president, and I hear things."

"Thank you," Eve said.

Blake and Zara left the room, and Hannah touched Eve's arm. Eve pulled it away and shook her head "no." They both sat in the two empty chairs and waited.

About thirty minutes later, two technicians walked into the room. They stopped and talked with the woman at the desk for a few minutes. After signing papers on a clipboard, they removed the wires from the dummies, then they picked them up and brought them toward Hannah and Eve.

Hannah and Eve got up, walked to the golf cart, and climbed in. The technicians returned and drove the cart across the hangar and up a ramp beside the middle plane. After parking at the top, they carried Eve and Hannah into the spaceplane, complaining about the weight of the dummies. They buckled them in and left.

Immediately, Hannah unbuckled herself and hair sprayed the cameras focused on her and Eve. Then she returned to her comfortable seat. Hannah was careful not to move, knowing the camera was only blurry. She could not see much, but her head was turned partially toward the window. About an hour later, she heard two people enter and assumed they were the astronauts based on their technical conversation. She could hear them going through a precheck and then closing the cockpit door. The outer door was sealed, and she saw the plane leave the hangar.

The three planes in conjunction took off. It felt like any other plane Hannah had ever ridden in. After about thirty minutes, loud knocking along the roof reverberated through the craft. Five seconds later, the rocket ignited and curved up.

The acceleration was incredible. Hannah's body pushed deep into the chair. Her face felt like peanut butter and she held on to the armrest with all her strength. After a few minutes of terror, Hannah heard Eve shout in her mind, *"Stop screaming!"*

"My mouth is shut! We should have space suits. The pilots have space suits! Why don't we have space suits?"

"Space suits won't help us if we crash."

"That didn't help!"

"Stop screaming in your mind. You're distracting me."

Hannah sucked in air, trying to calm herself. *I don't ever want to go into space again,* she thought. Being in zero gravity helped. She gazed out the window and could distinguish some of the larger craters on the lighted side of the moon. As she marveled at the sight, she noticed something change. It looked as if a small white toothpick intruded into the dark side of the moon, then, after a few seconds, it disappeared. She wished she could tell Eve but didn't want to distract her again.

The spaceplane descended back into the atmosphere. The ride back down was very turbulent but not as frightening as the ascent. The cabin heated up, and Hannah felt icy air blowing on her face from above and her seat turned very cold. It helped a little.

They landed at a military base near Okinawa, Japan. As soon as the plane stopped, trucks and soldiers quickly covered it with camouflage nets. Once inside the hangar, Eve dropped the crash dummy illusion. The door opened, and a man walked in with a lot of medals on his shirt. "Miss McAdam?" he asked.

"Yes," Eve replied.

"The hangar has been cleared and the cameras turned off. I have been ordered to escort you and your companions to a charter jet. I can ask no questions, and neither can you."

Ten minutes later, Eve and Hannah were seated in a small jet. Eve put a finger to her lips, telling Hannah to remain quiet.

Hannah believed what she saw was important, so she reached across the aisle and touched Eve. *"Something appeared close to the moon. I think Lotan is near."*

"Share your memories with me."

Hannah closed her eyes and recalled her glimpse of the moon.

Eve sighed. *"That was a leviathan."*

"Have you met one?"

"No, but I have read about them. If you could see it, so could the telescopes on Earth. Lotan's people made a mistake."

"What do you mean?"

"A leviathan will not willingly enter the gravity well of a star. It hurts them. Someone must coerce it. It is difficult to control exactly where a leviathan will teleport. This complicates things."

"They must really want to rescue the princess," Hannah said.

"Or capture me," Eve replied. *"I must think."*

They landed at Taipei International Airport, and taxied into a hangar for private planes.

After disembarking, Hannah followed Eve as she talked to Gertrude on her phone.

Eve walked past several planes, and Hannah spotted Mabel and Gertrude carrying duffel bags and escorting Mary Ruth toward them. It took a minute to cover the distance. Hannah almost didn't recognize them. They all looked younger. Eve and Mary Ruth hugged each other.

"It is so good to see you again," Mary Ruth exclaimed without a trace of a warble.

"Have you located Carla's plane?" Eve asked.

"Gertrude is linked to the airport tower. Carla, using an alias of course, radioed in a few minutes ago. She should arrive shortly."

"You look and sound so young," Hannah blurted. "Is this the result of Cain's manna?"

"Yes, it is. I don't feel a day over seventy-five."

Gertrude and Mabel looked at least ten years younger. "It really worked," Hannah said. "The manna cured your Parkinson's disease, made everyone younger, and did Gertrude lose some weight?"

Gertrude smiled. "I did, and I look forward to losing more."

"This is wonderful news," Hannah exclaimed.

"That isn't the best part." Mary Ruth looked at Hannah and smiled.

Hannah felt a bee buzzing on her head. She yelped and immediately removed her veil.

"You can coerce," Eve exclaimed. "The manna enhanced your mental abilities."

"Not coercion—illusion." Mary Ruth laughed. "I did not force her to remove her bonnet but created the illusion of a bee buzzing on her head. I can only create small illusions, but Gertrude is now a full telepath. What happened to your hand?"

Eve held up her bandaged hand. "Cain stabbed me."

"Oh my," Mary Ruth sympathized.

"Did you plant the seeds?" Eve asked Mabel.

"Yes," she replied, glancing at Hannah. "The flowers will begin to blossom in England a few hours after sunrise."

Hannah fixed her veil back and wondered which flowers would blossom. They walked toward the waiting room, which looked empty through the glass. Most of the jets were white, but one stood out because it was as black and dull as a lump of coal. She looked closer as they passed it and whispered, "That's Cain's plane."

Chapter Forty

Hannah felt nervous as she walked past Cain's plane.

"Don't worry, Hannah," Gertrude said. "Cain arrived several hours ago."

Eve stopped and gathered everyone around her.

"Is something wrong?" Mary Ruth asked.

Eve grasped Mary Ruth's hands in her uninjured one. "I met your son."

Mary Ruth sucked in a surprised breath and smiled. "How is Karl?"

Eve locked gazes with Mary Ruth. "She is doing well."

Mary Ruth's smile faded. "She?"

"You will meet her in a few minutes."

Mary Ruth let go of Eve and whirled around. "Please tell me my son isn't about to arrive in a pink plane."

"I'm afraid she is," Eve replied with regret. "I'm so sorry, but you cannot save him. Open your mind to me and let me share with you what I learned from his mind. We'll make it through this together."

Mary Ruth embraced Eve, who returned the hug gently. In the silence, Eve shared her knowledge with the mother of Carla Babb.

Hannah prayed for her friends.

Mary Ruth broke from Eve's embrace. "I can handle the sex change. She's my son, and I will always love him or her. What I can't tolerate is that she's a serial killer. We must move forward. My son should arrive soon."

They walked into the waiting room. Gertrude pulled out her laptop and opened it. "The cameras in here have been disabled. You can make us look like whomever you want, and it should fool any of Carla's guards."

Mabel passed everyone a face veil. She removed her patch to free her red camera eye. Then she handed Hannah Eve's cane.

"What am I supposed to do with this?" Hannah asked.

"The Mother said you know how to use it. You're my backup in case there are too many guards. The veils will filter the sleep gas. Don't spray Carla."

Hannah watched through the waiting room windows as a lone technician entered the hangar from a security door. Using his orange cone-covered flashlights, he motioned Carla's pink plane to a space close to the waiting room.

The door opened and two burly men, dressed in black suits and wearing dark sunglasses, stepped out of the plane. Carla, also dressed in black, followed and two more guards brought up the rear. The large bandage across the bridge of Carla's nose made her look like a boxer after a poorly executed fight.

Carla walked toward the waiting room with a cell phone to her ear.

Hannah raised her veil over her nose. She picked up a magazine, pretending to read it, and over its edge she watched Carla glance through the windows. Then Hannah looked at her own reflection in the glass, surprised to see an Asian woman looking back. Out of the corner of her eye, Hannah glimpsed Gertrude press a button on her laptop as Carla entered the waiting room. Carla removed the phone from her ear, looking annoyed when she peered at it. She moved the phone closer to her face to check the signal strength, or so Hannah assumed. Since she was not paying attention, she bumped into the burly guard frozen in front of her and dropped her phone. It fell at Hannah's feet.

Carla looked down at her phone, and Hannah knew by her shocked expression that Eve had removed the illusion. Hannah batted her eyes. "Fancy meeting you here."

"You! How did you get here before me?" Carla exclaimed.

"All things are possible when you trust in God," Hannah replied.

Carla glanced at her bodyguards, three of whom seemed frozen in place. The other guard struggled to escape Mabel's chokehold. As the guard slumped to the floor, Carla caught sight of Eve standing on the other side of the frozen bodyguards. "It seems you have me outnumbered."

Mary Ruth moved closer. She spoke with love in her voice. "Hello, son."

"I have no mother," Carla replied in a flat voice.

A tear welled in Mary Ruth's eye. "You were only three when Cain took you away, Karl."

"My name is Carla," she growled. "I'm older than I look. If you were my mother, you would be at least a hundred years old."

Mary Ruth smiled. "I'm over ninety years old, and I've benefited from Cain's manna too. Surely you remember something?"

Carla sucked in a breath and looked deep into Mary Ruth's bright blue eyes. Hannah hoped she would recognize the color since she saw it whenever she looked in a mirror. Carla then spoke in a tiny voice filled with sadness and longing. "Mom?" She hesitated for a few seconds then pulled a gun out of her coat pocket and pointed it at Mary Ruth's head. "I have no mother!"

Hannah considered pouncing on Carla's arm but worried her actions could accidentally fire the gun. She grasped Eve's cane and prepared to strike, but stopped when Eve shook her head.

"You won't kill your own mother," Mary Ruth said.

"I wouldn't bet your life on that," Carla snapped. "Now, back off." She pressed her gun against Mary Ruth's forehead. "I don't need a gun. I inherited my father's gift."

Mary Ruth let out a whimper of pain and gritted her teeth. "You have a gift I don't, but I have something greater that you will never have."

"And what is that?" Carla sneered.

"Friends."

Mabel took an aggressive step forward and growled. Eve spoke before Mabel could take another step. "That won't be necessary, Sister Mabel. However, I would appreciate it if you make sure these men don't injure themselves. Hannah, spray the guards. Just use a little."

Hannah approached each guard and lightly pressed the wings of the angel on each side of Eve's cane. Mabel caught them as they slumped.

Mary Ruth backed up, keeping eye contact with Carla. Eve approached. "I will not let you pull that trigger. Drop your gun."

Carla's hand shook. After a moment, she lowered her arm and dropped the gun. With one finger, Eve touched her cheek. "The last time we met, I didn't know the depth of your crimes, so I was gentle with you. When I told you I could turn you into a vegetable, I meant it. I believe you now feel the full strength of my power, do you not?"

Carla's eyes widened, and she nodded slowly.

"Cain changed the security code. Tell me what it is."

Carla didn't speak, but Eve smiled. "What else should I know?"

After a moment, Eve looked at Hannah. "Hannah, Carla is ready to sleep."

Hannah walked to Carla and sprayed her in the face. Carla tried to hold her breath. Her palms were bloody where she had dug in her fingernails. Mabel caught her as she collapsed.

Gertrude moved to a door marked "Employees Only." Mabel dragged the sleeping bodies to the door as Gertrude picked the lock. She also removed all cell phones and guns. "Hannah, there are zip ties and metal headbands in my bag. Get them and secure the prisoners."

Hannah did as she was told and helped Mabel drag the guards into a cleaning closet. Mary Ruth stroked Carla's cheek then placed a metal band around her head.

They entered a hall heading toward the main terminal. Hannah caught up to Eve and said, "If anyone deserves to be mindwiped, it's Carla. Why didn't you?"

"That would be the equivalent of murder," Eve replied.

"But God made provisions for the death penalty when someone was guilty of murder," Hannah stated. "You know, an eye for an eye and tooth for a tooth?"

"Jesus said otherwise."

"She isn't only a murderer, but a slayer of children. As a coercer, it will be difficult to put her on trial."

Eve looked at Hannah. "In my heart, I believe Carla Babb should die. Her soul is already halfway in hell. God might allow you to send her the rest of the way, but He does not allow me to."

"I don't understand."

"In the beginning, God gave Adam and me one command," Eve explained. "He said, 'You must not partake of the fruit of the tree of knowledge.' I disobeyed Him. When God expelled us from the garden, He gave us another command, 'Thou shalt not kill.' I disobeyed Him once. I shall not do it again."

Hannah remained quiet as she thought about Eve's words. When she spoke again, it was with reverence. "The Bible states that you had conversations with God."

Eve smiled. "Yes, and if God ever speaks to you, I would strongly advise you to listen."

Chapter Forty-One

U pon exiting the airport, Hannah found a taxi van. They piled in with Eve sitting in the front. Eve said something in Taiwanese. As the taxi pulled away from the curb, Hannah looked out the window and saw several hundred people performing the martial arts exercise routine called tai chi.

"Why did you miss one of the guards?" Hannah asked Eve.

"He had a mental shield," Eve said. "I couldn't take the time to break him and hold Carla in check too. Mabel read my signal, and I knew she could handle him. Cain will have an illusionist, a coercer, and possibly more at his office."

"Where are we going?"

Eve pointed out the front window. "It should be obvious."

The van topped a hill, and Hannah saw a breathtaking view of Taipei. Ancient temples positioned beside tall, modern apartments filled the city. One building, over a hundred stories tall, rose out of the sea of humanity. "Cain is at Taipei 101, one of the world's tallest buildings."

"Cain has been attracted to tall buildings ever since he designed the Tower of Babel," Eve replied.

"But it fell," Hannah exclaimed. "Wouldn't that make him want to avoid tall buildings?"

"You would think. Perhaps it's his way of defying God. Of course, he could just like the view. From what Carla shared with me, Cain is waiting for her to arrive to escort Princess Sela to an iron fortress in the mountains. He expects the rest of us to arrive much later, so we have a window of opportunity to surprise him."

Gertrude spoke from the middle row of seats. "Eden Pharmaceuticals is on the eighty-third floor of Taipei 101. The building has a state-of-the-art security system. We're going to avoid that by entering through a service entrance to the food court in the basement. We'll arrive before the mall opens, so everything is closed except for a few restaurants. Mabel has an umbrella for everyone in her bag if we need to avoid cameras. In case someone's watching, Eve will disguise us like she did in Nigeria."

"Excuse me," Hannah interrupted. "I've never been to Nigeria."

"Just try to walk like a man," Mabel said in her raspy voice.

"We'll walk through the food court to the elevators. Mary Ruth will get off on the fifth floor, which contains four banks and the security center. She'll provide distractions for the security guards. The rest of us will change elevators five times before reaching the eighty-third floor. Other than the elevator lobby, I don't know the layout of the office. Eve and Mabel will subdue anyone in the lobby. The rest is a guess until eight, when the staff arrives. We need to be out before then. I have an electronic scrambler and two sound suppressors, which will be useful if there is gunfire, but they have a limited range and a short duration."

"Are Cain and Princess Sela there?" Hannah asked.

"Carla didn't know Cain's whereabouts, but she believes Sela is there," Eve replied.

"To exit," Gertrude continued, "we'll climb up to the indoor observatory on the eighty-ninth floor. There's an express elevator that can get us back to the ground in less than a minute."

Hannah said, "Uh, what am I supposed to do?"

Gertrude smiled. "You're the only person Princess Sela will recognize. The rest of us have changed in the last few days. We don't want her screaming, so you'll be the first face she sees."

"It's a good plan," Eve complimented.

The taxi drove to an entrance underground and stopped by a loading dock. People were unloading merchandise from several trucks. Gertrude paid the driver. Everyone walked through several hallways and entered the food court. It was larger than Hannah imagined. She smelled chicken. McDonald's was open, and she really wanted an Egg McMuffin but knew she couldn't stop.

For the first time in her life, Hannah understood what it meant to be a minority. Everyone had dark brown eyes and straight black hair. She believed she was the only person out of the twenty-three million people on the island who had curly hair. She also felt as if she were walking on stilts since she was taller than anyone she saw.

Eve stepped back beside Hannah. "Don't make this more difficult. Try walking like a man."

Hannah looked at Eve, and the face looking back at her was Asian. She looked at Mabel and saw a heavyset Asian man. She wondered what she herself looked like. She tried spreading her legs farther apart, imagining how a man walked. Her knees bent awkwardly, and she felt like a frog, but Eve said, "That's better."

They got on the elevator and arrived at the fifth floor. Mary Ruth stepped out. She no longer looked like herself but instead like a young Asian woman wearing a gym outfit. A few early risers fast-walked around, waiting for the gym to open. Before the elevator doors closed, Mary Ruth fell and grabbed her ankle.

Hannah jumped to go help her, but Eve grabbed her arm. "She knows what she's doing. That's how she'll get into the security room." The doors closed, and she hoped Eve was right.

The team exited on the thirty-fourth floor to get on another elevator that went higher. At the third elevator transition, Gertrude pulled out her electronic scrambler and turned it on before entering. The door closed, and Gertrude donned a pair of microthin gloves. Hannah wrapped her face with her veil like the other sisters did.

Two seconds later, Eve pressed the button for the eighty-third floor. Eve changed their appearance. She now looked like Carla Babb, and every-one else looked like her bodyguards. The doors opened into a small foyer with a glass door on the other side. A palm print scanner with a keypad extended from the wall beside the door. Gertrude placed her gloved palm on the scanner, punched in a six-digit code, and whispered, "Let's pray this works."

Hannah held her breath, and Eve spoke to her mind. *"Gertrude is wearing Cain's palm print. She lifted it from the video when he visited the abbey. A latex copy of a holographic image is risky, but it could work."*

Eve glanced through the glass door then pushed it open. The others followed. A middle-aged man sat at a reception desk, his eyes as wide as saucers. He seemed frozen in place. Two more men rose from the couch with huge grins when they saw Carla Babb, and they moved forward. Eve smiled as she raised her cane in front of them, and two heartbeats later, they slumped to the floor, their lungs filled with green gas.

As Mabel dragged the men behind the receptionist desk, a drop of liquid appeared on the plush carpet in front of Eve's feet. Although the illusion of Carla Babb looked calm, underneath it, Eve was sweating.

The reception area opened to two hallways in opposite directions. Using an infrared heat scanner, Mabel looked for more bodies through the walls. Gertrude did the same in the other direction. Gertrude signaled that her side was clear and proceeded to the door marked "Maintenance."

Mabel approached the first room on her side of the hallway and stood to the side of the open doorway. As Eve and Hannah moved closer, Hannah heard voices and dice and tiles clicking together in a game of mah-jongg. Mabel reached into her pocket and pulled out a small red box and an aerosol spray can. She pressed the button on the red box, popped the top off the aerosol can, and tossed them both into the room. A green fog filled the space, and the sounds of the game stopped.

Mabel pivoted into the room and raised her fist just in time to punch the bottom of the boot only inches from her face. Hannah was not sure what to do, everything was happening so fast. The green fog dissipated as Mabel pushed into the room. Five men and one woman lay in awkward positions there. One man stood. The large Asian man wore a breathing apparatus and sported a band of metal around his head. The room was silent, and Hannah realized the orange box must be a sound suppressor. She ducked when she saw the Asian man pull a gun from a holster behind his back. Mabel's left foot slammed into his arm with enough force to break it. The gun flew across the room.

It slammed into the far wall, and a flash of fire and a wisp of smoke exited the barrel. The carpet close by exploded like a miniature volcano as the concrete beneath it tried to escape.

With no sound, it seemed like an old silent kung fu movie without the accompanying music. The attacking Asian man took a step backward when Eve removed the illusion of a large black man from around Mabel. Holding his injured arm across his body, he kicked Mabel in the mouth. Mabel spit out her false teeth, now covered in blood.

The two opponents circled the table in the center of the room. Mabel didn't allow the man to get closer to the exit. Using one of his companion's sleeping bodies as a springboard, the man did an amazing body flip and came straight at Mabel across the table. Mabel had been lifting weights and punching bags for more years than her opponent had been alive. With a grip like the jaws of a shark, she clamped on to one ankle and pivoted, taking the man straight to the floor. She followed with a punch that knocked him unconscious with at least a concussion and probably a broken jaw.

Mabel picked up her teeth and the small red box, which she switched off, and exited the room. Hannah heard a few faint snores and Mabel breathing a little heavier than normal.

"That was fun," Mabel whispered. She looked at her infrared scanner. "There are only two people within fifty feet."

Gertrude rejoined the group and Eve absorbed her back into the illusion, looking like the thugs who protected Carla Babb.

Hannah looked and saw several doors and a large potted plant down the hall. Suddenly, the hall grew longer, and she could not see the end. Several hundred doors appeared. "There's an illusionist nearby."

"I see her," Mabel said. She pulled out two zip ties and a metal band. She walked to the potted plant and placed the metal band on top. The plant turned into a middle-aged woman. Mabel forced her to turn around and put the zip ties on her hands and feet. She then gagged her with a white cloth.

Watching the scanner, she led them to a door farther down the hall. Instead of using her lock-picking tools, Gertrude inserted what looked like a rubber key into the keyhole. Three tiny lights flashed red three times and then turned green. Gertrude stepped back, and Mabel twisted the key, opening the door.

Hannah peered into the dimly lit room and saw Princess Sela lying on a comfortable-looking bed. Stainless steel covered every inch of the floor, ceiling, and walls. A chemical toilet and a small sink under a mirror stood in the corner. Hannah saw her reflection in the mirror, revealing that it was the same as it had been all her life. Other than a recliner and three books, the room was bare.

Hannah walked to the side of the bed and leaned over. She whispered to the beautiful woman lying there, "Princess Sela, wake up. We are here to rescue you." There was no response. She tried again a little louder. Still no response. Hannah shook the princess once and then again. She turned to Eve, who was standing beside the door. "I think she's drugged."

Eve motioned for Gertrude to enter the room. Gertrude approached, saying, "I was afraid of this." She pulled out a syringe of yellow liquid and tapped the side three times. "This is a small dose of adrenaline. I don't want to give her too much since her anatomy may be different. This could be poison to her system."

Hannah replied, "Cain stated in Chicago that preliminary tests showed she was genetically compatible with humans."

"I only need to give her enough to awaken. She's a healer and can cleanse her system of whatever they gave her." Gertrude turned Sela's arm over and sought a vein. She inserted the needle and pressed the plunger halfway. Less than a minute later, Sela's eyelids fluttered. Gertrude removed the needle and backed away, allowing Hannah to move closer.

Sela's purple eyes came into full awareness with a blaze of light and focused on Hannah. The princess reminded Hannah of a caged tiger that had found a way to lash through the bars. "I knew you were all in this together," Sela said in a dry and raspy voice.

"Oh, no, princess," Hannah replied with a kind and patient tone. "We're here to rescue you."

Sela cleared her throat. "Thank God," she replied with passion. "What took you so long?"

"It wasn't easy to find you, and certain incidents delayed our progress. We can tell you everything later, but right now we need to hurry. Can you walk?"

"Give me a few minutes, and I can fly."

Sela wore only a light gray cotton shirt and matching shorts. Hannah didn't find shoes or a robe. Sela moved her hands to her abdomen, and they glowed.

"Is there a problem?"

The princess narrowed her eyes. "No. Just clearing my system of drugs." Sela sat up and swung her legs to the side of the bed. Gertrude came forward to offer assistance. Sela wiped her eyes. "You look familiar. But my mind must not be totally clear yet."

"We met briefly in Mexico," Gertrude explained. "I looked a little older."

"You've used Cain's manna," the princess said.

"We found his stash, thanks to you and your ring."

"Cain wanted to show off." Sela took a wobbly step. "He took me to see where he will soon produce enough manna for the entire population. He needs his drugs to create more telepaths."

"I guess he didn't wish to babysit you," Hannah interjected.

"My abilities presented him with new difficulties. Without a metallic room, he knew he could not keep me contained. He tried to convince me he was the savior of the human race and how much good he could do with me by his side. He wants me to be his queen."

"Then he hasn't . . . ," Hannah began but was reluctant to finish the question.

"Raped me?" Sela finished. "No. It's difficult for a telepath to rape another telepath. He coerced me to sleep in Chicago, and with the help of his two coercers and one healer, I have remained drugged most of the time since."

"He has a healer?" Gertrude asked.

"As of two days ago, but he is untrained and weak. He can heal minor wounds or maybe a broken nose."

Sela walked more steadily, so they headed to the door. Hannah advised the princess that another member of their team was an illusionist and would disguise them all as they made their way out of the building. Hannah and Gertrude took Sela into the hallway. Gertrude again looked like the black man.

A split second after arriving in the hallway, the ornate mahogany double doors swung open. Standing there, wearing a half-buttoned white shirt, was Cain. He carried his pistol in a shoulder holster on his left side.

No one breathed.

Cain looked down the hall and grew angry. With a commanding voice, he called out, "Carla, when I told you to come straight to my office, that didn't mean you could stop by and see your Sacred M . . ." Cain paused as a drop of moisture fell to the plush carpet from Carla. He squinted, tilted his head, and continued, "Mother. Did you forget that Carla Babb has a broken nose?"

Cain drew his long-barreled pistol. He pointed it directly at Eve as she dissipated the illusion. He spoke with a calm, still voice. "I warned you, Mother, that the next time I saw you, you would get a bullet between the eyes."

The next thing Hannah heard was Cain's gun firing.

Chapter Forty-Two

Between heartbeats, Hannah looked down the hall and saw four bullets racing directly toward Eve, Mabel, Gertrude, and herself. The first bullet would strike Eve. It was less than twenty feet away. In a nanosecond, Hannah stepped in front of Eve. The bullet radiated heat only two inches from her face. Hannah felt her heart throb. A faintly glowing hand entered her view from the doorway.

Princess Sela's long manicured fingernail flicked the bullet away. Her voice sounded sweet and innocent while simultaneously projecting superiority and contempt. "Eloshin females always have two gifts. My second gift is telekinesis."

Cain growled like a dog determined to get his favorite bone back. He kept his gun pointed at Eve.

Mabel pushed Hannah against the wall as she charged down the hallway toward Cain. Sneering, Cain stepped back and closed the door. Mabel didn't slow her pace. A steel plate descended from the ceiling, reinforcing the door. She slammed full force into it, causing the walls around the door to vibrate. She bounced backward, dropping to one knee. Mabel rose with determination and looked at the walls.

Eve's commanding voice rang down the hall. "Mabel, that is not the plan, nor is this the time." Eve could not coerce Mabel into obedience because of her impenetrable metallic shield, but she knew what to say. "Your mother will be nearing exhaustion by now. It's time to leave."

Mabel reluctantly turned away from the wall. Rubbing her injured shoulder, she returned with eyes downcast. She led the way to the fire exit. An iron bar secured the door shut. Although easy to remove from the inside, a burglar would need a welding torch to break in. Gertrude severed the fire alarm, and Eve handed Mabel her cane. Mabel welded the fire door shut before heading up to the eighty-ninth floor to reach the express elevator.

On the eighty-fifth floor, Hannah heard banging from below as if someone was trying to break through Mabel's weld. Fire alarms rang out in the stairwell. By the time they made it to the eighty-eighth floor,

Hannah's ears were numb from the screaming alarms. She covered her ears, but it did little good, so she used her hands to pull her up the next flight of stairs. She noticed Gertrude panting. Eve slowed the pace. Sela seemed unwinded, and Hannah wondered why. She looked down and noticed Sela using telekinesis to travel up the stairs. Her bare feet never touched the floor.

∽⌒

Nearly a half mile below, Mary Ruth, looking like a young woman, sat in a comfortable chair inside the security office with a bandage around her dainty ankle. She chatted with the guards. Glancing at a bulletin tacked to the wall, she saw that it advised the security guards to report seeing any of the six women posted. Her own picture was there, but as an old woman dressed as a nun, as were two pictures of Eve, one young and one old.

Mary Ruth kept an eye on the multiple security monitors as the pictures rotated from camera to camera throughout the complex. Eight guards casually watched the monitors. When the first alarm rang, she did not react nor did anyone else. Using her newly acquired talent, Mary Ruth kept the room silent and the monitors clear of anything unusual. She knew there was trouble when she had to block four more alarms. Although to everyone else the monitors looked normal, Mary Ruth saw several dozen guards enter from the fifth floor and take the express elevator to the eighty-ninth floor.

Once the phones started ringing, Mary Ruth felt the stress of maintaining the illusion of silence. She missed catching a walkie-talkie when it squawked, but the security guard heard nothing but static. She was still a novice at creating illusions. Controlling sound was not too difficult. Altering what a person saw on a two-dimensional monitor was also not too difficult. But doing both for nine guards was becoming more than she could handle for a few more minutes.

Two police officers burst through the door, demanding to know what was going on. She could not hold the illusion any longer. Pandemonium erupted as dozens of lights on the security boards flashed bright red, every phone rang, several walkie-talkies squawked, and the police screamed at the security guards. Before anyone had time to notice, Mary Ruth left.

When the team reached the eighty-ninth floor, Mabel checked her infrared scanner for anyone who might be awaiting them on the other side of the door. She shouted over the screeching fire alarms, "There are at least twenty people in stationary positions around the stairwell exit. We should assume each one will have a gun."

Gertrude clipped the wires on the fire alarm, and the ringing diminished. Eve closed her eyes and faced the door. "The nearest guards are wearing metal helmets. I can't freeze them."

"We could toss a few gas bombs out there," Gertrude suggested.

"I believe they're wearing gas masks," Eve replied.

"We have to find a way past them," Gertrude stated.

Eve turned to Sela. "How many bullets can you block?"

"It's not possible for a telekinetic to affect anything made of metal," Sela replied. "I compress air molecules to reduce the velocity of the bullets. Telekinesis is not my primary gift. If the bullets keep coming or are from different directions, I will not be able to stop them all."

Eve sighed. "Can you block all the bullets for thirty seconds?"

Before the princess could answer, the lights went out. "They cut the power. I think we just lost the express elevator." A crashing sound from below indicated that Cain's men had broken through the welded door, eliminating the option of fleeing down.

"You call this a rescue?" the princess demanded.

"I'm open to suggestions," Eve replied through gritted teeth.

The emergency lights snapped on. Hannah heard footsteps getting closer from below. She looked at Eve. "There's more than one way off the top of a building."

Eve looked intently at Hannah then turned to the princess. "How much weight can you lift?"

"I'm used to measuring my telekinetic ability in mass units," Sela explained.

"We're about to die here," Hannah quipped.

"I would give a rough estimate of two thousand pounds if I were at full strength, which I'm not."

Hannah heard footsteps a few floors below. "Does fear increase your strength?"

"Yes," Sela confessed.

"Good. Follow me." Hannah climbed the next set of steps to the ninetieth floor, with everyone following her.

Sela spoke to Eve. "I don't understand."

"If you lower your shield, you can read Hannah's surface thoughts," Eve said over her shoulder.

"You know I can't do that," Sela replied.

"Then do whatever Hannah tells you."

Hannah stopped at the ninety-first floor. "This is the open air observation deck."

Mabel quickly scanned the walls. "There are only six people close by."

Eve motioned for Mabel to lead the way. Hannah followed her through the door and saw six people. Three of them wore metal bands around their heads. Everyone had guns pointed at Mabel. Hannah knew Eve could not force the two to freeze, so she looked at her for directions. Hannah saw Princess Sela where Eve should have been. She looked at Mabel and saw Princess Sela again as she zigzagged toward one of the guards wearing metal. She missed her swing but grabbed his headband.

Turning around, Hannah saw ten more princesses coming through the doorway and realized what Eve had done. Cain would have given his goons instructions concerning whom not to shoot. Instead of four women dressed in black and one in a light gray shirt and shorts, they saw several dozen identical women wearing light gray shirts and shorts, and each one glowed.

Most of the men were confused, but the two with metal were not. They began shooting, but Sela blocked their bullets. Hannah didn't know which one was the real Sela. Hoping the men with guns didn't speak English, she yelled, "Sela, gather the dust around us and create a small tornado above me."

"Which one are you?" the princess cried.

"Follow my voice." Hannah knew the guards would also follow her voice. Sure enough, a few bullets pinged off the concrete floor around her.

She felt a sharp pain on top of her left foot and looked down to see a hot bullet smoldering on top of her shoelace. She flicked the bullet away, and her shoe almost came off.

A hand touched her arm. *"I cannot do this."* Sela's voice trembled.

"You have to. It's our only option."

"You have no idea how much trouble I will be in if I create a whirlwind."

"If we fail, Cain will kill me. Your fate will be much worse."

"Interfering is against our rules."

"It's better than being dead."

Sela muttered something in a different language that sounded like, "I'm going to be in so much trouble," but a vortex of air began to swirl on the observation deck.

At least twenty princesses spread out and began an intricate dance, weaving in and out of the steps and metal handrails. Mabel managed to knock out one of the guards wearing a metal headband. The rest of the men turned in circles, pointing their guns at each identical woman, but none fired. A commanding voice spoke Taiwanese from the stairwell door. The guards, along with several others who had arrived from the fire escape, fired their weapons at each woman's feet. Hannah admired the logic, for an injured princess could heal herself, while the rest would bleed.

Bullets passed through three pairs of feet. The guards focused on new targets and continued firing. Sela stumbled to the ground as a bullet lodged in her ankle. Blood covered her bare foot as she fell and screamed. Hannah was thankful the guards had only shot an illusionary Sela, which Eve made bleed to look real.

"We are all here," Eve whispered to Hannah as a bullet whizzed by her foot. Gertrude passed out umbrellas to everyone.

Hannah heard a familiar ding and looked at the elevator. The doors opened, and several police officers unloaded, taking up positions around the doors. Their uniforms changed from blue to green. Their emblems changed from police to Chinese military. Their weapons were out, and one of them fired. Cain's guard turned and shot back at the Chinese military.

"Cover your face and link arms!" Hannah exclaimed. As the five women joined together, Hannah spoke to Sela, "Surround us with your vortex."

"This is going to hurt."

"Then levitate us over the guardrail and then down."

"I can't do both!" Sela looked through the bars to the city below. "It's too far."

"Just get us to the top of the Grand Hyatt Hotel across the street," Eve interjected. "I will guide you."

Hannah felt a blast of wind laced with dirt whip past her shoulders.

Linked arm in arm, the five jumped from the ninety-first floor of Taipei 101.

Chapter Forty-Three

As the wind whistled past her ears, Hannah screamed, as did Mabel and Gertrude. Hannah tried to see the ground, but Sela kept the dirt swirling tightly so that no camera could glimpse inside the vortex. Hannah continued screaming. Eve's commanding voice spoke into her mind. *"Shut up!"*

A few seconds later, Eve yelled, "Now, Sela!"

Hannah felt her blood flow to her legs as the princess halted their downward plunge. The vortex dissipated, and her veil was no longer threatening to detach itself from her head. Her stomach lurched as Sela moved the group sideways, and she felt her damaged left shoe fly from her foot. She prayed it wouldn't hit anyone.

"As soon as your feet touch, open your umbrella," Eve commanded.

Hannah felt her stocking-covered foot touch warm pavement, and she opened her umbrella. They landed in a red circle with a white cross, which she recognized as the helicopter pad on top of the Grand Hyatt. Gertrude pulled out her electronic scrambler. A dozen people stared in wide-eyed amazement through the glass windows of the heliport. One shook her cell phone camera in frustration.

Eve snapped open her umbrella, and Hannah caught her own reflection in the window. She appeared to be Mary Poppins. Everyone else looked like Mary Poppins too. The group of flying nannies dressed in black, with bodices cinched tight, long and flowing skirts, and frilly white blouses, walked with dignity to the heliport entrance. One Mary Poppins hobbled as if she were missing a shoe.

The women marched through the heliport waiting room as if they owned it. Everyone stared with mouths hanging as each one smiled and winked as she passed. They entered the elevator, and as the doors closed, Sela nearly fainted. Hannah caught her and looked at Eve, who also looked pale and weak. Sweat glistened on her face, and her pierced hand bled through the bandage. Gertrude reached in her pocket and passed out Snickers bars. Sela devoured hers, but Hannah noticed she was no longer glowing.

Though exhausted, Eve transformed everyone just before the elevator opened on the ground floor. Minutes later, five elderly Chinese women, dressed in the uniforms of the cleaning staff of the Grand Hyatt, exited the building. They walked slowly down the sidewalk and used their umbrellas, like many other pedestrians, to protect themselves from the early-morning sun. Once they were aboard a large transit bus heading east, Hannah felt the tension in the air lessen. Hundreds of commuters got off the bus heading to work, but few got on. With a nearly empty bus, Eve allowed her illusion to fade. Everyone took seats near the back and rode in silence for several miles.

After a few moments, Sela, who sat beside Hannah, wrinkled her nose and sniffed the air. "What is that smell?"

Eve looked at Hannah.

Hannah blushed. She tucked her leg under and sat on her bare foot. "Sorry, I seem to have lost a shoe somewhere."

"Good heavens, child," Sela whispered. "Is it a fungus?"

"No," Hannah sighed. "It's genetic."

"Then, there is nothing I can do," Sela replied sadly.

Hannah turned to look at Eve. "Why did you make us look like Mary Poppins?"

Eve seemed distracted and took a few seconds to reply. "The media considers reality to be a hoax and reports hoaxes as reality. I wanted to make it easy for them."

Before the bus turned to continue its circular route heading back toward Taipei 101, the five elderly Chinese women debarked and walked across the street. "We need discreet transportation," Eve said.

Hannah pointed out a plumbing repair truck parked in front of a large apartment complex. "No one would look for us in there."

Eve spoke Taiwanese to the driver. The small man shook his head in refusal. He changed his mind after Gertrude handed him a large roll of currency.

Mabel opened the back of the truck, and the heavy smell of raw sewage wafted out. Princess Sela stepped back and crossed her arms. "I'm not riding in there."

"Which is why this is the best choice," Eve explained.

"There are some things princesses don't do."

Eve stepped closer to Sela. "I'm exhausted, but Mabel can make you get in there."

"You wouldn't dare," the princess sneered.

Mabel circled behind the princess, and Eve smiled. "Try me."

With a disgusted sigh, Sela climbed into the back of the truck. She hovered in place, and Hannah stood on one foot, refusing to allow the unprotected foot to touch the putrefying van floor.

In the back of the truck, Eve dropped her illusion and nearly collapsed. She caught herself and hung on to the PVC pipes along the side wall. There was one seat, but it was a broken toilet that reeked.

Nearly gagging from the odor, Sela asked, "Was this part of the plan?"

"Has anyone heard the princess say thank you?" Eve snapped.

Sela narrowed her eyes at Eve. "You are the old lady who started this whole mess. Why should I thank you?"

"Since you don't consider kidnapping a crime, we could have left you where you were. We did not have to rescue you. We chose to. If you're a princess, then act like one."

Sela began to glow.

"I can turn her over my knee if you want," Mabel suggested.

Eve looked at Sela and raised an eyebrow. Sela remained silent for a moment, then her glow diminished. "Please forgive me. My manners seem to have deserted me during my incarceration. I humbly thank you all for the efforts you have taken to rescue me. I apologize for being rude."

"You're welcome," Eve replied and turned to the greasy window.

The plumbing van stopped in the service area of the smaller Tao Yuan airport. Five smelly plumbers exited from the rear and headed toward the terminal. People veered away from the smell, clearing a path to the maintenance department.

Mabel drove an airport transit vehicle toward Eve's pearly white plane idling on the tarmac. Mary Ruth met them at the hatch and welcomed everyone aboard. As Sela reached the landing, she paused. "You are the other old lady who entered my home in Mexico."

Mary Ruth smiled. "I am Sister Mary Ruth, and you are still much older than me."

"So, Cain's manna really works."

Mary Ruth nodded and directed Sela to take a seat. As she escorted Eve to her customary chair, she asked, "I take it all went well?"

"No," Eve replied. "There were a few problems after Cain made an appearance. I'm exhausted and am anxious to get in the air."

"Getting in the air might be more difficult than we originally expected."

"What has he done?"

"Twenty minutes ago, Taiwan declared a state of emergency. All air traffic is temporarily suspended."

"Cain is going to make this difficult. We're going to have to use every resource we have to make it back home."

"We can block their radar," Mary Ruth suggested. "But with the military on high alert, the people in the control tower will see and hear us take off. Now that I can create illusions, I can stay behind."

"Absolutely not," Eve said. "I need you with me." By their facial expressions, Hannah assessed that Eve and Mary Ruth continued their conversation mentally. Eve pressed a button on the arm of her chair and spoke. "Captain Bob?"

"Yes, ma'am."

"I trust Mary Ruth has updated you?"

"Yes, ma'am. I barely took off from Taipei before they closed the airport."

"Prepare to fly to international waters. Once you're out of detection range, turn on the stealth and change the transponder registry to one originating from Singapore. What's the fastest route back to England?"

"Crossing the heart of China."

"That's not an option. Have you had any interesting visions lately?" Eve asked.

"More than usual," Captain Bob replied. "I was going to share them with you as soon as you made yourself comfortable."

"I'm as comfortable as I will be for a while."

"My first child will be born in two years," Captain Bob said.

"I didn't know you were dating someone."

"I'm not."

"Interesting. Did you have any visions pertaining to our immediate future?"

"Just a moment ago. Black planes will attack us in midair. I saw a missile strike our left wing."

Chapter Forty-Four

Silence reigned in the plane for a few awkward seconds until Princess Sela spoke. "If he is a precognitator, you should heed his warning."

"I always heed his warnings," Eve replied. "But precognition isn't an exact science. Knowing what the future holds allows us to change our course of action, so the vision may become invalid. We will avoid flying where we can easily be shot."

"And we should keep an eye out for Captain Bob's future wife," Hannah interjected with a touch of humor she didn't feel.

Gertrude handed Hannah her spare pair of shoes.

"How are you going to get this big, noisy plane in the air without alerting the military?" Sela asked, keeping her voice calm.

"I'm not sure," Eve confessed. "I'm not used to getting caught." She pressed a button and spoke to Captain Bob. "You'll need to turn on the stealth before we take off."

"Ma'am, when we turn on the stealth, our own radar will be useless. I strongly advise against this. Another plane could be approaching the runway. I would also not know if someone shoots a missile at us."

"The airport is closed right now, so there should not be any planes approaching. We must remain undetectable for as long as possible. Any military fighter jet can fly at twice our speed. But if they can't find us, they can't shoot a missile at us."

"We won't show up on radar, but we'll still be visible to the naked eye and satellites. I'll have to adjust our course continuously to stay within the clouds."

"Asia is Cain's domain. We won't be able to enter Chinese airspace," Eve advised. "We'll have to take a northern route. Fly a hundred miles out from the Pacific coast. Return us to the continent above North Korea, and then cross Russia."

"Flying low will be dangerous and difficult. It will also increase our fuel consumption, so we'll have to make at least one stop," Captain Bob explained with enough anxiety to cause his Texas accent to thicken.

"I have every confidence you'll get us home."

"Yes, ma'am."

"Cain would not expect us to go south," Sela interjected. "We have a secret base in Fiji. My people can hide you until it is safe to return to your home."

Eve frowned. "There was a volcanic eruption there two days ago. That base is closed."

Sela looked stunned. "Well, if you're heading north, you can stop at Tokachi, Japan, and drop me off."

"Once you're off this plane, Cain will not hesitate to blow us out of the sky. Besides, there was a volcanic eruption at Tokachi two days ago also. Your people overreacted when they decided not to trust me. They've closed all of your bases."

Sela turned pale. "Land anywhere, and Lotan will pick me up."

Eve stood, moved across the aisle, and bent over Princess Sela's chair, placing her hands on the armrests. Eve's face was only inches from Sela's, and she spoke with iron control. "My name is Eve. I am six thousand years old, and I outrank you."

Sela's jaw dropped open, and her glow diminished to nearly nothing. "That's not possible."

"Anything is possible in God's universe," Eve responded.

"Then, Cain is your son," Sela spoke with disgust.

"And he intends to kill me. Does that make you happy?"

"Of course not," Sela objected.

Eve stood. "I do not need your help or your advice or your talent. I do not even need your conscious. If you interfere in any way, you will go back to sleep. Do I make myself clear?"

"Perfectly," Sela replied.

Eve met the eyes of each person in the cabin. "We need to figure out how to get in the air without anyone noticing. I'm sure Cain will have inspectors at every airport in the next fifteen minutes, reporting on every plane present. First we have to cut communications."

"I can cut the landlines," Mabel suggested. "And if I can get my signal scrambler close to the cell tower, I can block all cell phones."

"We don't need to do that," Hannah interjected. "There's a swamp by the runway. I bet it's full of birds."

Five minutes later, Mabel returned from attaching sound suppressors to the engines. The small devices wouldn't last long, but they needed the engines silent for only a few minutes.

Eve stood in the open doorway of the plane with a rope tied around her waist, staring at the swamp. Mabel secured the rope to the cockpit door and a chair then took her seat. Hannah looked out the window. Thousands of birds rose from the swamp and headed toward the plane and control tower.

The plane began accelerating. "Keep the birds out of my engines," Captain Bob said over the speaker.

So many birds came into view that Hannah could no longer see the control tower. It felt odd to move down the runway at breakneck speed while the engines remained silent, but the wind flowing in the open door was intense.

After ten minutes of being in the air without a military challenge, Hannah felt the tension drain from her body. A few minutes later, the sound dampeners ran out of power and the muffled roar of the engines returned. Hannah realized she had barely slept in two days.

Eve rose, told Mary Ruth to keep an eye on the princess, asked Gertrude to track down her old friend, General Kerchenko, and motioned for Hannah to follow her to the sleeping quarters. As the airplane skimmed the surface of the Pacific Ocean, Hannah drifted off to sleep.

Hannah woke when the wheels of the plane made contact with the pavement. Eve raised the shutter on the window, and Hannah looked upon a stark white world. "Where are we?"

"I don't know," Eve replied.

Hannah followed Eve, rocking and swaying along the way as the plane slid to a stop near a small snow-covered airport terminal.

"Where are we?" Eve asked Mary Ruth as she looked out the window.

"Magadan, Russia, on the Okhotsk Sea. Captain Bob believes this is a safe place to stop. There is very little air service to Magadan in the wintertime, which lasts six months."

A fuel truck refilled the tanks. Captain Bob handed the parka-clad truck driver a large amount of cash.

"Captain Bob had to turn off the stealth before approaching Magadan," Gertrude informed Eve.

"Anything else?"

"We made the news." Gertrude turned her monitor so everyone could see. She replayed the coverage from Fox News. The story led with a few snapshots taken during the construction of Taipei 101 and led to the question of how much skyscrapers affected localized weather patterns. The reporter called the small whirlwind a "sirocco." A sand-colored mini-tornado drifted off the top of Taipei 101, descended rapidly, then moved laterally to stop on top of the Grand Hyatt. From another angle, a video camera tracked the same whirlwind but shifted and followed a black shoe until it struck the street below. Hannah felt the blood rush to her cheeks.

A brief interview followed with two of the people who worked at the Grand Hyatt helipad. The only words Hannah could understand were "Mary Poppins." The newscaster explained what the people were saying, and along with her cohost, traded a few comments about pranks.

"That could have been worse," Eve commented. "Was there any news concerning Eden Pharmaceuticals?"

"They're claiming to be the victim of corporate espionage."

Everyone huddled under blankets until the captain restarted the engines. He took the plane to a higher altitude, and Eve instructed him to leave the stealth off for a short while. Eve asked Gertrude if she had tracked down General Kerchenko.

"Yes," Gertrude replied. "I have his phone number and private email address, used only by his mistress."

"Excellent."

"Are you sure you want him?" Mary Ruth objected. "He is not your old friend and he holds a grudge."

"Surely not after twenty years," Eve responded. "He spun the blame on someone else and was promoted two years later. Besides, he's the only military officer with enough power to aid us who also happens to be a patron of the Russian Museum of History."

Eve placed the call using the speakerphone. She spoke fluent Russian to a secretary and waited for the general to answer. When he did, his speech was deep, angry, heavily accented English. "Mother Evelyn?"

"It's pleasant to hear your voice again, comrade," Eve said.

"I vish I could say zee same," General Kerchenko replied. "Vhy are you not dead yet?"

"Come now. This is a new age. We're not adversaries anymore."

"Vat do you vant?" The general asked.

Eve clicked a button on her computer. "I would like to give you a present."

The general laughed. "Zee last present you gave me exploded in my face."

Eve chuckled. "If you'll check your email, I sent you a picture of an artifact I'm sure you would love to donate to your favorite museum."

There was a pause on the line. "Zere is nothing in my email."

"Check your other account, the one your wife doesn't know about."

"I really hate you," the general muttered in Russian, and the sounds of people leaving came through the phone. A minute passed, and then he said, "Is zat vat I zink it is?"

"Yes, comrade. That is the legendary cup of Rasputin."

"No. Zee cup was lost in zee river when he drowned under zee ice."

"I have kept it well preserved. Rasputin's blood is still on the cup. You can analyze it, but I assure you, it's authentic."

After another long pause, the general asked again, "Vat do you vant?"

"My plane entered Russian airspace a short while ago at Magadan. A ruthless individual who intends to shoot me down is pursuing me. I need an escort across your territory."

The general cleared his throat. "Have you been in Taiwan rezently?"

Eve's reply held a touch of annoyance. "I see you're still in the espionage game."

The general let out a guttural, harsh laugh. "Here is zee deal. I get zee cup of Rasputin and a zample of zee drug you stole from Eden Pharmzeuticles."

Eve sighed. "It's a deal. But you'll want to keep this sample secret. It will take ten years off your life."

The general laughed. "My mistress vill be pleased."

"You can expect delivery in seven days." Eve ended the call.

"We must leave the stealth off so our escort can find us, but that will make it easier for Cain to find us too," Gertrude said.

"We're above the clouds," Mary Ruth stated. "Cain has probably already found us."

"Which is why I want an escort," Eve said. Assuming we'll make it across Russia, we still need an escort across Europe. Who do you think would want Hitler's atomic bomb, the Germans or the French?"

"The Germans," Mary Ruth replied.

"Then start digging. We need to find the right German to talk to. I've wanted to get rid of that ugly monstrosity for a long time."

Hannah used the workstation beside Gertrude to cross-reference high-ranking military officers who were also patrons of the various World War II museums in Germany. Eve worked on something else across the aisle, while Mary Ruth and Mabel kept a watchful eye on Princess Sela.

Gertrude presented two options to Eve. She made her choice and placed a call speaking German. Eve's satisfied look indicated that they would have a military escort across Europe.

Everyone returned to the passenger compartment to enjoy the meal Mabel had prepared. Hannah raised the window shade and saw the aurora borealis. "It's beautiful," she said. The atmosphere seemed alive as sheets of red light traveled in rapid waves as far as she could see. Pink, yellow, and green occasionally flowed along the strands.

"That's not a naturally occurring borealis," Sela stated.

"What's wrong?" Hannah asked.

"It's the wrong color and much too bright," Sela replied.

Eve didn't seem to take the princess's concern seriously. "Red auroras are uncommon but do happen occasionally. It's really nothing to worry about."

Sela's skin glowed bright. "I have worked with Lotan, the solar weatherman, for several years. Red only occurs in the extremely thin oxygen two hundred miles above us, not ten miles from the surface."

"Why does this make you angry?" Mabel asked.

"Because someone seeded your atmosphere with ferric oxide."

"There was a major solar flare two days ago," Mary Ruth suggested. "Perhaps ferric oxide was carried by the solar wind. Or perhaps our planet is passing through a stellar cloud."

"Ferric oxide is a manufactured chemical. This is not a natural occurrence," Sela stated.

"I know why you're so upset." Eve spoke in an intense low tone. "You were expecting your people to track you and make a midair extraction. But since every camera in the northern latitudes will be pointing toward the sky, they can't because your spacecrafts become visible in an energized atmosphere."

"The thought had occurred to me. I am a princess of the Eloshin. My people will break laws to get me back. If they know you are trying to rescue me, they would track your movements."

"And our lives would be forfeited," Eve stated bitterly.

Sela's eyes flashed. "I don't want your deaths on my conscience. I would not abandon you unless we could provide you with a robotic simulacrum of myself. The robot would accompany you until your safety was secure."

"I appreciate your honesty and forethought."

"Unfortunately, that option has been taken away from us," Sela replied sadly.

Hannah remained silent during the interesting conversation. A jigsaw puzzle formed in her mind. One of its pieces had "seed" written on it.

"May I see your hand?" Sela asked Eve.

"I don't wish to place you in an awkward position with your people by asking you to heal me."

"Please," Sela said quietly. "I am a healer. I cannot just sit here while you bleed. Besides, I serve God first and my government second."

Eve stretched out her arm and allowed the princess to place her hands around her wound. Sela's hands glowed. Eve sighed. "Thank you."

"May I ask you a question?" Hannah asked Sela.

"Yes, but I may be constrained from answering."

"What's your world like?"

Sela smiled, and her face glowed. "That I can answer. We have mountains, rivers, and thousands of lakes, but no oceans. My world is actually a moon and revolves around a gas giant similar to Jupiter. When we move behind the giant, it gets very dark."

"Is that why you glow?"

"Yes."

"You told Cain you have three husbands? Is that true?"

"Our nights are very long." Sela laughed. "Eloshin men are handsome and loving but not too bright. Our Adam sinned, but our Eve did not. God stripped men of their talents and some intelligence and gave it to the women. Men outnumber women three to one, but all leadership falls to the women."

"That sounds nice."

"I think I'm going to take a nap now before you ask a question I cannot answer," Sela said as she rose from her seat.

"Mabel snores," Hannah warned.

Captain Bob's voice screamed through the speaker, "Incoming!"

Hannah's stomach flipped over as the plane banked hard and dove down. She looked out the window and saw a long, narrow missile strike the left wing of the plane.

Chapter Forty-Five

The plane shuddered, and Hannah heard a loud clang as metal struck metal. She didn't understand why she was still alive. Captain Bob had aimed the plane toward the ground.

"Report!" Eve commanded from her seat.

The captain spoke with haste. "Two short bogies at seven and nine alpha plus three thousand."

"Turn the stealth on so they can't get a missile lock. Pull up!" Eve's computer screen flashed warnings. Hannah heard beeps and buzzes from the open microphone in the cockpit.

Eve spoke into the microphone embedded in her computer. "I have control of stealth, defenses, and communication. Try to avoid any more midair contacts."

"Acknowledged," Captain Bob replied. "I need radar."

"Stealth is off for thirty seconds in five," Eve replied.

"Hello, Mother," Cain's mellow voice echoed through the cabin. The air felt as if an arctic chill were passing through. "That was a warning shot across your bow."

"You hit my bow!"

"Lucky for you my missile was not armed. If you land now, there will be no need to damage your plane further."

"Not a chance," Eve stated flatly.

"Then I will blow you out of the sky."

"You wouldn't want to kill your beautiful bride before you have consummated your relationship, would you?"

"How do I know she's still with you?"

"You are a pig," Princess Sela exclaimed.

After a pause, Cain said, "That will do."

"Stealth is on," Eve informed the captain. The plane accelerated straight up into the sky. Low-level static emanated from the cockpit. A half minute later, the static cleared and Eve spoke again. "I don't think she wants to return to your loving embrace, Cain."

"Land the plane now, and I will allow you to survive."

Eve stared into Gertrude's eyes. Gertrude opened several programs on her computer. Hannah nearly jumped when Gertrude touched her arm. *"We need two computers. Open the program titled 'Signal Analyzer.' I will divide the antennas on each wing between us and route only the signal from the left wing to you. We need to triangulate Cain's position."*

Hannah opened the program and waited for Gertrude to send her the information. Mary Ruth stared intently out the window. "There is too much metal, and they are traveling too fast for me to interfere."

"I don't think illusion or coercion is an option," Eve remarked as she typed commands into her computer.

Hannah looked into the workroom and saw Mabel talking on her phone. Sela sat very still, glowing a slight shade of green.

Eve held her fingers poised over her keyboard. "It seems we are at an impasse. You can't blow me out of the sky, or you will kill the very prize you seek. I can't land. You will kill me and all my friends. You didn't plan this attack very well, did you?"

Cain laughed. "On the contrary. I came prepared to force you to land. Captain Bob?"

"I am here," Captain Bob replied calmly.

"How good are you at playing dodgeball?"

The plane banked sharply to the left. Cain's laughter didn't mask the sound of a targeting computer attempting to lock on to a moving target. The first few beeps were slow, but they quickly accelerated. When the computer locked on, the beeping became one long and frightful tone.

Nearly four seconds passed before Eve pressed a button on her computer and shouted, "Bank right!"

As soon as she pressed the button, the tone-lock stopped, as did Cain's laughter. The next maneuver shoved Hannah against the left side of her seat. She felt an odd vibration beneath her feet and heard a roar as the captain deployed the landing gear. Hannah waited for the expected clang of another unarmed missile strike.

The landing gear retracted, and the plane leveled off. Cain's voice returned. "Nice move, Mother. Tell me, how many decoys did you manage to pack?"

"How many missiles did you bring?"

"I'm betting I brought more missiles than you brought decoys. I have the advantage since all I have to do is damage one of your engines. Of course, if I run out of missiles, I can use bullets. I brought lots of bullets."

Eve performed the same dodge, released the decoy, and turned on the stealth two more times before speaking to Gertrude. "We can't keep this up. Have you located Cain's transmission?"

"We just did," Gertrude replied. "He's two hundred miles to the south in his personal jet, merging toward us."

"How typical of him to lead from the rear," Eve said. "If two planes are approaching each other at six hundred sixty miles per hour—"

"Nine minutes." Hannah calculated the math quicker than Eve could type.

"Bob," Eve commanded, "change course fifty-four degrees to the south, and rise to thirty thousand feet. Maintain maximum speed."

The plane responded. Twice more, the aircraft made abrupt maneuvers. Every time a missile came close, Cain's semihysterical laughter blared through the speakers.

Hannah tucked her head between her shoulders as if to add protection from the missile that ricocheted off the top of the plane. She listened for a hiss of air, which would mean the hull had been pierced.

"Bob, I'm sending you a new course," Eve commanded. She spoke to the sisters and Sela. "That was our last decoy. Pray that Cain remembers the lessons his brother taught him."

Hannah didn't understand what Eve referred to but said a silent prayer anyway.

Eve opened the channel. "Cain?" she said, her voice calm and pleasant.

"Yes, Mother."

"There have been several times over the past few centuries that I could have easily taken your life."

"Oh, please, Mother," Cain sneered. "You can't possibly believe that I owe you one."

"Do you know why I have let you live?"

Hannah heard Cain breathing heavily. He probably hadn't expected to have a heart-to-heart chat with his mother while shooting missiles at her. "I suppose it's because you're afraid of that sevenfold curse your God placed on me."

"That's right," Eve said as if speaking to a small child. "However, if you and I were to die at precisely the same time, then that curse wouldn't matter much, would it?"

After a long moment of silence, Cain replied, "What are you doing, Mother?"

"I'm tired of playing dodgeball. How about a game of chicken? Ram him, Bob!"

The captain banked sharply to the left. Through the window, Hannah saw Cain's coal-black plane on a course that would intersect with their own in less than a minute.

Sela looked pale and sick. She spoke to Eve in a dry voice. "You do realize suicide is wrong, don't you?"

"I have no intention of dying today," Eve said with a smile. "Neither does Cain. He always lost the game of chicken to his brother, Abel." Eve closed her eyes and concentrated. "Captain Bob, when Cain takes the high ground, maneuver underneath him as close as you can."

Eve opened her eyes. "When I turn the stealth off again, the communication line will automatically open. If we're going to survive this, I need all of you to scream as if we are about to die." She took a deep breath. "One, two, three!"

Hannah screamed along with everyone else. She looked out her window and saw Cain's plane less than ten feet away. The jets shook as the wind streams surrounding them collided. Captain Bob slipped right underneath Cain. The black wings loomed to either side of the windows right above their own. Hannah screamed again.

Captain Bob maintained his position ten feet below. Cain banked left. So did Bob. He tried several other maneuvers, but Captain Bob was better than Cain's pilot, and with his precognition could see what was about to happen. Cain could not make sudden maneuvers, or their wings would touch. Cain was trapped. Two fighter jets flew parallel, seemingly doing a mating dance in the sky.

Cain's voice returned to the speaker. "Captain Bob, how much is my mother paying you?"

"Quite a bit."

"How would you like to triple your salary?"

"Not interested."

Cain sighed. "You can't keep this up for long, Mother. One of us will make a mistake, or we will cross some turbulence."

"Then we'll all die."

"Then taste this!"

Hannah felt the plane lurch, and everything went silent. The sound of the engines was gone. The black plane shot away as the white plane lost speed and altitude. Hannah pressed against her seatbelt as the nose of the plane dove toward the ground.

"What happened?" Eve demanded.

Captain Bob sounded strained. "He opened his fuel valve and sprayed us with jet fuel. I had to shut off the engines, or they would've caught fire."

Eve looked at Mary Ruth and shrugged. "I can't see down every path."

"Jet fuel evaporates almost instantly," the captain explained as the plane began to spin. "Five more seconds, and I can restart."

Five seconds! Hannah prayed. She heard the engine sputter and stall as if it were flooded with gas. Hannah watched the ground loom closer. About the time she could distinguish individual pine trees that would soon become part of her funeral pyre, the engines came to life. They were so close to the ground, she saw snow fall from the tall conifers as they swooped past.

For several heartbeats, Hannah could not breathe. She started to black out. Relief finally came, but it was short-lived. The two fighter jets returned and lined up behind them. Captain Bob rocketed skyward for maneuverability room.

Hannah lurched forward as Captain Bob slowed the plane to a crawl. The fighter shot missiles several times, but with the stealth on, they could not lock on the target. The captain alternated speeding up and slowing down as he turned left and right, making an accurate shot by the fighter jets difficult. However, without decoys, eventually one of the missiles would do enough damage to make them land, if it didn't kill them.

Captain Bob's voice came over the speaker, sounding frustrated. "We have a problem."

No kidding, Hannah thought.

"What is it?" Eve asked.

"Two more fighter jets are heading toward us from the west."

"How close?" Eve sat up straight and closed her eyes.

"Two minutes."

"Fly directly toward them!" Eve shouted. "I'm turning off the stealth. Level the plane, and let the two fighters behind us take their shot."

"You're kidding?"

"Trust me," Eve replied. "In ninety seconds, slow to minimum speed and pivot ninety degrees."

"You're the boss."

Hannah counted the seconds in her head. She leaned against the side of her chair as Captain Bob pivoted the plane, pointing one wing toward the ground.

"I've turned the stealth back on," Eve said.

Hannah saw one missile streak past her window as the plane decelerated. When the missiles lost the lock on the plane, they streaked past, targeting the two new jets approaching from the opposite direction. The captain leveled the plane back, and the twin explosions lit the sky.

"They have armed their missiles," Sela exclaimed. "Cain has tired of this game and plans to kill us all!"

"I don't think so," Eve replied with a smile of excitement.

She turned the stealth off, and the speaker came to life. A male voice spoke Russian then English. "Aircraft of the Taliban, you are trespassing in Russian airspace and have fired upon us without provocation. You will land immediately or be destroyed."

The message repeated in what sounded like Arabic. Cain's two fighters streaked southward. The two Russian fighters pursued immediately. A black parachute opened as one of Cain's jets broke in half and burst into flames. The two Russian jets pursued the last invader.

Eve turned the stealth back off. Cain's growl of frustration carried through the speakers. Eve chuckled. "What's the matter, son? Disappointed? Angry? Frustrated? Are you upset that you're now associated with the Taliban? I wonder if this will make the six o'clock news. Perhaps I should send your picture to CNN."

"You win round one, Mother," Cain replied, sounding like he spoke between gritted teeth.

"I believe this was round two. Round one was in Taiwan."

"Well, round three will be a knockout."

Chapter Forty-Six

Hannah breathed a sigh of relief. Her hips felt bruised, and her neck hurt.

Eve and Gertrude worked on their computers. Gertrude calculated the amount of fuel used during their recent maneuvers. Eve finished typing and called the captain.

"Thank you for keeping us safe. Your skill is unparalleled."

"It was my pleasure, ma'am."

"When we find your bride, I'll buy you a nice house in the country."

"That's very generous, Mother Evelyn, but unnecessary."

Eve pursed her lips. "You may change your mind once you see where I intend to land. Our left wing is dented, and there's a major crease along the top of the passenger cabin. We're not losing any air or fuel, but I think another dogfight would cause it to rupture."

"I've already compensated for the drag on our left wing, and I'll try to avoid any more dogfights. I'm going to lower our altitude in case we experience decompression."

"I think that's wise," Eve replied.

"We'll be on reserve fuel when we reach London," Gertrude said. "Cain will have to stop to refuel since he used his fuel as a weapon. We'll arrive at least an hour before he does."

"God works in mysterious ways," Mary Ruth added with a shrug.

Eve turned off the speaker and looked at Sela. "Are you okay?"

"That was not an experience I wish to repeat, but I'm fine. I have a question though. Why did you continuously goad Cain? It seemed as if you were intentionally making him angry."

"If you goad a human into thinking with their emotions instead of their mind, they will react instead of respond. Most bad decisions are made because they react to a situation instead of taking the time to think about it. An angry man acts like a child."

"And this is good for us?" Sela asked.

"I want Cain angry. I don't want him to think of creative ways to stop us."

Hannah felt her throat constricting and gulped down her fear. "If I were Cain, I would place snipers around every airport within fifty miles of the abbey."

"Which is why we're not landing at an airport." Eve rose from her seat.

"I would also have an army stationed around the abbey," Hannah added as Eve walked past her.

"And where would he get an army on short notice?"

"Ireland?"

Eve stopped walking.

"There are many contributors to the IRA. What are the odds that the most violent chapter paints a red hand on their face?"

Eve locked gazes with Hannah then looked at Mary Ruth. "Evacuate the abbey. Leave only four inside to maintain security."

"Yes, ma'am." Eve turned to proceed to the workroom.

Mary Ruth called the abbey then spoke to Sela. "Gertrude, Mabel and I are going to rest. There is a fourth bunk. You are welcome to join us."

"I may join you in a little while, but right now I don't want to close my eyes."

Hannah knew how the princess felt. Adrenaline and endorphins coursing through her veins made her jumpy. She stretched her back and looked at Sela. "You said that you were going to be in trouble. Why?"

Sela smiled sadly. "The Council of Elders placed your world under surveillance and protection over a thousand years ago. The rules are strict about noninterference."

"Won't they make allowances for extenuating circumstances? After all, you were kidnapped."

"They might for someone like Lotan. But I am royalty and held to a higher standard."

The two Russian jets returned and took up positions on each side of the plane. Although she knew the pilots could not see her, Hannah saluted. "Our escort has returned."

"That makes me feel a little better," Sela acknowledged.

"Can't you pull some strings?" Hannah asked.

"I am the last daughter of my mother, the queen. I will probably have to abdicate my position."

"I'm sorry."

Sela sighed. "I do not mind so much for me, but my daughters will lose their privileges and status. I think I will rest now."

◡

For the first time in nearly a week, Hannah was alone. She checked the news and saw that the Taiwanese stories had already dropped out of the top twenty items of interest. The police search for Karl Bujold, also known as Carla Babb, remained at number twelve. Hannah was disappointed to see that some movie star's newest relationship ranked higher than the search for a child killer.

While checking her email, Hannah noticed two German jets replaced the Russians as escorts, probably somewhere over Europe by now. After a few searches, she opened her Bible. She knew there was a huge difference between memorizing the words and studying them.

In the beginning, God created the heavens and the earth.

As Hannah researched new insights in the first six chapters of Genesis, she developed a new understanding for things she couldn't grasp before. This led to questions. She hoped Eve would supply the answers someday.

Eve walked past Hannah to consult with Captain Bob speaking on the phone to someone about a potato farm. When she returned, she was talking to someone else. Hannah listened to the one-sided conversation.

"Yes, Sir Alfred, the Bentley," Eve stated. "I know you have newer and nicer limousines, but I prefer the Bentley. The others are too long."

After a pause, Eve replied, "Yes. I'll be escorting an important dignitary. Did you add rear passenger airbags in the recent upgrade? Good. No, it isn't the Pope, and no, you don't need to call the police for an escort."

After another pause, Eve looked annoyed. "Sir Alfred, my abbey has been a client of the Bank of England for longer than you've been alive. I know you would not like to see our funds in the care of another institution, so do not question my request any further. Sister Elizabeth will be there in a short while to get the keys." Eve sighed and rolled her eyes. "I know you didn't mean to offend me. Goodbye.

"Bankers," Eve stated as she hung up the phone. "They are almost as bad as lawyers."

Hannah sat up straighter as the others returned to their seats. Captain Bob walked through to ensure all compartments were closed and tray tables put away. He stopped beside Eve. "This plane will never fly again."

"Then I'll buy you a better one."

Captain Bob returned to the cockpit.

The plane tilted forward, preparing for descent. Hannah looked at Eve. "Can you tell us what's going on?"

Eve smiled and spoke with a sweet tone. "I don't want to frighten you."

Hannah's pulse sped up. "I'm already frightened."

"Don't worry, dear. Captain Bob is the best pilot in the world. We need to make this look good so he doesn't lose his license."

"Make what look good?"

"Why don't you explain to Princess Sela how to assume the crash position."

Alarm bells rang in Hannah's head. She wondered what Eve planned to do, but there was no time to ask. She showed Sela how to tuck her head as close to her knees as possible and cover it with her hands. Everyone looked frightened except Eve and Mary Ruth.

Hannah looked out the window and saw the familiar lights of London. Judging by the minimal amount of lights in homes and businesses, she assumed the time must be around midnight. Hannah could make out a few landmarks. The Tower of London was a blaze of light, as was Westminster Abbey and Buckingham Palace. The giant Ferris wheel was clearly visible along the Thames River, highlighted in neon blue. Another string of blue lights caught her eye as the plane descended toward the multiple runways of Heathrow Airport.

The cabin was deathly quiet. Hannah held her breath, waiting for Eve to indicate when they should assume the crash position. When Eve remained calm, Hannah allowed herself to breathe. Perhaps Eve and Bob were going to fake a crash at the airport so they could use an ambulance to escape any snipers. She was about to ask when she realized how silent everything was. Too silent. She should be able to hear the wind whipping past the landing gear.

Hannah looked out the window and saw that they were almost on the ground. A fast buzzing alarm sounded from the cockpit as the blue lights came closer. Captain Bob shouted over the screaming alarm, "Tower, our landing gear failed to deploy."

Hannah looked at Eve, who had still not assumed the crash position. With only a few feet to spare and the white lines of the runway whizzing past, Captain Bob gunned the engines and streaked back into the sky. The bruises on both sides of Hannah's hips screamed as the acceleration pressed her firmly back into her chair.

After a few minutes of flying only a few hundred feet above rooftops, the captain shouted again, "Tower, I can't circle around while you prepare a runway! I've been flying on reserve fuel and am sucking fumes."

The cabin lights went out, the hum of the engines stopped, and a video camera dropped from the ceiling with its own light source. Eve assumed the crash position.

Hannah prayed with her eyes open. She looked out the window. They were close to the ground, but she saw only a few lights. They were thirty or more miles out from Heathrow. She shouted to Eve, "Couldn't you have foreseen this?"

Eve looked Hannah in the eye. Hannah screamed. Princess Sela, Gertrude, and even Mabel joined in.

The first touch of the ground felt light but sounded odd. The second touch grabbed the plane with brutal force as the wheels dug in. Hannah doubled over, and the seatbelt cut into her waist. The plane lurched, bounced, vibrated, and rumbled as it plunged down what felt like a boulder farm. Hannah looked out the window. The only lights she saw were the ones attached to the wings. They didn't highlight smooth cement of a runway or even a road. They showed dirt. She blinked twice and saw potatoes. Eve had landed her plane on a potato farm.

Potatoes flew everywhere. At the speed they were traveling, they sounded louder than missiles when they struck the plane. The engines sucked in potatoes and dirt. Massive dents and a gaping hole were visible on the wing. The sound of crashing glass indicated that the windshield must have given in to the tremendous pounding. Hannah prayed for Captain Bob and the copilot, James.

The plane slid to a stop. Eve rose to check on Captain Bob and James. Hannah followed. The cockpit had a layer of dirt and potatoes on the floor, but the crew was relatively uninjured. Mabel opened the door, lowered a ladder, and everyone departed. Eve's cane tapped rhythmically against the metal steps, and she assumed the lead.

Upon reaching the ground, Hannah turned back and looked at the plane, now a dented mess. The few spots not covered with dirt glowed eerily as the red aurora borealis illuminated the sky. The heat of the engines must have cooked the potatoes, for the air smelled like greasy French fries. Hannah looked at the others. Eve looked like an old crone, as did Mary Ruth.

Sister Elizabeth arrived driving a 1972 Bentley. The mud of the potato field clashed with the mirror-polished finish of the black paint, as if the Bentley was too dignified to place its wheels on such humble earth. The chrome bumpers reflected the lights from the plane. Sister Elizabeth got out of the car and conferred with Eve.

"Is the abbey evacuated?" Eve asked.

"Yes, Mother Evelyn," Sister Elizabeth replied. "All have evacuated except the five who remain to maintain security."

"I ordered only four to remain," Eve stated and tapped her cane in the dirt.

"The novice Mykaela refused to leave. We considered forcing her, but she hid and we could not find her."

"We will have words when I return."

When Eve moved to take the driver's seat, Sister Elizabeth looked to Mary Ruth with alarm. "You're not considering driving, are you?"

Mother Evelyn smiled. "I may be old, but I'm not dead yet."

Elizabeth appealed to Mary Ruth. "I thought you refused to ever ride with her again."

"I'm making an exception this time."

Hannah offered to sit in the back, but with a discreet shake of her head, Mabel directed her to the front. Hannah understood when Mabel and Gertrude sandwiched Princess Sela between them. In the front, Mary Ruth sat in the middle and Hannah took the passenger seat.

Two items waited for each of them on the burgundy velour seats. Hannah donned a Kevlar vest but didn't wish to put on the iron welder's helmet, knowing it would be difficult to see through the small eye slot. She felt relieved when Eve instructed everyone to keep the helmets close at hand.

"That was an inventive landing," Mary Ruth said as Eve shut her door.

"Thank you." Eve drove slowly across the uneven farmland until she reached a paved road. "It was also expensive. Cain may have already landed by now. He'll be rushing to get to the abbey before we do, but I've arranged a little traffic snarl for him. He'll be late, but some of his forces at the airport will be able to join those already in place at the abbey."

"Do you think they'll try to break in?" Mary Ruth asked.

"Not without Cain present." Eve increased her speed. "Gertrude, keep your contact with the abbey security to a minimum, as we don't want any of Cain's hackers to discover a link is open. The abbey is at defense level five. At the last moment, you'll need to lower the defense to level three and use the emergency releases on the drawbridge. We're only ten miles away from the abbey. Things may get rough, so be prepared."

Hannah figured they must be traveling over a hundred miles an hour down the dark and winding county road. Two headlights came to life behind the car and drew her attention to the side mirror. Eve slowed down for a series of nasty curves, and the headlights from behind moved closer. "I think we have company."

"Keep an eye on them," Eve requested. "I need to concentrate on what lies ahead."

Hannah focused on the headlights. When the lights spread farther apart, she said, "Two motorcycles are approaching fast." They took the curves much faster than the Bentley, so they gained even more ground.

A few feet behind the rear bumper, the motorcycles split and drove to either side of the car. Hannah looked out the window and peered down the wrong end of a gun barrel. A flash of fire left the tip of the pistol.

Chapter Forty-Seven

A firecrackerlike sound exploded against Hannah's window. She screamed then realized if she were dead, she probably couldn't scream. A motorcyclist peered inside, seeing Hannah smiling through the Bentley's bulletproof glass.

The motorcyclist raised his pistol again to fire at the window, but Eve bumped him with the side of the Bentley. He dropped his gun and fought to keep control of his bike. As he dropped behind the car, another motorcyclist shot forward and swerved in front of the Bentley.

The gunman pointed his semiautomatic behind him. Hannah again heard firecrackers and chips of glass flew from the windshield. Hannah cringed, but Eve didn't even flinch. The next salvo of bullets created star-shaped white spots about two inches across. There was no such thing as bulletproof glass, only bullet-resistant glass. Hannah wondered how many hits the windshield could take before a bullet made its way through its multiple layers of glass and polyvinyl plastic.

"Mary Ruth," Eve said, "that motorcycle is in my way."

The motorcyclist stole glances behind him, trying to aim his gun while maneuvering the twisting curves. Eve swerved around the next one. The driver faced forward as a wall of lights appeared before him. A Mack truck blew its horn as it approached from the other direction. The motorcyclist swerved out of the way, flew over a gully, and slid across freshly plowed dirt.

The truck continued and was only a second from crashing into the Bentley. Hannah braced herself against the dash. The truck faded from existence as Eve drove through Mary Ruth's illusion.

The first motorcyclist returned and shot more bullets at Hannah's window with a semiautomatic. More stars appeared on her window. This time when Eve bumped into him, he lost control and landed in a ditch.

"A hollow illusion may not work against snipers, especially if they're wearing metal helmets." Eve slowed down. Farms gave way to residential neighborhoods on the outskirts of town.

"If the illusion has some substance, they will have less of a reason to disbelieve," Mary Ruth said.

"What are you thinking?" Eve asked.

Mary Ruth turned to Sela. "I know the Mother said she did not need your help. Will you do it anyway?"

"I would be happy to," the princess replied, "but I'm not allowed to interfere."

"Is there not an exception for minor action when your life is at stake?" Mary Ruth asked.

"It would have to be very minor, but since several lives are at stake I will try. What did you have in mind?"

"You can lift two thousand pounds. How much can you push?"

Eve skidded to a stop at a used car lot. She scanned their immediate surroundings while looking into the future. Gertrude exited the car before it came to a complete stop and ran to the driver's side door of an older-model Rambler. The metal along the undercarriage was eaten through by rust. The price on the car was only four hundred pounds. Hannah doubted the engine ran, but the tires were inflated.

The driver's window was missing. A minute later, the engine turned over, and with a little extra gas, sputtered to life. A cloud of black smoke exited the tailpipe. Gertrude moved the transmission into drive, but the car just sat there.

Gertrude got out of it and picked up a big rock. She placed it against the gas pedal, and the car began to move. Sela concentrated then frowned. "There is too much metal in that machine," she said with exasperation.

"Don't worry about the metal," Mary Ruth said. "Just move the rubber wheels. The steering wheel is coated with a hard plastic, so it should be easy. Can you grasp it with your mind through the glass?"

"I think so," Sela replied, sounding tense. "I have not trained for this."

"You did just fine with the bullets," Eve complimented.

"Every transmuter and telekinetic who travels to Earth is trained to defend against bullets. Bullets are the favorite weapon on most Nephilim worlds."

The Rambler blew smelly black smoke in front of the Bentley as it increased speed to about thirty miles per hour. As they entered the warehouse district, Eve scanned the tops of the buildings with three or four stories. "This will be our first gauntlet," she mumbled.

Hannah saw the black Bentley in front of them. She knew it was an illusion, but since she was not wearing metal around her head, she could not discern the white Rambler beneath the illusion. She looked down the hood of the Bentley, but instead of seeing shiny black she saw rusted white. What anyone else would see was a shiny black Bentley followed by a rusty white Rambler.

Seeing Eve's gaze sharpen, Hannah looked to the tall warehouses built to the edge of the sidewalks on both sides of the street. She had traveled this road a few times but had never noticed that gargoyles lined the tops of the buildings. The gargoyles were spaced evenly, twenty feet apart, and were backlit by rooftop lights and the faintly glowing red sky. One gargoyle moved. It was holding a gun. Gunfire echoed through the canyon of buildings. Not a single bullet pinged against their car as it slowed, but the Bentley in front of them was taking a beating. Hannah saw one tire explode in a puff of dirt and dust. Black smoke poured from the back of the car as the trunk ignited. She could not see any flames but assumed that Mary Ruth and Eve hid the fire with illusion. The Rambler made it to the end of the block before Sela gasped in frustration. "All the tires have been deflated, and the engine is dead. I can't push it anymore."

"Let it go." Eve swerved around the black Bentley parked in the middle of the road, maintaining the illusion of the white-and-rust Rambler. Still no bullets stung the Bentley disguised as a Rambler.

They passed the city park and entered the shopping district. There were almost no other vehicles. Hannah caught their reflection as they passed a large storefront window and would have sworn she was riding in a produce delivery truck.

"Here we go again," Eve said.

The shopping and financial districts blended along the main road, making a six-block stretch of buildings, each four to eight stories tall. In the darkness, silhouetted by an occasional flash of the red aurora borealis, the gargoyles looked more sinister. Each one sported a pair of glowing green eyes.

Eve let her latest illusion drop. "There will be no more illusions tonight."

Another set of bullets slammed into the windshield. They were not the small, rapid bullets of a semiautomatic machine gun, but large bullets from high-caliber rifles. Each one left a snowflake of broken glass in the windshield the size of a baseball. A minute later, the windshield was completely frosted. Eve drove using only her memory and precog talent.

Hannah's side windows looked like a thick sheet of crushed ice. She figured Cain's mercenaries had been given instructions about where to shoot since there was not a single chip out of the rear windows.

After hundreds of firecracker sounds pounded the Bentley, Hannah jumped when Eve screamed, "Helmets!"

Hannah put on the welder's helmet. Eve was the only person not wearing one. Without turning her head or opening her eyes, she shouted, "Hannah, raise your chin three inches."

Hannah did as instructed. A second later, a bullet pierced the poly-vinyl plastic and smashed into her helmet. With her head braced against the headrest, the impact pushed the helmet deeper into the support. Had her chin been three inches lower, the bullet would have flown right through the opening for her eyes.

More bullets rang against the roof of the car. Hannah hunched her neck. They were less than a mile from the abbey, but at twenty miles an hour with bullets screaming down, that was a long way. Gertrude let out a yelp when a bullet slammed into the rear window.

Eve shouted, "Cain must have arrived! He is confident that Princess Sela will protect herself."

"Why that arrogant pig!" Sela yelled.

Hannah wondered how she could hear the princess so well until she realized Sela had removed her helmet. Every window in the vehicle blew out with an explosive wave of telekinetic strength. The sounds of the bullets slamming into the car faded as they met a wall of compressed air.

The hood of the Bentley was no longer black but had large gray craters filled with spent bullets. It reminded Hannah of the hailstorms in Tulsa, except hailstones in Tulsa were made of ice.

Eve kept her eyes partially shut. A few minutes later, she slammed on the brakes. "We have a problem."

"What?" Mary Ruth asked.

"Cain has positioned bulldozers at both ends of our street. I can't drive through a bulldozer. Sela can't move one. The moat is on one side of the road and the home for abused women is on the other."

"Our garage is across from the abbey. The front offices with glass windows face our drawbridge," Hannah suggested.

Eve gunned the engine again. "Gertrude?"

"I'm on it."

Eve turned one block early. "Hannah, open the glovebox and turn off the airbags. When we're through the office, turn them back on. Gertrude, it takes six seconds for the drawbridge to fall into place. Release the chains one second before we enter the garage."

Hannah opened the glovebox and pushed the airbags' "off" buttons. She remembered Eve's comment to Sir Alfred from the bank about the stretch limo being too long. "Mother, this car won't fit into the foyer. We won't be able to close the drawbridge with the tail of the car sticking out."

"This car will be two feet shorter in about fifteen seconds," Eve replied.

As they approached the garage, the door was almost open. Eve cut the wheels sharply and gunned the engine. The bottom of the door scraped across the top of the Bentley. Eve slammed the car into the back wall of the garage. The wall, made of sheetrock and wood, exploded in a cloud of dust and splinters as the Bentley plowed through. The next room whizzed by in an instant, and as they crashed through the next wall, Hannah saw her home across the street through the large window of the front office. The drawbridge fell. She turned the airbags back on.

The scraped, dented, and torn Bentley crossed the street so quickly that Hannah only caught a glimpse of the bulldozers blocking the entrance to their street. When Eve hit the drawbridge, she sped up. The Bentley entered the foyer and slammed into the reinforced iron wall at the back of it. Unlike the plaster and wood walls, this one didn't budge.

The airbags exploded, hitting Hannah hard. She had difficulty breathing. The airbag deflated almost as quickly as it inflated. Her ears rang, and stars floated in her vision. Eve climbed out of the car, stumbled to the front of the vehicle, and smiled. From her expression, the Bentley was two feet shorter than it had been fifteen seconds earlier.

Chapter Forty-Eight

Hannah's muscles ached so badly that she nearly fell out of the car when she opened her door. Knowing the others could be in worse shape, she carefully opened the rear passenger door to help Gertrude. Mabel assisted Sela, who looked stunned.

As soon as the drawbridge closed, Sister Julia opened the inner door carrying a fire extinguisher. She sprayed the Bentley down with white powder. Eve headed toward the door. "Gertrude, move us to defense level six. Mabel, check the perimeter. Mary Ruth, assist Sela. Hannah, find Mykaela and bring her to my office."

Gertrude opened her computer on the hood of the car and logged into the security program. Hannah waited with Gertrude to see if she could find Mykaela electronically. While Gertrude reset the defense grid, Hannah asked, "What is defense level six?"

"We've never used the sixth."

"What does it do?" Hannah asked.

"It adds a grid of high-intensity lasers over the courtyard and the Glass Chapel. I don't understand the technology, but it will prevent us from being affected by an electromagnetic pulse, radiation, or toxic gas. It will also keep anyone from getting in through the courtyard. It can turn on lasers to stun anyone entering the garden too."

"Why didn't you use it when the boys attacked?"

"There was no need. It also makes the courtyard glow green."

"Can you find Mykaela?"

"I need to disable the electronic functions of the drawbridge first. It's our most vulnerable spot."

Hannah stood behind Gertrude and watched her work. The screen showed a schematic of the abbey. Hannah saw ten glowing dots representing the people there. Three dots glowed in the foyer, and six moved about in the security center. One dot remained stationary in the courtyard. "Mykaela is in the garden," Gertrude said.

Hannah headed toward the door but noticed that Sister Julia looked pale and was watching Gertrude with wide eyes. "Eve forgot to put her illusion back. I think she's about to go into shock," Hannah whispered.

Gertrude placed an arm around Sister Julia's shoulder. "Are you feeling okay?"

"Mother Evelyn looks so young," she stammered.

"I'll explain everything as soon as you feel better," Gertrude said.

Gertrude looked at Hannah. "Go find Mykaela."

Hannah walked through the halls and entered the garden. A fine mesh of green lines glowed at the top of the courtyard, making the garden seem like it was on another planet. Every plant and flower looked different. Green leaves looked black while the flowers bloomed with abnormal colors.

Hannah saw movement by the fountain. "Mykaela?"

"Hannah?" a timid voice called back.

"Yes. Are you okay?"

"No," Mykaela replied as Hannah approached the fountain. "I need to talk to Mother Evelyn."

Sensing that Mykaela was on the verge of tears, Hannah gently said, "Mother Evelyn is anxious to talk to you too."

"Is she mad?"

"She's not happy."

"I didn't think it was safe for me to leave the abbey."

"Why?"

"Because something is wrong with me," Mykaela cried.

"We have talked about this before. If you don't feel called to be a nun, you shouldn't take the vows. There are many ways to serve God, and wanting to have children is normal."

"My commitment isn't what's wrong."

"Then what's the problem?"

Mykaela stretched out her hand. A small jet of water leaped from the fountain and shot toward her, but it didn't touch her hand. It formed a perfectly round sphere and hovered three inches above her open palm.

Hannah looked into Mykaela's eyes. "You have been given a wonderful gift."

Mykaela looked surprised. The water globe fell apart and drenched her arm. "That's not the reaction I expected."

"Let's just say I've seen stranger things than a floating globe of water in the past week."

"Then you know what's happening to me?" Mykaela asked with hope.

"Yes, but I think it would be best for Mother Evelyn to explain things to you."

"Will you come with me?"

"Of course," Hannah replied.

"I've also started hearing voices, and I'm pretty sure it's what people are thinking."

"Yes, I know," Hannah said.

"Perhaps this isn't the best time to talk to Mother Evelyn."

"I think it's necessary though."

Mykaela gulped. "Let's get a bite to eat first. I'm starved."

Believing Mother Evelyn would be forgiving of the delay, Hannah agreed.

Eve opened her office door and was surprised to see Sister Betty sitting behind her desk. Sister Betty knew the rules and should never have entered Eve's office without permission. Since it was out of character for her, Eve sent her mind to see what she was thinking and was surprised to find a solid mental wall. "Do you realize that you're the first male to ever enter this sanctuary for women, Lotan?"

Sister Betty looked at Eve and spoke with Lotan's voice. "You can still say no human male has entered this place."

"You have violated a quarter century of tradition."

"You entered my house first uninvited."

Eve shifted her cane slightly, preparing to use it if necessary. "So much for your policy of noninterference." She could easily see through another person's illusion, but she could not see through Lotan's. A chill traveled down her spine as she wondered what security he might have compromised. "How did you get in here?"

"We've been walking unnoticed among your people for more than a thousand years," Lotan replied through Sister Betty's mouth. "Holograms are fairly easy, and our technology is vastly superior to yours. Even your pheromone sensors were fooled."

Eve relaxed a little. "Where is the real Sister Betty?"

"She evacuated with the other nuns."

"Did you interact with my people or alter their memories?"

"Just a little," Lotan confessed. "I did not alter any memories, but those that stayed thought I should make supper for you and the rest."

"Sister Betty is the cook."

"I chose her because she is the tallest. I did not know she was the cook. I apologize if supper is not up to your usual standards."

"What did you fix? I hope you haven't poisoned my people."

"On my world, we mostly eat fish. I used fish from tin cans and added pond sauce."

"Probably anchovies," Eve surmised. "What was on the sauce label?"

"Ponds. Fish live in ponds."

"How revolting. That was hand lotion. I'd better warn the others." Eve pulled her cell phone from a pocket.

"No." Lotan pointed a red gun at Eve. "You will not call anyone except to get Princess Sela down here. I can stun you faster than you can prevent me."

"I see no reason to put it to the test. The princess will be here shortly, or you can call her with your mind if you wish."

Lotan touched a button on a band around his left wrist. The image of Sister Betty winked out. He had been healed of his injuries, but he was tense and had dark circles under his eyes. Lotan wore his light blue cool-suit. "Where have you taken her?"

"Princess Sela is taking a shower and trying on clothes. It may be a while, but she will arrive eventually. Now, I have a lot of work to do, so get out of my chair." Eve took a step toward her desk.

"That is close enough." Lotan shifted his gun with menace. "I am only interested in getting Princess Sela off your godforsaken planet."

Eve wondered how fast Lotan could pull the trigger. Cain could be tearing down a wall while she was stuck in a standoff. "God has not forsaken us. Do you realize that you are trapped here?"

Lotan smiled. "I am holding the gun."

"Cain has an army waiting outside these walls. You won't get the princess out of here without my help."

"You are bluffing," Lotan sneered.

"Oh, for heaven's sake, Lotan. I need to plan for Cain's impending attack. Let me access my computer, and I'll show you."

Lotan hesitated. A knock on the door interrupted his thoughts. Eve was not sure if she should feel frustrated or relieved. Lotan touched his wrist and looked like Sister Betty again. "Do not try anything funny, or I will stun you."

"Sister Betty would never sit in my chair."

Lotan moved to the couch, keeping his gun pointed at Eve.

"Enter," Eve called out.

Hannah opened the door and held a glass of tea and a saucer with an egg salad sandwich. She felt tension emanating from Mother Evelyn and knew something was wrong. "I brought you some supper."

"Thank you," Eve said. "Just put it on the coffee table."

Hannah put the sandwich and tea on the table then looked at Sister Betty on the couch. "Hello, Lotan."

"How did you know it was me?"

"The real Sister Betty would have shown up on the computer when Gertrude scanned the abbey. I only know one person who can live and breathe while their body temperature is a chilly sixty-eight degrees. Also, Sister Betty would never make food that awful."

"Have a seat," Lotan said and waved the red gun in her direction. "We will all wait patiently for the princess to arrive."

"She may be awhile. She's not happy wearing black. Black is not your color either, but the dress fits nicely."

Lotan sighed and shut down his hologram.

"What's Cain doing?" Eve asked.

"Gertrude said he finished talking with the police and they left. He set up a perimeter guard around the abbey, and they are searching for weaknesses. Eight in scuba gear are searching the moat."

"Cain is really here? You were serious?"

"Deadly."

Lotan looked at Hannah, and she knew he was reading her surface thoughts. He lowered his gun. He pulled out a gold rope from his cool-suit and tossed it to Eve. "Put this on."

Eve tied the rope around her head and moved to her desk.

"You need to eat, Eve," Hannah said.

"Give it to Lotan. He has time to eat. I don't."

Lotan looked at the sandwich. It was cut into four pieces. He picked up one triangular sandwich but hesitated. He looked at Eve and put the sandwich back down. "How do I know it is not poisoned?"

Eve looked up from her computer. "It's going to be a long night. You've scanned Hannah already. Scan her again if you wish. Eat or don't eat. I don't care."

"Only if you eat one too."

Eve rolled her eyes and motioned Hannah to bring her a piece. Eve took a bite. A few seconds later, so did Lotan.

As they chewed their third bite, Hannah saw Lotan's eyes widen in alarm as Eve dropped the remainder of her sandwich and slumped over her desk. He looked at Hannah and fell sideways across the couch.

I never knew what Mabel planned. She made sure I didn't, Hannah thought. She heard the door open. Gertrude entered with a stethoscope around her neck and her medical bag. Mabel held her infrared scanner.

"What did you give them?" Hannah asked Gertrude.

"Nothing serious. The stethoscope is for listening through the door."

Hannah grabbed Lotan's wrist. Knowing Mykaela would soon arrive and thinking it would be wise not to shock her with the appearance of a blue alien sitting in Eve's office, she pressed the button on Lotan's wrist and his appearance changed to a snoozing Sister Betty.

"We need to hurry," Mabel rasped. "Mary Ruth can't delay the princess much longer."

"Why would we need to delay the princess?" Hannah asked.

"She's not aware that Lotan tried to kidnap Eve. We have more important matters to attend to, and she could complicate things."

Gertrude produced a small syringe from her bag, found a vein in Eve's arm, and emptied the contents into her bloodstream. Less than a minute passed before Eve opened her eyes. "I loathe being drugged."

"That's why I drugged the egg salad, which you also loathe."

"I hoped that was why you sent it." Eve shook her head. "And you did very well disguising your thoughts, Hannah."

"I didn't," Hannah replied. "No one told me the plan."

"Mabel, get the floater so you can get Lotan into the basement. Gertrude, tell Mary Ruth to bring the princess here and then monitor Cain. Keep me informed of his progress. Hannah, did you find our missing novice?"

"Yes, ma'am."

"Tell her she is restricted to her room. I'll deal with her later."

"Excuse me, Mother, but I think you should deal with her now," Hannah said. "She read my mind before I came down here."

"Gertrude used her as a test subject for Cain's manna. I forgot how quickly it works. She would have been safe outside the abbey."

"I thought the abbey was invincible," Hannah objected. "Are we not safe?"

"No. I believe Cain will attack before dawn."

"Can we call the police?"

"They've already investigated the sounds of gunshots. Cain dismissed them. The only evidence of a crime is the theft of a beat-up old Rambler with multiple bullet holes. Bulldozers across the street will provide a plausible explanation for the damaged building. Cain will kill anyone who gets in his way, including the police."

"How could he get in?"

"He has guns and explosives, which the boys from Kappa Lambda Omega did not."

"Where will he enter?"

"I would blow a hole in the back wall of the Glass Chapel and move my troops in. Cain is more experienced in warfare than I am. I'm sure he will surprise us."

"Then how are we supposed to keep the princess safe?"

"Daylight is Cain's worst enemy. Even for the princess, he won't risk exposure."

"Can you spare the time to talk to Mykaela?" Hannah asked.

"I suppose I will have to," Eve sighed. "Go get her."

Hannah ushered in Mykaela, who walked in with her head bowed. The hologram-clad Lotan had been moved to a sitting position on the couch. Mary Ruth and Eve sat on it, facing Sister Betty. Hannah wondered which one maintained the illusion of two old crones.

"Have a seat." Mother Evelyn's voice betrayed no emotion.

Mykaela and Hannah sat beside Sister Betty, each with their hands clasped in their lap.

"Why are you here?"

Mykaela's alabaster skin turned pink. "Because you ordered me to come to your office."

"You had no problem disobeying the evacuation order earlier today." Mother Evelyn's voice reflected displeasure. "So why are you here?" she asked again.

Mykaela stiffened. "I did not feel obligated to follow your orders."

Mother Evelyn smiled. "I know about your doubts about your call to serve the Church. If you cannot reconcile your desire to be a mother and a wife, you should not take the vow to become a sister of our order, or any order."

Mykaela glanced at Hannah, who smiled to encourage her. "My parents are going to be very disappointed."

Mother Evelyn chuckled. "Be at ease, child. Parents are often disappointed with their children. However, children return a special gift to their parents that removes all past transgressions. That gift is grandchildren."

Mykaela smiled. "You're probably right."

"Now, Miss Mykaela, why are you here?"

"I know something bad is about to happen since the abbey and the women's shelter have been evacuated. According to the older nuns, the abbey has never been evacuated. I thought this was the safest place in the world. At least it has been for me. Mary Ruth has been a mother to me."

"And you have b-been like a d-daughter to me," Mary Ruth fake warbled.

"I want to help. I don't understand it, but I can read Hannah's mind."

"You gift has awakened," Mother Evelyn said.

Hannah started to reach out a hand to offer Mykaela support but felt a compulsion to stop.

Mother Evelyn pursed her lips. "Perhaps you can explain why all my furniture is hovering six inches off the floor."

Mykaela let out a squeak as almost every piece of furniture slammed back down. Her face turned ashen. Apparently, the altar was attached to the floor.

"Dear child, did you think you were alone?"

Mykaela looked up and saw confusion on Hannah's face.

"There are only a few gifted people in this world," Mary Ruth said.

Mykaela looked at the two old women. "You can do this too?" she stammered.

"Not exactly," Mother Evelyn admitted. "We each have our own gift. We call your gift 'telekinesis.' Mary Ruth's gift is called 'creativity.'"

"You can create things?"

"Only God can create things. Another name for my talent is 'illusion.' Watch closely."

Mykaela's eyes widened in amazement as Mother Evelyn and Mary Ruth turned much younger.

"We can't go into much detail right now. You would have been safe if you left with the nuns. There is a telepath with a hundred mercenaries outside, ready to storm the abbey. You would be a great prize for him, and we must not allow that to happen. Our adversary is a coercer, as am I."

"A co-coercer?" Mykaela stammered.

Eve's face turned cold. "Stand up!"

Mykaela nearly jumped off the couch.

"Stand on your head."

Mykaela hastily tied her skirt into a knot, placed her hands on the floor, and stood on her head.

"Resist my command."

"I can't," Mykaela cried.

"Turn and face my desk."

Within two seconds, she turned and faced the desk while still standing on her head.

"On my desk lies a black cane with a white top. Pick it up, and move it in front of Sister Mary Ruth."

The cane floated in the air and moved to hover a few feet in front of Mary Ruth.

"Now," Mother Evelyn commanded, "turn back around and shove the cane through Mary Ruth's heart."

Hannah glanced at Mary Ruth, who wore a gentle smile on her elderly face as she sat placidly on the couch.

The cane quivered in the air as Mykaela tried to resist. Tears flowed from her eyes and ran down her forehead. The cane zoomed through the air and struck Mary Ruth in the middle of her chest. Hannah screamed.

"You may relax."

Mykaela toppled forward. She wiped Mary Ruth's gooey blood out of her eyes. Blood covered the carpet, the ceiling, and both couches.

"That was disgusting," Hannah said.

"Too much?" Mary Ruth said from behind the couch with the cane sticking through it.

"Why would you do such a thing?" Mykaela gasped.

"To show you my power," Mother Evelyn replied. "Our adversary will break into our home very soon. He is also a coercer. I intend you to fear him."

Eve retrieved Lotan's gold rope from her desk. "You will wear this without question. It will prevent you from using your powers and protect you from coercion. Sister Mabel will give you a Kevlar vest. Go to your room and stay there. If you're captured, don't fight. You are to surrender, but don't remove your metal band. Do you understand?"

"Yes, ma'am."

"If we survive, there is a friend of mine who is a pilot I would like you to meet. The two of you would make beautiful grandchildren. Now, go to bed."

Mykaela blushed as she left the room.

Eve removed her cane from the hole in the couch. "She is extremely strong."

"Is she strong enough to teleport?" Mary Ruth asked.

"She doesn't know that teleportation is an option."

"Wouldn't it be safer to move everyone to the basement?" Hannah asked.

"The basement is our last resort. If we go down there, we're trapped."

"It seems we're trapped now."

The secret door to the basement opened, and Mabel stepped into the room pushing a wheelless cart that floated in the air. Hannah helped Mabel roll Lotan onto the cart, and Mabel took him down the steps.

Gertrude entered carrying her laptop. "Half of Cain's forces are quietly departing, and most of the rest are moving to the back of the abbey."

Eve sat at her desk and pressed a few commands into her keyboard. "I'm filling the Glass Chapel with foam. Cain will have a difficult time when he gets in. Gertrude, move the second magnetic repulser to the back to slow him down."

Mabel returned from the secret passageway. Mary Ruth hugged her. "Try not to get shot again."

Eve looked at Hannah. "Cain isn't ready yet. Go to the security room. Mary Ruth and I will keep watch and alert you if anything happens. Find some metal to wear."

"Princess Sela is waiting in the hall," Mabel said.

"Bring her in. We'll take her with us downstairs."

Mabel paused while opening the door. "Why did Cain pull half of his troops away?"

"I don't know," Eve replied. "One of us is overconfident. I hope it's not me."

⌣

Hannah felt exhausted and had a slight headache as she turned the lights on in the security room. She found a box opener and cut a cord from a lamp. She sat down, placed the cord on the desk, and woke up the computer. She leaned back in her chair, allowing the fatigue to drain out, and was asleep in just a few seconds.

Hannah woke in a panic. She had forgotten to set her alarm. Gertrude had told her to ring the morning bell. She looked at the clock and realized she had only three minutes to get to the bell room. She jumped up, raced down the hall, and reached the room, located beside the drawbridge.

She reached for the heavy chain and pulled hard. A loud bong let the community know it was time to begin its day. She pulled the chain three more times. The sound reverberated off the bell room's walls. Faint music drifted down the hall, and she assumed that Mykaela must be awake. The music sounded mournful and sad. As Hannah pulled the chain a fourth time, she closed her eyes, enjoying the music.

After the fifth pull, Hannah froze. *The Abbey of Saint Margaret does not have a bell. If I'm not ringing the bell, then what am I doing? There was only one chain in the abbey.*

Her eyes flew open, and she looked at the chain in her hands. It was a dream. Cain's laughter rang in her head as the massive chain slipped through her grasp. The drawbridge landing on the other side of the moat was loud. Cain must have entered her mind before she fell asleep. She had betrayed everyone. Hannah felt her head nearly explode. Suddenly, the oil on the drawbridge chain was on fire.

Hannah screamed like she had never screamed before. "MOTHER!"

Chapter Forty-Nine

Eve watched Cain's men on her computer in the Templar chamber. Mary Ruth sat beside her, and Sela stood behind both of them. The vault door stood open.

"Burglar alarms at three separate banks," Mary Ruth said.

"Cain used half of his men to create a diversion," Eve replied. The bedrock trembled. A cloud of dust and debris flew out from the back wall of the Glass Chapel. The same hardened foam that filled the chapel covered the cameras inside, so she could only assume that Cain's men had blown a considerable hole in the back wall.

Eve looked up as a shock wave assaulted her mental barrier and heard, *"MOTHER!"*

"Did you hear Hannah?" Mary Ruth asked. "She just screamed through thirty feet of solid rock. I can't even do that."

"I think Hannah is finally awake. And she won't be dependent upon Cain's manna for her talent like Mykaela will be."

"That will make Cain happy. One of his goons has a crossbow with C-4 on the tip of a bolt. There's no metal to repulse."

Eve typed commands on her keyboard. "The drawbridge is down. A bulldozer has just rolled onto it. It's too big for the magnetic repulser to affect it." A second bulldozer lumbered onto the drawbridge, moving backward. The first bulldozer crossed the bridge and rammed into the front of the gatehouse. Another shudder passed through the rock. It wouldn't take long for the wall to crumble.

"Drop the gatehouse floor and send the Bentley into the moat," Eve called to Gertrude.

"We have another problem," Mary Ruth said.

"What?" Eve demanded.

"The drawbridge chain is on fire."

"Hannah must have awoken as a transmuter. She might have inadvertently caused a chemical reaction to take place on the object her fear focused upon."

"But the chain is metal," Mary Ruth objected.

"The oil on the chain is not."

A crossbow bolt with its explosive-laden load stuck to the magnetic repulser. A flash of light from the explosion lit Eve's screen, and the camera stopped. She switched views to two men using fire extinguishers to spray the flames running along the drawbridge. "The chain passes through a closet in the kitchen. I'm turning the sprinklers in the kitchen on just to be safe."

"That isn't just a closet. That's where Sister Betty stores the wine and other alcohol. If the glass breaks, the vapors will ignite," Mary Ruth replied.

"I will see what can be done," Eve said.

Hannah's pulse quickened almost as fast as the thoughts flying through her mind. The flames raced up the metal chains of the drawbridge, and she knew she had caused the fire. She ran to the hall, where Sister Julia left the fire extinguisher.

She jumped back as something massive slammed into the rock wall of the foyer. She grabbed the fire extinguisher, but it felt almost empty. She returned to the drawbridge control room and emptied the extinguisher. The fire died, but she saw flames through the hole in the ceiling where the chains passed through.

Hannah raced up the stairs and into the dining hall, where sprinklers suddenly came on and soaked her with ice-cold water. Ignoring the freezing rain, she ran across the dining hall and into the kitchen, where smoke flowed from under the closet door. She opened it. The chain burned, and the wooden shelves, holding bottles of alcohol, smoldered. Hannah looked for another fire extinguisher but found an empty holder beside the stove where the extinguisher should be.

Eve watched as the bulldozer crashed through the first wall. Gertrude pivoted the floor of the foyer and dumped the crumpled Bentley into the moat. The driver of the bulldozer jumped off, but the dozer kept rolling. It tipped over and fell on top of the Bentley.

The second bulldozer driver also jumped just before the bulldozer rolled backward and fell on top of the first dozer. The large flat blade on the front made an almost level floor for Cain's mercenaries to cross the foyer. Two men with welding torches began cutting through the heavy iron door. A few minutes later, a swarm of men entered the abbey.

Eve pressed a button, and the basement corridor filled with foam. The basement video feed turned white on her computer screen.

As the soldiers approached the open door to the gym where the veiled Mabel hid, she wished she could attack by surprise but thought someone might shoot her. Knowing she faced mercenaries, she chose to play to their egos. She knew mercenaries were usually not disciplined enough to serve in a regular military structure, but their desire to fight remained for personal reasons. A man with a big ego could not resist the challenge of physical combat.

Mabel moved into the hallway and twirled her pugil sticks. Twenty soldiers rounded the corner wearing metal helmets, gas masks, and tinted goggles. Each soldier held a large gun with two strings of bullets draped across their chests. Various knives and other small weapons were strapped to their brown camouflage uniforms.

She tossed one pugil stick to her other hand and motioned for the men to come and get her. The first row lowered their guns and sprang forward. Mabel danced around them with her pugil stick, only aiming at the gas masks. She took several blows to her body but managed to knock six gas masks off. Six soldiers slumped to the floor.

Another four grabbed their guns. Mabel jumped through the gym door and tucked behind a desk. One took point, leading the rest, who cautiously spread out along the hallway. Mabel looked at the stun lasers mounted on the gym ceiling and hoped that Gertrude would time them well to surprise the remaining soldiers.

Adrenaline coursed through Mabel's veins. She heard a commander shout instruction. One man led the rest down the hallway. Mabel knew that Cain had come prepared to win. She heard the soldiers position themselves on both sides of the door. The first soldier tucked into the gym, hugging the right-side wall. A heartbeat later, the second entered and moved to the left. Mabel smiled. They failed to look up.

Above the door, she had set up a collapsible shelf with weights. As several others entered, she pulled out a remote control and heard two small explosions from above the door. The weights crashed down. Two soldiers were hit hard enough to knock them out. Three more gas masks were damaged, and the solders dropped.

The remaining dozen soldiers rushed into the gym. Lasers rained down from the ceiling, striking several, but they had no effect. Mabel went into a frenzy pounding soldiers with her pugil sticks. She hit several in the face and cracked their gas masks. She swung at the soldier to her left, but her pugil stick crashed against the butt of his rifle. She spun, and her left foot slammed into the side of another soldier's face. As he crumpled, another man caught her foot. Mabel lifted her right foot and pivoted the man holding her ankle over her head. Someone punched her in the face, and she fell on her back. She shifted just in time to avoid a rifle butt that slammed into the floor where her face had been.

~ↄ

Gertrude shifted her attention from one computer screen to another. Sitting at the Mother's station, she monitored five screens while adjusting security functions to the abbey. She could not fight like her sister, nor could she cast illusions like her mother, but she did have a formidable intellect.

Fire doors slammed in front of the enemy. Sprinklers sprayed large volumes of water. Alarms rang through every corridor. Lights turned off. She would put them back on when she could see the solders put on their night googles. She knew she could not win and would be captured soon. Mother Evelyn had told her to do one thing: "Slow Cain down. Make him angry enough to muddle his thinking but not so angry that he starts killing people."

Looking at the monitor, she saw Cain enter the abbey. A few of his soldiers talked with him for a few minutes. He picked up an umbrella from the front hall and climbed the stairs to the kitchen level. She knew Hannah was there.

She glanced at the gym monitor, praying for her sister as she watched Mabel dislocate a large soldier's shoulder. Unable to keep her tears from welling, she saw soldiers spreading through every corridor on all the monitors.

Gertrude assumed the Mother had a plan but could not figure it out.

The alarm woke Mykaela. She jumped out of bed, threw on her robe, and sprinted down the hall in her bare feet. When she heard men's voices coming up the stairs, she halted. She ran to the only place of safety she could think of, her own room. She heard men opening the doors and shouting, "Clear!"

With her ear pressed to the door, Mykaela heard a cell phone ring. After a muffled conversation containing the word "gym," some of the soldiers' footsteps sounded like they were leaving. Two men continued checking each room. She saw no place to hide. Her armoire was too small to fit inside, and her bed too low to hide underneath. If she could use her talent, she could raise the bed six inches and squeeze underneath it, but the Mother's instructions were clear. If she had obeyed in the first place, she would be safe.

Remembering not to resist, Mykaela sat on her bed and placed her hands on top of her head in the traditional position of surrender. She closed her eyes and began to pray. With every door she heard crash open, she flinched. With every shout of "Clear," she prayed harder. The voices grew closer and louder.

With a quick turn of the knob, the door slammed against the wall. The soldier smiled and said, "Now, what do we have here?"

Mykaela looked up. Both men wore a gas mask loosely on top of their head and had red hands painted on their faces. They leered at her. The Red Hand Defenders considered nuns and priests to be their primary targets. They both unzipped their pants.

Fourteen men down and six to go. Mabel barrel-rolled across the gym, avoiding most of the kicks. Her face felt numb from many blows. A rifle butt slammed into the small of her back, knocking her off-balance. The six remaining men surrounded her. One turned his gun around, but the leader stopped him from raising it. Mabel took advantage of the distraction and swept the feet from beneath one soldier who had stood behind her. She cracked the fallen soldier's gas mask and hurled the stick across the circle, which struck the mask of the man who'd raised his gun.

Mabel somersaulted over the fallen man and felt another sharp blow to her back. She spun and knocked the air out of his lungs with her right foot. He was not out of the fight, but he would be stunned for a minute or two.

Only three left. Mabel leaped on top of a table, and the men surrounded it. The leader pulled out his pistol and pointed. The bullets slammed into Mabel's Kevlar vest, knocking her down.

More gunshots rang out. Mabel could not breathe.

Hannah looked around the wine closet. If the bottles burst, half the abbey could burn down. She considered finding a large pot to fill with water but didn't know where the pots were, and the sink was on the other side of the kitchen. It would take too long to fill them with water anyway. She opened several cabinets, looking for flour to smother the fire.

Suddenly, a voice whispered into her mind, and she froze. It was Mother Evelyn. Her mental voice was faint but firm. *"Hannah, you must put out the fire."*

"I know!" Hannah mentally screamed. *"Where are the pots?"*

"Forget the pots. There's no time. You are a transmuter. Transmute something!"

Hannah didn't know how to transmute anything. She walked into the closet, which felt like an oven. Wine in several bottles was starting to boil. She looked at the bottles. *"If Jesus could turn water into wine, maybe I can turn wine into water."*

She closed her eyes and concentrated, imagining all the bottles contained water instead of wine. Her vision blurred as she focused on the wine molecules. She began to see the amazing molecular structure of the beverage. The majority of the wine molecules contained hydrogen and oxygen. She pictured the molecules breaking apart and coming back together in the simpler form of H_2O. Unsure what to do with the leftovers, she melded them into the glass.

She picked up a big bottle of Dom Pérignon and threw it at the fire. The bottle broke, and the flames diminished. She picked up several more bottles, and with each strike, the fire died out.

"I'm impressed," Cain said from behind her. Hannah froze. "Do you know how rare a bottle of 1945 Mouton is?"

"It was only water."

Hannah turned around. Cain stood in the middle of the kitchen with four guards, all holding umbrellas. He wore a tuxedo and held his gun. Hannah raised an eyebrow.

"Why don't we step out of the rain?"

"The gun is not necessary."

"The last transmuter I crossed had a tendency to turn everyone into stone. She was difficult to kill."

"Medusa?" Hannah asked.

"I gave Perseus a metal shield, helmet, and sword. It was still difficult."

"You're kidding." Hannah would have laughed had she not been looking down the barrel of Cain's gun.

"Medusa the transmuter, Mercury the telekinetic, Zeus the coercer, and Hera the illusionist. I killed them all. Do you know that a good precog can still see after you blind them?"

"I can't say the thought has ever occurred to me," Hannah replied, cold water drizzling down her back. "Perhaps you shouldn't have killed them all since you are now looking for a telepathic bride."

"I see Mother has not told you the whole story." Cain looked at her from under his umbrella and tilted his head. "Maybe I will tell you sometime why the pacifist farmer killed his brother the hunter, but there are more pressing matters to attend to now, such as killing my mother. Where is she?"

"I don't know." Hannah was glad she could answer the question honestly.

Cain used his gun to motion Hannah toward the kitchen door. "Then I suggest we go find her."

$\backsim$

Mykaela climbed on top of her bed and huddled against the corner of the wall. Seeing nothing to use as a shield except her pillow, she covered her chest with it. The first man spoke, his voice dripping with lust. "Come, now, my pretty. I've never had a virgin."

She kicked her foot at the leering face coming toward her. "And you won't be having this one."

The soldier caught her foot and dragged her across the bed. His friend came around to the side of the bed and snatched the pillow from her hands.

She pulled her lips back in anger, showing her teeth. The man at the foot of the bed placed his rough hand on the inside of her thigh. The other stoked her hair and removed the metal band from around her head.

With a thought, she hurled both men through the door. They struck the far wall so hard that they stuck to the stone surface for a moment, then they slowly slumped to the ground. Even though they were unconscious, Mykaela telekinetically zipped their flies, ripping through tender flesh.

The doors burst open, and Gertrude pressed a key on the computer and placed her hands on top of her head. Four guards walked in, followed by Cain. Gertrude recognized two of the guards from his entourage in Taiwan. Two more guards escorted Hannah, who looked miserable and wet. Her hands remained behind her back, and she wore a metal band around her head.

Gertrude looked at Cain. "Hello, Father."

"Don't try to play games with me, Gertrude," Cain replied with a cold tone.

"Why the tux? Are you supposed to be James Bond?"

"I always dress up for weddings and funerals." Cain gazed into Gertrude's eyes. "Where is she?"

"Where you can't find her." Gertrude heard the computers shutting down and tried to stall. She felt waves of intimidation flowing from Cain, but his eyes shifted to the right to one of the monitors. He pointed to it. "Which corridor is that one? And don't even think of lying to me."

Gertrude looked at the monitor. It showed the corridor where Mykaela was. She tried to shield her mind with a prayer litany, but a flash of pain broke her concentration. She had no choice but to answer. "East corridor, second floor."

Cain spoke to one of his guards. "Bind them, and put a metal band around her head. Don't harm them unless they try to escape. If they do, shoot them in the foot. I will return shortly."

Four personal guards followed Cain and left the room. A moment later, three soldiers dragged Mabel through the door and dropped her on the floor. Her face looked bruised and pale, and her eye was wide with shock.

~⌒

Mykaela tightened her robe and ran. She didn't know where she could go. The flagstones felt cold against her bare feet. Reaching the stairs, she grasped the rail and swung around the corner, taking the steps two at a time. She hoped she could reach the safety of the courtyard.

At the last stair, Mykaela turned the corner and ran straight into the chest of a man wearing a tuxedo and carrying an umbrella. He looked handsome except for the red hand painted on his face.

The four guards behind him lifted their guns. Looking down the hall, she saw a chair fifty feet away. Hoping to distract them long enough to escape, Mykaela grasped the chair with her mind and hurled it at the man in the tuxedo.

He ducked with the grace and speed of a master of the martial arts. A guard behind him crumpled under the impact of the flying chair. The man in the tuxedo smiled. She felt his mind forcing her to relax as he reached out and grabbed her arm and said, "Hello young lady. My name is Cain."

Mykaela screamed, wishing she could be anywhere else. Her head swam, and she heard a pop.

The hallway turned dark, and the fountain and trees of the courtyard appeared before her eyes. The man in the tuxedo stood beside her.

~⌒

Gertrude looked at her sister with alarm. Mabel was turning blue. "She can't breathe!"

The soldiers looked at Mabel then ignored her. When Mary Ruth stood up, one of the guards pointed his gun at her foot.

"Shoot both my feet, and I'll still try to save my sister!" Gertrude shouted.

The soldier continued to stand with his gun drawn. Gertrude knelt, and because her hands were tied behind her back, she used her chin to force Mabel's mouth open. She breathed air into her lungs and used her shoulder to force the air back out.

Turning her head, she exchanged the air and repeated the process. After the fifth exchange, Mabel groaned and coughed. Gertrude began to hyperventilate. A soldier walked over and placed several zip ties around Mabel's feet and hands.

Mykaela tried to scream but felt her jaw lock shut. Her eyes widened as a green laser flashed, striking the top of Cain's umbrella. Another one struck her on the hip, funneling energy through her. She went numb as the sensation traveled up her spine. A second later, Mykaela felt nothing.

In Eve's office, Mary Ruth watched Cain carry Mykaela inside. The umbrella blocked multiple lasers as they struck from above. Mary Ruth turned to Eve. "Is it time?"

"Not yet."

Chapter Fifty

Hannah felt relief when Mabel breathed by herself. Her relief turned to dread when the door opened and Cain walked in carrying Mykaela. He walked to a couch and placed her gently upon it. He looked at one of his guards, and the guard placed a metal band on Mykaela's head.

Another guard escorted Gertrude to her chair. Cain removed her metal headband, and she cringed. He leaned forward and placed his hands on the armrests of the chair. "Where is she?"

"Whom do you seek?" Gertrude asked.

"You know whom I seek," Cain said, narrowing his eyes.

"What is your favorite color?" Gertrude asked.

"Do not play games with me. Now, tell me where my mother is."

"I thought you were looking for the princess."

"My mother has already given me a transmuter and a telekinetic. A healer would be nice. I control the abbey. Where is she?"

Hannah saw Gertrude's finger stick straight out.

Gertrude slumped in her chair.

Cain rose from bending over Gertrude and turned to his men. "There is a secret passage out of the Mother Superior's office. Send someone to raise the drawbridge. Bring these four along and follow me."

Everything is going wrong, Hannah thought.

One of the soldiers carried Mykaela. Another dozen followed Cain to the stairwell leading to the basement. They reached where the stairwell should be but saw a wall of stone instead. Cain touched it. "Delaying tactics, Mother? I expect better from you."

He motioned to one of his men, who withdrew a long dagger and threw it at the wall. The dagger sank into the stone. Cain reached out and twisted the knife. It moved easily, and the wall crumbled into pieces of Styrofoam.

Cain looked at Hannah. "This is supposed to take me hours to cut through, but I have a better idea." He removed her metal headband and veil and wrapped the veil around his face. "Can you transmute it into something useful, like air?"

Hannah turned pale. "I don't know how."

"If you can turn wine into water, surely you can turn Styrofoam into air."

A tear trickled down her cheek. "Truthfully, sir, I don't know how."

Cain whipped out his gun and placed it against her temple. "Will this help?"

Hannah froze. "I can't do it if I'm dead."

"Good point." Cain moved the gun to point at Mabel's head. "Perhaps this will bring more enlightenment."

Hannah felt nauseous. "I will try. But please read my mind. I really don't know how to do it."

"I'll be reading you, and if you try anything foolish, Mabel will pay the penalty. Do you understand?" Looking deep into Hannah's eyes, Cain frowned. "You really don't have a clue, do you?"

"No."

"I can't teach you how to transmute one item into another, but my father said he could visualize the individual particles that make up an object. Just separate the elements back into their basic forms."

Seeing no choice but to cooperate, Hannah closed her eyes to concentrate and relax. She opened her eyes and stared at the Styrofoam. Just as when she looked at the wine, the molecular structure of the Styrofoam materialized before her. She could see that it was composed of hydrogen and carbon, spaced widely apart, with chambers for air. If she could separate the hydrogen and carbon, the hydrogen would mix with the remaining air and disperse through the ventilation while the carbon would make a fine dust on the floor. Hannah touched the first group of molecules.

"Careful," Cain warned. "It's easy to cause the molecules to combust, and you wouldn't want to burn your sisters."

Hannah lost her concentration.

"Focus."

Hannah looked intently at the Styrofoam wall again. After a few seconds, it began to crumble. She formed a narrow tunnel, and the transmutation seemed to flow easier the further she progressed.

She had to stop and rest for a moment. Transmutation took a lot of energy. She could not just simply give up and give in. She had to do something. Her mind reached out to a guard. She could turn their uniforms into hard plastic. If she could eliminate the threat from his soldiers, Cain might be vulnerable. As soon as she locked on to the fabric, her mouth turned dry and a blinding flash of light seared her eyes. She stumbled and fell to one knee.

Cain said, "That was stupid. There is metal woven into the fabric of their uniforms. You can't change metal. Sorry, Mabel. Hannah is not taking me seriously. That one will cost you a leg."

Hannah heard Cain's gun cough. Mabel and Gertrude screamed.

Deep underground, Mary Ruth slammed her fist onto the table.

Eve looked at her. "It is time." She brought Mary Ruth into her arms and held her in a comforting embrace. After a moment, the two nuns took Princess Sela into the vault and closed the door behind them.

Hannah slumped on the floor and leaned against the Styrofoam wall as guilt crashed into her soul. Her mind spun. If God didn't want her to use such a powerful gift just as the greatest villain in history invaded her home, why did He give it to her? She didn't believe He gave her the power to transmute in order to help Cain kill his mother. As Gertrude sobbed behind her, Hannah realized her chance of altering their situation was as thin as one of Eve's illusions.

She blinked a few times, and her vision cleared. She choked at the sight of Mabel's blood. Cain stood in front of her and tapped his umbrella against the flagstone floor, bringing Hannah's attention back to him. "Should I shoot her other leg?"

Hannah's eyes widened with fear. "No."

"If you give me your word you won't try to alter anything to harm me or my people, I'll allow my medic to bandage Mabel's leg. Otherwise, she will bleed to death."

Gertrude cried as she held Mabel's head in her lap. "Do what he says. Don't try to be a hero."

"Thank you, daughter," Cain said without taking his eyes off Hannah.

"Don't call me that," Gertrude spat.

Hannah looked at Cain. "I promise not to harm you by changing any item in your presence."

"See? That wasn't so difficult."

"For twenty-four hours," Hannah added.

Cain laughed. "Fair enough."

He motioned to one of the soldiers. The medic bandaged Mabel's thigh. Mykaela awakened, looking frightened and confused. She flinched as a guard locked on to her arm.

Cain looked at Hannah. "Get to work."

Hannah turned back to the Styrofoam tunnel. It took a while to transmute the first hundred feet of foam, then her vision became blurry again and she seemed to run out of energy. Her stomach growled.

Remembering a high school chemistry lesson, she grabbed a handful of Styrofoam and concentrated. She turned it into a giant marshmallow, took a few bites, and felt a little better. Looking at Cain, she asked, "Would you like some?"

"What is it?"

"A marshmallow. It's only one molecule away from Styrofoam."

Cain smiled but refused.

Hannah turned back to the Styrofoam. Before long, the tunnel reached Mother Evelyn's office door. It was locked. Cain shot the lock, and a soldier opened the door. Six soldiers led the way into the office looking for traps.

Cain entered and looked around the room. He noticed a hole in the sofa and looked at Mykaela. "Did you do that?"

Mykaela shook her head "no."

Cain walked to the Bible on the pedestal and opened it to Genesis 4:14. "Come, Gertrude, open the secret door."

When Gertrude crossed her arms, a soldier pushed her from behind to the pedestal.

"Interesting verse. I know it well. Is my mother trying to send me a message?"

"I hope so."

Cain grabbed Gertrude's hand and placed it on the Bible. The altar receded into the floor, revealing a dark stone staircase leading down. Six guards led the way using flashlights. Cain followed, keeping a firm grip on Mykaela's arm. Ten guards escorted Hannah and Gertrude behind Cain. The final four helped Mabel hobble down the stairs after cutting the zip ties around her ankles.

The bottom of the stairs led to the small room carved into the bedrock. The air became cloying, and several guards fidgeted. Cain spoke loudly. "This is ingenious, Mother. Any thief would think they had reached the end of the road. If they blasted through where the door looks to be, they would only find more stone."

Cain motioned a guard to bring Gertrude forward. He forced her to wave her hand over the plastic flowers. He touched the opposite stone, and his hand passed through it. "The secret door opens, but the thief would not realize it since the hologram where the door is looks identical to the rock wall."

As Mykaela became more alert and frightened, Hannah felt concerned for her.

The lead soldiers passed through the illusion, and florescent lights came on revealing the main computer and six workstations in a semi-circle near the back wall. The computers displayed a big yellow smiley face bouncing slowly across their screens. The smiley face whistled the song "Don't Worry, Be Happy."

After everyone filed into the room, Cain commanded one of his soldiers to bring Sister Mabel forward. Blood covered her face, and her leg left drops of blood on the stone floor. Her fake eye was swollen shut, and her good eye had turned purple and continued to show defiance and loathing. She grunted as the soldier brought her to a halt in front of Cain.

"I have always admired you, Mabel," Cain said. "You are Attila the Nun. You have character. I can't read your mind and force the combination out of you, but I have a healer upstairs. If you will help your sister open the vault, I will have him heal your wounds. I will allow you, your sister, and your mother to go free."

"And if I refuse?" Mabel rasped.

"If you refuse," Cain explained gently, "then you will watch Gertrude die slowly and painfully before you meet your own end. Your mother will die too. I can blow the vault door if I must. The choice is yours."

Mabel looked at her sister and slumped her shoulders. With a slow nod, she hobbled to the rock wall on the north side of the door. Gertrude moved to the south side. The two sisters touched three stones on the wall at the same time. Hannah heard a faint grinding as if stone rubbed against stone, and the wall sank behind the computers and into the ground. Behind the descending wall, Hannah saw the vault door. Gertrude stepped forward and put in her combination on the left dial attached to the door. Mabel did the same on the right then moved to the vault and turned the spindle. With a loud click, the vault door opened.

A short, curvy hallway had a low, iron-plated roof, making the tunnel feel cramped. Cain followed his men with a triumphant bounce in his steps. The nuns and several more soldiers brought up the rear. The leading soldiers entered the Templar Sanctuary twenty feet in front of Hannah. She heard one of the men whistle in amazement through his gas mask.

Mabel looked pale. Ten feet before reaching the sanctuary entrance, she leaned against a wall and slid down, unable to continue. Cain looked at her, narrowed his eyes, and motioned two guards to stay with her.

Cain reached the threshold and ignored the crates, boxes, glass cases, iron ceiling, and ancient carvings in the rock walls. The stacks of gold bars consumed the soldiers' attention. At least fifty pallets, each with hundreds of gold bars, filled a large portion of the room. Iron chains secured the pallets to the floor with interlocking metal bands.

The soldiers fanned out, and Cain dropped his umbrella while keeping one hand wrapped firmly around Mykaela's arm. With his free hand, he pulled out his long-barreled pistol from his tuxedo jacket. He led Mykaela across the room. When he reached the center, florescent lights came on, revealing two women sitting in thrones on the far side of the room. One was Princess Sela and the other was . . . Princess Sela.

Chapter Fifty-One

Hannah sucked in a breath as Cain raised his gun and pointed it at both princesses. He moved it back and forth. With a mocking tone, he said, "Come now, Mother, it is time to die, not play illusion games."

The soldiers took positions behind mounds of gold, steel pillars, and antiques large enough to shield their bodies.

Hannah felt her nerves jump as Eve's voice came from the princesses' mouths. "Cain, son of Adam, son of Eve, I charge you with eighty-seven thousand six hundred thirty-one counts of murder in the first degree and three hundred million counts of murder in the second degree. How do you plead?"

"More games, Mother?" Cain laughed. "I think your estimates are a little low."

"Is that an admission of guilt?" Eve asked.

"Yes, but I want to add you to the list." Cain tilted his head. "You can drop the illusion, Mother. You are on the right, and Mary Ruth is on the left."

As Cain focused on his mother's illusion to the right, Hannah edged toward a metal support post where a gnarled shepherd's staff leaned.

"As your elder, I place you under my judgment," Eve said. "You are cursed from the earth. A fugitive and a vagabond you shall be. You shall wander around the earth until the end of your days."

"I've had that curse before." Cain aimed his gun to the right. "It didn't stop me then, and it won't stop me now. No more games, Mother. It is time to die."

"I don't think so," Eve replied.

Hannah grabbed the staff, but before she could bring it around, Cain shot his gun three times. She cringed as a loud hum rang from the ceiling, making her spine tingle. A large sword crashed through its glass case and flew to the ceiling, where it stuck. Coins, swords, chalices, and suits of armor crashed through their cases and sprayed glass shards in all directions. Cain's men screamed. Guns ripped from their hands and slammed into the ceiling, followed by their bodies. Eve had magnetized the iron ceiling.

On the thrones, both princesses smiled. Cain's bullets rose above them, and his gun flew from his hand.

Hannah considered whacking Cain with the wooden staff but decided to wait and see what else her Mother Superior planned. Cain's metal cufflinks forced his arms up until the cufflinks ripped from his sleeves. The metal buttons on his shirt worked loose, leaving him looking like a puppet struggling against a master marionette.

Hannah almost felt sorry for the twenty soldiers attached to the ceiling by their metallic-laced uniforms, helmets, and gas masks, reminding Hannah of mosquitoes on flypaper.

The metal bands securing the pallets of gold quivered. When she heard the vault door close, Hannah realized that Mabel and Gertrude had left her side.

Eve allowed her illusion to fade, and she and Mary Ruth sat in their comfortable thrones. Cain looked at Hannah. Other than Mykaela, whom Cain gripped tightly, Hannah was the only person left in the room. "You will not win, Mother!" Cain screamed.

Hannah decided it was time to act. She grasped the shepherd's staff in both hands and swung it like a baseball bat. It jerked from her fingers and flew with the speed of a crossbow bolt and the force of a bullet, striking Eve squarely in the chest.

Chapter Fifty-Two

Hannah stared in shock at the staff piercing the Mother's heart. Mykaela fainted. Eve looked down at the protruding staff. Sparks of electricity crackled around it, and Eve's black robe faded into blue. In her place sat a mannequin wearing a blue dress with gold cross-stitched embroidery.

"You can see through my illusions," Eve said as she moved from behind the thrones. "But you can't see through a hologram. You should know. You gave me the dress." She removed a net of electrodes from around her body.

Hannah stepped back behind an iron column. She didn't want Cain to use her as a tool against the Mother. She snuggled against the column, placing her cheek against the cold iron. It rubbed against something sharp, and Hannah glanced at the annoyance. She saw a serial number embedded in the iron. Looking below the number, she noted the manufacturing date of 1947. Hannah's eyes widened as she realized the significance of the date.

Cain's voice dripped with venom. "I do not need metal weapons to kill you, Mother."

He reached down and picked up a thick shard of glass with a pointed end. Blood dripping from his hand, he took a few steps toward Eve.

"Do you not realize that I planned for this?" she asked.

"What do you mean 'planned for this'?" Cain stopped walking. "You could not predict what I would do. If anyone is unpredictable, it is I."

"Oh, there have been a few twists and turns along the way," Eve said, "but I knew you would not be able to resist my bait."

"Don't you see," Hannah said and felt frightened when Cain focused on her instead of Eve. "When you crashed Lotan's spacecraft in 1947, she figured out what you were after. You wanted to create a master race, and you needed a fully telepathic bride. Since the human race wasn't developing talents fast enough, you thought about our alien observers. Unfortunately for you, the aliens wouldn't cooperate. They were more careful after your attack at Roswell, and they hid too well for you to find them. So, she built this magnetic chamber but had to find a way to entice you to come down here."

"You are wrong," Cain interrupted. "I scanned you and Gertrude, looking for some kind of plot. There was nothing."

"Of course Gertrude and I didn't know. Mabel, with a metal plate, knew. Eve has been controlling events since you arrived the first time. She allowed you to believe what you wanted to believe."

Cain stepped forward again.

"She set up Kappa Lambda Omega, supposedly to test her defenses, but in actuality it was to challenge you. Much to her annoyance, you never took the bait. Did you notice the red lights in the sky?"

"That's just the aurora borealis."

"But it was red. That's not normal. She has satellites up there. Mary Ruth seeded the atmosphere with ferric oxide to prevent Sela's people from interfering. Ferric oxide negates the effects of their stealth system, just as it did when a Mexican Air Force plane recorded them for fifteen minutes."

Cain narrowed his eyes.

"I imagine you looked for the alien hideout but you couldn't find it. You assumed that your mother would know where they hid. But she tricked you into believing you used your cunning to lure her into helping locate the aliens."

"You have a vivid imagination," Cain sneered. "She didn't trick me. I attached a transponder to her plane and knew where it landed."

"Which is why I know Mabel was part of the plan." Hannah glanced at Mabel, who leaned against a wall in the hall, outside the magnetic field. Mabel winked. "She checked the plane for tracking devices but left yours in place. Eve could have turned on her stealth equipment and you wouldn't have been able to track us. She wanted you to follow, and she led you to Sela's front door."

"She could not have known where the Elohim were. They have precogs to block any probes. I know, I have tried."

"She used technology."

Cain's anger showed. The mark on his face darkened. Hannah felt a tendril of his mind try to grasp her as he attempted to entice her. "Join me. I will make you queen of the world. I will shower you with gold. People will worship you."

Hannah pressed her body more firmly against the iron column. "I am a nun. I don't desire riches and power. Besides, I am now a transmuter, and I can change garbage into what I want."

"Then, after I kill my mother, I will kill you."

A chill traveled down Hannah's spine. Cain turned and swept his broken-glass dagger at Eve, and blood splattered all around him.

Eve stood silent and still as Cain slowly approached. She reached behind her and brought forth a thick golden pole with a spiraling design along the shaft and three narrow forks on the top. She pointed the weapon at Cain. "Do you recognize this?"

"That is the trident of Zeus. I have felt its sting once, long ago. I survived."

"You were in a lake that diffused the electrical charge. You're not in a lake now. Get down on your knees and place your hands on top of your head."

"Who are you trying to fool, Mother?" Cain maneuvered around a shattered showcase. "You could have killed me from a distance at any time in the last six thousand years, but God's little commandment keeps getting in your way. *Thou shalt not kill!* You chose the wrong weapon."

Eve did not flinch as Cain closed the gap by just a few feet. "I have some bad news for you, son."

"Oh? What is that?"

"This is not the trident of Zeus."

Chapter Fifty-Three

Hannah felt as if she were on fire as a cone of amplified sound waves nearly stunned her senseless. She clamped her hands over her ears, but her skin went numb, her knees quivered, and her teeth ached like a tuning fork with a sour pitch.

Cain received the full force of the blast and slumped to the floor, unconscious.

Mary Ruth removed earplugs from beneath her veil then placed zip ties around Cain's wrists and ankles.

Hannah heard a voice above her head. "We surrender. Can we get down now?"

"Not yet." Eve walked around the room under the hanging soldier, raised her hand, and said, "Forget."

The soldier fell asleep. Eve performed the same memory erasure on each of the remaining soldiers. By the time she made a circuit around the room, the ringing in Hannah's ears diminished.

"How are we going to get them down?" Gertrude asked as she walked from behind a large wooden chifforobe.

"I can help," Mykaela offered.

"Yes, you can," Mary Ruth replied. "Eve, you have places to go and duties to fulfill. You should be on your way."

"I can stay awhile and help with the cleanup. There are still many soldiers in the abbey above us."

"Do not be concerned about them," Cain said, his voice resonating through the chamber.

Hannah looked at where Mary Ruth had been, the location from which the voice came, but saw Cain standing in her place. Mary Ruth allowed her illusion to fade. "I will order the rest to leave. They will believe that Cain and his soldiers found an underground passage leading from your office, which allowed his quarry to escape. After Gertrude compensates them out of Cain's account, I believe they will be glad to leave, especially since the police may arrive soon."

"Very well." Eve looked at Mykaela. "I'll begin training you when I return. Telekinesis is easy to learn, but it takes lots of practice to be safe. Don't teleport until I get back. Mary Ruth will explain the dangers of metal."

"Every minute he remains here increases the risk," Mary Ruth interrupted and pointed at Cain. "We know what to do, but you must get going."

Eve nodded. "Hannah will come with me."

"I will?" Hannah asked, confused.

"Where are you going?"

"I must take Cain to a more secure location."

"Hannah, do you realize what we've accomplished?" Eve asked. "Imagine a man spreading radioactive dust over every square inch of the United States, Canada, and Mexico, and a few days later, everyone dies. Would you despise that man?"

"Of course," Hannah replied.

"I am very happy." Eve pointed to Mary Ruth, Mabel, and Gertrude. "We managed to capture Cain without anyone dying. I've faithfully adhered to God's commandment. I have not killed nor accidentally caused anyone's death."

Mary Ruth clapped. The rest joined in.

Eve looked at Hannah. "You're coming with me because you're now a transmuter. Someone needs to train you before you blow something up. Help Gertrude load Cain on the cart and follow me."

Gertrude pushed the floating cart to where Cain was sprawled unconscious. Hannah helped Gertrude lift him onto the cart. Mary Ruth and Mykaela lowered one of the unconscious soldiers from the ceiling and floated him to the hallway, where Mabel waited.

Eve walked across the chamber to the old iron door. "I thought you said there was nothing behind that door except a caved-in passageway?" Hannah whispered to Gertrude.

"Apparently, I was wrong. If I had known there was anything beyond that door, Cain would have too."

Eve inserted a key and turned the lock. On the other side of the door, Lotan and Princess Sela sat in two office chairs watching a monitor sitting on a table. Sela stood as Eve approached. "That was interesting."

"Thank you for bearing witness," Eve said. "I'm sure when you share your memories with the council the repercussions you might face for assisting us will be mitigated."

Lotan remained sitting in his chair with metal cuffs binding his feet and hands, a metal helmet covering his head, and a mask covering his face.

Eve unlocked the hasp on the side of the helmet. "You should feel honored to wear the mask of Eustache Dauger." She removed the gag in Lotan's mouth. "I apologize for the rough treatment, but I could not take a chance on you interfering."

Lotan was dark blue with anger. After spitting dust out of his mouth, he spoke with forced politeness. "The gag was not necessary. We are not allowed to interfere."

"The very air you breathe is interference. Do you remember a factory worker in Minnesota named Mark Carter? You abducted him six years ago for two hours. Of course, he doesn't remember the abduction, but he remembers the night. He carries a lot of guilt because he was two hours late for work. He knew the valve on pump number five needed replacing, but his assistant didn't. Because he was late, the valve burst, causing the entire plant to burn down. Two people died, seven were injured, and a thousand people were out of work for nearly a year. Don't tell me you don't interfere."

Eve removed the cuffs from his ankles. "Hannah, bring Cain along, and why don't you explain the principles of chaos theory and the butterfly effect to our distinguished guests."

Hannah smiled, warming to one of her favorite subjects. She enjoyed telling Sela and Lotan about the theory as she pushed Cain on the cart.

Eve smiled as she approached the pile of rubble blocking the passageway. She pressed her hand on three rocks in the wall, and the entire pile of stones slid to the side, revealing another short passage and a large room at the end.

Entering the room, Hannah realized that if the Templar Sanctuary were under the Glass Chapel, this room would be under the courtyard.

The room was about sixty feet across with a high ceiling. A decrepit-looking airplane about twenty feet wide and forty feet long nearly filled it. Hannah wondered how Eve had gotten the World War II cargo plane into a chamber thirty feet below the ground. Its dull gray paint was chipped and flaking in several places, and carbon stains from the large twin engines had turned the undersides of the stubby wings nearly black.

Eve walked toward the plane and Lotan barked, "You can't expect me to risk the princess's life in such a pitiful example of your flying machinery. It does not look safe, and we are beneath the ground. Don't you need a runway or something?"

As Eve reached the side of the plane, a set of stairs extended down to the ground, looking like flowing mercury. She took the first step and a door opened, spilling bright light from the interior of the plane. At the top of the stairs, she turned and gave Lotan a cynical smile. "Lotan, you were right. My genetically pure children survived. To hide from Cain, we created technology superior to yours. I won't share that information."

"Where are they?" Lotan asked.

"None of your business." Eve walked inside the plane.

Hannah pushed the cart to the bottom of the stairs. She touched a button marked with an up arrow, and the cart rose. She moved it up the stairs and into the plane. Lotan and Sela trailed behind her.

The interior of the World War II cargo plane reminded Hannah of Lotan's spacecraft. Eve told Hannah to place Cain in one of two boxes that looked like coffins. She rolled Cain off the cart and into the box, and the lid shut automatically. Without a wall between the pilot area and the passengers, the spacecraft felt roomy. Smooth chairs and cabinets seemed to flow seamlessly into the walls and floor.

Lotan spoke to Eve. "We closed the base in Antarctica, but we can make a rendezvous with my people over the South Pole."

"Why don't I take you to the leviathan on the far side of the moon instead?"

Sela glowed bright. "You forced the leviathan into the inner solar system?"

"Not me," Lotan said, "the admiral."

"And you closed all the bases because of Eve?" Sela asked.

"Every base has been compromised."

"I can't say I'm sorry," Eve said.

"A lot has happened while you were gone," Lotan said. The blue around his eyes lightened. "I will tell you about it later."

The stairs turned into a mercurial liquid and were absorbed into the bottom of the plane, and the wings flowed into the side. The door closed by itself, and Eve motioned for Hannah to join her in the front. The craft tilted up, but there was no sensation of movement from within. A moment later, they were perpendicular to the floor, yet Hannah felt like she was flat on the ground.

"You have antigravity," Princess Sela stated.

"Antigravity is a misnomer," Eve replied. "I have gravity control and inertialess engines."

The chamber ceiling looked like solid stone, but it opened to form a round hole barely larger than the body of the craft. From the side window, Hannah watched the stubby wings as they dissolved into the side of the plane.

She saw water flow by as they rose and exited from the fountain in the courtyard. The craft turned horizontal and increased speed and altitude. The wings had returned, and the propellers on the fake engines looked as if they were turning at a high velocity.

Eve said quietly to herself, "I don't think anything can go wrong now."

Chapter Fifty-Four

Hannah watched the sun break on the horizon as they traveled at super-sonic speed over the Atlantic Ocean in a craft that looked like a Learjet. They pierced the atmosphere and headed toward the moon.

"If you have all this marvelous technology, why did you need to create such an elaborate ruse to capture Cain?" Sela asked.

Eve swiveled her chair to face her guests. "Between Cain, Anak, and the flood, most of my pureblood children and grandchildren died. A few used Anak's shuttle to survive. Since there has been no trace of them for five thousand years, Cain assumed they were all dead. Actually, they hid in Peru and studied galactic technology. If I tried to capture Cain with unworldly technology and failed, he would know my children survived and would find a way to kill them."

"But you are Nephilim. You could have killed him anytime."

"I do not kill. Cain is cursed to wander the earth. He is also a powerful coercer. No ordinary prison will hold him. It took a long time to build one that would."

"Where is it?" Lotan asked.

"Again, that's none of your business," Eve replied. She looked back at Sela. "This was not my first attempt to capture Cain. In 1859, I used specially trained ninjas during the Taiping Rebellion. I tried drugging him in 1914 in Austria. He no longer eats or drinks in public. In the middle of World War II, I had him, but I had to let him go. It was a choice between keeping him or helping Mary Ruth prevent Hitler's atomic bomb from reaching London."

Hannah watched the moon grow larger and marveled at its beauty.

Eve piloted the craft toward the dark side to avoid Earth telescopes. "We'll be in range of the moon in an hour. Contact your people so they can send a shuttle to pick you up after we leave."

"Eve," Lotan said, "I'm still required to arrest you."

"She cannot come with us. That would be illegal," Sela interjected.

"Lotan kidnapped Hannah and me several days ago. Needless to say, we escaped."

"The council ordered her arrest for crimes against humanity. I must obey my orders. I will call my people now." Lotan touched one of the buttons on his wristband.

Eve swiveled around and touched some holographic buttons.

"Would you like to hear Lotan's version of our trip around Mercury or mine?" Hannah asked Sela, then she noticed Lotan looking out the window. "What are you watching, Lotan?"

"Nothing."

Hannah thought for a few seconds. "Eve, I believe Lotan signaled to his people where we are."

"They can't track us," Eve replied.

"But they can track his signal."

Eve raised an eyebrow.

Hannah heard something go "pop" behind Sela, then she saw four people in skintight thermal suits and facemasks crouched down behind Sela's seat. Three of the four newcomers were large men and looked human. The fourth was a green-skinned petite woman. The men carried handguns, all pointed at Eve.

Eve stood. "Welcome aboard. I've been expecting you. Unfortunately, you cannot teleport out."

The green woman glanced at the sides of the plane and said, "There is an electronic force field around this ship that was not there a second ago. I cannot teleport through it."

"I've had enough of this," Princess Sela said. "Eve is staying, and we are leaving."

"We must follow our orders, Princess." Lotan turned toward the guards and pointed at Eve. "Stun her."

All three men shot a beam of light at Eve. It diffused against an invisible wall between the pilot's area and the passenger section. "There is also a force field between her and us," the green woman said.

"Lotan, do you really want to take me on?"

Lotan turned almost purple as he looked at Eve. "When reinforcements arrive, we will take your whole ship."

"I don't think so," Eve said. "Hannah, the force field can't block your talent. I know you are new to this, but can you lock on to those weapons?"

Hannah smiled. "I'll try." She concentrated and felt the buzz of the force field. She focused on one of the guns pointed at Eve and saw the complex molecules within. "This weapon contains a lot of energy. I wouldn't want them to explode."

"Just melt the tip a little."

Hannah looked deeper at the molecules. The gun began to droop. The man dropped the gun. Hannah melted the rest of the armed weapons.

"You cannot escape us. We have the resources of thousands of worlds."

"I suggest you take a seat."

Eve sat, her fingers dancing across the holographic keyboard. Hannah leaned closer. "Where are we going?"

"To prove a point."

Eve drove the spacecraft to the far side of the moon. Not long after passing the transition line, Hannah noticed several sources of light emanating from a high orbit. Eve swiveled her chair to speak to her guests. "Princess Sela, it has been a pleasure meeting you. I apologize for involving you in our problems and hope you do not suffer any further consequences from my decisions."

She continued, "Lotan, take this message to all the psychologists and scientists who are observing my world: Every time you abduct one of my children, I shall abduct one of theirs. As for you, Lotan, the first person you discover missing may be your wife."

"Do not threaten me."

"It's not a threat. It's a promise. I know where your planet is. Warn the Council of Elders that their families are vulnerable too. I will not harm them, but I will erase their memories just like you do. You are a coercer. Have you ever piloted a leviathan?"

"No," Lotan replied. "A leviathan obeys the strongest coercer."

Eve smiled. "And you brought a leviathan in close proximity to the most powerful coercer ever known."

Hannah looked out the windshield and saw a creature that looked like a whale but was as thin and fragile as a jellyfish and as large as the state of

Rhode Island. A multitude of lights shone through its nearly transparent exterior, revealing what looked like multiple levels of habitations, with streets and parks scattered throughout.

Eve looked at the leviathan and said, "Boo!"

The leviathan disappeared.

"Where did they go?" Sela asked. "My husbands are within the leviathan along with some of my youngest children."

"They are several billion miles above the ecliptic and are quite safe. I will provide you with space suits and drop all of you off on the moon. Once you are free of the force field, you can signal your shuttle to pick you up. The space suits are in the closet behind you."

"She will not kill us. If you do not put on that suit, she cannot force us out of her ship," Lotan said.

"You have lost, Lotan," Sela replied. "She's letting us walk out of her ship with dignity. She could render us unconscious with a gas and push us out. I am ordering you to put on the space suit."

Lotan grabbed a suit. He looked at Hannah, smiled, and turned a lighter shade. "You will be the first human female to land on the moon."

Excitement coursed through Hannah as Eve landed on the moon. Dust swirled around the windshield. Eve turned on exterior lights so Hannah could see. The four new aliens sealed their suits, and Sela and Lotan donned their helmets. Lotan caught Hannah's eye and silently mouthed, "I'm sorry." A few seconds after they departed, the ship rose into the sky.

Chapter Fifty-Five

Hannah spent several days in the spacecraft learning everything Eve could teach her about transmutation. Not being a transmuter herself, Eve wasn't an expert, but she did help Hannah understand the basics of her new talent. By the end of each day, Hannah's head hurt. Every piece of plastic had its own unique molecular structure. Every breath of air contained an assortment of molecules different from the majority. Every drop of water held minute impurities undetectable by almost any instrument. With concentration, Hannah could see every molecule.

She practiced for hours, changing oxygen into hydrogen and helium atoms. It was easier to dismantle a molecule than to reconstruct it into something else. She sneezed once while converting hydrogen, and it exploded in a little puff of fire, slightly singeing her eyebrows.

To break the monotony, Hannah experimented expanding and contracting the molecular bonds between atoms. She practiced compressing hydrogen until it became a liquid and expanding it again when she felt her hand start to burn from the chill.

On the third day, Eve had removed two dozen frozen oranges from the freezer of the food storage unit and requested that Hannah turn one into an apple. Hannah looked deep into the orange. She could change it, but the result was definitely not an apple. It was a mushy blob that smelled a little bit like fruit. She chose not to taste it.

Hannah saw much more than simple chemicals and molecular bonds in the orange. Since it had once been alive, it was at least ten thousand times more complex than Styrofoam. She could not master the technique, especially since she didn't know the molecular structure of an apple. Knowing the structure of a marshmallow, she could change an orange into that, but an apple seemed impossible. When she ran out of oranges, Hannah grew frustrated.

"I don't expect you to succeed," Eve said. "I allowed you to ruin my oranges to show you how much you need to learn. When we return to Earth, you shall change your major at Oxford University. I'll expect you to graduate in four years with doctorates in chemistry and biology. You will learn quickly how to transmute an object that was once alive. I strongly suggest you wait several years before attempting to transmute something that is still alive. The results are rarely what you hope they will be. Only God can create life. You can change it, but it will no longer be of God's perfection."

To relax, Hannah watched the stars. As the sun's light diminished from the distance, the light from the stars became brighter. Orion blazed bright orange and Centauri a clear blue.

The ship resembled a small asteroid made of black ice traveling randomly through space. After leaving the asteroid belt, Eve showed Hannah how to fly the ship in an emergency and added her DNA as a signature to the computer.

On the fifth day, far beyond the orbit of Saturn, Eve turned on the floodlights, revealing a large asteroid as they approached it. Since the asteroid blended with the darkness of space, Hannah could not be sure of its size but estimated it to be at least ten miles wide and five miles tall. The lights reflected frozen water here and there, but even the ice looked black. She stirred with excitement, anticipating entering a massive city within the asteroid built by Eve's technologically superior children.

Eve maneuvered her craft inside one of the large cavities on the side of the asteroid. Hannah felt disappointed to see only a single flat place cut in the rock where Eve could settle her ship. No crowds greeted them, and no buildings were visible to indicate that another person was within a million miles.

Eve landed on the small section of smooth surface. The door opened, and cold air brushed against Hannah's face. Eve moved to the coffin containing Cain. She pushed one end and guided its floating mass out the door and motioned Hannah to follow.

Having experienced zero gravity, Hannah grabbed the rail, feeling unsafe. Eve continued walking, and Hannah stepped on the smooth surface. Hannah didn't feel weightless. The surface had normal gravity. She also realized that a force field must be keeping the air from flowing into space.

The lights from Eve's ship revealed several tunnels leading into darkness. Eve pushed Cain into one, and Hannah followed. Eve turned on a flashlight, which lit rough black walls and a smooth floor. They moved deeper into the asteroid. The air felt frigid and smelled odd. Hannah played with the molecular structure of her robe, thickening it and forming layers of insulation from carbon molecules she absorbed from the asteroid. Without asking permission, Hannah thickened Eve's robe but wasn't sure that Eve noticed.

They walked in silence for an hour, seeing nothing except rough-hewn rock and ice crystals reflecting in the beam of light from the flashlight. They approached a massive steel door larger than the vault door in the Templar Chamber. Eve entered several codes, alternating between a retina scan, blood test, and pheromone sweep. The door opened, and Hannah followed Eve inside.

They found themselves inside a single room thirty feet wide, thirty feet long, and thirty feet tall with no doors. Each wall curved gently into the floor and ceiling. Looking at the bed on the ceiling and the table on the wall, Hannah realized that each surface was also a floor, with its own source of gravity. The room looked comfortable, if a little austere without any decorations or personal touches. On the floor they stood on, a recliner chair faced a large television screen tuned to the Nickelodeon channel. On the wall behind the flat television, Hannah saw several exercise machines.

Eve pressed some buttons on the coffin, then jumped straight up, spun in midair, and landed beside a bed that to Hannah's perspective was on the ceiling. The coffin floated up to Eve, and she pushed it toward the bed. After spinning the coffin on its side, Eve opened the lid, sprawling Cain unceremoniously on the bed.

Hannah could see that Cain remained unconscious. Eve touched his cheek gently, and a tear fell and landed on the bed. Sighing deeply, she walked to the kitchen on another wall and continued back to the floor where Hannah stood.

The empty coffin followed Eve as she exited through the massive vault door and closed it behind her. The walk back to the spacecraft was solemn. After a while, Eve said, "He will not awaken for at least six hours. When he does, I don't want anyone within ten thousand miles of this place."

Hannah felt relieved once they boarded the spacecraft. Eve accelerated away from the asteroid and continuously checked her instruments. Hannah sat in silence. Several hours passed before Eve seemed to relax.

She changed the windshield into an electronic viewing screen that showed Cain still asleep on the bed.

Eve broke the silence by sharing a few stories of Cain as a child and her joy of raising her first son in a world where everything was new and unknown. She cried once, but only for a moment. Hannah wanted to comfort her but wasn't sure what she could say to a mother who had imprisoned her first and only living son. Realizing there was nothing she could say that didn't sound trite, Hannah remained silent.

An hour later, Hannah saw Cain stir on the windshield view screen. He awoke abruptly and jumped into a defensive crouch. He looked around at his surroundings, and his expression turned to anger. His facial mark darkened. "Where am I, Mother?"

Eve pressed a button and spoke. "I will give you a hint. Every seventy-six years or so, you can wave as you wander around Earth."

"Halley's Comet!" Cain exclaimed.

"Very good."

"You think you have won?"

"It certainly looks that way."

"You think you are the only person who can plan ahead?" Cain laughed a full minute. "Did the princess mention what I took from her?"

Hannah felt a chill run down her spine as she remembered Princess Sela placing her hand on her pelvis when she woke in Taiwan.

Cain moved toward the television. He found the camera and brought his face close to the lens. Hannah leaned back in her chair as his marked face filled the screen. "Remember, Mother, you set events into motion, not I. You introduced me to the princess. You ate the forbidden fruit first, and now it will be you who ushers in the Antichrist."

"What have you done?"

"You should have killed Carla when you had the chance." Cain fell backward on the bed and laughed.

"What have you done?" Eve demanded again.

Cain continued to laugh.

Eve touched a few buttons, and the spacecraft accelerated away from Halley's Comet. After a few minutes, Cain's image faded to static as they flew out of range.

Hannah reached out and touched Eve's arm. She felt a lump in her throat when Eve turned to look at her. With reluctance, Hannah said, "When the princess woke up in Taiwan, she healed herself. She placed her hands over her womb, and they glowed. Cain stole some of her eggs."

Eve's eyes widened. "He's going to father another race."

"Carla has been sacrificing children to usher in the Antichrist. She has the eggs of an Eloshin. I can only imagine what she can do."

"I hope you're wrong," Eve said.

"Can we stop her?"

"We'll try, but if that's part of God's plan, we will not succeed."

Hannah spent the next two days practicing transmutation, but she kept making mistakes. Her mind spun through the words that Eve and Sela had said. As Saturn approached, she asked, "Can we access the Internet?"

Eve quirked an eyebrow. "What do you need?"

"Archeology research."

"The computer downloads world news and has stored much of our history. The archeology information it contains is probably extensive. I'll grant you access to the files."

"Thank you."

Eve turned back to her station and typed a series of commands. A holographic screen formed in front of Hannah along with a keyboard. Eve rose from her chair. "I need to rest." She turned and sat in the back row, leaned her chair back, and slept.

Hannah turned to her holographic keyboard, typed a few commands, and started reading. By the time Eve returned, Hannah felt prepared to ask Eve questions. "You are not the mother of humankind, are you?"

Eve hesitated and replied in a small voice, "No. I am the mother of mankind."

"And there is a difference between mankind and humankind, isn't there?"

"Yes."

Hannah took a deep breath. "Princess Sela and Lotan called us half-breed. Lotan questions if we have souls. He also said I was the first human to land on the moon. You call your hidden children 'purebloods.' Cain wants to kill all of them. Cain wants to father another race."

Hannah looked at Eve, knowing the question would hurt her. "Why did Cain kill Abel?"

"You won't like the answer."

The interior of the ship darkened, and a firepit glowed in front of Hannah's eyes. Hannah could still feel the chair beneath her, but every other sense told her that she sat inside the cave that Adam and Eve originally called home.

Hannah, through Eve's eyes, shucked beans from their pods. Adam sat cross-legged beside her, weaving what looked like cotton thread into a blanket. Cain, on the other side of the cave, mixed some kind of paste in a clay bowl. Two young girls, whom she knew to be the twins born a few years after Abel, watched Cain. Both girls' fingers were dark red, and she saw a partially finished painting in simple colors on the cave wall. The sound of chirping crickets filling the cave overrode the occasional pop and crackle of the fire in a pit toward the front. The air felt chilly but not enough to cause Hannah to shiver.

A teenage boy entered the cave carrying several long skewers of meat. Hannah recognized him as Abel. Adam looked up from his weaving and smiled. "What has the greatest hunter in the world caught for us tonight?"

"Father," Abel replied in a deeper voice than his father's. He glanced at Cain with a sneer. "Other than you, I am the only hunter in the world."

"And you are a much better one than me," Adam said.

"That is because you can't lure the animals to you by tricking their senses like Abel does," Cain said bitterly.

"Can't the two of you go one night without bickering?" Eve said.

"God gave me power over the animals, and I intend to use it." Abel placed the skewers of meat across two rods bracketing the fire.

Cain lowered his eyes. "God gave you the power so you can gather the animals to help bring forth food from the ground, as I do."

Adam sighed. "Your brother will understand one day that death is a part of life. Let him be."

Eve spoke quietly to Adam. "Your condescension does not help. You know he feels their suffering when the animals die."

"It is not normal," Adam whispered back.

"Who is to say what is normal?" Eve watched Abel turn the meat above the fire. "You mean Abel is like you and Cain is like me."

Adam tied the cotton string in a knot and set it aside. "What are you cooking, son?"

Abel looked at his father. "It's a surprise. We have never tasted this animal before."

"We have lived in this valley for three seasons," Adam stated. "I thought we'd named and tasted everything by now."

"I traveled half a day toward the rising sun and found a new herd drinking from the river."

"It smells interesting." Adam said as a sweet smell wafting through the cave.

"I think it's done." Abel removed the skewers from the fire and passed them to everyone except Cain. Cain dipped vegetable stew from a clay pot beside the fire and gave everyone a clay bowl.

Hannah tasted the meat as Eve took a bite. It was sweet but tough to chew. She swallowed the bite and looked at Abel. "Did you give the new animal a name?"

"I didn't have to." Abel looked at Cain. "It was a wild herd of hues, and we have never tried hues before."

Hannah's stomach convulsed as Eve spat the meat in the bowl of vegetables and looked toward Abel. Cain stood in the way. From his posture, Hannah could tell that he was about to strike his brother.

Adam's voice stopped Cain's fist. "You will not bring violence against your brother! Do not add a crime greater than Abel has committed."

Cain turned and glanced at Adam. Cain's eyes were furious, and his voice quivered with suppressed rage. "You were right, Father. I understand."

Adam stood and glared at Abel. "God gave us the hues to help us tame this world. They are ten times more intelligent than any other animal."

"But they do not have a soul," Abel objected.

"You knew it was wrong to eat them, yet you killed one just to anger your brother."

"I'm sorry!" Abel yelled.

Adam moved to stand within a breath of Abel. He spoke with deliberate calmness. "Since you do not respect the gift of the hues that God gave us, you will plow the fields and pick the fruits of the plants alongside them until the first snow."

"But, Father."

"I have spoken."

Abel turned from his father. He mumbled something Hannah could not hear, but Cain obviously did, for he glared at his brother and stormed out of the cave.

Eve rose, and Hannah felt the sensation of movement as she ran after Cain. She stood at the mouth of the cave and searched for him with her eyes and mental senses but could not find him. She returned to the cave, sat against the wall, and sobbed quietly.

"I have seen enough," Hannah said to Eve, using her own voice.

The lights of the ship returned. Eve's voice sounded strained as she finished her story. "The next day, I found Abel dead in the field. Cain and all the domesticated hues were gone, along with his favorite pets, the platypuses. He traveled to the east, where Abel found the wild hues, but we never found him."

"I'm sorry you had to endure that memory again," Hannah said, feeling her throat constrict with sorrow. "I saw the hues in the picture in Cain's office, but I didn't make the connection. The hues were Cro-Magnon, weren't they?"

Eve sighed. "God created them with the animals millions of years ago. They were not intelligent enough to develop more than a crude language of grunts and gestures, but we could communicate with telepathy. They were gentle and responded well to love. They were easily frightened but protected their young and had a sense of family."

"While you were asleep, I researched Cro-Magnons. The archeologists say they were nomadic and sparse. Yet for some unknown reason, starting six thousand years ago, cultures sprang from the Cro-Magnon all over the world, almost simultaneously."

"A few hundred years later, Cain returned and declared himself the father of the human race, and he no longer minded killing," Eve said.

Hannah took a deep breath. "Cain is the missing link."

Epilogue

Carla Babb walked down the hall of the medical research facility deep underground. Though late at night, she wore large sunglasses that hid most of her face. Bandages covered her nose, ears, and cheekbones. Her long, jet-black hair flowed almost to her waist. She wore a black business suit with a slit up the side of the skirt and a low-cut blouse. Her tailor-made jacket accentuated her large breasts.

As Carla passed through a set of security doors, a doctor and two medical assistants rose from their seats and left the laboratory without even glancing at her face. They passed through the doors and left her alone.

She removed her sunglasses, revealing bruises under her eyes. She looked at the thirteen glass containers connected to small tubes and wires. "Good evening, children. I know you cannot understand me yet, but when your ears develop, you will learn to love the sound of my voice. Each of you has been designed to be the most magnificent human ever to walk the face of Earth."

The woman giggled. "Did you see the beautiful lights that heralded your conception? Half the people on Earth witnessed the heavenly display. The sky shivered with life, and the sun and moon were covered in blood."

Carla walked to the first canister and stroked the glass barrier. "You, my beautiful little boy, have had a few cosmetic genes altered to make you look like the most perfect Chinese samurai to ever grace the continent. China and many other Asian nations will be your kingdom."

She peered inside the next canister. She could barely see the red-tinted organic mass inside. Tiny black pinpricks seemed to look back at her from what almost looked like a face. A microthin tube, which fed the fetus nutrients, connected where an umbilical cord would normally be. "You, my Nubian warrior, shall rule all of Africa."

Carla touched the next four canisters and spoke to the fetuses as if they were already conscious of their destiny. When she reached the seventh, she paused and turned to look at the six she had already addressed. "Of course, if any of you disappoint me, I can replace you with one of your brothers or sisters. Please keep that in mind when you consider defying me."

She moved to a canister farther down the line. "I have a special plan for you, my half brother. Our father is gone now, so I will guide you. You will learn from the greatest warriors and assassins so you can walk beside me and kill anyone who interferes with my plans. I will train you from the beginning to loathe the enemy as I do. You shall be my instrument of death."

Carla placed both hands on the last canister. "You, my most special child, will be blessed with more gifts than your brothers, and you shall rule us all. Your name shall be Susej. I believe you will look just like your handsome father did before the arrogant enemy marred his perfect face."

She backed up to address her silent audience. "Your eyes will glow as your sacred mother's did when she used her powers, which will be quite dramatic when you grow older. Each of you shall have wonderful lives. I've carefully selected your adoptive parents, and they anxiously await your birth. They are all rich and powerful because of me. They will teach you whom to worship.

"Don't worry about Father's manna. I stopped the construction of those huge facilities. We wouldn't want the whole world to be telepathic, now would we? The factories I will build will be much smaller, and only those I choose will benefit from the manna."

Carla paused. "Who am I, you ask?" She laughed. "I've gone by several names. I was born Karl Bujold, but you will never learn of that. The name I loved was Carla Babb, but due to some unfortunate events, I have changed it again.

"You may call me Charlotte, but someday you will call me The Harlot."

THE END